THORNS of DESIRE

By LINDSEY FINCH

Thorns of Desire

The Ivy & Bloom Trilogy: Book 2
A Dark Mafia Romance

By Lindsey Finch

AVIARY
PUBLICATIONS

ISBN: 978-1-966627-01-2 (eBook)
ISBN: 978-1-966627-16-6 (Paperback)

Thorns of Desire is a work of fiction. Any references to historical events, real people, real places or crimes are used fictitiously. Names, characters, places, and events are products of the author's imagination. The author does not condone or support the horrible acts portrayed in this fictional work.

.

Front cover design and book design by Aviary Publications, LLC.

Printed in the United States of America.
First printing edition 2025.

www.instagram.com/aviarypublications

Books by Lindsey Finch

THE IVY & BLOOM TRILOGY

Petals of Sin
Thorns of Desire
Blossoms of Lust

THE WHITE LOTUS SERIES

The Keeper's Mark
The Keeper's Key
The Keeper's Reign
The Keeper's Empire
The Keeper's Legacy

THE CITADEL SERIES
(STANDALONES)

Silent Obsession
Surrendered Will
Crimson Chains
Possessive Claim
Dark Dominion

Disclaimer: this novel may contain elements not suited for every reader. If any of the following offends you, please do not read this book. This novel contains: elements of domination, submission, control, crossing personal boundaries, financial leverage, organized crime, and dark romance.

"She was the thorn in his side;
he was the fire she couldn't resist.
Together, they would either bloom or burn."
—Unknown

CHAPTER ONE

The air inside the Rolls-Royce was a claustrophobic weight, pressing against my chest as the engine hummed softly around me. Each moment that had led to this felt like a jagged reel of film unspooling in my mind, every memory razor-sharp and cutting.

It hadn't been long since my world had tilted on its axis: my father's gambling, Cassian's calculated arrival, and the bitter realization that Ivy & Bloom—my sanctuary—was no longer mine. Cassian Moreau had stepped into my life with the precision of a scalpel, carving away any illusions of control I thought I had. He wasn't merely a man of power; he was power incarnate—dangerous, unyielding, and, against all reason, fiercely protective.

The lines between ally and captor had blurred almost instantly. Cassian's ownership of the shop had been just the beginning. Resentment and rebellion on my part had morphed into something far more convoluted—a dance of defiance and desire. He demanded submission with his presence alone, but I had refused to yield completely. And somewhere in the chaos, I had realized there was no escaping him. Perhaps, I didn't even want to.

But every step deeper into his world came with rising stakes. It wasn't just the shadow of his criminal empire looming over me—it was the enemies that trailed it. Rivals who whispered threats, shadows that shifted at the edges of my vision, and now, this.

Abram's warnings echoed relentlessly in my mind: Cassian's world was not one of safety, but survival. And tonight, that truth had come crashing down with brutal clarity. Cassian wasn't invincible. He wasn't untouchable. The man's words earlier had confirmed it—Cassian could bleed, and it seemed he was bleeding because of me.

Now, as the car moved further from the life I'd known and deeper into the unknown, the weight of my choices bore down on me like an anchor. My pulse raced, carrying with it a single, unrelenting question I didn't dare voice aloud: *What have I done?*

The glow of passing streetlights flickered over the man seated across from me, illuminating every austere line and shadow. He sat with a deliberate ease, his posture unyielding yet deceptively relaxed, like a predator in no rush to pounce. His appearance was meticulously curated—he exuded the kind of controlled intimidation that came from decades spent mastering the art of power.

He looked to be in his late fifties, his pale skin taut over high cheekbones that caught the light like carved stone. Deep lines etched his forehead and mouth, evidence of years steeped in intrigue, danger, and unrelenting calculation. His eyes, dark as obsidian and cold as winter frost, didn't simply see; they penetrated, stripping away pretense and laying bare the truths you might not have realized about yourself.

A faint scar sliced through his right eyebrow, vanishing into his iron-gray hair, which was combed back with the kind of precision that spoke of discipline rather than vanity. A meticulously groomed beard framed his jawline, flecked with silver strands that caught the light like slivers of ice. Everything about him—his tailored three-piece suit, his crimson silk tie, even the heavy gold signet ring on his left hand—radiated a kind of power that was not just wealth, but legacy.

When he finally spoke, his voice matched his appearance: low, smooth, and weighted with deliberate menace. Each word felt measured, like pieces of a puzzle he was revealing one agonizing fragment at a time.

"What intrigues me," he began, leaning forward slightly, "is how you seem so unafraid when you should be utterly terrified. Are you naive, or are you simply blinded by... love?"

The word hit like a physical blow, its meaning twisting in the suffocating air around us. His gaze locked onto mine, cold and merciless, and it pinned me in place as effectively as chains. Beneath his calm exterior, I could sense a brewing storm, a coiled violence restrained only by his need to study me further.

"Fear and love aren't mutually exclusive," I said, forcing my voice to remain steady even as my chest tightened. "Maybe I've realized neither will save me here."

His lips curved into the faintest semblance of a smile, though it was anything but kind. "Interesting," he murmured, tilting his head slightly, as though I were an enigma he was intent on solving. "But love—true love— clouds even the sharpest mind. And fear?" His smile darkened, a cruel edge sharpening his words. "Fear is a far more useful tool. It's biological, primal—designed to keep us alive."

"Fear is learned," I said sharply, my tone colder than I'd intended.

His chuckle was soft, calculated, a sound that wasn't meant to soothe but to unsettle. I didn't press further, unsure if silence would mark me as weak or defiant. Instead, I turned toward the window, watching the city blur into streaks of sterile light and shadow. The familiar streets melted away, replaced by towering structures of iron and stone, their imposing facades emanating power and history.

The world beyond the glass was shifting, just as my place in it had. And for the first time, I wondered if there was any part of myself I would recognize when this was over.

The man said nothing more, content to let the silence grow thick and consuming around us. The only sounds were the low rumble of the engine and the occasional soft creak of leather as he shifted, his movements deliberate, his gaze cutting toward me from the corner of his eye. I refused to meet it, clinging to the fragile sliver of control I still possessed. If this was a game, I wouldn't give him the satisfaction of seeing me falter first.

The Rolls-Royce slowed as we approached a massive structure that seemed hewn from the earth itself. A sprawling, European-style building loomed before us, its towering arches and heavy stonework bathed in the understated glow of bronze sconces. The façade was both imposing and elegant, exuding a kind of grim opulence that spoke not of wealth but of legacy. This was no place for visitors—it was a labyrinth meant to ensnare them.

The car turned sharply, descending into a hidden passage beneath the building. The warm glow of the sconces faded into the sterile, fluorescent light of an underground garage. The space was immaculate, as meticulously maintained as the man beside me. Rows of sleek black vehicles gleamed like predatory animals lying in wait. This wasn't just a garage—it was a fortress, and every detail told me it was designed with precision and purpose.

The car rolled to a stop, and the driver stepped out without a sound, his movements forced and unpracticed, unlike Cassian's men. The door beside me clicked open, and a rush of cold air prickled against my skin.

"Ladies first," the man ordered, his voice sharp yet quiet, like the whisper of a blade unsheathing.

I hesitated, glancing toward him instinctively for some sign of reassurance, but his expression remained inscrutable, his cold, unyielding eyes offering nothing.

Reluctantly, I stepped out, my boots clicking softly against the polished concrete. The underground chill seeped into me, mingling with the unease that coiled tighter around my chest.

Before I could take a step, a hand gripped my arm—firm, unrelenting, but not painful. A younger man, broad-shouldered and built like a monolith, had appeared at my side. His expression was neutral, detached, as he guided me forward. There was strength in his hold, a silent warning that resistance would be futile. He wasn't rough, but his grip left no room for argument.

The older man stepped out behind me, smoothing the lapels of his suit with the grace of a monarch descending from his throne. He gestured toward a set of heavy iron doors at the far end of the garage, and without a word, we began to move. The younger man's hand didn't loosen as he escorted me across the expanse, his presence more sentinel than captor—but the distinction felt meaningless.

As we neared the doors, intricate carvings in the surrounding stone came into focus. Wreaths of laurel, snarling beasts, and symbols I couldn't decipher adorned the entryway, their meanings obscured by time but no less foreboding. The wrought iron doors themselves gleamed faintly under the overhead lights, their dark surfaces bearing a mirror-like sheen.

The older man paused before them, his gold-ringed hand brushing the iron with a reverent touch. He turned to me, his voice carrying the weight of inevitability. "Inside," he said softly. "The next steps are yours to take."

I wanted to ask what that meant, but my throat felt paralyzed. Before I could summon the courage to speak, the doors creaked open with a resonant groan, revealing a corridor shrouded in shadow. My pulse thundered as I stepped forward, my movements hesitant, the younger man's grip ensuring I didn't falter.

The older man's voice followed me, soft and deliberate. "Don't waste this opportunity, Miss Quinn."

The corridor stretched long and narrow, its walls composed of cool, exposed stone. The dim lighting emanated from recessed sconces, their amber glow flickering faintly, as though the building itself was alive. The faint scent of oak and caramel hung in the air, mingling with the tang of iron and something older, muskier—a scent that seemed to seep from the ancient stone itself.

The younger man remained stoic, his grip steady as he

guided me forward. Each step echoed against the stone, a rhythmic reminder of my isolation. Behind us, the older man followed, his presence like a shadow that could become lethal at a moment's notice.

We emerged into a larger space, the air warmer, thicker, and heavy with the rich aroma of whiskey. Massive copper tanks loomed on either side of the room, their curved surfaces catching the faint light like burnished shields. Pipes snaked around them in intricate, coiled patterns, carrying liquid through what was unmistakably the heart of a distillery. The machinery emitted a low, constant hum, a vibration that traveled through the floor and into my legs.

The path wove past towering stacks of casks, their surfaces marked with bold blood red script denoting dates and batch numbers. The scent of aging whiskey mingled with the earthy aroma of the wooden barrels, creating a strange, almost hypnotic atmosphere. It would have been beautiful if it weren't for the suffocating presence of the men at my sides, their silence more oppressive than any words.

Another set of doors awaited us, heavier and more imposing than the first. Their ornate iron handles gleamed faintly as the younger man pushed them open without hesitation. We stepped through into a quieter space, the air cooler, tinged with the faint acrid scent of smoke. The shift was deliberate, like crossing an invisible boundary between function and exclusivity.

At the end of the hall, a final door came into view. Its surface was a polished black, its sheen reflecting the dim light like a pool of still water. The younger man opened it with a silent efficiency, stepping aside as the older man gestured for me to enter.

The room beyond was vast and commanding. A massive stone fireplace dominated one wall, its flames crackling softly and casting flickering shadows across the space. A long table stretched the length of the room, carved from dark mahogany and surrounded by high-backed leather chairs that exuded authority. The ceiling rose impossibly high, crisscrossed with heavy beams of dark wood in intricate patterns.

The walls were lined with shelves, but instead of books, they bore rows of whiskey bottles, their amber contents glowing softly in the firelight like captured embers. The room was both intimate and intimidating, a space designed to inspire reverence while concealing its intentions.

And as I stepped inside, I realized the room wasn't meant to impress me. It was meant to remind me of one thing: power.

At the head of the table, Cassian sat, his posture imperious, a commanding force despite the disarray of his appearance. His split lip was a raw slash of red against the pale canvas of his skin, and his knuckles were bruised and bloodied, the evidence of violence still fresh. Yet, even battered, he exuded the unyielding aura of a king—one who had fought tooth and nail to defend his throne and emerged victorious.

Two men flanked him, their hands resting on holstered weapons that glinted faintly in the firelight. Their expressions were impenetrable, masks of calm that belied their readiness to spring into action. The tension in the room was suffocating, a palpable weight that wrapped around me as I took another hesitant step forward.

"Rosalie," Cassian said, his voice low and gravelly, the edges frayed by fatigue yet underscored with unmistakable relief. "You shouldn't be here."

The older man entered behind me, the quiet *click* of the door sealing the room with a chilling conclusiveness. He moved with measured grace, his presence a disquieting counterpoint to the restrained violence surrounding Cassian. Taking his place at the opposite end of the table, he exuded a cold satisfaction, his sharp gaze flicking between the two of us like a hawk assessing its prey.

"I disagree," the older man said smoothly, his tone laced with quiet authority. "She's exactly where she needs to be."

I glanced at Cassian, my chest tightening at the sight of him. His injuries were stark and undeniable, the bruises darkening beneath the flickering firelight. Yet his gaze remained locked on mine, the usual razor-sharp intensity

in his gray eyes softened by something more profound—
something raw and unspoken.

He didn't speak, but his silence conveyed everything I
needed to understand: This wasn't over. Whatever battle
had been fought to bring us here, it was only the beginning
of something far more dangerous.

CHAPTER TWO

The older man stood at the head of the table, his hand resting on the back of the chair, his sharp eyes darting to the men flanking Cassian. His expression remained composed, but the faint tightness in his jaw betrayed a simmering discontent.

"Where are my men?" he asked, his voice smooth but threaded with quiet steel. He stepped away, stopped a few paces from the table, his hands clasped behind his back, studying Cassian with an air of forensic scrutiny.

Cassian leaned back slightly in his chair, his posture deceptively relaxed. His lips twitched—whether it was the beginning of a smirk or a grimace of pain was unclear. Slowly, he flexed his bruised and bloodied knuckles, letting the movement speak volumes before he responded.

"They're not dead, if that's what you're wondering," he said, his tone low and measured. "Though I should kill them—and you—for this little stunt." His words hung in the air, sharp and deliberate, like a blade poised to strike.

The older man's lips pressed into a thin line, his gaze narrowing. "How considerate of you," he said dryly, though the undercurrent of menace in his tone was unmistakable.

Cassian didn't flinch. He inclined his head toward the men flanking him, their hands still resting on their weapons. "They'll return once they remember who they work for."

The tension in the room thickened, a silent storm brewing beneath the surface. The older man stepped closer, his movements unhurried but purposeful, circling the table until he came to stand behind me. The weight of his presence at my back was daunting, the firm grip of his hand on my shoulder a subtle but undeniable reminder of control. It wasn't painful, but it left no room for defiance.

Cassian's eyes flicked to me, softening for a fleeting moment before the steel returned to his gaze. "Come here, Rosalie," he said, his voice quiet yet commanding, a thread of pressure woven through the calm.

The older man didn't release me immediately. His hand lingered, a silent challenge directed at Cassian. When he finally let go, his fingers brushed deliberately against the back of my coat, as if reluctant to relinquish his hold. I stepped forward hesitantly, my body stiff with uncertainty, every nerve on edge.

Cassian's eyes never left mine as I approached. He remained rigid in his seat, his hands resting on the table in front of him. The cuts on his knuckles were deeper than I'd realized, the dried blood a stark contrast to his skin. I stopped a few feet away, unsure if I should move closer—or if I even wanted to.

"Rosalie," Cassian said, his tone softening just enough to reach me, though it still carried the weight of command. "Are you hurt?" His eyes, however, remained fixed on the older man, his jaw taut.

"No," I whispered, my voice barely audible. "He didn't hurt me."

"What's happening?" I asked, struggling to steady the tremor in my voice. "Why am I here?"

Cassian didn't answer right away. His jaw tightened, his gaze briefly shifting to the older man before returning to me. The silence stretched taut, a cord ready to snap.

"You're here because some people believe you're a weakness I can't afford," Cassian said finally, his voice deliberate, each word laden with restrained fury. "And I'm here to remind them they're wrong."

Behind me, the older man chuckled, the sound cold and sardonic, devoid of humor. "It seems your priorities have... shifted." His eyes flicked toward me, and though I didn't dare meet his gaze, I could feel his scorn. "Have I not taught you anything?"

The chuckle faded, leaving behind a silence that pressed against my ribs like a vice. I couldn't decipher the game being played, but the stakes were rising with every word unspoken. Cassian's gaze met mine again, and for a moment, the tension in the room receded, replaced by something quieter—something that felt like a lifeline meant only for me.

"Rosalie," he said again, softer this time, "come closer."

I hesitated, torn between the compulsion to obey and the mounting dread clawing at my chest. The older man's presence lingered behind me like a shadow, his words circling in my mind like a warning. Yet it was Cassian's steady, unyielding gaze that pulled me forward, cutting through the chaos unraveling around us.

I took another step closer, but the older man's voice sliced through the silence, halting me mid-stride. "You've grown soft, Cassian," he said, his tone sharp and cutting. He moved toward the table with the same measured ease, commanding the room effortlessly. "I taught you better than this."

Cassian's hands curled into fists, his knuckles whitening as he leaned back slightly, his voice dropping to a deadly calm. "You taught me plenty," he said, his tone like iron. "Including how to bury the dead."

The older man smirked, his cold amusement flickering like a shadow across his face. "Ah, yes. And yet, here I stand."

The words hung in the air, charged with a meaning I couldn't fully grasp. For the briefest moment, Cassian's expression faltered, something raw and unguarded flashing across his features before he masked it once more. His voice, when it came, was quiet but cutting.

"You're supposed to be dead," Cassian said, the words slicing through the air with surgical precision. "The

Reapers made sure of that."

The older man paused at the edge of the table, his hand hovering over a decanter. "The Reapers tried," he said evenly, his fingers curling around the glass. "They cut me, stabbed me, and weighted me down like a sack of garbage." He poured the whiskey into three glasses, the rich amber liquid glinting in the firelight as it splashed into the crystal. His voice lowered, quieter now, but no less sharp. "And then they threw me into the Chicago River."

He slid two glasses across the table, one toward Cassian and one toward me. My fingers remained frozen at my sides, unwilling to touch it. Cassian didn't move either, his eyes locked on the older man with a fiery intensity.

The older man lifted his glass with deliberate slowness, the movement precise and controlled, as though daring us to take the next step in a game only he seemed to understand.

That's when I saw them—the scars.

The flesh around his wrists was ragged and uneven, a jarring contrast to his otherwise immaculate appearance. Thick, pale lines carved jagged paths around both wrists, as though something sharp had bitten into his skin over and over again. A chill crawled up my spine as he lifted his glass and took a slow, deliberate sip, his movements exuding control despite the raw evidence of past brutality.

"They thought I'd sink and disappear," he said, his voice steady but laced with a quiet, smoldering fury. "They underestimated how much fight I had left. I clawed my way free, Cassian... after they left me for dead."

Cassian's knuckles whitened as he flexed his hands, the deep cuts on his own skin glinting faintly in the firelight. Though his gaze never wavered from the older man, the conflict in his eyes betrayed him—a storm of emotions barely contained. Anger, disbelief, perhaps even a trace of guilt.

"Why now?" Cassian asked at last, his voice low and measured, though his barely-restrained anger hummed beneath the surface. "Why come back after all this time?"

The older man swirled the whiskey in his glass, his

expression inscrutable as he weighed his response. "Because the game has changed," he said simply. "And because you needed to remember who you are."

Cassian's lips pressed into a thin line, but he said nothing. The weight of his silence was deafening, the tension between them sharp and electric. I stood frozen between them, the oppressive force of their words pressing against me. I didn't know the full story—only fragments of a past riddled with pain, betrayal, and unspoken truths— but it was impossible to ignore the simmering intensity between them.

The older man's dark, penetrating gaze turned to me, sharp enough to feel like a physical blow. "And this one," he said, his tone almost clinical, as though I were a curiosity he intended to dissect. "What role does she play in all of this? Because from where I'm standing, she'll be your undoing."

Cassian's chair scraped loudly against the floor as he stood abruptly, his towering frame casting a shadow that swallowed the flickering firelight. His voice, low and razor-edged, carried a warning that left no room for argument. "Don't," he said, his words measured but seething with restrained fury. "Don't fucking touch her."

The man smiled faintly, the gesture devoid of warmth, like a predator baring its teeth. "Protective, aren't we?" he murmured, his tone mocking but thoughtful. "Interesting. Very interesting."

The fire crackled softly behind them, the only sound in the room as the weight of their unspoken history hung heavy in the air. I remained rooted in place, my heart pounding as I struggled to piece together the jagged edges of the puzzle unfolding before me. The past and present seemed to collide in this room, leaving no space to breathe.

The older man leaned forward slightly, his voice dropping to a conspiratorial murmur that sent a fresh wave of unease rippling through me. "You and I, Cassian, we're going to have to talk. But first, why don't you tell her what kind of man you really are?"

Cassian's jaw clenched, his shoulders taut as though

bracing for impact. His eyes darted to me for the briefest moment, a flicker of regret flashing across his face. When he turned back to his father, his voice was steady and resolute. "She already knows," he said, each word deliberate. "And I don't need your approval."

The older man chuckled, the sound low and malevolent, reverberating through the room like the ominous roll of distant thunder. "Approval?" he echoed, his gaze darkening with predatory intent. "No, son. You need my help."

The finality in his words sent a chill down my spine, the implications hanging heavily in the air. Cassian's hands remained clenched, the tension in his frame coiled tight enough to snap. Whatever battle lay ahead, it was clear that the stakes had just been raised.

CHAPTER THREE

The silence in the room stretched, heavy and stifled, like a taut wire ready to snap. Cassian stood at the head of the table, his bloodied knuckles braced against the polished mahogany, his glare locked onto the man seated opposite him. Mr. Moreau leaned back in his chair, exuding a calculated ease, the whiskey glass balanced delicately between his fingers as though the confrontation was nothing more than a casual exchange.

"You've let yourself get sloppy," the man said, breaking the silence. His voice was low, deliberate, each word laced with quiet derision. "A man in your position should have known they'd come for you."

Cassian's jaw tightened, the muscle ticking as he straightened, his frame vibrating with restrained fury. "I know exactly who they are and what they want," he said coldly, his tone sharp enough to cut. "But I'll admit—this was a surprise. I never expected to see you still breathing after seven years. Or still meddling."

A faint smirk tugged at the man's lips, his calm demeanor unbroken. "Meddling?" he repeated, his tone almost amused. "You call this meddling? No, boy. This is a reminder—of the empire you're squandering."

Cassian's laugh was dry, devoid of humor. "Don't mistake my restraint for weakness, old man. You weren't here when I rebuilt everything they tore apart. You don't get to walk back in and question how I've run things after abandoning it—and me."

The smirk faded, replaced by a cold, unyielding expression. Cassian's father placed the whiskey glass on the table with deliberate slowness, the sharp clink of crystal against wood slicing through the room. "You've built a house of cards," he said, his voice low and measured. "And now it's starting to collapse because you've let sentimentality cloud your judgment."

Cassian's hands curled into fists, the bloodied cuts stretching against his knuckles. "This isn't about sentimentality," he snapped, his voice rising just enough to betray the crack in his composure. "This is about control—control I earned after you left it in ruins. You abandoned me to chase a rival you could never defeat."

His father's gaze darkened, his expression hardening like granite. "Control?" he echoed, his voice dipping to a dangerous octave. "If you truly had control, we wouldn't be here now. If you had control, she wouldn't be your weak spot."

Cassian's breath hitched for a fraction of a second, a subtle but damning reaction. His eyes narrowed, his expression hardening as the air between them grew electric, charged with years of unspoken conflict and betrayal.

"I bet you said that about my mother, too." Cassian's words struck like a gunshot, reverberating through the room, but his father's gaze didn't falter, but something flickered behind his cold eyes—a shadow of pain buried beneath layers of steel.

"You're not as different from me as you'd like to think, Cassian," he said, his voice quieter but clear. "The only difference is that I knew how to separate my heart from my decisions. You still don't."

Cassian's jaw clenched, his shoulders rigid as though bracing for another blow. Before he could respond, I stepped forward, my voice cutting through the tension like a thread on the verge of snapping. "Why now?" I asked, keeping my tone steadier than I felt. "Why come back after all this time? Clearly, there's unresolved tension here."

Both men turned their attention to me, their stares so intense I fought the urge to retreat. My pulse thundered in my ears, but I pressed on. "Seven years," I continued. "You've been gone for seven years, and now you expect us to believe you care enough to return? That you care about him?" I hesitated, swallowing hard. "I don't even know your name."

Elias tilted his head slightly, as though weighing my audacity. Then, to my surprise, his lips curled into a faint smile—one that didn't reach his eyes. "My name is Elias Moreau," he said smoothly. "Not that it matters to you. But it will. Soon enough."

Cassian scoffed, his expression twisting into a bitter sneer. "She doesn't need to know your name, because you'll vanish as quickly as you appeared."

Elias ignored him, his focus still fixed on me. "You asked why now," he said, his voice dipping into a tone that felt heavy with significance. "I'll tell you why. Because the boy sitting at that table refuses to listen to anything but a goddamn explosion."

"I listen," Cassian snapped, his voice low and dangerous. "I just don't listen to ghosts."

Elias chuckled, the sound dark and caustic, shaking his head. "No, you don't listen. Not when the Reapers started creeping back into your territory. Not when their alliances are spreading like weeds. And the things I hear—you're saving cops now?" He leaned forward, planting his hands on the table, his voice hardening to iron. "Meanwhile, the Reapers are finding ways to burn everything you've built to the ground."

Cassian's body stilled, his expression hardening into something implacable. "If you've come to play doomsayer, save it," he said icily. "I'm not the boy you abandoned. I've survived worse without you."

Elias exhaled slowly, his gaze steady and unflinching. "And yet, I came back," he said. "Because what's coming is bigger than either of us. Bigger than you."

Reaching into his pocket, Elias withdrew a folded piece of paper and slid it across the table toward Cassian. "This is just the beginning," he said, his voice softening, though his words lost none of their gravity. "Names, places, movements. They've been planning this for years—waiting for you to get comfortable."

Cassian didn't touch the paper. His expression remained unreadable, but the tension radiating from him was palpable. Elias straightened, his presence monumental as his eyes flicked between us.

"This isn't about sentimentality, Cassian," he said, his voice quieter but no less cutting. "It's about survival. You can hate me all you want—curse me, spit at me, fight me. But if you don't deal with this, there won't be anything left for you to fight over."

The fire crackled softly, the only sound breaking the suffocating silence. My gaze shifted to Cassian, whose hands were still clenched into fists at his sides. His focus remained on Elias, his face a mask of controlled fury. My stomach twisted as the full weight of what was happening began to settle—the storm on the horizon wasn't just looming. It had already arrived.

Elias's sharp, appraising gaze shifted to me, his expression almost amused. "And you," he said, his tone as smooth as it was unsettling. "You're the wild card, aren't you? The one thing they didn't anticipate." He took a step closer, and I fought the instinct to retreat. "Let's hope you prove to be more of an asset than a liability."

Cassian moved before I could respond, his body a blur of precision as he stepped between us. The swiftness of it made my breath hitch. "Don't," he warned, his voice low and smoldering, every syllable carrying the weight of restrained fury. His gray eyes burned, locking on Elias with a ferocity that left no room for misinterpretation. "Don't drag her into this."

Elias smirked faintly, his reaction as calculated as it was infuriating. "Oh, son," he said, his tone soft yet barbed, "she's already in it."

Cassian's gaze flicked to the table, his jaw tightening as

his hand closed around the gun resting there—a weapon that had been a silent threat the entire time. He lifted it effortlessly, the action fluid, practiced. It wasn't the presence of the weapon that struck me—it was the way he held it, like an extension of himself, a tool as familiar as his own breath.

Without a word, Cassian snatched up the folded paper from the table, his movements sharp and purposeful. He tucked it into his pocket with a controlled aggression that betrayed the storm simmering beneath his surface. His shoulders were rigid, his jaw set with a tension that felt almost unbearable to watch.

"Let's go," he said, his voice clipped and devoid of softness. His hand settled firmly on the small of my back, the heat of his touch a stark contrast to the icy tension radiating from him. He guided me toward the door, his pace brisk, almost impatient.

I hesitated, glancing back at Elias. His expression was calm, almost resigned, but there was something unnerving in the way his gaze lingered. He didn't make a move to stop us, didn't utter a word—until Cassian's fingers brushed the door handle.

"When you figure out that I'm telling the truth," Elias said, his voice quiet but carrying the weight of inevitability, "I'll be here. Waiting."

Cassian didn't reply. He pushed the door open with a force that sent its hinges creaking, the sound reverberating into the hallway. The air outside felt colder, heavier, the encounter in the room pressing on my chest like an immovable weight. Cassian's hand remained steady on my back, his touch the only thing grounding me as we moved through the corridor.

We stepped into the underground parking garage, the sterile hum of fluorescent lights buzzing faintly overhead. The sharp contrast between the polished concrete and the tension thickening the air made the space feel suffocating. Cassian's pace was quick and unrelenting as he led me toward the sleek black SUV waiting at the far end of the garage.

He reached the passenger door before his driver could move, his actions sharp and decisive as he pulled it open. His impatience hung in the air like an unspoken reprimand. I slid into the seat, and turned to watch him. Cassian circled the car, his footsteps echoing faintly off the walls, before climbing into the seat beside me. The door slammed shut, the sound reverberating in the enclosed space.

"Drive," he barked, his voice edged with authority.

Cassian's hands curled into tight fists in his lap, his knuckles pale against the shadows that cloaked the interior of the car. His jaw remained locked, his gaze fixed ahead, though it was clear his mind was still in that room, replaying every word, every moment.

I shifted in my seat, the silence pressing against me like a tangible force. "Cassian..." I began, my voice tentative, barely audible.

"Not now," he snapped, his tone sharper than I'd ever heard before. He glanced at me then, and though his gaze softened slightly, the frustration etched into his features was undeniable. "Not yet."

I nodded, leaning back into the seat as the engine roared to life. The SUV surged forward, its tires squealing faintly as we sped out of the garage and into the night. The city lights streaked past in a blur of gold and white, the hum of the engine filling the charged silence between us.

Cassian didn't speak, and I didn't press him. His shoulders remained tense, his eyes unyielding as he stared out at the city. Whatever storm Elias had warned him about, it was clear that it wasn't over—not for Cassian, not for me. It was only beginning.

CHAPTER FOUR

The ride back to Cassian's penthouse was suffocatingly quiet, the air inside the car heavy with unspoken words. The city's lights blurred past the windows, their brilliance muted against the turbulence of emotions that lingered between us. I glanced at Cassian's profile—his jaw tight, his lips pressed into a firm line, and his hands resting in his lap, still smeared with dried blood.

Whatever Elias had said weighed heavily on him—that much was clear. But there was something else, an inescapable tension in his posture that went beyond the fallout with his father, a stiffness that spoke of something more profound.

When the car finally pulled into the underground parking of his building, Cassian opened his door before the driver could. He rounded the car quickly, his hand finding my arm as I stepped out, guiding me toward the private elevator with a silent, unyielding pressure.

The elevator doors slid open, revealing the familiar warmth of Cassian's penthouse. The soft glow of recessed lights and the faint scent of spice and cedar filled the space, but the usual tranquility felt at odds with Cassian's energy. He moved ahead of me, his strides sharp and purposeful, his silence more suffocating than any words.

As we stepped into the foyer, two of his men approached

him. They spoke in hushed tones, their words too low for me to catch. Cassian's expression remained unreadable, his gaze flicking briefly toward me before he nodded once. Whatever they told him, he didn't share it.

"Cassian?" I ventured, my voice breaking through the heavy silence. "Is something wrong?"

He didn't respond immediately. Instead, he turned toward me, his gray eyes impenetrable as he gestured for me to follow. "Come," he said simply, his voice clipped and controlled.

I hesitated, torn between demanding answers and giving him the space he so clearly needed. I chose the latter, following as he led me through the familiar hallways to his bedroom. My heart pounded as he shut the door behind us, the soft *click* of the lock reverberating in the stillness.

Cassian stood with his back to the door, one hand resting against the wood as though steadying himself. I watched him, unsure whether he was grappling with Elias's sudden reappearance or something deeper. The tension in the room shifted as he turned to face me, his gray eyes no longer guarded but dark and incisive, the intensity in them making my pulse quicken.

"You really don't understand what you've done, do you?" he asked, his voice low and steady—a calm so unnerving it felt like the prelude to a storm.

I blinked, my stomach twisting at the weight of his words. "What are you talking about?" I asked, though part of me wasn't sure I wanted to know.

Without a word, he reached into his pocket and pulled out my phone. He tossed it onto the armchair nearby, the soft thud unnervingly loud in the silence.

"You left this behind," he said, his tone eerily calm. "On purpose."

I swallowed hard, my throat dry as realization dawned. "Cassian, I—"

"Don't," he interrupted, his voice sharper now, though it remained quiet. "Don't try to explain it away. You slipped your guards. You left your phone. And because of that, Elias was able to get to you." He stepped closer, his presence towering and unrelenting. "Do you have any idea what could have happened if it hadn't been him?"

My lips parted, but no words came. His frustration wasn't misplaced—I knew that—but beneath the anger, I sensed something else: fear, raw and visceral.

"Do you think this is a game?" he continued, his tone darkening. "Do you think I assign guards to you for show? That I don't mean it when I tell you to stay safe?"

"I didn't mean—" I tried, my voice trembling.

"I don't care what you meant," he snapped, closing the space between us until there was barely a foot between our bodies. "What you did was reckless, dangerous, and unacceptable."

I tried to hold his gaze, but the sheer intensity in his eyes was overwhelming. "I'm sorry," I whispered, the words fragile and uncertain.

Cassian exhaled slowly, his expression softening for a fleeting moment before the darkness returned. His jaw tightened again, and the tension radiating from him, the heat rolling off and seeping into me.

"I'm glad you're sorry, Rosalie," he said, his voice dropping to a chilling calm. "But that doesn't mean there won't be consequences."

My breath hitched, my chest tightening painfully. "What? You can't be serious, are you?"

Cassian tilted his head slightly, his gray eyes steady, unyielding. "It means you deliberately put yourself in harm's way. And that will not go unpunished."

A shiver ran down my spine at the quiet finality in his words. He moved past me, his steps deliberate, each one echoing in the stillness as he approached the armchair farthest from the door.

It was intentional—I think.

Sitting down, he exuded an air of quiet dominance, his posture deceptively relaxed, though every line of his body radiated authority.

"Come here," he said, his voice low but firm, a velvet-wrapped command that left no room for refusal.

I hesitated, my feet rooted to the floor as panic clawed at

my chest. I shook my head, fearful of the sudden turn of events. "Cassian, I—"

"Rosalie," he said, his tone hardening just enough to send a tremor through me. "Come here. Now."

My legs moved before my mind could catch up, carrying me across the room until I stood in front of him. His gaze roved over me, not with the familiar heat I had come to recognize, but with something colder—an assessment, as though he were deciding just how far to take this.

"You're going to understand," he said slowly, his voice as steady as it was unyielding, "exactly how serious I am about your safety. And exactly why you don't get to make decisions like that on your own."

The realization of his meaning settled over me like a heavy weight, my breath catching in my throat. "Please..."

"I'm going to spank you, Rosalie," he said, his voice calm and unyielding, as if he were simply stating a fact. "And I'm going to make sure you never forget this moment."

My breath hitched at his words, the measured authority in his tone sending a ripple of unease—and something else I couldn't quite name—down my spine. It wasn't just what he said but how he said it, a conviction that left no room for pleas.

"No," I began, my voice trembling slightly. "You don't have to do this."

He sat on the edge of the bed, his posture deliberate and commanding. His gaze remained locked on mine, unwavering. "No, Rosalie. I do. Because clearly, words aren't enough for you."

His hand reached for mine, his grip firm yet controlled as he guided me closer, positioning me between his knees. The proximity was damning, the heat of his body radiating against mine. I shivered, uncertain if it was from the gravity of the moment or the closeness we now shared.

"You're going to count each one," he instructed, his voice low, deliberate, as though issuing a decree. "Do you understand?"

I hesitated, my pulse roaring in my ears. "This isn't necessary—"

"Do you understand?" he repeated, the implacable tone of his voice leaving no space for defiance.

I swallowed hard, closing my eyes before I spoke, my words barely audible. "Yes."

His fingers moved with slow precision, unfastening the button of my jeans. My breath caught, but I didn't move. The zipper slid down, the soft hum unnervingly loud in the quiet room. With deliberate care, he peeled the denim away, exposing the thin barrier of my underwear. His touch was steady, methodical, as he guided me sideways and bent me over his lap. My palms pressed against his thighs, warm and solid beneath me, the duvet tantalizingly close to my cheek but out of reach.

"Good," he murmured, his hand settling on my lower back, grounding me. "Now, count."

The first swat came before I could process the command, sharp and unexpected. I gasped, the sting blooming across my skin as I struggled to form words.

"One," I whispered, my cheeks burning with more than the heat of the strike.

"Louder," Cassian instructed, his voice calm but unrelenting. "I want to hear you."

"One," I said again, louder this time, my voice betraying the vulnerability clawing at me.

The second swat followed swiftly, the sound of his palm meeting my skin echoing through the room. My breath hitched, and I forced the number out between clenched teeth.

"Two."

Each strike was measured, precise, the force enough to sting and bite without crossing a line. The rhythmic impacts rippled through me, leaving my body tense yet compliant.

"Three."

"Four."

"Five."

By the sixth, my voice wavered, emotion bubbling to the surface. This wasn't just a punishment—it was a reprimand, a lesson wrapped in intimacy. The humiliation of being bent over his knee, of submitting so completely, brought tears to my eyes, not from pain but from the sheer rawness of it all.

When the final swat landed, I barely choked out the number, my breath uneven and shallow.

"Ten," I whispered, my body trembling against his lap.

Cassian's hand stilled, resting gently on the small of my back. He leaned forward, his voice softer now, the sharp edges replaced with something almost tender. "Good," he murmured. "You took that well."

His fingers brushed aside the fabric of my underwear, the warmth of his palm soothing the burn. It wasn't invasive, just deliberate—a silent reassurance that he hadn't gone too far.

With care, he helped me up, his hands steady as he guided me back to my feet. He lifted my jeans and fastened them with the same meticulous precision, careful not to add to my discomfort. My legs felt unsteady beneath me, the vulnerability of the moment leaving me raw.

His thumb brushed my cheek as he tilted my chin, forcing me to meet his gaze. The tenderness in his touch was at odds with the storm still brewing in his eyes. He wiped away a tear I hadn't realized had fallen, his movements slow and deliberate.

"Do you understand why I did that?" he asked, his voice low but laced with genuine concern.

I nodded, my throat tight as I tried to find the words. "Yes."

"Say it," he pressed, his fingers cradling my chin. "I need to hear you say it."

"Because you care," I whispered, my voice cracking under the weight of the admission. "Because you don't want to lose me."

"You're right," he said softly, his thumb tracing small circles against my skin. "I don't. But I can't protect you if you're careless with your life."

For a moment, the air between us felt impossibly heavy, thick with unspoken promises and unacknowledged truths. Then, without warning, Cassian pulled me into his arms, holding me as though I were something fragile yet fiercely cherished. His chin rested lightly against the top of my head, his breath warm against my hair.

"I won't let anything happen to you," he murmured, the words a quiet, immutable vow. "Even if I have to protect you from yourself."

His arms around me were unyielding, grounding me as the tremor in my limbs slowly subsided. I pressed my face into his shirt, the familiar scent of cedar and spice anchoring me. It was maddening, this need to both resist him and lean into his strength.

I hated that he was right. Hated the way he reminded me of my responsibility—not just to him, but to myself. But what I hated most of all was how alive I felt, the fire in my chest and the butterflies stirring awake after what felt like an eternity of quiet.

Tears welled in my eyes again, though I blinked them back quickly. His hand, still resting on the small of my back, radiated warmth that seeped into my core. He didn't speak further, didn't demand more from me. But his presence alone was a reminder of the line I'd crossed and the trust I'd nearly broken.

And, somehow, I felt safer in his arms than I had in years.

Pulling back slightly, I glanced up at him. His gaze had softened, the sharp edges blunted, but the storm still brewed in the depths of his gray eyes, a reminder of everything left unsaid. "I'm sorry," I whispered, the words trembling on my lips, fragile yet sincere. "I wasn't thinking."

"No," he said, his tone firm but free of cruelty. "You weren't. And next time, I hope you will, or you'll be counting higher than ten."

His words weren't meant to wound—they were meant to anchor me. They landed with quiet precision, cutting through my guilt and leaving behind a reminder that stung in its simplicity. I nodded, letting the truth of it settle in my chest, heavy but necessary.

Cassian brushed his thumb over my cheek again, the

rough pad of his finger surprisingly gentle against my skin. "Rosalie," he murmured, his voice low and weighted with intent. "I need you to understand something. Every risk you take, every reckless decision—it doesn't just affect you. It affects me. My men. My entire operation."

The vulnerability in his words struck me harder than any rebuke. It wasn't anger driving him; it was fear. Fear disguised as control, wrapped in the armor of his unyielding nature.

"I understand," I said softly, my voice barely audible, my chest tightening under the weight of his gaze.

"Good." His hand slid to the back of my neck, his fingers tangling lightly in my hair as he leaned closer, pressing his forehead against mine. The intimacy of the gesture stole my breath, his touch both grounding and disarming. The raw emotion in the space between us was palpable, charged with something I couldn't name but felt to my core.

"Let's shower," he said, his voice softer now, tinged with an almost imperceptible ache. The weight of his words lingered, heavy and certain, settling in the air around us. For the first time, I understood—truly understood—how much I meant to him. This wasn't just possession or control; it wasn't the domineering need to keep me tethered to his side. It was something deeper, something that both scared and grounded him.

It scared me too.

I let myself sink into the moment, into the quiet strength of his presence. His touch was steady, his warmth undeniable, and in that instant, I knew I wasn't just another piece on the board in his carefully constructed world. I was something more, something that could shatter him just as much as he could shatter me. And the thought of it left me both terrified and irrevocably drawn to him.

CHAPTER FIVE

Cassian's hands lingered at my hips before sliding to the small of my back, his touch a quiet reassurance that steadied the erratic rhythm of my breath. The soft click of the door shutting behind us echoed in the tiled space, sealing us away from the tension simmering in the bedroom beyond.

The bathroom mirrored the opulence of the rest of his penthouse—sleek marble surfaces, warm recessed lighting, and a shower so expansive it looked as though it belonged in a sanctuary of indulgence. The glass walls stretched from floor to ceiling, and steam began to rise as he twisted the shower handle, the rush of water filling the space with a soothing, rhythmic hum.

Cassian didn't speak as he adjusted the temperature, his movements precise and almost ritualistic, every action exuding control. His jaw remained tight, a muscle feathering beneath his skin, but the anger from earlier had dissipated. What lingered now was something more visceral, more potent.

He turned toward me, his gray eyes burning with an intensity that sent a jolt through my chest. Without a word, his fingers grazed the hem of my shirt, lifting it slowly as his gaze held mine, unwavering. My arms rose automatically, letting him pull the fabric over my head. The cool air pricked my skin, but the weight of his attention burned hotter than the water cascading behind him.

Piece by piece, he undressed me. Each action was deliberate, as though he were stripping away more than just clothing—each motion a reminder of the power he wielded, not just over my body, but my heart. When he crouched to unlace my boots, his fingers brushed against my ankles, the fleeting contact sending a shiver racing up my spine. Finally, his hands moved to the band of my underwear, hesitating for the briefest of moments before slipping them down.

When I stood bare before him, my arms instinctively crossed over my chest, a vain attempt to shield myself from the vulnerability of the moment. Cassian shook his head, his expression softening with something unspoken. "Don't," he murmured, his voice firm but gentle. "You don't need to hide from me."

His hand met mine, slowly wrapping around my wrist as he pulled my rms down. No longer shielding myself, my breasts hung free, my nipples hard in the cool air. Cassian smirked, a devilish twitch of his lip as he rolled my nipped between his thumb and forefinger. Something inside me came alive.

"Be still."

Heat rushed to my face, but I obeyed, letting my arms fall to my sides. He stepped back then, his gaze roaming over me—not with lust, but with a quiet reverence that left me feeling more exposed than any lack of clothing ever could.

Then, as if to even the playing field, Cassian began to undress himself. His shirt came off first, revealing the sculpted lines of his chest, each muscle defined and marred by faint scars—etched into his skin like silent testaments to the life he'd lived. The soft clink of his belt echoed in the space, followed by the whisper of fabric as his slacks pooled at his feet. When he finally stood before me, stripped of everything but the intoxicating power he carried so effortlessly, my breath hitched.

Cassian turned back to the shower, testing the water

once more before stepping aside and gesturing for me to enter. "Go on," he said softly, his voice laced with a gentleness that both calmed and unnerved me. "It's warm."

I hesitated for a moment, unsure if the trembling in my legs was from the lingering sting of his earlier lesson or the vulnerability of this moment. But I stepped forward, the steam curling around me like the heart of a sauna as I moved beneath the spray. The hot water cascaded over my skin, soothing the ache in my muscles and washing away the weight of the night.

Though the shower was vast, Cassian's presence was inescapable as he followed me in. He didn't touch me again, didn't speak. He simply stood close, his gaze fixed on mine, the silence between us charged with an intensity that stole the air from my lungs.

The water flowed over us, the sound drowning out the world beyond the glass walls. The heat from the shower was nothing compared to the fire in his eyes. He took a single step forward, closing the distance between us, and his hand reached out to tilt my chin upward. His thumb brushed against my cheek, the deliberate motion sending a tremor through me.

"Rosalie," he murmured, his voice rough and low, like the growl of a storm approaching.

I barely had time to react before his lips claimed mine. The kiss was fierce, possessive, leaving no room for hesitation. His hand slipped from my face to cradle the back of my neck, holding me in place as his mouth moved against mine with unrelenting precision. I gasped, and he seized the opportunity to deepen the kiss, his tongue sweeping past my lips with an intensity that left me breathless.

His other hand found my waist, pulling me flush against him. The heat of his body melded with mine, the water cascading over us a mere backdrop to the fire igniting between us. I clung to his shoulders, my fingers curling into the slick muscle as I tried to anchor myself against the storm he unleashed.

Without breaking the kiss, Cassian bent slightly, his hands sliding to the backs of my thighs as he lifted me effortlessly. A soft gasp escaped me, and my legs wrapped around him instinctively, my arms tightening around his neck as he pressed me against the cool tile wall of the shower. The contrast of the chilled surface against my back and the scorching heat of the water sent a shiver coursing through me, but his presence anchored me.

His grip on my thighs was firm, unrelenting, a silent reminder of his dominance. Yet his lips, as they trailed along my jaw and grazed the sensitive curve of my neck, held a tenderness that left me trembling. Each kiss was deliberate, a balance of power and vulnerability, as though he were carving his claim into me with every touch.

In that moment, Cassian wasn't just a man of control or power. He was my storm, my anchor, my reckoning—and I surrendered completely.

"You drive me insane," he murmured against my skin, his voice a low growl that resonated through me, igniting a spark in places I dared not acknowledge. "You reckless, infuriating woman."

There was no malice in his words, only raw, unrestrained emotion—a concoction of desire and frustration so tightly interwoven it made my pulse stutter. I opened my mouth to respond, to defend myself, but he silenced me with his lips, crashing against mine with a ferocity that stole my breath and left me spinning.

Before I could steady myself, I felt him—hard and unyielding, pressing against me with a promise not yet fulfilled but impossibly close. My breath hitched as his hips flexed, his entry deliberate, stretching me inch by torturous inch.

His lips brushed my ear as he leaned in, his voice a velvet warning that sent a shiver cascading down my spine. "This isn't for you," he rasped, each word dripping with authority. "Don't you dare come."

It was the only warning he gave before he began to move, his thrusts measured and controlled despite the storm of emotion he carried. Each movement was calculated, his mastery evident even in his conflicted state.

I bit down on my lip, my body trembling as I fought to

obey him. He filled me completely, each stroke igniting waves of pleasure that threatened to pull me under. The tension within me coiled tighter, an unbearable ache just out of reach. I knew better than to surrender without his command.

Cassian's pace quickened, his breath warm and ragged against my neck. The steady cascade of the shower mingled with the heat radiating between us, the sound of rushing water punctuated by the sharp rhythm of our bodies. His grip on my thighs was firm, fingers pressing into my skin as he drove deeper, claiming me with every unrelenting thrust.

My head fell back against the cool tile, the sharp contrast between its chill and his molten heat making my senses reel. The battle between my mind and body raged, each collision of his hips with mine blurring the line between torment and ecstasy.

A ferocious growl rumbled in his throat, primal and unrestrained, before his mouth found mine again. His kiss was fierce, devouring, his tongue tangling with mine as though he intended to claim not just my body but my very will. My fingers clung to his shoulders, nails grazing the taut muscles beneath his skin as I sought to steady myself against the relentless pace he set.

His rhythm was hypnotic—repetitive, commanding, and maddeningly addictive. Each thrust was deliberate, pushing me closer to the precipice he had forbidden me to cross. "Don't you fucking dare," he growled, his voice a dark promise as his hand slid to the back of my neck, tangling in my damp hair. His grip was possessive, tilting my face up until our eyes met, the heat in his gaze leaving me breathless.

The room was alive with the symphony of our movements—the slap of skin against skin, the hiss of water striking tile, and the shared, involuntary gasps that neither of us could contain. His thrusts became rougher, more erratic, the control he usually wielded so effortlessly beginning to unravel as he neared his peak.

I whimpered, the effort of holding back leaving me

trembling in his arms. The tension coiled within me threatened to snap, each nerve frayed and sparking with the unrelenting pressure. But his command was law, and I refused to betray it.

With a final, powerful thrust, Cassian froze, his body rigid and trembling as a low, rough groan escaped his lips. The sound reverberated through me, a mix of release and possession that left me trembling. He pulled out at the last moment, the warmth of his climax spilling against me as he pressed me firmly against the tile. His chest rose and fell with the effort of catching his breath, his forehead resting against mine.

For a moment, the world stilled, the tension between us replaced by the faint hum of the shower and the steady beat of his heart against my chest. His hands softened their grip on my thighs as he lowered me gently to my feet. My legs wavered, unsteady beneath me, but his arms remained, holding me upright.

"Good girl," he murmured, his voice a low rasp as he reached up to brush a wet strand of hair from my face. His touch was tender, at odds with the dominance he had just displayed, and the duality of it sent a shiver through me.

The simple praise seared through me, reigniting the embers of the need he hadn't allowed me to quench. My body still trembled, the ache of denied release coiling tighter in my core, and his knowing smirk only deepened the tension. His hand trailed down my side, the lightness of his touch leaving goosebumps in its wake.

CHAPTER SIX

The dim light slipping through the heavy curtains painted the room in muted grays, a quiet testament to the lateness of the hour—or the earliness, depending on one's perspective. My eyes adjusted slowly, taking in the soft texture of the sheets against my skin and the cold, empty space beside me. Cassian's side of the bed had long gone cold, leaving only the faint imprint of his presence.

Frowning, I sat up and glanced at my phone. The numbers glared back: 2:13 a.m. The penthouse was silent—too silent. The kind of silence that didn't speak of tranquility but of something unresolved, lurking just out of reach. My chest tightened as memories of the evening filtered back, a tangle of tension and tenderness, dominance and vulnerability.

Slipping out of bed, I let the cool hardwood guide me, the sensation grounding my unease. I wrapped a throw blanket around my shoulders and padded into the hall, the recessed lighting casting faint shadows that seemed alive with unspoken tension. The penthouse felt vast and hollow, its usual warmth replaced by an unsettling stillness.

I checked the living room first, half expecting to find him sprawled on the couch with a glass of whiskey, but the space was untouched. The kitchen was the same—pristine, sterile in its quiet. Then, a faint glow caught my attention, emanating from down the hall like a beacon in the dark. My pulse quickened.

The study.

The door was ajar, and the soft hum of activity slipped through the crack, an audible confirmation of his presence. Pushing it open gently, I found him.

Cassian sat at his desk, his silhouette outlined by the warm glow of the desk lamp and the faint, cool blue of his computer screen. Papers lay scattered across the polished surface, interspersed with maps, notes, and symbols I couldn't decipher. His sleeves were rolled up, exposing the sinew and strength of his forearms, while his normally impeccable hair was slightly disheveled—a sign of hours lost to relentless focus.

He hadn't noticed me yet, his gray eyes scanning the screen with unwavering intensity. His fingers tapped lightly against the desk, the only sound breaking the quiet rhythm of the room.

"It's late," I said softly, my voice hesitant, as though afraid to disrupt the delicate balance.

His head snapped up, his eyes locking onto mine in an instant. For a moment, his shoulders tensed, but when recognition set in, the tension melted slightly. Exhaustion etched deep lines into his face, but his gaze was as sharp as ever.

"You should be asleep," he said, his voice low, the concern beneath it unmistakable.

I stepped further into the room, the blanket trailing behind me like a shield. "I could say the same for you. What are you working on?"

Leaning back in his chair, Cassian ran a hand over his face, a rare moment of lapsed control slipping through his composed exterior. "Research," he replied, though the weight in his tone suggested it was far more than that.

I moved closer, my bare feet silent against the plush rug. My eyes flicked to the chaos on the desk, scanning the scattered papers, maps, and his meticulous handwriting. "The Reapers?" I guessed.

His jaw tightened, and he gave a curt nod. "My father's

list," he said, his voice tight. "Names. Places. Movements. Enough to know they're planning something, but not enough to stop it. Yet." His last word carried a quiet, deadly resolve.

I hesitated, the weight of Elias's warnings settling heavily in my chest. "Cassian..." I began carefully, "you don't have to do this all tonight. Come back to bed."

His gaze flicked to where my hand had rested on the desk, brushing lightly against his. His expression softened for the briefest of moments, the sharp edges of his demeanor blunted by something I couldn't name. But just as quickly, the walls came back up.

"I can't," he said firmly, his voice leaving no room for argument. "Every minute I waste, they gain ground. This isn't something I can afford to set aside."

My frown deepened, the ache in my chest growing at the sight of his exhaustion. "You're running yourself into the ground," I said quietly. "You can't protect anyone if you burn out. You'll make mistakes."

His hand stilled, the tension in his shoulders visibly tightening. "You don't understand," he said, his voice quieter now but no less resolute. "If I lose focus, they'll destroy everything. My work, my men... you."

The unbidden conviction in his voice sent a chill down my spine. His gaze met mine, holding me captive in its intensity. "They're coming for me, Rosalie," he said softly, "and means you too. I can't let that happen."

I wanted to argue, to tell him he couldn't carry the weight of the world alone, but the certainty in his eyes stopped me. Instead, I stepped back, wrapping the blanket tighter around myself. "Fine," I said quietly, though my heart twisted at his resolve. "But I'm not leaving you alone. Not tonight."

Cassian arched an eyebrow, the faintest flicker of surprise breaking through his exhaustion. "Rosalie—"

"I mean it," I interrupted, cutting him off. "If you're going to fight this battle tonight, then I'm staying too."

He sighed, shaking his head, a ghost of a smile tugging at his lips despite the tension. "You're impossible," he muttered, though there was no bite to the words.

"I've learned from the best," I replied, my voice soft as I grabbed a throw blanket draped over the armchair and settled myself onto the couch in the corner of the room. If he wouldn't rest, I'd keep watch with him.

The plush cushions cradled me as I sank into the chair, tucking my legs beneath me and wrapping the blanket tightly around my shoulders. The warmth cocooned me, a stark contrast to the early morning chill lingering in the air.

Cassian's eyes lingered on me, his expression unreadable but heavy with something that tugged at the edges of his sharp features. "You don't have to do this," he murmured, his voice softer now, stripped of its usual command.

I held his gaze, the words tumbling out before I could second-guess them. "And you don't have to do this alone."

The faintest flicker passed through his gray eyes, a shadow of surprise quickly buried beneath layers of composure. He didn't argue, didn't protest—just exhaled quietly and turned back to his work. The subtle shift in his posture spoke louder than anything he could have said.

The room settled into a rhythm of quiet activity. The soft scratch of his pen on paper, the rustle of documents being shifted, and the occasional low sigh from Cassian filled the space. The desk lamp cast a warm halo over him, its light catching the planes of his face as he worked with relentless focus. His presence, steady and unyielding, seemed to fill every corner of the room, grounding me in a way I hadn't expected.

I watched him through heavy-lidded eyes, trying to commit the moment to memory. The determined set of his jaw, the slight furrow in his brow as he made notes in his precise, angular handwriting—it all spoke of a man carrying far more weight than any one person should. My chest ached at the sight of his resolve, his determination to protect everything and everyone he cared about, no matter the cost to himself.

Sleep began to creep in, pulling at the edges of my

38

consciousness. The events of the night replayed in fragments—the heat of the shower, the way his hands steadied me when I felt most vulnerable, the quiet authority in his voice. They intertwined with the present moment, wrapping around me like a lullaby I couldn't resist.

My eyelids fluttered shut despite my efforts to stay awake, to share in the burden he refused to set down. The last thing I saw before sleep claimed me was Cassian's profile, illuminated by the soft glow of the lamp. His features, etched with determination, blurred into the haze of my dreams as I drifted into the quiet comfort of knowing he was there, tirelessly guarding the world he'd built—and me.

CHAPTER SEVEN

The soft stream of morning light filtered through the heavy curtains, spilling across the study and warming my skin as I stirred. The blanket draped over my shoulders slipped slightly as I sat up, the plush cushions beneath me a quiet reminder of the night before. Blinking against the glow, I let the events of the past hours settle in my mind—Cassian's resolve, his intensity, and the quiet determination that had anchored him to the desk long after I'd fallen asleep.

I stretched slowly, the ache in my back from sleeping on the couch tugging gently at my muscles. The study was still, the only sounds the faint hum of the penthouse beyond and the distant rustle of city life filtering in from the windows. The desk lamp was off, and Cassian's chair was empty, the papers that had been spread across the surface now stacked neatly in a way that was unmistakably his.

Rising to my feet, I pulled the throw blanket closer, savoring the lingering warmth as I moved toward the door. The penthouse was quiet, its usual hum subdued, but the calm didn't unsettle me. If anything, it reminded me that this was how Cassian worked—moving purposefully through the stillness to stay one step ahead of his enemies. He wasn't one to linger in the same place for long, and I had no doubt he was already immersed in whatever plans or preparations the morning required.

The warm glow of the sun poured through the tall windows, bathing the penthouse in a golden light as I padded toward the kitchen. The faint aroma of coffee reached me before I saw it—Cassian's untouched cup sitting on the counter. I smiled faintly, shaking my head at his usual habits. He'd make it, let it cool, and forget it entirely while his focus consumed him elsewhere.

After pouring myself a glass of water, I leaned against the counter, letting the cool marble press against my palms as I took in the peaceful stillness. It was rare to find moments like this in Cassian's world—moments that weren't charged with tension or veiled threats. I let it linger for a beat longer before heading toward the bedroom to get dressed.

Sliding open the closet door, I chose a pair of fitted black jeans and a soft gray sweater, something practical and comfortable. Cassian had insisted on maintaining a wardrobe at his place given I spent a good deal of my time here. As I dressed, I thought about Cassian—about the way he'd held my gaze last night, his words filled with both command and care. There was a weight to everything he did, a gravity that pulled me closer to him even when I wasn't sure I could carry it all.

Once ready, I smoothed a hand through my hair, leaving it loose over my shoulders, and grabbed my phone from the nightstand. The clock read 7:15 a.m.—early, but not so much that the day hadn't already begun for him. Slipping my phone into my pocket, I ventured back into the main hallway, the faint sound of rhythmic thuds drawing my attention.

I slipped my phone into the pocket of my jeans, grabbed my bag, and slung it over my shoulder. The routine of Ivy & Bloom called to me—a sanctuary of order amidst the chaos of the past twenty-four hours. I longed for the familiarity of arranging bouquets and welcoming customers, something *normal* to counterbalance the storm Cassian's world seemed determined to draw me into.

The elevator was just down the hall, its sleek metal

doors gleaming faintly. My footsteps were measured, purposeful as I pressed the button and waited for the lift to arrive. But before the soft chime of its arrival, a voice broke the quiet.

"Miss Quinn."

I turned to find one of Cassian's security guards approaching. Broad-shouldered and clad in a tailored black suit, he looked every bit the part of the stoic sentinel, his expression calm but firm.

"Yes?" I asked, my tone polite but edged with impatience. I wasn't in the mood for interruptions.

"I'm sorry, but you're not permitted to leave the residence at this time," he said evenly, his tone leaving no room for negotiation. "Per Mr. Moreau's instructions."

I blinked, taken aback. "Excuse me?" My voice rose slightly. "I have a shop to run. I can't just—"

"Mr. Moreau's orders were clear," he interrupted, though his tone remained respectful. "For your safety, you're to remain here."

My grip on the strap of my bag tightened, a surge of frustration flaring in my chest. "I'm not a prisoner."

"I understand, Miss Quinn," the guard replied, his calm demeanor never wavering. "But I cannot let you leave."

The truth in his words wasn't up for debate; Cassian's orders were absolute. I exhaled sharply, the heat of my anger simmering beneath the surface as I turned and headed back down the hallway. Fine. If Cassian thought he could keep me here indefinitely, I'd confront him myself.

The faint hum of rhythmic strikes guided me toward the private gym at the far end of the penthouse. As I approached, the sound of controlled breathing and the steady impact of fists meeting a heavy bag became clearer. Pushing open the door, I stepped inside and found him.

Cassian stood in the center of the room, his bare torso glistening with sweat, the intricate lines of his muscles shifting with each deliberate movement. The heavy bag swung under the weight of his strikes, his muscles taut with controlled, precise power. His focus was unyielding, every motion accurate, every punch resonating with the tension of a man who carried the weight of an entire world on his shoulders.

"Cassian," I said, my voice cutting through the rhythm of his strikes.

He didn't stop immediately, landing a final blow before turning to face me. His chest rose and fell steadily, his gray eyes locking onto mine. There was a flicker of something in his gaze—irritation, perhaps, or curiosity. He grabbed a towel from a nearby bench, wiping his face before draping it over his shoulder.

"Rosalie," he said simply, his tone neutral. "Did you sleep well?"

"Well enough," I replied, crossing my arms as I leaned against the doorframe. "But it seems I'm under house arrest."

Cassian's expression hardened, the faintest trace of a frown pulling at his lips. "For good reason."

"Cassian, I have a business to run," I said, keeping my tone calm but firm. "I can't just stay here indefinitely."

He stepped closer, the intensity of his presence making the room feel smaller. "The Reapers are out there," he said quietly. "Until I know exactly what they're planning, I'm not taking any risks."

"This isn't your decision to make," I countered, my voice steady but edged with determination. "I appreciate your concern, but I'm not some possession you can lock away whenever it suits you."

For a moment, his jaw tightened, and I thought he might snap back. Instead, he exhaled slowly, his gray eyes softening just enough to stir something in my chest. "You don't understand what's at stake, Rosalie," he said, his voice low but resolute. "When you show me you can follow directions, we'll revisit this."

"Directions?" I asked, narrowing my eyes. "I'm not one of your men, Cassian. I don't take orders."

He didn't respond, his gaze steady as he turned away and grabbed his phone from a nearby bench. "Yes, directions.," he said over his shoulder, his words broken by his breathing.

I trailed him through the penthouse, my frustration simmering. He led me into his office, pausing at his desk for a moment while I shut the door behind us; his men didn't need to hear the rest of this conversation. Tossing the towel onto the back of a chair, Cassian tapped something on his phone before nodding toward the door.

"Come in," he called, his voice sharp.

I sighed, realizing my attempt was overruled.

The door opened, and two figures stepped inside. Their presence was as commanding as Cassian's, though in entirely different ways.

"This is Sierra," Cassian said, gesturing to the woman who stood to the left. Her blonde hair was pulled into a sleek ponytail, her sharp blue eyes assessing me with precision. She exuded a quiet confidence, her fitted suit emphasizing her lean, athletic frame. "She's former military. She'll shadow you at the shop and on errands."

He turned to the man beside her. "And this is Marcus." Broad-shouldered and calm, Marcus had the kind of steady presence that demanded respect. His dark suit fit impeccably, his deep brown eyes steady but kind. "Marcus will handle your transport and be your shadow when I'm not here."

I blinked, glancing between the two of them. "My security detail," I said slowly, the words tinged with disbelief.

"Yes," Cassian said simply. "You're not going anywhere alone, Rosalie. Not anymore."

The word *shadow* reverberated in my mind, but in truth, they weren't just shadows—they were chains, binding me to a reality I hadn't chosen. I studied Sierra and Marcus, my frustration simmering beneath a begrudging respect for the way they carried themselves.

"You can't be serious," I said, directing the question at Cassian. "Where are the other guys?"

"They're lucky they're not in a ditch somewhere," Cassian replied sharply, his tone clipped and unyielding. His jaw tightened, the tension in his expression unmistakable. "This isn't a joke, Rosalie. You've already demonstrated that you're incapable of following the most basic safety protocols. So now, I'm handling it."

Sierra's face remained impassive, her posture as steady as a statue, but Marcus offered a faint, reassuring smile. "We'll stay out of your way as much as we can, Miss Quinn," he said, his deep voice a soothing contrast to Cassian's sharpness. "But our priority is your safety."

I exhaled sharply, crossing my arms over my chest. "This feels like overkill."

"No," Cassian said, his voice as firm as the granite edge of his desk. "This is necessary. And if you don't understand that yet, you will by the time the doctor arrives."

"The doctor?" I echoed, my brow furrowing as memories of the older gentleman who had stitched me up after Victor's attack resurfaced.

Cassian leaned back slightly against the edge of his desk, his arms crossing over his chest. "Routine follow-up," he explained, his tone softening just enough to be almost disarming. "That gunshot wound wasn't minor, Rosalie. Just because the stitches are healed doesn't mean we can ignore the possibility of complications."

The memory of that night surged forward—the chaos, the blinding pain, and Cassian's arms carrying me to safety. The bullet Victor had fired wasn't meant for me, but I had been caught in its path. The gash it left along my side had required more than just stitches—it had demanded weeks of recovery and a forced dependency I hadn't been ready to face.

"That was months ago," I argued, though even as I said it, the faint ache in my side reminded me of its permanence. "I'm fine."

Cassian's gray eyes softened, though his resolve didn't waver. "Humor me," he said, his voice dropping just enough to take the edge off. "Dr. Ellison will be here later today. And if you're feeling restless, I'll have some arrangements brought from Ivy & Bloom. You can work on them here."

I sighed, his protectiveness settling over me like a weight I couldn't shake. "Fine," I said, relenting but far from satisfied. I gestured toward Sierra and Marcus, my irritation simmering. "But that doesn't mean I'm okay with all of this. I'm perfectly capable of taking care of myself."

Cassian's lips curved into a faint smirk, though it carried none of the warmth I'd hoped for. "Forgive me if I don't take your word for it," he said, his voice laced with quiet authority.

As I turned to leave the room, his voice followed me, sharp and commanding as he addressed my new *shadows*. "The first one to lose sight of her outside these walls will answer directly to me."

The weight of his words hung heavy in the air, and I didn't need to look back to know his eyes were already on me, watching, ensuring that the world I'd stepped into wouldn't swallow me whole.

The word *shadow* had lingered in my thoughts, but as I slipped into Cassian's office, the sensation was sharper—more tangible. I stood in the middle of the penthouse, pacing back and forth as frustration clawed at my chest. Cassian's heavy-handed control was starting to wear on me. The bodyguards, the restrictions, the constant feeling of being watched—it was too much. I couldn't live like this, locked away and powerless, waiting for someone else to take care of things.

The quiet hum of the penthouse, the faint trickle of water from the shower down the hall, and the soft rustle of papers under my fingertips were the only sounds drawing my attention to the hear and now. I closed the door behind me, careful to press it shut without a sound, sealing myself into his world of meticulously constructed secrets.

The desk loomed in front of me, an altar to Cassian's precision and control. His familiar scent of cedar and spice still lingered in the air, a subtle reminder of the man who occupied this space only an hour ago. Papers lay in organized chaos, his sharp handwriting etched across notebooks and documents, mapping out a network of connections that stretched far beyond the penthouse walls.

Sliding into the high-backed leather chair, I felt the cool surface press against me, comforting me as I began to sift through his work. Names, dates, locations—all scattered like shards of glass, each piece reflecting a fragment of a larger, darker truth. My fingers hesitated over a notebook, flipping through pages marked with his steady script, only to falter where his handwriting became less controlled. The weight of his exhaustion was evident, the lines trailing off as though written in the grip of relentless pressure.

The computer screen sat dark, its black mirror a silent guardian of its secrets. I nudged the mouse, the screen springing to life only to demand a passcode. Of course. My lips pressed into a thin line as I turned back to the papers, determined to uncover what I could without digital access.

Taking a deep breath, I approached the desk and slid into the chair, the leather cool against my skin. My eyes scanned the papers, trying to piece together what he'd been working on. Names, dates, places—it was all there, scattered like pieces of a puzzle.

I reached for a notebook, flipping through the pages slowly. Cassian's handwriting was sharp and deliberate and first but there were visible signs of when the lack of sleep had set in, each word written with less control than the next. Patterns began to emerge as I traced my fingers over the notes. Meetings, movements, shipments. The Reapers weren't just operating in the shadows; they were moving pieces on a much larger board.

The sound of water running in the distance was a constant reminder of the limited time I had before he returned. I grabbed a blank sheet of paper and began jotting down my own notes, trying to make sense of the patterns in his research. If I could find something—anything—that might help him connect the dots, maybe he'd see that I wasn't just some liability to be protected. I was a partner in this mess.

I tapped my pen against the desk as I scanned the documents in front of me. My notes were starting to take shape, a web of connections slowly forming as I pieced together the fragments of information Cassian had collected. There were dates and shipment records that didn't match up, locations marked on maps that didn't correspond to the supposed activities in those areas.

Something wasn't adding up, and the more I looked, the more the inconsistencies stood out.

Leaning forward, I pulled a stack of shipping manifests toward me, carefully comparing them to the transaction records Cassian had printed out. My heart sped up as I spotted the first discrepancy. A shipment marked as "delivered" in the port logs wasn't accounted for in the corresponding inventory list. Another had been rerouted at the last minute to a warehouse that wasn't even registered in the original delivery chain.

I scribbled furiously in the notebook, circling the names of the involved parties and tracing the patterns. All the shipments in question seemed to funnel back to one company: Apex Logistics. The name was innocuous enough, but the irregularities screamed otherwise.

Biting my lip, I opened my phone since Cassian's laptop was password protected. A quick backward search of the company's business registry led me to its parent corporation, a seemingly unrelated entity called Astra Holdings. But when I dug further, my stomach turned. The CEO listed on the registry was none other than Damon Cross.

The name was vaguely familiar, but as I searched Cassian's files, I realized why. Damon Cross had been flagged in Cassian's earlier research as a suspected Reaper affiliate—a financier with a clean public image but deep ties to their operations. If Apex Logistics was tied to him, it meant the Reapers were using legitimate business fronts to mask their movements. And judging by the shipment patterns, they weren't moving small-scale goods. This was something big.

I jotted down everything I found, mapping the connections between Apex Logistics, Astra Holdings, and Damon Cross. Every piece of data I uncovered painted a more alarming picture. Apex's activities weren't confined to one area—they were nationwide, even international. Shipments from ports in New York, Los Angeles, and even overseas all pointed to a systematic operation designed to avoid detection.

The clock on the desk ticked past the two-hour mark since I'd started, but I barely noticed. My focus was razor-sharp as I dug deeper, uncovering records of financial transactions that hinted at bribes and under-the-table deals with port authorities. Whoever was running this operation wasn't just well-funded—they were meticulous, just like Cassian.

I leaned back in the chair, the pages of notes in front of me a mix of adrenaline-fueled discoveries and growing dread. This wasn't just a threat—it was a ticking time bomb, and Cassian was sitting in the middle of it.

The soft click of the door opening snapped me out of my thoughts. My head whipped up to see Cassian standing in the doorway, his hair now dry from the shower, his shirt was buttoned and neatly tucked into a pair of dark slacks. His gray eyes narrowed as he took in the scene—me at his desk, papers spread out, and the giant map sprawled across the floor, an array of new sticky notes on the surface.

"What the hell do you think you're doing?" he asked, his voice low and dangerous. The calm before the storm.

I froze under Cassian's intense gaze, my mind scrambling for the right words. The calm fury in his tone made it clear he wasn't in the mood for excuses. But I'd come too far, uncovered too much, to stop now.

"I'm helping," I said, lifting my chin despite the nerves twisting in my stomach.

Cassian stepped further into the room, his eyes darting to the scattered papers and my hastily scribbled notes. "Helping," he repeated, his voice laced with disbelief. "Do you have any idea what you've just done?"

"I've made sense of this." I gestured to the chaos on the desk and floor. "Cassian, look. There are discrepancies in these shipments—patterns you might not have noticed yet. They all trace back to Apex Logistics. That company is a front, and it's owned by Damon Cross."

His eyes narrowed slightly at the mention of the name. "I know who Damon Cross is."

"Then you know his ties run deep," I pressed, pointing to one of my notes. "He's using legitimate businesses to funnel... something. I don't know what exactly, but it's not small. And it's not isolated. This isn't just a local problem, Cassian—it's global."

He leaned over the desk, picking up one of the pages I'd marked. His gray eyes scanned the data, his brows furrowing as he processed the connections I'd outlined. For a moment, I thought he might actually thank me, but then his sharp gaze turned back to me, colder than before.

"This isn't your fight," he said, his voice low and controlled. "You shouldn't have touched this."

"Cassian—"

"No." His tone hardened, cutting me off. He slammed the paper back onto the desk, the sound making me flinch. "Do you understand what you've done? The second you started digging, the second you know their names, the more someone can use it against you."

I opened my mouth to argue, but the words stuck. He was angry—furious, even—but beneath that, I could see the fear. It wasn't just about me meddling; it was about the risk I'd taken without understanding the stakes.

"I couldn't just sit back and do nothing," I said finally, my voice quieter but no less resolute. "This affects me too, Cassian. You've made sure of that."

His jaw tightened, and he dragged a hand through his hair. "You think you're helping, Rosalie, but this? This makes you a liability."

The word stung, but I refused to back down. "A liability? You don't mean that."

"You don't know what I mean." His voice dropped to a rough whisper as he took a step closer. "These people—the Reapers—they don't leave loose ends. If they find out you've been looking into this, if they even suspect you know anything, they'll come after you."

"And you'll stop them," I shot back, my heart pounding. "Because that's what you do, isn't it? Protect the people you care about."

His breath hitched slightly, the faintest crack in his composure. "You don't understand what you've put yourself into," he said, quieter this time. "Knowledge is dangerous,

Rosalie. Even in your hands."

"And ignorance keeps me helpless," I countered. "You're fighting this battle alone, Cassian. I'm trying to help you."

For a long moment, neither of us spoke. The tension between us was palpable, the air thick with unspoken emotions. His gray eyes locked onto mine, searching for something I wasn't sure I could give him—obedience, maybe. Trust. But I'd already crossed the line.

He finally exhaled, a sharp, frustrated sound, and stepped back. "You don't see the full picture, and that's exactly why you need to stay out of this."

I opened my mouth to respond, but he held up a hand, silencing me. "Enough, Rosalie. The doctor is waiting for you in the living room. Go, now."

The sharpness of his command left no room for argument. My chest tightened as I gathered the scattered notes and tossed them into the small trash can beside his desk. I couldn't tell if I was angrier at him for shutting me out or for refusing to even look at what I'd discovered. But as I left the office, I couldn't shake the feeling that I'd struck a nerve—one he wasn't ready to confront.

CHAPTER EIGHT

Dr. Ellison hummed softly as he removed the blood pressure cuff from my arm, his movements efficient and practiced. He adjusted his glasses, squinting slightly as he made notes on his tablet.

"Well, Rosalie," he said finally, his voice warm but detached, "you're in excellent health. Your wound has healed well. I see no reason for further follow-ups unless you experience any complications."

I nodded, relieved but eager to end the visit. "Thank you, if only you could relay that to Cassian."

His smile was brief, professional. "Of course, take care of yourself, and don't hesitate to reach out if you need anything."

As he packed up his bag and left, I sat in the stillness of the living room, the weight of the morning pressing down. The penthouse felt too large, too quiet. Cassian was somewhere, likely orchestrating another unseen plan, leaving me to fend off the stir-crazy feeling clawing at the edges of my mind.

I pulled out my phone and dialed Lena. Her clipped, no-nonsense voice answered on the second ring.

"Rosalie. What is it?"

"I need supplies," I said. "Bouquet-making materials. Enough to keep me busy for a few days."

Lena didn't hesitate. "I'll have it sent over. Anything specific?"

"No," I replied. "Just make sure there's a good variety."

The line went dead with a sharp click, and I exhaled, already dreading her involvement. But if it kept her at arm's length for a while, it was worth it.

An hour later, a knock at the door announced the delivery. Two men wheeled in carts overflowing with fresh flowers, vases, ribbons, and tools. The scent of lavender, roses, and eucalyptus mingled in the air, momentarily soothing the tension knotted in my chest. I tipped them and directed everything to the solarium.

The solarium.

I hadn't spent much time there lately. It was tucked at the far end of the sprawling space, hidden behind a pair of frosted glass doors. When I pushed them open, the room felt like a different world.

Sunlight poured through the massive floor-to-ceiling windows, casting the room in a golden glow. Potted plants and small trees dotted the corners, their lush greenery lending the space a vibrant, earthy feel. A glass table sat in the center, its sleek surface reflecting the light, surrounded by plush chairs upholstered in soft, neutral tones. It was serene, quiet, almost untouched—a sanctuary amidst the chaos of everything Cassian had pulled me into.

I rolled up my sleeves and began arranging the materials on the table. Buckets of fresh water went under the windows, while vases and floral foam lined the surface. The hum of the city outside was faint, almost drowned out by the rustling leaves of the plants around me.

As I worked, threading stems through greenery and adjusting blooms, the tension began to ease. My fingers moved instinctively, muscle memory taking over. For the first time in days, my mind quieted. This was familiar, grounding. Here, amidst the flowers and the sunlight, I could almost pretend I was back at Ivy & Bloom, untouched by Cassian's world.

Almost.

I glanced out the window at the skyline, my gaze

catching on the towering buildings that stretched into the horizon. This wasn't my life—not really. It was his. And no matter how hard I worked, how deeply I buried myself in the comfort of flowers and memories, I couldn't escape that truth.

The arrangements I crafted began to take shape, each one a little more elaborate than the last. I didn't stop until the sun began to dip below the horizon, casting the solarium in shades of amber and crimson. Exhausted but satisfied, I stepped back to admire my work. Bouquets lined the table, each one a testament to the pieces of me I refused to let slip away.

But as I stood there, the weight of Cassian's presence pressed in again, invisible yet inescapable.

It wasn't a feeling I could shake or ignore—it lingered, heavy and magnetic, drawing my awareness even before I turned.

"You're talented," his voice broke the silence, soft yet resonant, carrying a warmth I wasn't accustomed to. "I didn't want to interrupt."

I startled, spinning to find him standing just a few feet away, his frame relaxed against the doorway. The light from the solarium caught on the faint sheen of his tailored shirt, his burgundy jacket absent for once. He looked... different. Not disarmed, exactly—Cassian was never disarmed—but something in his expression was less guarded, softer around the edges.

"How long have you been standing there?" I demanded, the sharp edge of my words an instinctive reaction to the way he always seemed to slip past my defenses.

"Long enough," he replied evenly, pushing away from the door and stepping further into the room. His movements were unhindered, cautious, as if he were careful not to shatter the delicate atmosphere.

I crossed my arms, my fingers curling against the fabric of my sleeves. "You could've said something."

"And ruin the moment?" His lips curved into a faint smile, one that didn't carry the usual smugness but still made my stomach twist. "You looked... at peace. It's rare to see that."

I turned back to the table, pretending to inspect one of the arrangements. "Maybe that's because I don't get much of it."

He didn't respond immediately. Instead, I felt the quiet shift of his presence as he moved closer, the space between us shrinking. His voice, when it came again, was lower, quieter. "You're right."

I frowned, glancing at him over my shoulder. "Right about what?"

"About me," he said simply, his gaze steady. "About how I've treated you. I owe you an apology, Rosalie."

The words landed with the weight of something rare, something that felt as unexpected as the man himself. Cassian Moreau didn't apologize—not unless it served a purpose. And yet, here he was, his tone calm, his expression uncharacteristically earnest.

I didn't trust it.

"For what exactly?" I asked, unable to keep the skepticism from my voice. "The constant interference? The threats? Or just existing in general?"

He tilted his head, a faint sigh escaping him. "For pushing too hard. For not giving you the space to adjust. I can be... harsh." His lips pressed into a thin line, as though the admission cost him something. "It's not an excuse, but it's the truth."

I stared at him, searching for the catch, the hidden agenda. But his gray eyes met mine, steady and unflinching, and for once, I couldn't find the shadow of calculation I'd come to expect.

"Why now?" I asked quietly. "Why apologize now?"

"Because I've been watching you," he admitted, gesturing toward the table of bouquets. "Because I see how hard you're fighting to hold on to something that feels yours, even when the world around you isn't. I understand that more than you think."

I blinked, caught off guard by the sincerity in his voice. "You're saying you understand me now?"

"I'm saying I see you," he corrected gently, stepping

closer until the faint scent of his cologne wrapped around me. "And I admire the strength it takes to stand your ground, even when it feels impossible."

A lump rose in my throat, but I forced it down, refusing to let his words affect me more than they already had. "You don't get to just say that and expect everything to be fine."

"I don't expect anything," he said, his voice steady but soft. "I only want you to know that I see the weight you carry—and that you're not alone in it."

The words hung between us, heavy and charged. For a moment, I let myself believe him, let myself feel the strange comfort his presence offered. But the vulnerability was fleeting, gone as quickly as it came. I turned back to the table, brushing an imaginary speck of dust off a vase.

"You could start by giving me more room to breathe," I said, my tone lighter than the emotion in my chest.

Cassian chuckled softly, the sound low and warm. "That's something I'll have to work on."

The corner of my mouth tugged upward despite myself, a faint smile that I quickly hid by busying my hands with the flowers.

Before I could even register the shift in the air behind me, strong arms wrapped around me, lifting me effortlessly.

"Cassian!" I gasped, the word barely more than a startled breath. My hands instinctively reached for his shoulders, my palms meeting the firm press of muscle beneath his shirt. "What are you doing?"

His gray eyes caught mine, a faint glimmer of amusement flickering in their depths, but his tone was steady, unrelenting. "Giving you the space you asked for."

"This isn't what I meant," I said, my voice rising slightly, though the fight in it faltered under the weight of his gaze.

"No?" he murmured, his lips curving into the barest hint of a smile. "Then maybe you should clarify."

The warmth of his breath brushed against my temple as he carried me, his stride unhurried, deliberate. I should have pushed back, demanded that he put me down, but the words tangled in my throat. Instead, I clung to him, my heart pounding in my chest—not with fear, but with something far more dangerous.

"I meant... You can't just sweep me off my feet—disarming me..." I began, my voice trailing off as we crossed the threshold into the hall. His grip on me tightened, firm yet strangely gentle, and my protest melted into the quiet hum of his presence.

"I can," he replied softly, his gaze unwavering as he glanced down at me. "And I will."

The air shifted around us, growing heavier with each step. I was acutely aware of every sensation—the faint scent of his cologne, the steady rhythm of his breathing, the way his hands cradled me like I was something precious. It was maddening, intoxicating.

"Cassian," I said again, softer this time, almost a plea.

He didn't answer. Instead, he pushed open the door to the bedroom, the room awash in the soft amber glow of the city lights spilling through the floor-to-ceiling windows. The faint hum of the world outside was a distant echo, muted by the stillness that stretched between us.

His steps slowed as we entered, the plush rug muffling the sound of his movements. Gently, he set me down, my feet barely touching the floor before his hands slid to my waist, steadying me. I looked up at him, my breath catching at the intensity in his gaze—sharp, focused, and utterly consuming.

For a moment, neither of us moved, the space between us charged with unspoken words, unacknowledged truths. Then, with deliberate care, his hand rose to brush a stray lock of hair from my face, his fingers lingering against my cheek.

"I see you, Rosalie," he murmured, his voice low, almost reverent. "And I don't want to push you away, but I don't know how else to keep you safe in a world where demons lurk around every corner. I'd do anything for you, Rosalie—and I think you know that."

I swallowed hard, the knot in my chest tightening as I struggled to find my voice. But before I could speak, his hand moved, cupping the back of my neck as he leaned in.

The heat of his breath skimmed my skin, and everything else—my doubts, my fears, my carefully constructed walls—faded into nothingness.

The door clicked softly shut behind him, sealing us in.

And   then,   the   world   fell   away.

CHAPTER NINE

The solarium was bathed in the soft light of a crisp morning, the golden glow casting delicate shadows on the table where breakfast was laid out. Fresh blueberry muffins, chocolate croissants, crispy bacon, fluffy eggs, sliced fruit, and steaming coffee filled the air with their subtle aroma, but my appetite was as absent as the warmth in Cassian's chair across from me.

I sat alone at first, picking at a perfectly flaky croissant as I listened to the faint sounds of movement filtering through the penthouse. Cassian's voice drifted closer—low, steady, though I couldn't make out the words. The sound had an anchoring effect, despite the storm still brewing from my unexpected house arrest.

When he finally appeared, I glanced up from my barely-eaten plate to find him entering the solarium, a shirt draped loosely over his shoulders. His tie hung untied around his neck, and his hands moved with practiced ease, buttoning his shirt as he walked.

He looked out of place among the serene greenery and soft light—too sharp, too commanding—but he didn't seem to notice.

"Good morning," he said, his tone casual as he approached the table. He didn't wait for a response before pouring himself a cup of coffee, his movements calm and efficient.

"It would be a *great* morning, if I could go outside," I muttered, sipping from my own mug. The heat from the coffee did little to thaw the chill lingering in my chest, the product of too many questions and too few answers.

Cassian's eyes flicked to me as he adjusted his collar, a faint smile curving his lips. "You don't look like someone who got much sleep."

"Hard to sleep when you keep throwing curveballs," I replied, my tone taunting.

His smile deepened slightly, a glint of amusement in his gray eyes. "I'll try to keep my pitches straighter next time," he said lightly, reaching for his tie.

I scoffed, though I couldn't stop the corner of my mouth from twitching. "How generous of you."

Cassian didn't respond immediately, his attention focused on the knot he was tying. His fingers moved deftly, looping and pulling the silk with a precision that spoke to years of habit. The tie—a deep charcoal that blended sharply with his black shirt—settled perfectly against his collar.

"I have a meeting today," he said finally, breaking the silence. His voice carried an undertone of something heavier, though he kept his gaze steady as he straightened the cuffs of his shirt. "At The Marquess."

I frowned, the name unfamiliar. "The Marquess?"

"It's a private club downtown," he explained, his tone carefully neutral. "Lucrative, exclusive, and notoriously selective about its clientele. The security is... tight, to say the least."

I raised an eyebrow, unsure where he was going with this. "Sounds *regal*."

Cassian smirked, reaching for his jacket. "It serves its purpose." He slid his arms into the sleeves, smoothing the fabric with a practiced motion before looking back at me.

"And what purpose is that?" I asked, setting my coffee cup down.

"Maintaining order," he replied simply. "It's a meeting place for people who deal in power—whether it's money, influence, or information. Everyone plays by the rules because no one can afford not to."

The casual way he said it sent a ripple of unease through me, though I kept my expression neutral. "And why are you telling me this?"

Cassian's smile returned, softer this time as he stepped closer to the table. "Because I thought you might like a change of scenery."

I blinked, unsure if I'd heard him correctly. "You're suggesting I go with you?"

"Why not?" he said, his tone easy but his gaze piercing. "It'll give you a chance to see a different side of this city—and of me."

I narrowed my eyes, trying to decipher the layers beneath his words. "And what would I do while you're having your meeting? Sit quietly in a corner and pretend not to notice all the power plays happening around me?"

Cassian chuckled, the sound low and rich. "Something like that," he said, leaning down to meet my gaze. "Or, you could observe. Analyze, much like you did with the map in my office."

I was shocked. He'd actually taken a look at my work, and what was that? A hint of appreciation? A stark contradiction to yesterday afternoon's dismissal.

His words hung between us, heavy with implication. He wasn't just offering me a distraction—he was inviting me deeper into his world, the one I'd spent so much time trying to resist.

I glanced down at the table, my hands tightening around my coffee cup. "I don't know if that's a good idea."

Cassian straightened, adjusting the lapels of his jacket. "I didn't say it was a good idea," he said, his voice lighter now, almost teasing. "But it's an opportunity. The decision is yours."

He stepped back, his gaze lingering on me for a moment longer before turning toward the door. "Think about it," he called over his shoulder as he left.

The solarium felt emptier without him, though his presence lingered, woven into the air like an inescapable thread. I stared at my coffee, the warmth of it doing little to soothe the knot tightening in my chest.

The decision should've required more thought, but I was on my feet before I could stop myself, the chair scraping faintly against the floor as I pushed it back. My heart pounded, not with fear, but with something else— something reckless and insistent that propelled me forward.

"Cassian, wait!" I called, my voice breaking the stillness of the moment.

His footsteps paused just beyond the door, and I heard the faint rustle of fabric as he turned. By the time I reached him, his gaze was already locked on me, a flicker of something unreadable in his gray eyes.

"I'll go," I said breathlessly, my hands twisting nervously at my sides.

The faintest smile tugged at his lips, more satisfaction than amusement. "Are you sure?"

"No," I admitted, lifting my chin. "But I'm coming anyway."

Cassian stepped closer, his presence overwhelming even in the quiet restraint of his movements. "Good," he murmured, brushing past me and heading down the hall. "But you can't wear that." He gestured to my baggy sweater and short shorts, hidden beneath the sweater's hem.

His strides were long and unhurried, but there was an air of purpose to them, one that left me trailing slightly behind as we reached his bedroom. He pushed the door open, into the bedroom full of dark woods, the muted grays and blues, the faint scent of his cologne lingering in the air. He headed straight for the walk-in closet he'd had stocked for me.

Cassian moved with precision, his fingers skimming over hangers as he considered his options. "You'll need something that fits the room," he said, more to himself than to me. "Something elegant but understated. Powerful, but not ostentatious."

I crossed my arms, raising an eyebrow as I leaned against the doorframe. "You've put a lot of thought into this."

He glanced over his shoulder, a faint smirk curving his lips. "You've seen the kind of people I deal with, Rosalie. First impressions are currency in my world."

His hand paused on a sleek black dress, the fabric gleaming faintly in the light. He pulled it from the rack, holding it out to me. The silhouette was simple but striking, the kind of piece that spoke volumes without saying a word.

"Try this," he said, his tone leaving no room for argument.

I took the dress hesitantly, the weight of his gaze following me as I stepped back into the bedroom. "What's wrong with what I'm wearing?" I asked, half-joking, though I already knew the answer.

Cassian arched an eyebrow, leaning casually against the doorway of the closet. "You mean besides the fact that you look like you're about to rearrange bouquets all day?"

I shot him a glare, but the warmth in his voice softened the jab. "Fine," I muttered, clutching the dress a little tighter.

He didn't move, his steady gaze unnerving me as I stood there, frozen between defiance and a strange, inexplicable thrill.

"Do you need help?" he asked smoothly, his lips curving into a knowing smirk.

The heat that flared in my cheeks only deepened his amusement. "No," I snapped, turning toward the edge of the bed, laying the dress down. "But I think you'd like a show, wouldn't you?"

His chuckle followed me before he said, "There's no time. Raincheck."

I slipped into it quickly, the cool material sliding over my skin and settling perfectly against my frame. When I turned around, Cassian was waiting, his gaze sweeping over me with a deliberateness that sent a shiver down my spine.

"Perfect," he said softly, his voice carrying a weight that made my pulse quicken.

I swallowed hard, smoothing the fabric nervously. "Is

this how you get all your business associates to follow you around?"

Cassian's lips curved into a slow, knowing smile as he stepped closer, his presence commanding every inch of space between us. "Only the ones who matter," he murmured, his hand brushing mine as he adjusted the line of the dress on my shoulder.

The faintest contact sent a ripple of heat through me, but I forced myself to hold his gaze, refusing to let him see how much he affected me.

"Let's go," he said, his voice a quiet promise as he turned toward the door.

And just like that, I followed him into the unknown, the pull of his world impossible to resist.

Before we knew it, we were in the back of Cassian's SUV, the dark-tinted glass, the hum of the engine a low, steady presence beneath our feet. Cassian sat beside me, his posture relaxed yet commanding, his elbow propped casually on the door. Despite the calm demeanor he projected, there was a sharpness in his gaze as he glanced out the window, scanning the street as though calculating every possible risk.

The convoy was unmistakable—our vehicle flanked by another identical SUV behind us. I'd caught a glimpse of the men stepping into the second car before we left, each of them dressed in unassuming dark suits, their movements sharp and efficient.

"Isn't this a bit much?" I asked, breaking the silence. "I thought you said The Marquess is a fortress."

"It is," Cassian replied, his gaze flicking toward me briefly before settling back on the road ahead. "But a fortress isn't impenetrable. Precautions are necessary."

"For you," I countered, folding my arms. "Not me."

His lips curved faintly, though the amusement didn't quite reach his eyes. "You're with me, Rosalie. That makes you a target, we've discussed this or does your bottom need a reminder so soon?"

My cheeks instantly turned red. The words settled uncomfortably in the pit of my stomach, heavy with implication. "It remembers just fine."

Cassian turned his full attention to me then, his gray eyes sharp. "Are you sure?"

I opened my mouth to argue but stopped, unsure what to say. His presence was overwhelming in the confines of the car, not just physically but in the way he carried himself—so assured, so resolute. He wasn't being dramatic or overly cautious. To him, this was simply reality.

The SUV rolled to a slow stop at a traffic light, the other vehicle halting in sync behind us. Cassian leaned back in his seat, the faintest tension still lingering in his shoulders as he turned to me.

"There are rules you need to follow," he said, his tone steady, businesslike.

"Rules?" I echoed, raising an eyebrow.

His lips twitched slightly. "Yes, rules. The Marquess operates on them, as do I. First, you don't leave my side. Not for a moment. Do you understand?"

I nodded, though a flicker of irritation sparked in my chest. "I can handle myself." Though we both knew that was me trying to be braver than I was.

"While I question your capabilities, we don't have time to die into that rabbit hole," he said smoothly, his tone softening just enough to take the sting out of his words. "But this isn't about you. It's about the message your absence might send."

I frowned, trying to unpack the meaning behind his words. "What kind of message?"

"That I can't protect you," he said simply. "And if they think I can't protect you, they'll wonder what else I can't protect. Perception is power, Rosalie. Never forget that."

The weight of his explanation settled over me, the gravity of his world pressing closer. "Fine," I said, my voice quieter. "I'll stay close."

"Good," he said, his expression approving. "Second, you don't speak unless I tell you to. This isn't your world, and the less they know about you, the safer you'll be."

I bristled at the rule but nodded, recognizing the practicality behind it. "Anything else?"

He tilted his head slightly, his gaze softening. "Just one more. If I give you an order, you follow it without hesitation. No questions, no arguments."

I narrowed my eyes. "That's convenient for you."

"It's necessary," he corrected, his voice calm but firm. "I'm not asking you to trust me blindly, but I need you to trust that I know what I'm doing."

His words hung in the air, heavy and unyielding. I wanted to push back, to challenge his control, but the intensity in his gaze left little room for argument. He wasn't just being protective; he was setting boundaries in a world I barely understood.

The SUV eased forward again, the convoy moving in sync as we neared the club. The buildings outside grew taller, sleeker, their mirrored facades reflecting the late-morning sunlight.

"I'll follow the rules," I said finally, my voice quieter. "But don't expect me to like them."

Cassian's lips curved into a faint smile, one that carried the barest trace of amusement. "I wouldn't dream of it."

CHAPTER TEN

The SUV came to a smooth stop in front of a building that exuded quiet elegance. Nestled between towering office complexes, its facade was sleek and understated, a blend of matte black stone and glass that absorbed the morning light rather than reflecting it. Above the entrance, a single brass plaque bore the club's name—The Marquess—in regal script, the engraved letters gilded and shining faintly in the muted daylight.

The design was subtle but unmistakable, a declaration of exclusivity for those who knew what to look for. The intricately engraved brass doorframe beneath it hinted at secrets within, framing an entrance meant for those with power, wealth, or both.

Cassian stepped out first, his movements measured as he scanned the quiet street. I followed closely, my heels clicking against the pavement, the sound sharp and out of place in the eerie stillness of the late morning.

The man at the door—a tall, broad figure in a perfectly tailored suit—opened it without a word, his sharp nod an acknowledgment of Cassian's presence.

"Mr. Moreau," the man said, his voice low and clipped. His gaze shifted to me briefly, his expression unreadable.

Cassian gave a curt nod and placed a hand on the small of my back, guiding me inside.

The interior was a world apart from the cold, modern exterior. Stepping into *The Marquess* was like stepping back in time. The space was a study in old-world opulence, its design evoking an era where power was synonymous with sophistication.

A grand staircase dominated the entryway, its dark mahogany bannister polished to a mirror-like sheen. Crimson carpet lined the steps, bordered with gold stitching that glinted faintly under the warm light of an enormous chandelier suspended above. The walls were paneled in rich, dark wood, interrupted only by ornate light fixtures that cast a soft, ambient glow.

Cassian led me further inside, his stride relaxed yet purposeful. As we moved through the space, I couldn't help but take in every detail—the velvet curtains framing tall, arched windows that stretched nearly to the ceiling. The glass was tinted so heavily that it allowed natural light to filter in without revealing anything to the world outside. The floors were polished black stone, smooth and gleaming like a mirror, reflecting the soft glow of the warm ambient lighting. The faint but intoxicating scent of leather and expensive cigars lingered in the air, a subtle reminder of the kind of power that frequented this place.

Even empty, the club felt alive, as though the walls themselves carried the weight of countless whispered secrets and silent deals.

"This is... extravagant," I said quietly, my voice swallowed by the sinfully dark space.

"It's intentional," Cassian replied, glancing at me out of the corner of his eye. "Power isn't just about control; it's about perception. The Marquess was designed to remind its patrons of their place—whether that's at the top of the food chain or scrambling to climb it."

He paused as we approached a pair of heavy double doors, their surface adorned with intricate carvings of the British royal crest—lions, stallions, and a crown framed by laurel leaves. The craftsmanship was meticulous, every detail etched into the dark wood with an almost reverent artistry. His fingers brushed the polished brass handle, the ornate design shaped like a heraldic lion's head. He paused briefly, turning to me before pushing the doors open.

"This is the heart of the club," he said. "The main lounge. It's where most meetings take place. It won't look the same now as it does when it's open, but you'll get a sense of it."

With a smooth motion, he pushed the doors open, revealing a sprawling room that managed to feel both vast and intimate.

The lounge was dominated by a circular bar at its center, a masterpiece of black marble and brushed gold. Shelves behind the bar rose to the ceiling, lined with an impressive array of bottles that shimmered in the soft light filtering through frosted skylights above. Scattered around the room were clusters of low, leather armchairs and polished tables, each space arranged with deliberate care to create a sense of privacy without isolation.

Above it all, a mezzanine wrapped around the room, its railing lined with gold filigree. Private booths were tucked into the shadows of the upper level, their velvet curtains half-drawn as if awaiting their next occupants.

Despite its grandeur, the room felt shrouded in confidentiality. The muted colors—deep greens, golds, and rich burgundies—along with the absence of windows, created an atmosphere that was both seductive and secretive.

Cassian's hand rested lightly on my back again, drawing my attention.

"This isn't a place for the faint of heart," he said, his voice low and steady. "Everything you see here—the opulence, the elegance—it's all a facade. Behind it, every person who walks through these doors is here for one reason: leverage."

I swallowed, my gaze sweeping the room again. It was beautiful, but now, with Cassian's words lingering in the air, it felt like a gilded trap.

"And what about you?" I asked, glancing up at him. "What's your reason for being here?"

His lips curved into the faintest smile, though it didn't reach his eyes. "Leverage," he repeated. "But this time, it's for both of us."

Before I could ask what he meant, footsteps echoed through the lounge, sharp and deliberate. A man emerged from a side door near the bar, his tailored suit impeccable and his expression carefully neutral.

"Mr. Moreau," the man greeted, his voice smooth as he extended a hand. "Everything is prepared."

Cassian shook his hand but didn't let go immediately, his grip firm. "Thank you, Herald," he said, his tone carrying a quiet authority that filled the space. "Let's not waste time."

The man nodded, his gaze flicking briefly to me before stepping aside and motioning toward a private room.

Cassian turned to me, his expression unreadable. "Stay close," he said, his voice dropping to a near whisper. "And remember the rules."

I nodded, the weight of his words settling heavily on my chest as I followed him toward the room, my steps quieter than my racing heartbeat.

We were led through another set of heavy doors; they creaked open, revealing a room that matched the grandeur of the rest of the club. The space was vast yet intimate, its lighting low and warm, casting shadows that softened the sharp edges of the furniture. A massive oak table dominated the center, its surface tinged and dented, as if the remnants of a battle ram. The table was surrounded by high-backed chairs upholstered in deep maroon suede. Along the walls, bookshelves lined with volumes of law, finance, and history gave the room a scholarly air, though the faint scent of brandy and cigars betrayed its true purpose.

Cassian's hand rested briefly at the small of my back, guiding me forward. The subtle touch steadied me, though it did little to ease the unease curling in my stomach. This was his domain—luxurious, powerful, and shrouded in secrets—and I was an outsider, standing on the edge of something I didn't fully understand.

Two men were already seated at the far end of the table, their conversation low but tense. Both looked up as we entered, their gazes abrupt and scrutinizing. One was older, his silver hair neatly combed back, his tailored three-piece suit a shade too traditional for the modern opulence around him. The other was younger, his scarred jaw and piercing eyes giving him the look of someone accustomed to having the upper hand.

"Moreau," the older man greeted, rising from his seat. His tone was neutral, but his eyes carried the weight of years of dealings—perhaps alliances, perhaps rivalries. "It's good to see you—I think."

"Time will tell," Cassian replied smoothly, his expression unreadable. He motioned for me to take a seat at his right before he moved to claim his place at the head of the table.

The younger man's gaze lingered on me, his lips curving into a faint smirk. "And you've brought a guest. That's unusual."

Cassian's eyes cut to him, jagged and cold. "Keep your dick in your pants," he said simply, his tone leaving no room for argument.

The smirk disappeared, replaced by a brief, tight nod. "Of course."

Before the conversation could continue, the door to a side room opened, and another figure stepped out. He was lean, his tailored suit impeccably pressed, his movements efficient and precise. In his hands, he carried a slim black case, the kind that screamed importance.

I watched as the man approached one of the bookshelves, pulling a hidden lever that revealed a small compartment behind the rows of leather-bound volumes. Carefully, he placed the case inside, locking it with a thumbprint scanner before stepping back.

The entire exchange lasted less than a minute, but the tension in the room sharpened, as if an invisible line had been crossed.

"Discrete as ever," the younger man muttered, leaning back in his chair.

The silver-haired man shot him a warning glance before turning to Cassian. "Shall we begin?"

Cassian nodded, but his focus shifted briefly to me. His hand brushed mine under the table, a subtle reminder to remain composed.

"Proceed," he said, his voice steady and commanding.

As the conversation began, I tuned out the specifics, instead focusing on the undercurrents in the room. The way the silver-haired man's fingers twitched when he listened, the way the younger man's smirk returned every time he spoke—it was a game of chess, every word and gesture a calculated move.

But my attention kept flickering to the case tucked behind the bookshelf. Whatever it held wasn't just valuable; it was vital to this meeting. The way the room had shifted when it appeared told me as much.

The atmosphere grew heavier with each passing word, every exchange charged with the kind of tension that didn't need raised voices to be felt. The silver-haired man leaned forward, steepling his fingers as he addressed Cassian directly.

"The product is secure, as you've seen," he said, his tone calm but laced with warning. "But that won't matter if distribution falls apart. The Reapers are pressing on your northern routes. The shipments are vulnerable."

Cassian's expression didn't falter. He leaned back in his chair, his posture casual but his eyes razor-sharp. "The Reapers press because they think there's weakness to exploit. Let them try. My men are prepared."

The younger man, still lounging in his seat, chuckled softly, the sound grating in the tense silence. "Prepared? That's a bold word, Moreau. How many of your shipments have been intercepted in the past month alone? Five? Six?"

Cassian's gaze shifted to him, cold and deliberate. "Two," he said evenly, his voice carrying a quiet authority that silenced the room. "Both recovered. And if I'm not mistaken, those routes wouldn't have been compromised if certain... information hadn't leaked."

The smirk on the younger man's face faltered, his hand tightening briefly on the armrest of his chair.

"Let's not turn this into a blame game," the silver-haired

man interjected smoothly, his tone an attempt at diplomacy. "What matters is ensuring that the next shipment reaches its destination without interference. The buyers are growing restless, and the Reapers' influence grows daily."

Cassian's jaw tightened, his hand brushing briefly over the table as if weighing his next words. "I have contingencies in place. The northern routes are a temporary problem, not a permanent one. What I need from you," he said, directing his focus to the older man, "is confirmation that the shipment is still on schedule. Delay it, and we risk more than restless buyers."

The older man hesitated, glancing briefly at the younger one, who met his gaze with an almost imperceptible shake of the head. It was subtle, but I caught it—and so did Cassian.

"Let me make this clear," Cassian said, his voice dropping, dangerously threatening. "If the shipment is delayed because of hesitation or second-guessing, you'll be answering to more than just me. That is—if you believe in a maker."

The warning settled, undeniable and echoing the depths Cassian would go to. The silver-haired man nodded with measured reluctance, his carefully maintained composure giving way to a brief glimmer of apprehension.

"It's on schedule," he said finally. "We'll have it routed to your designated point by the end of the week."

The conversation shifted then, moving into logistics and security protocols that I didn't fully follow. My attention drifted back to the case behind the bookshelf, the way it had been placed there with such precision, as if it contained more than just documents or cash.

"What's in it?" I whispered, the words barely audible.

Cassian's hand brushed mine again, a subtle gesture that silenced my question before it could linger. He didn't look at me, his focus remaining on the discussion, but the tension in his grip was answer enough.

The meeting wound down after another fifteen minutes, concluding with stiff handshakes and curt nods. The silver-haired man stood first, smoothing his jacket as he glanced at Cassian.

"We'll hold up our end," he said. "See that you do the same."

Cassian's smile was thin, cold. "I always do."

The younger man lingered, his gaze darting to me one last time before he followed the older man out of the room.

As the doors closed behind them, the silence left in their wake felt almost deafening. Cassian didn't move immediately, his eyes fixed on the now-empty chairs as if lost in thought.

"What's in the case?" I asked again, my voice steadier this time.

He finally turned to me, his expression inscrutable. "It's better if you don't know."

I frowned, my frustration bubbling to the surface. "That's not an answer."

"It's the only one you're getting," he said, his tone soft but final. He stood then, offering me his hand. "Come on. We're done here."

Reluctantly, I took his hand, letting him guide me to my feet. But as we left the room, the weight of the case and the secrets it held stayed with me, a quiet reminder that Cassian's world was far more dangerous—and far more complex—than I'd ever imagined.

CHAPTER ELEVEN

The gentle hum of the SUV filled the quiet as the city blurred past the tinted windows. Morning had given way to midday, the sun casting sharp streaks of light that the glass muted into a soft, golden glow. I glanced out at the familiar streets, the landmarks of my world, and tried to anchor myself in their simplicity.

Ivy & Bloom was close now, just a few more blocks. The thought of returning brought a sense of relief, a tether to something normal amidst the chaos Cassian's world had drawn me into. My phone sat in my lap, the screen still dark despite my urge to call Lena and check on the shop.

"Thinking about the business?" Cassian's voice cut through my thoughts, low and steady.

I turned to find him watching me, his expression unreadable, though there was something sharper in his gaze than the casual tone suggested.

"Lena's been running things without me for longer than I expected," I admitted. "I just want to make sure everything's running smoothly."

"As she should—that's why I pay her more than most of my men," he said with a faint curve of his lips. "She's also got more balls than half of them."

I chuckled, but my anxiety resurfaced. His reassurance

didn't entirely soothe the worry gnawing at me. "True. But she doesn't handle details the way I would. Sometimes I just—"

"Like to be in control?" he finished, the faintest trace of amusement slipping into his tone.

I shot him a look. "I like to make sure things are done right."

Cassian's chuckle was low, almost indulgent. "You're not wrong for wanting that. Control is important. Which is why I'm curious what you noticed during the meeting."

The shift in his tone drew my attention fully to him. He was watching me now, his gray eyes searching mine, though his posture remained casual.

"What do you mean?" I asked, wary of the question's weight.

"You were there," he said simply. "You saw the same things I did. I want to know what you observed."

I hesitated, my hands tightening slightly in my lap. "You're testing me."

"I'm curious," he corrected, leaning back slightly. "It's one thing to follow instructions, another to understand the dynamics at play. Show me you understood."

I let out a slow breath, replaying the details of the meeting in my mind. The silver-haired man's measured tone, the younger man's subtle defiance, the tension that sharpened when the case appeared. Every detail felt like a piece of a puzzle I wasn't sure how to assemble.

"The older man," I began carefully. "He's the stabilizer, isn't he? He's the one keeping everything together—too experienced to act rashly, but not confident enough to push back if it means risking disruption."

Cassian's expression didn't change, but I caught the faintest flicker of approval in his eyes.

"And the younger one?" he prompted.

"He's dangerous," I said without hesitation. "Not because he's clever—though he is—but because he's impulsive. He wanted to push back, challenge you, but the other man kept him in check. If he were alone, I think he'd be more reckless. Riskier."

Cassian nodded slightly, his attention unwavering. "And the case?"

I faltered, the weight of the question settling heavily in my chest. "It's... pivotal," I said finally. "Whatever it holds, it's tied to something bigger than just the deal. The room changed when it appeared—like it held more than just its contents. It felt like leverage."

He studied me for a moment, the silence stretching between us, thick and heavy. Then, slowly, he nodded again, his lips curving into a faint smile.

"Not bad," he said quietly. "Not bad at all."

"Is this what you wanted?" I asked, unable to mask the edge of frustration in my voice. "For me to see what you see the board the way you do?"

His smile faded slightly, his gaze softening. "No," he said simply. "I want you to understand the board. Because whether you like it or not, you're at my side now."

The words hit harder than I wanted to admit, their weight settling uncomfortably in my chest. I turned back to the window, watching the familiar streets slide by as Ivy & Bloom came into view.

The SUV came to a smooth stop in front of the shop, its familiar green awning fluttering gently in the breeze. My heart lifted slightly at the sight, the unpolished brass lettering on the window glinting in the midday sun. For a moment, I could almost forget the morning's tension, the chess game of power and leverage that I'd just witnessed.

Cassian opened the door and stepped out first, his sharp silhouette cutting against the sunlight. I reached for the handle, but before I could push it open, he was already there, holding the door for me.

"Don't wander too far," he murmured as I climbed out, his voice steady but carrying that same undercurrent of authority I was learning to recognize all too well.

I didn't bother responding, my focus shifting to the shop as the familiar scents of flowers and earth carried on the breeze.

But before we could take more than a step toward the entrance, Cassian's phone buzzed in his pocket. He pulled it out, his brows furrowing slightly as he checked the screen.

"I have to take this," he said, his tone clipped, already stepping a few paces away.

"It's fine," I said, brushing past him toward the door. "I'm twenty feet away. What could possibly happen?"

"Rosalie," he called, his voice firm enough to stop me in my tracks.

I turned back to see him motioning to the two guards who had been trailing discreetly behind us. Their broad shoulders and dark suits blended into the city background, but their sharp eyes missed nothing.

"Go with her," Cassian instructed, his gaze flicking between them and me.

"Seriously?" I asked, crossing my arms. "It's twenty feet, and you'll still be in sight."

His eyes met mine, steady and unyielding. "Go. With. Her."

I let out an exaggerated sigh, rolling my eyes as I turned on my heel and stalked toward the shop. The guards followed silently, their presence more annoying than reassuring.

The bell above the door jingled as I stepped inside, the familiar sound accompanied by the warm, earthy scent of the shop. For a brief moment, the tension melted away, replaced by the comfort of the familiar.

"Lena?" I called, glancing toward the back.

"In the office!" her voice rang out, slightly muffled.

The guards stopped just inside the door, their imposing figures completely out of place among the delicate arrangements and soft pastel decor. I shot them a look but didn't bother addressing them as I made my way toward the back, determined to get back to something normal— something that didn't involve hidden cases or tense power plays.

Lena was perched at the desk, her usual sharp efficiency on full display as she flipped through a clipboard stacked with papers. Her hair was pulled back into a tight bun, and she didn't bother looking up as I stepped inside.

"Busy as ever," I remarked, leaning against the doorframe.

She glanced up briefly, her eyes narrowing just enough to convey her usual impatience. "Big orders coming up," she said briskly. "Two corporate events and a retirement ceremony. And before you ask, yes, we're handling it. Though your absence hasn't exactly helped streamline things."

I raised a brow but didn't rise to the bait. "Can you walk in that direction," I pointed to the door where Cassian paced beyond, "and repeat that a little louder?"

Her lips twitched, though it wasn't quite a smile. "Cassian has been... generous," she added, flipping another page on the clipboard. "He's made arrangements for additional materials to be delivered to the penthouse. Apparently, you'll be working out of there for some of these orders."

I blinked. "The penthouse? That's not exactly the best space for—"

"His words, not mine," Lena interrupted, finally meeting my gaze. "You should've seen the delivery list. Top-quality flowers, imported greenery, tools I didn't even know existed. He's pulling out all the stops, Rosalie. I'd say you should be flattered, but I think we both know there's more to it than that."

My chest tightened at her words, but I forced myself to nod. "Let me know if there's anything else you need to keep things running smoothly here. And keep the deliveries reasonable. I don't want to drown in roses."

"Noted," Lena replied, already turning back to her clipboard.

Before I could press her further, the bell above the shop door jingled faintly. The sound carried through the quiet, and I glanced over my shoulder, expecting another customer.

Instead, a petite woman stepped inside, her heels clicking softly against the wooden floor. She was a little over five foot, but not much taller, her slim frame wrapped in a thick cream coat that matched the glossy beige of her manicured nails. Her blonde hair was swept into an elegant knot, and she moved with a purposeful grace that immediately caught my attention.

I stepped out of the office, meeting her as she approached the counter. Her eyes—dark, intelligent—swept over the shop with careful precision, lingering on the arrangements lining the walls.

"Can I help you?" I asked, keeping my tone professional.

The woman turned to me, offering a small but polished smile. "I certainly hope so. I'm not here to buy flowers, though. I'd like to discuss the possibility of expanding Ivy & Bloom."

Her words hit like a splash of cold water, and I straightened instinctively. "Expanding?" I repeated, caught off guard.

"Yes," she said, her smile widening slightly. "I've followed the shop for quite some time—your designs, your reputation. They're impeccable. I believe there's an opportunity to elevate Ivy & Bloom into something even greater. Perhaps a chain or a collaboration with larger brands."

I blinked, unsure how to respond. This wasn't a conversation I'd expected today—or ever, for that matter.

"Forgive me," I said carefully. "But who are you, exactly?"

The woman extended a hand, her grip surprisingly firm for someone so slight. "Sophia Brandt," she said smoothly. "Business consultant. I specialize in brand development and expansion."

Sophia's calm confidence unsettled me slightly, but I forced myself to maintain composure. "I appreciate your interest, Ms. Brandt, but Ivy & Bloom isn't exactly positioned for that kind of move."

Her head tilted slightly, her expression unflinching. "Perhaps not yet. But with the right guidance, the possibilities are endless. You have something rare here, Ms. Quinn. A foundation that could grow into something extraordinary."

I hesitated, unsure how much to say. "This is... a family

business," I said, my voice softening slightly. "We've always operated on a smaller scale."

Sophia's smile didn't waver. "Sometimes small beginnings lead to the biggest opportunities. I'd love to discuss this further, if you're open to it. Perhaps an informal proposal over lunch?"

Before I could answer, Lena's voice cut through the moment. "Rosalie, we have those invoices to review for the McMullen retirement."

Sophia's gaze flicked to Lena briefly before settling back on me. "Think about it," she said, pulling a sleek business card from her coat pocket and placing it on the counter. "I'll leave this with you. Call me when you're ready to talk."

She turned on her heel and strode toward the door, her movements as precise as her words. The bell jingled faintly as the door swung shut behind her.

I picked up the card, running my thumb over the embossed gold lettering. It felt heavier than it should have, weighted with possibilities I wasn't sure I was ready to consider.

Guilty almost.

"What was that about?" Lena asked, stepping out of the office.

"An offer," I said simply, slipping the card into my pocket. "One I'm not sure we need."

Lena arched a brow but didn't press, her attention already shifting back to the clipboard in her hands.

I glanced out the window, my eyes searching for Cassian. He stood a short distance away, still on his call, his silhouette sharp against the backdrop of the city.

For the first time, I wondered what he would think about Sophia's offer—and whether Ivy & Bloom's future would be mine to decide at all.

CHAPTER TWELVE

Cassian was still on the phone when I emerged, which was a rare occasion. Sierra and Marcus had followed me out, a silent shadow while Cassian held the door open for me.

I climbed in and he followed suit, keeping his responses short and cryptic, with a dissatisfied grunt here or a agreeing murmur there.

The silence in the SUV stretched thin as Cassian ended the call, his expression unreadable. He slipped the phone back into his jacket pocket, leaning back against the seat with a sharp exhale.

"We're making a detour," he said, his voice low but firm, his attention on the driver.

I frowned, glancing out the window at the streets we were passing. "Where?"

"To one of my businesses," he replied, his tone clipped, leaving no room for questions. But his gaze flicked to me, softening just slightly. "You'll understand when we get there."

I wanted to push for more information, but something about the way his jaw tightened stopped me. Whatever the call had been, it wasn't good news.

The SUV pulled into a narrow alleyway lined with brick

buildings, their facades weathered and unassuming. The bustling sounds of the city faded into the background, replaced by a faint hum of activity that seemed to emanate from behind the metal doors of a nearby building. Cassian didn't wait for the car to stop fully before opening the door and stepping out, rare impatience infecting him.

I hesitated, glancing at the building. Its exterior was plain, almost forgotten, with a faded industrial sign that read Rosemont Imports above the main entrance. A loading dock at the far end was busy, men in uniforms unloading crates with lackadaisical energy.

Cassian glanced back at me, his eyes narrowing slightly. "Rosalie."

That was all it took to shake me from my hesitation. I climbed out of the SUV, my heels clicking softly against the cracked pavement. He was already walking toward the building, his long strides forcing me to quicken my pace to keep up.

"What is this place?" I asked as we approached the door, which a guard opened with a brief nod.

"One of my holding facilities," he replied without breaking stride. "It's where shipments are processed before they move further down the chain. Think of it as a crossroads for information and goods."

I followed him inside, stepping into a wide, open space that smelled faintly of wood and metal. Stacks of wooden crates lined the walls, each marked with nondescript labels that revealed nothing about their contents. Workers moved with precision, clipboards in hand as they checked off inventory lists or communicated through radios clipped to their belts.

The air was cool and carried a sense of controlled chaos, the kind of place where every move was calculated even if it didn't seem that way.

"Why are we here?" I asked, my voice low, though the hum of the space swallowed it almost entirely.

Cassian stopped abruptly near a corner office, his hand brushing mine as he turned to face me. "You're here because I want you to understand something."

"Understand what?" I asked, my unease growing with every passing second.

"This," he said simply, gesturing to the organized chaos around us. "This is what makes control possible. You think Ivy & Bloom is separate from this, but it's not. Nothing I touch is. I need you to see that."

Before I could respond, a man stepped out of the office nearby, his face tight with tension. He was broad-shouldered, his button-up shirt rolled to the elbows, exposing tanned forearms marked by faint scars.

"Mr. Moreau," the man said, nodding in greeting. "We've got an issue."

Cassian's jaw tightened. "What kind of issue?"

"Shipment out of Baltimore didn't clear customs," the man explained, his voice low and hurried. "And now it's sitting in a yard with half the staff asking questions they shouldn't be."

Cassian's expression darkened, and he glanced at me briefly before motioning for the man to follow him into the office. "Wait here," he said to me, his tone leaving no room for argument.

I stayed rooted in place, watching through the glass walls of the office as Cassian and the man spoke. The conversation looked heated, Cassian's gestures calloused and tense, though his face betrayed little of the frustration I could sense radiating off him.

Unable to stand still, I wandered a few steps away, my gaze sweeping over the space. A row of crates near the far wall caught my attention, their markings more deliberate than the others—numbers scrawled in black ink and symbols I didn't recognize etched into the wood.

"You shouldn't touch those," a voice said behind me, low and calm but carrying a quiet authority.

I turned to see another man, his appearance as sharp as Cassian's but less intimidating. He had an air of quiet confidence, his hands tucked casually into his pockets.

"I wasn't going to," I replied, narrowing my eyes. "What's in them?"

He smiled faintly, though it didn't reach his eyes. "You

don't want to know."

Before I could press further, the office door opened, and Cassian stepped out, his expression colder than before. His gaze flicked to me and then to the man who'd spoken.

"Rosalie," he said, his voice steady but firm. "Come with me."

I followed him out of the building, my thoughts churning with unanswered questions. As the SUV pulled away, I glanced at him, searching his face for any hint of what he was thinking.

"What was in those crates?" I asked finally, breaking the silence.

Cassian's jaw tightened briefly before he replied. "Something that doesn't concern you."

"Everything concerns me now," I shot back, unable to keep the edge from my voice.

He sighed, his gaze softening as he turned to me. "There are some things your moral compass can't handle."

The answer did little to satisfy me, but the weight in his tone silenced any further argument. As the city blurred past the windows, I found myself wondering how much of his world I was truly prepared to understand—and how much I wanted to.

The SUV cruised down the narrow streets, the industrial sprawl giving way to a more familiar skyline. But the tension from the warehouse lingered, settling like a heavy fog between us. Cassian stared straight ahead, his fingers drumming softly on the armrest, his mind clearly elsewhere.

"Handling it," I muttered under my breath, repeating his earlier words. "That seems to be your answer for everything."

Cassian turned his head slightly, his gray eyes locking onto mine. "Because it works."

"Does it?" I challenged, leaning back against the leather seat. "Because from what I just saw, it looks like parts of your empire are crumbling. People asking questions they shouldn't. Shipments not arriving where they're supposed to. That's not control, Cassian. That's chaos."

His jaw tightened, and for a moment, I thought he might snap back. Instead, he let out a slow breath, his voice calmer than I expected. "You don't understand how these things work. Chaos is inevitable—it's the way you respond to it that matters."

"And sending people to 'handle' things?" I asked, my voice sharper now. "What does that solve?"

"It solves the problem," he replied evenly. "Quickly and effectively." I realized that even I had begun to master speaking in riddles, still uncomfortable with the notion that if Cassian wanted someone to disappear, he could easily do it.

I scoffed, shaking my head as I turned to the window. The buildings outside blurred together, the familiar streets of the city doing little to ground me. "That's not solving anything. It's a band-aid. You can't keep patching holes in a sinking ship."

Cassian shifted in his seat, his gaze heavy as it settled on me. "And what do you suggest, Rosalie? That I walk away? That I abandon everything I've built because it doesn't fit into your rose-colored lenses?"

"No," I said quietly, my throat tightening. "But maybe stop pretending it's perfect."

He didn't respond immediately, his silence more cutting than any retort. Finally, he leaned forward, resting his elbows on his knees, his hands clasped together. "Perfect isn't the goal," he said, his voice low. "But failure is not an option."

The weight of his words hung in the air, and for a moment, I didn't know how to respond. He was right, in a way. His world wasn't about ideals or morals—it was about staying one step ahead, no matter the cost.

The SUV slowed to a stop at a red light, the faint hum of the city outside filling the silence. Cassian's phone buzzed again, and he pulled it out, glancing at the screen with a frown.

I resisted asking him what was wrong, not because I didn't care but because I suspected he wasn't going to tell me. His walls were going up and there was nothing I could do to stop them.

As we pulled up to the curb outside his building, Sierra and Marcus were out of their vehicle first, but Cassian made no effort to move, not right away. I sensed the tension in his shoulders, the way his jaw clenched with unresolved anguish.

"You're not coming up, are you?" I asked, finally, the silence eating at me.

"No," he paused, "I'm not."

My chest tightened, the irritation bubbling up before I could stop it. "So I just sit and wait while you run around playing damage control?"

His lips twitched, but there was no humor in his expression. "Yes. That's exactly what you do."

I opened my mouth to argue, but Cassian motioned to Marcus who approached on my side. He opened the door and stepped aside, but I stayed seated, my eyes locked on Cassian.

"This isn't working," I said finally, my voice quieter now. "You drag me into your world, show me everything, and then push me aside like I'm just... an accessory. You're hot then cold, up, then down, you bring me into the fold and then you isolate me."

Cassian's eyes softened, but his voice remained firm. "You're not an accessory, Rosalie. You're not, but there are things that you can't recover from."

"Then stop keeping me in the dark," I said, my frustration spilling out. "Stop shutting me out when things get hard."

His hand brushed mine briefly, a fleeting gesture of connection. "We'll talk tonight," he said, his tone softening. "Right now, I need you to trust me."

I stared at him for a moment longer before stepping out of the SUV. The door shut behind me with a heavy finality, and the car pulled away, leaving me standing on the curb, my shadows lurking.

I glanced up at the towering building, its sleek exterior a stark reminder of just how far I'd come from my old life— and how much further I'd fallen into Cassian's.

"This way, Miss Quinn." Marcus ushered, directing me toward the building.

"No," I turned away from him. "I think I'll have a drink instead."

I turned without their approval and walked down the street toward the first pub I could find. Their hurried steps behind me, frustrated and angry, but I didn't care. I was tired of forfeiting my freedom.

CHAPTER THIRTEEN

My phone buzzed against the sticky bar top, the faint vibration cutting through the low hum of chatter and the clinking of glasses. I didn't need to look at the screen to know who it was—only one person could make the air feel heavier from miles away.

Still, I swiped it off the counter and unlocked it. Cassian's message was as sharp as his voice, practically vibrating with restrained anger.

Cassian: What the hell were you thinking going to a bar?

I sighed, taking another sip of my drink—something sweet and vaguely fruity the bartender had recommended when I asked for "anything that doesn't taste like alcohol." The drink was fine. The tension coiling in my chest wasn't.

Rosalie: I needed air, sometimes I think you forget I'm human too. I typed back, my fingers trembling slightly despite my effort to appear nonchalant.

The response came instantly, as though he'd been waiting, his temper simmering on the other end of the line.

Cassian: This isn't about air, Rosalie. It's about pushing back when you're not in control. Where are you?

I stared at the screen, debating whether to answer. He didn't own me—at least, that's what I kept telling myself. I'd made it clear to Marcus and Sierra that I wasn't interested in their escorting services tonight. They had followed me into the pub, but kept their distance, lingering near the door like frustrated parents unable to scold their rebellious child.

I was willing to stake my entire business on my shadows already informing Cassian, but then again—I didn't own it anymore. Cassian had made that clear from the beginning.

I glanced toward them now. Marcus was watching me with a level of patience I didn't deserve, while Sierra leaned against the wall, her arms crossed and her expression icy. They weren't happy, but they weren't stopping me either.

Rosalie: A place called Hargrove's, but you knew that. I typed reluctantly, pressing send before I could overthink it.

Cassian's reply came immediately.

Cassian: Stay put. I'm on my way.

I was already on my second drink, and could quite easily go for a third before he appeared, his dark and broody mood souring the rest of the evening.

I groaned, setting the phone down a little too hard. The bartender gave me a curious glance, but I ignored him, swirling the remains of my drink in its glass.

The truth was, I didn't know what I was doing here. Coming to the bar had felt like a small act of rebellion, a way to push back against the constant walls Cassian had placed around me. But sitting here, surrounded by strangers and the faint stench of spilled beer, I didn't feel free—I felt untethered.

The sound of the pub door opening pulled my gaze. I half-expected to see Cassian storming in, his presence filling the room like it always did, but it was just another group of patrons, laughing and shoving each other as they made their way to the bar.

Sierra appeared beside me, her voice low and even. "He's going to be furious."

"I know," I muttered, not looking at her.

She didn't say anything else, just stepped back to her post by the door, leaving me to stew in the weight of my own choices.

When the door opened again, I knew it was him without

even looking. The energy in the room shifted, a ripple of awareness moving through the air.

Cassian's stride was deliberate, his coat trailing behind him as he made his way toward me. His expression was unreadable, but his gray eyes were stormy, locking onto me like I was the only thing in the room.

The pub seemed smaller with him in it, the noise dulling to a faint buzz.

"Rosalie," he said, his voice calm but threaded with steel. "What exactly are you trying to prove?"

I turned to face him fully, my chin lifting in defiance. "That I can still make my own decisions."

"By walking into a bar alone?" he asked, his tone sharp but quiet enough not to draw attention. "Do you have any idea how stupid this is?"

"I'm not alone," I shot back, gesturing toward Marcus and Sierra. "They're practically glued to me—you made sure of that."

"That's not the point," he said, his voice dropping lower, more dangerous. He stepped closer, and I could feel the tension radiating from him, a tightly coiled storm barely held in check.

"Then what is the point, Cassian?" I asked, my voice rising slightly. "That I can't even breathe without your approval? That every step I take has to be monitored, questioned, controlled?"

His jaw tightened, and for a moment, I thought he might snap. But instead, he leaned in closer, his gaze piercing. "The point is that—" he stopped, something inside him shifting. His gaze was a smidge less intense, his posture less rigid, his tone a degree softer. "Finish your drink," he said finally, his voice quieter now. "Then we're leaving."

I hesitated but nodded, picking up the glass and draining the rest in one go. The sweetness tasted cloying now, sticking to the back of my throat. "I was done anyway."

As I stood, Cassian's hand brushed against the small of my back, guiding me toward the door. His touch was firm but not forceful, grounding me even as the frustration simmered beneath the surface.

The cool night air hit me as we stepped outside, and for a moment, the tension eased. But as Cassian led me toward the waiting SUV, I knew this wasn't over.

Not by a long shot.

The ride back to the penthouse was silent, the tension simmering beneath the surface like a current too strong to ignore. Cassian sat beside me, his presence imposing but no longer sharp. He'd stopped speaking after his curt instructions to the driver, leaving me to fidget with my phone and stare out the window, my emotions tangled between defiance and regret.

By the time the elevator doors slid open, depositing us into the cool, understated luxury of his penthouse, my frustration had waned. But the energy in the room shifted again the moment we stepped inside. Cassian and I walked into the bedroom; he closed the door behind us with a deliberate click, the sound reverberating in the stillness, and my mind instantly raced.

Was he going to draw me over his knee again?

I turned to face him, bracing for another lecture, another sharp reprimand. But what I saw in his eyes wasn't anger—it was something deeper, something hotter, that stole the breath from my lungs.

"You're wild," he said finally, his voice low, steady, and thrumming with an intensity that sent a shiver down my spine. "And stubborn."

"I—" I started, but the words caught in my throat as he stepped closer. "I am."

"And you make me insane," he continued, his hands coming to rest lightly on my arms. His grip was firm but not rough, his touch grounding me even as my heart raced. "Do you have any idea what you do to me, Rosalie?"

His words, barely more than a murmur, carried more weight than I was prepared for. "I just needed to make my own decisions," I said quietly, though even as the words left my lips, they felt weak. "I needed to be free for a moment. I needed space."

"Space?" Cassian repeated, his lips curving into a faint,

humorless smile. "You don't need space. You need someone to remind you who you are."

The heat in his voice sent a pulse of electricity through me. Before I could respond, he closed the remaining distance between us, one hand sliding up to cup the back of my neck. His fingers tangled in my hair as he tilted my head back, his gaze locking onto mine with a searing intensity.

"I'll remind you," he said, his voice rougher now, his breath warm against my lips. "But not like this."

His mouth covered mine, the kiss deep and demanding, igniting every nerve in my body. My protests, my frustration, all melted away beneath the fire of his touch. His hands roamed, one sliding down to my waist while the other stayed tangled in my hair, holding me against him as though letting go wasn't an option.

I gasped as his teeth grazed my bottom lip, the sharpness sending a jolt of heat straight through me. His grip tightened, pulling me closer, until there was no space left between us—only the overwhelming sensation of his body against mine, his control eclipsing everything else.

"Cassian," I managed, my voice barely above a whisper.

He pulled back just enough to meet my gaze, his expression dark and filled with something I couldn't quite name. "Say it again," he murmured, his voice rough and raw.

"Cassian," I repeated, his name falling from my lips like a plea.

That was all it took. He lifted me effortlessly, his hands firm as he carried me to the bed. The cool air against my skin did nothing to quell the heat building between us, the pull of his presence drowning out every coherent thought.

The world blurred as he climbed on top of me, the shadows of the room wrapping around us as, the world falling away.

CHAPTER FOURTEEN

The brisk air stung my cheeks as I stepped onto the cracked pavement, the city's muted hum enveloping me. Ivy & Bloom's familiar façade came into view, the warm glow of its windowed display fighting against the shadows creeping along the street. My steps slowed as I neared the corner, and an ache I hadn't anticipated took root in my chest.

I stopped just short of the door, my fingers brushing the textured fabric of my coat as I hugged it tighter around me. For a moment, I was no longer twenty-four, navigating the chaos of debts and threats. I was a little girl again, barely able to see over the counter, standing on this same sidewalk as my father unlocked the shop for the day.

The memory hit me with startling clarity—the way the sunlight would catch on the glass vases in the display, scattering tiny rainbows across the walls inside. My father would whistle a tune I could never quite place, his hands steady as he carried in fresh bundles of roses and lilies. He'd let me pick one flower each morning, claiming it was my "duty" to choose the centerpiece for the day's arrangements.

I could almost feel the weight of that responsibility again, my small hands trembling with excitement as I carefully selected a single bloom. Back then, Ivy & Bloom wasn't just a shop—it was magic, a world where everything felt alive and bursting with possibility. The sweet scent of jasmine and eucalyptus had been my lullaby, the vibrant colors my earliest muse.

Now, as I stood outside, the magic felt distant, cloaked in the suffocating weight of my father's mistakes and the danger Cassian's world had brought to our doorstep. Yet, even as the ache in my chest deepened, there was still a flicker of that childhood wonder, stubbornly refusing to be extinguished.

I exhaled a shaky breath, blinking back the sting of tears as I let the memory fade. The glass reflected a faint silhouette of myself—a woman far removed from the girl who once danced between the rows of blooms. But it also showed Ivy & Bloom, standing resilient against the encroaching shadows. And that, I reminded myself, was why I was here.

Adjusting the strap of my purse, I stepped forward and grasped the cold handle of the door, pushing it open. The bell above jingled softly, its sound a balm against my frayed nerves. The familiar scent of freshly cut flowers wrapped around me, a fleeting comfort as I stepped into the shop.

It didn't matter that Cassian would be furious when he found out I'd left the penthouse. Ivy & Bloom wasn't just a business—it was a piece of me. And no amount of danger would keep me from it.

The bell's soft jingle faded as I stepped further inside, the familiar scent of eucalyptus and garden roses enveloping me. My boots clicked softly against the polished floor, and I took in the changes with a mixture of curiosity and unease.

The large oak counter, once the centerpiece of Ivy & Bloom, had been shifted closer to the back wall. The quaint wooden displays that once carried a mix of terracotta pots and vintage watering cans had been replaced with sleek white pedestals adorned with glossy vases. Even the arrangement of the flowers themselves had changed.

The daffodils and hyacinths that heralded spring were

front and center, a vibrant explosion of yellows, pinks, and purples catching the eye. It was beautiful, undoubtedly, but it felt foreign—too curated, too polished. The shop's once-chaotic charm had been stripped away, replaced with a calculated elegance that didn't quite feel like home.

My gaze landed on the wall where my mother's photograph used to hang. The space was now bare, the faint shadow of its outline the only indication it had been there at all. My chest tightened, a flare of irritation sparking as I turned to scan the room. There it was, tucked near the corner by the employee entrance, partially obscured by a hanging fern.

I crossed the room, my movements brisk, and carefully lifted the frame from its misplaced perch. My fingers brushed over the glass, the familiar photo inside steadying me. She was captured mid-laugh, her apron dusted with pollen and a bouquet of peonies cradled in her arms. It was how I always remembered her—vivid, alive, and endlessly in love with this shop.

Without hesitation, I walked back to the original spot on the wall. The tiny nail still protruded, and with one fluid motion, I hung her picture back where it belonged. I stepped back, crossing my arms as I surveyed my work. Better.

A polite cough behind me broke the moment. I turned to see Sierra standing a few paces away, her sharp blue eyes tracking my every move. Marcus hovered near the door, his tall frame impossibly still, but his gaze missed nothing.

"Did you find what you were looking for?" Sierra asked, her tone professional but tinged with curiosity.

I didn't bother answering directly. "Why are you two still here?" I asked instead, adjusting the frame slightly. "You've been following me like shadows since I left."

"Mr. Moreau was very clear," Marcus replied, his voice a low rumble. "We're here to ensure your safety."

"Ivy & Bloom isn't exactly a hotbed of danger," I said, turning to face them fully. "I don't need babysitters."

Sierra's expression remained neutral, though I caught the faintest flicker of amusement in her gaze. "It's not our call, Miss Quinn."

Pulling my phone from my purse, I glanced down at the screen. Sure enough, there was a message from Cassian, his tone practically dripping from the words.

Cassian: You left. We'll discuss this later.

I clenched my jaw, resisting the urge to throw the phone into one of the flower displays. Instead, I slipped it back into my pocket and turned back to the picture.

"He can't control everything," I muttered, more to myself than anyone else.

But the sharp glances exchanged between Sierra and Marcus told me they'd heard every word.

The irritation simmering in my chest slowly ebbed as I fell into the familiar rhythm of Ivy & Bloom. My hands moved on autopilot, arranging stems into an intricate bouquet for a waiting customer. The scent of fresh-cut lilies and lavender mingled with the earthy undertones of the shop, soothing my frayed nerves.

A mother and daughter wandered near the succulents, their quiet laughter blending with the soft hum of conversation around me. For a moment, it felt like nothing had changed—like I hadn't spent the last few weeks navigating a minefield of danger and control.

"Perfect as always," the customer said with a bright smile, taking the bouquet. Her words brought a fleeting warmth to my chest as I handed over the arrangement.

"Thank you," I replied, a genuine smile finding its way to my lips. "Enjoy."

As she left, I turned back to the counter to tidy up, my hands deftly organizing the scissors, twine, and ribbons scattered across the surface. That's when my eyes landed on something out of place—a small, sleek business card tucked between the folds of a delivery invoice.

Sophia Brandt.

The elegant black lettering on the cream-colored cardstock caught my attention immediately. Her name had come up during one of Cassian's more veiled conversations about alliances. A businesswoman with a reputation for thriving in circles where power, influence, and secrecy ruled. She'd been a regular at Ivy & Bloom before my life had spiraled, her penchant for unique and extravagant floral designs ensuring she was one of our most prominent clients.

I ran my fingers over the edge of the card, a sudden idea taking root. Sophia was more than a customer—she was a connector. If anyone had a pulse on the subtle undercurrents of influence in this city, it was her. And if I could get her to talk, maybe I could uncover something useful. Something that might help Cassian and, by extension, me.

I hesitated for only a moment before pulling out my phone. Her number was printed neatly on the card, along with the logo of her interior design firm, Brandt Collective. I tapped the number into my phone and hit call, my pulse quickening as the line rang.

After two rings, a cool, professional voice answered. "Sophia Brandt."

"Sophia, it's Rosalie Quinn from Ivy & Bloom," I said, keeping my tone light and casual. "I came across your card and thought maybe you could explain more what you can offer me?"

There was a pause on the other end, then a small laugh. "Rosalie, I'm glad you reached out. What a pleasant surprise."

"I was hoping we could meet for lunch," I continued, leaning against the counter. "I'd love to hear about the projects you've been working on—and maybe even pick your brain about a few things."

Sophia's laugh softened, her tone turning almost conspiratorial. "You know I can never resist a good lunch invitation. When were you thinking?"

"Two days from now?" I suggested, glancing at the calendar pinned to the bulletin board behind the counter. "Around noon?"

"Perfect," she replied smoothly. "Let's meet at Léon's. It's quiet, discreet, and the wine list is divine."

"Sounds wonderful. I'll see you then."

We exchanged goodbyes, and I ended the call, my grip

on the phone tightening slightly as I set it back on the counter. My heart thudded against my ribs, a mix of excitement and trepidation coursing through me. If Sophia could provide even a sliver of insight into the chaos surrounding Cassian and the Reapers, it would be worth it.

"What are you planning now?" Sierra's voice interrupted my thoughts, her sharp gaze fixed on me as she leaned against the counter.

"Lunch," I said simply, slipping Sophia's card into my pocket again.

Sierra arched an eyebrow, but she didn't press further. Marcus lingered near the entrance, his quiet vigilance a constant reminder of Cassian's orders. I ignored the weight of their scrutiny and turned back to the arrangements waiting for me.

For the rest of the morning, I immersed myself in the work I loved, letting the feel of the flowers in my hands and the hum of the shop steady me. But no matter how much I tried to focus, the upcoming lunch with Sophia lingered in the back of my mind—a spark of rebellion and hope wrapped into one.

The rhythm of the shop, once so familiar and comforting, felt strange now—like trying to wear a coat that no longer fit. Every corner I turned revealed more evidence of how much control I'd lost in my absence.

The bookkeeping station in the back room was no longer mine. Neat piles of invoices, order forms, and receipts were meticulously sorted, each one labeled in Lena's sharp, precise handwriting. The delivery schedule was pinned to the corkboard above the desk, a new name scrawled next to daily routes—someone I didn't even recognize. Lena had hired a delivery person. A good move, objectively, but it gnawed at me that I hadn't been the one to make it.

As I passed the supply shelves, I noted new stock I hadn't approved—spring-themed ribbons, pastel wrapping paper, and some exotic flowers I would have hesitated to order due to their cost. But here they were, tucked neatly among the staples I'd always relied on. I paused, running my fingers over the petals of a strikingly vibrant orchid. I couldn't decide whether to be impressed by Lena's initiative or irritated by her overreach.

The clinking of the cash register drew my attention to the front of the shop, where Lena was balancing the day's books. She moved with ease, her sharp eyes darting between the receipts and the ledger, her expression calm and focused. I'd taught her some of those skills when she'd first started, but now she handled it all without a second thought.

This was her shop now. Or at least, that's how it felt. A pang of jealousy flared in my chest, but I swallowed it down. It wasn't Lena's fault. She was doing what needed to be done to keep Ivy & Bloom running. Still, it stung to realize how much of my place here had been quietly erased.

By the time we locked up for the night, the weight of it all sat heavy on my shoulders. Lena flipped the sign to "Closed" and snapped the lock on the front door, her movements brisk and efficient.

"You look exhausted," she said, glancing at me as we stepped onto the sidewalk. The city air was crisp, the faint glow of the streetlights casting long shadows across the pavement. "Are you okay?"

I nodded, though I wasn't sure it was true. "Yeah, just a long day."

Lena didn't press, which I appreciated. She adjusted her bag on her shoulder and gave me a small smile. "You should get some rest. Tomorrow's going to be just as busy."

"Thanks, Lena," I said, my voice softer than I intended. "For everything."

She paused, her expression shifting to something warmer. "It's your shop, Rosalie. I'm just holding it down until you're ready to take the reins again."

The words were kind, but they didn't quite settle the unease in my chest. I watched as Lena headed down the street toward her car, her figure disappearing into the glow of the city lights.

As I turned and began walking toward my own apartment, I pulled out my phone. Cassian's name hovered at the top of my recent messages. I typed out a quick note before I could second-guess myself.

Rosalie: I'm staying at my place tonight. I'll take Blondie and Mr. Buff with me.

I stared at the screen, my thumb hovering over the send button. Cassian wasn't going to like it. He'd probably argue, maybe even show up uninvited. But after everything—after feeling like a stranger in my own shop—I needed space. I needed to reclaim some part of myself, even if just for one night.

With a deep breath, I hit send. The message marked as delivered immediately, and I shoved the phone back into my pocket before I could overthink it. The night stretched ahead of me, quiet and uncertain, but for the first time in a long while, I felt like I was making a choice for myself.

CHAPTER FIFTEEN

The familiar creak of my apartment door greeted me as I stepped inside, the quiet solitude wrapping around me like a heavy blanket. It was strange, almost surreal, being back here after spending so many nights in the towering luxury of Cassian's penthouse. The modest warmth of my little apartment felt both foreign and comforting at the same time.

I kicked off my shoes near the door, my toes curling against the cool wood floors. The faint hum of the city beyond my window reminded me that I was home—a small haven tucked away from the chaos that had consumed my life lately. Ivy & Bloom, the Reapers, Cassian... everything seemed so far away here, like whispers behind a locked door.

Dropping my bag onto the kitchen counter, I headed straight for the bathroom. The day had clung to my skin like grime, and all I wanted was the hot embrace of a shower to wash it away.

The bathroom mirror was fogging up by the time I stepped under the spray, the heat enveloping me instantly. I closed my eyes, letting the water cascade down my back as the tension began to ebb from my shoulders. My fingers worked shampoo into my hair, the soothing rhythm helping to clear my mind. For the first time in days, I felt... normal. Just a woman standing in her shower, with no shadowy threats lurking around the corner and no Cassian hovering like a storm cloud waiting to burst.

But even as I told myself I was alone, my thoughts betrayed me. The memory of his touch, the way his eyes darkened when he was angry—or worse, worried—lingered in the back of my mind. It was maddening how he managed to invade my thoughts even when he wasn't around.

Rinsing the suds from my hair, I shook my head, trying to dispel him from my mind. Tonight was about reclaiming my space, my independence. Cassian Moreau and his consuming intensity could wait.

The water turned lukewarm, nudging me to wrap up my time in the shower. I turned off the faucet and stepped out, grabbing a towel and wrapping it tightly around me. The cool air nipped at my damp skin as I padded back into the main part of the apartment.

And that's when I smelled it.

The unmistakable scent of takeout—soy sauce, sesame, something rich and garlicky—wafted through the air. My heart leapt into my throat as my eyes darted to the kitchen.

There he was.

Cassian stood at the counter, casually unpacking a collection of Chinese takeout containers. His gray shirt clung to his broad shoulders, and his dark slacks were tailored perfectly, as usual. A bottle of wine sat open beside him, two glasses already poured. He looked impossibly relaxed, like he belonged here, in my space, as though the weight of his world hadn't followed him across the threshold.

"Cassian," I blurted, clutching the towel tighter around me. "What are you doing here?"

He didn't look up immediately, his movements measured as he set out chopsticks beside the containers. "Having dinner," he said simply, finally meeting my eyes with that infuriating calm of his. "You didn't think I was just going to let you sulk in here all alone, did you?"

"I didn't invite you," I snapped, though the heat in my

cheeks betrayed the bite in my tone.

He arched an eyebrow, the corner of his mouth twitching in faint amusement. "You also didn't explicitly tell me not to come. That's practically an invitation."

I opened my mouth to argue, but his logic—or lack of it—left me fumbling. Instead, I crossed my arms over my chest, trying to ignore the way his gaze flickered briefly to the bare skin of my shoulders.

"This is my apartment," I said, my voice firmer now. "You can't just waltz in whenever you feel like it."

Cassian leaned against the counter, his fingers curling around the stem of a wineglass. "Rosalie, I own the building. Technically, I can waltz in whenever I like."

I groaned, pressing a hand to my temple. "That's not the point."

"The point," he said, stepping closer, his tone softening just slightly, "is that you left my penthouse without telling me. You didn't answer my texts. And you decided it was a good idea to stay here alone, without security, while there's a target painted on your back."

His proximity sent a shiver down my spine, but I refused to back away. "I took your goons with me, didn't I and besides, I told you, I needed space."

"And I'm giving you space," he said, a faint smirk tugging at his lips. "I'm just doing it with dinner and wine. Call it... supervised space."

I glared at him, but the smell of the food and the promise of the wine were quickly eroding my resolve. "You're diabolically insane." I muttered.

"And you're starving," he countered, setting a pair of chopsticks into my hand before I could protest further.

As much as I hated to admit it, he was right. *Again.*

Cassian carried the takeout containers into the living room, his movements commanding the space, while I trailed behind, chopsticks in hand. He had already arranged the coffee table with napkins, plates, and the open bottle of wine. It was annoyingly domestic, like he'd planned this moment long before I left the shop.

I settled onto the couch, adjusting the towel around me

as Cassian handed me a plate. I scooped a small portion of sesame chicken and rice onto it, the rich aroma making my stomach rumble. He poured the last of the wine into our glasses and took a seat at the other end of the couch, his posture casual, one arm slung along the backrest. But even relaxed, his presence was consuming.

"This is better than the delivery guy mixing up orders again, isn't it?" he asked, his tone deceptively light as he picked up a dumpling with his chopsticks.

I rolled my eyes, stuffing a piece of chicken into my mouth so I didn't have to answer right away.

"You always have to be in control, don't you?" I finally said, taking a sip of wine.

Cassian's gaze slid to mine, the intensity behind his gray eyes cutting through the casual atmosphere. "If it means you don't get yourself killed, then yes."

I bristled, setting my plate down on the table with a little too much force. "I'm not helpless, Cassian. I don't need your constant surveillance or your bodyguards to follow me around like shadows."

His lips curled into a faint smirk, though there was no humor in it. "You think you're invincible? That you can handle whatever comes your way just because you're stubborn enough to try?"

"No," I shot back, heat rising in my cheeks. "But I can handle my life without you deciding what's best for me."

Cassian leaned forward then, setting his plate aside. The easy facade he'd maintained began to crack, his expression darkening with something more potent. "Your life isn't just yours anymore. You've made decisions— whether you realize it or not—that have brought you to this point in life. And every decision has either a reward, a consequence, or both. You have to learn to accept that."

I reached for my wine glass, needing the liquid courage to keep from folding under his intensity. "And what about my freedom? My ability to make choices for myself?"

He didn't respond immediately, taking a measured sip from his own glass before leaning back again, his gaze never leaving mine. "Freedom doesn't mean recklessness,

Rosalie. It doesn't mean making choices that endanger your life just because you can."

The conversation hung in the air, the unspoken tension simmering beneath the surface of his words. I hated how easily he turned everything into a battle of wills, how he could twist my arguments until they lost their footing.

"Why do you care so much?" I asked quietly, my voice barely above a whisper.

Cassian's expression softened for the briefest moment, a flicker of something raw flashing in his eyes before he masked it again. "Because I have to," he said simply, his tone firm yet laced with an edge of vulnerability that caught me off guard.

We sat in silence for a moment, the wine bottle now empty, the remnants of our takeout forgotten on the table. I watched him as he gazed out the window, his jaw tight, his hands resting on his thighs. There was so much I didn't understand about him, about why he felt the need to shoulder every burden, every threat, on his own.

"I'm not trying to make things harder for you," I said finally, my voice softer now. "I just... I can't stand feeling like a prisoner in my own life."

Cassian turned to me, his gray eyes studying my face as though searching for something he couldn't name. "You're not a prisoner, Rosalie. You're protected. There's a difference."

"Sometimes it doesn't feel that way," I admitted, surprising even myself with the honesty of the words.

His lips pressed into a thin line, and for once, he didn't have a sharp retort. Instead, he reached out, his hand brushing against mine in a gesture so unexpected that it sent a jolt through me.

"I'll try," he said after a moment, his voice quieter now. "But you need to try too."

I nodded, the faintest trace of a smile tugging at my lips. For the first time in what felt like forever, it wasn't a victory or a loss—it was something in between. A truce. For now.

Cassian stood, collecting the takeout containers and

wine glasses in one smooth motion. His quiet efficiency should have been calming, but the smirk tugging at the corner of his lips hinted that the night wasn't over—not by a long shot.

I watched him as he placed the empty glasses on the counter, his movements deliberate. He turned back to me, his gray eyes smoldering as they locked on mine.

"Come on," he said, his voice low and velvety as he extended a hand.

"What now?" I asked, even as I placed my hand in his.

"You'll see," he replied, his smirk widening.

He led me down the hall, the soft light of the living room fading into the shadows of the bedroom. The space was warm and inviting, the bed freshly made, the faint scent of cedar and spice lingering in the air. Cassian's presence filled the room, commanding and magnetic.

He turned to me, his gray eyes alight with something that made my pulse quicken. "Left, right, or both?" he asked, his voice a blend of mischief and challenge.

I frowned, tilting my head in confusion. "What does that mean?"

"Choose," he said, his tone playful but firm.

I hesitated, curiosity battling with apprehension. "Both," I said finally, unsure of what I'd just agreed to.

Cassian's smirk deepened, satisfaction flickering across his features as he reached into his pocket. "Good choice."

Before I could question him further, he guided me to the bed, his hands firm but gentle on my waist. He turned me so that the backs of my knees hit the edge of the mattress, and with a light push, I found myself sitting.

He leaned down, his hands on either side of me, his face inches from mine. "Trust me?" he murmured, his voice a soft caress.

"Yes," I whispered, though my heart pounded in my chest.

"Good," he said, his voice dropping to a low rumble.

In one fluid motion, he climbed onto the bed, straddling me as he reached into the nightstand drawer. The glint of metal caught my eye, and I realized what he was holding—

handcuffs.

"Wait," I said, my breath hitching.

Cassian chuckled, the sound warm and rich as he leaned down, his lips brushing against my ear. "Relax, Rosalie. You don't want to feel like a prisoner, but I promise, after I'm done with you, you'll be begging for more."

His words sent a shiver down my spine as he took my wrists in his hands, guiding them above my head. The cool metal of the handcuffs clicked softly as he secured them to the headboard, his movements careful but deliberate.

I tugged lightly at the restraints, testing them, and Cassian's smirk widened. "Comfortable?" he asked, his tone teasing.

"Define comfortable," I muttered, trying to suppress the nervous excitement building in my chest.

He laughed, the sound low and intimate, as he leaned down, his face mere inches from mine. "You look perfect like this," he murmured, his lips brushing against mine in the faintest of kisses. "Now, let's see how well you follow directions."

The weight of his words hung in the air, promising a night I wouldn't soon forget.

Cassian's eyes gleamed with wicked intent as he slowly trailed his fingers down my arms, over my collarbone, and along the edge of the towel still wrapped around me. His touch was light, teasing, sending shivers across my skin.

"First rule," he murmured, his voice low and commanding, "this is a game of choices, you must choose. Understood?"

I nodded, my breath catching in my throat.

"Good girl," he purred, rewarding me with a slow, deep kiss that left me dizzy.

He pulled back, his hands moving to the knot of my towel. With agonizing slowness, he undid it, letting the fabric fall open. Cool air kissed my exposed skin, and I fought the urge to squirm under his intense gaze.

"So fucking gorgeous," he breathed, his eyes roaming over my body.

Cassian's hands skimmed along my sides, barely

touching, igniting a fire beneath my skin. He leaned down, pressing soft kisses along my jaw, down my neck, across my collarbone. Each touch was feather-light, building a desperate ache within me.

"Oh," I whimpered, tugging at the handcuffs.

Cassian chuckled against my skin, the vibration sending tingles through my body. "Patience, Rosalie," he murmured. "We're just getting started."

His lips continued their torturous path down my body, pausing at the swell of my breasts. He looked up at me, his gray eyes dark with desire. "Left or right?" he asked, his voice husky.

I swallowed hard, my mind foggy with want. "Left," I breathed.

Without breaking eye contact, Cassian lowered his mouth to my left breast, his tongue swirling around my nipple before taking it between his lips. I arched into him, a moan escaping my lips as he sucked and teased the sensitive flesh.

His hand came up to cup my right breast, kneading it gently as his mouth worked its magic on the left. The dual sensation was overwhelming, and I pulled at the handcuffs again, desperate to touch him.

Cassian released my nipple with a soft pop, a smirk playing on his lips. "Good choice," he said, his voice low and approving. "Now, let's see what other decisions you'll make."

He trailed kisses down my stomach, his stubble scratching deliciously against my skin. When he reached my hips, he paused, looking up at me with a wicked glint in his eyes.

"Inner thigh or outer?" he asked, his breath hot against my skin.

I bit my lip, considering. "Inner," I decided, my voice barely above a whisper.

Cassian's smirk widened as he pressed a kiss to my inner thigh, just inches away from where I needed him most. His tongue darted out, tracing patterns on the sensitive skin, and I couldn't help but whimper.

"Please," I gasped, my hips lifting off the bed.

"Please what?" Cassian teased, his fingers ghosting along my other thigh. "You have to be specific, Rosalie. Remember, every choice has a consequence... or a reward."

I groaned in frustration, my body on fire with need. "Please touch me," I begged.

"Where?" he pressed, his breath hot against my core. "You have to choose."

"There," I gasped, beyond caring about embarrassment. "Please, Cassian."

He chuckled, the sound sending vibrations through me. "As you wish."

Without warning, he buried his face between my thighs, his tongue finding my clit with unerring accuracy. I cried out, my back arching off the bed as pleasure shot through me. Cassian's hands gripped my hips, holding me in place as he devoured me with single-minded focus.

Cassian's tongue moved in expert circles, alternating between broad strokes and pinpoint precision. I writhed beneath him, my wrists straining against the handcuffs as waves of pleasure washed over me. His stubble scraped deliciously against my inner thighs, adding another layer of sensation to the overwhelming experience.

"Ahh," I moaned, my head thrown back against the pillows. "Cassian, please..."

He hummed against me, the vibration sending sparks of electricity through my body. One of his hands left my hip, and I felt his fingers teasing at my entrance. He looked up at me, his eyes dark with desire.

"One or two?" he asked, his voice husky.

I was beyond thinking clearly, consumed by the need for more. "Two," I gasped.

Without hesitation, Cassian slid two fingers inside me, curling them in a way that made me see stars. He resumed his attention on my clit, his tongue and fingers working in perfect synchronization. The dual stimulation was almost too much to bear, and I could feel myself hurtling towards the edge.

"That's it," Cassian murmured against me. "How's it feel

to be the captain at the helm, every decision... every choice... yours."

I couldn't form coherent words, my mind lost in a haze of pleasure as Cassian's fingers and tongue worked their magic. The contrast of being restrained yet in control of the choices was intoxicating. My hips bucked against his face, chasing the release that was building rapidly within me.

"Cassian," I moaned, pulling at the handcuffs. "I'm so close..."

He hummed in acknowledgment, the vibration sending shockwaves through my body. His fingers curled inside me, hitting that perfect spot while his tongue flicked rapidly over my clit. The dual sensations were overwhelming, pushing me closer and closer to the edge.

"Come for me, Rosalie," Cassian commanded, his voice low and husky. "This one's mine."

His words were the final push I needed. My back arched off the bed as waves of intense pleasure crashed over me. I cried out Cassian's name, my body shuddering as the orgasm ripped through me. He didn't let up, working me through every aftershock until I was a quivering mess beneath him.

As I came down from my high, Cassian placed soft kisses on my inner thighs, slowly working his way back up my body. He hovered over me, his gray eyes dark with desire as he took in my flushed face and heaving chest.

"I enjoy watching you unravel at my fingertips," he murmured, leaning down to capture my lips in a searing kiss. I could taste myself on his tongue, and it sent a renewed spark of arousal through me.

Cassian pulled back slightly, his forehead resting against mine. "Ready for more?" he asked, his voice low and teasing.

I nodded, still breathless. "Yes," I whispered.

He smirked, reaching up to unlock the handcuffs. As soon as my wrists were free, I wrapped my arms around his neck, pulling him down for another passionate kiss. Cassian responded eagerly, his hands roaming my body as our tongues danced together.

Breaking the kiss, he sat back on his heels, his eyes roving over my naked form. "On your knees or on your back?" he asked, his tone challenging.

I considered for a moment, biting my lip. "On my knees," I decided, feeling bold.

Cassian's eyes darkened with approval. "Good choice," he growled, helping me into position.

I heard the rustle of fabric as he quickly stripped off his clothes. The anticipation built as I felt the bed dip behind me, Cassian's strong hands gripping my hips. He leaned over me, his chest pressed against my back as he whispered in my ear.

"Remember, Rosalie," he said, his voice low and commanding. "Choices sometimes have consequences too."

With that, Cassian positioned himself at my entrance, the thick head of his cock teasing me. I whimpered, pushing back against him, desperate for more.

"Patience," he chided, his grip on my hips tightening. "Fast or slow?"

"Fast," I breathed, beyond caring about anything but having him inside me.

Cassian chuckled darkly. "As you wish."

In one swift motion, he thrust into me, burying himself to the hilt. I cried out at the sudden fullness, my fingers gripping the sheets tightly. Cassian didn't give me time to adjust, setting a punishing pace that had me gasping with each thrust.

His hands roamed my body as he pounded into me, one sliding up to cup my breast while the other snaked around to rub circles on my clit. The dual stimulation was overwhelming, pleasure building rapidly within me once again.

"Fuck, Rosalie," Cassian groaned, his hips snapping against mine. "You feel so good."

I moaned in response, unable to form coherent words as he hit that perfect spot inside me over and over. The sound of skin slapping against skin filled the room, punctuated by our gasps and moans.

Cassian leaned over me, his chest pressed against my

back as he nipped at my earlobe. "Touch yourself or have me do it?" he asked, his voice strained with exertion.

"You," I gasped, arching into him. "Please," I begged.

His fingers increased their pressure on my clit, rubbing tight circles that had me floating among the clouds, high on the ecstasy. I could feel myself approaching the edge again, my walls clenching around him.

"That's it," Cassian encouraged, his thrusts becoming more erratic. He grabbed my hips, thrusting harder and faster. "Fuck Rosalie. Fuck!"

His words pushed me over the precipice, and I cried out as waves of pleasure crashed over me. Cassian followed shortly after, groaning my name as he spilled inside me.

We collapsed onto the bed, a tangle of sweaty limbs and heaving breaths. Cassian pulled me against his chest, pressing soft kisses to my shoulder as we came down from our high.

"Was that supervised enough for you?" he asked teasingly, once I'd caught my breath. Cassian grinned sheepishly at me.

I chuckled, my voice soft and drunk on endorphins. "I think we can call it a successful supervision," I murmured, nuzzling his neck.

As we lay there, basking in the afterglow, I couldn't help but wonder what other choices – and consequences – lay ahead of us. But for now, wrapped in Cassian's arms, I felt safe, satisfied, and strangely free.

CHAPTER SIXTEEN

The chill of the afternoon air brushed against my cheeks as I stepped into the restaurant, a soft blush warming my skin from more than just the cold. The soft hum of conversation filled the space, blending with the gentle clinking of silverware against porcelain. Warm light from vintage pendant lights bathed the room, creating a cozy contrast to the wintery gray outside.

I paused at the entrance, my coat wrapped tightly around me, but it wasn't just the cold that made me hesitate. My thoughts were still tangled in the events of the previous night, Cassian's voice low and commanding in my ear, his hands firm yet reverent as he claimed every inch of me. I swallowed hard, the memory of his touch sending heat curling low in my stomach. Even now, I could feel the phantom press of the handcuffs on my wrists, the way his gray eyes had burned into mine as if I were the only thing that mattered.

Shaking the thoughts away, I scanned the room until I spotted Sophia Brandt sitting at a table near the back. She was a picture of elegance, her dark hair swept into a polished bun, her tailored coat draped over the back of her chair. A small smile played on her lips as she caught sight of me, and she gestured for me to join her.

I crossed the room, shedding my coat as I approached. The heat from the restaurant's fireplace was a welcome reprieve from the biting cold outside, but it did little to cool the warmth still lingering in my veins.

"Rosalie," Sophia greeted warmly as I reached the table. She rose to give me a polite embrace, the faint scent of her floral perfume enveloping me. "It's so good to see you."

"You too," I said, managing a smile as I took the seat across from her. "Thank you for meeting me."

"Of course," she said, her dark eyes sharp yet inviting. "I was thrilled when you reached out. It's not every day someone as interesting as you crosses my path."

Her words carried an undercurrent I couldn't quite place, and I smoothed my napkin over my lap, forcing myself to focus. Whatever this meeting would bring, I couldn't let myself be distracted by thoughts of Cassian. Not here. Not now.

Sophia signaled to the waiter, who promptly arrived with a menu and poured us both glasses of water. As I glanced over the options, the warmth of the room and the steady rhythm of Sophia's voice grounded me, pulling me back to the task at hand.

But no matter how hard I tried, the memory of Cassian's smirk, the weight of his body above mine, and the way he'd unraveled me so effortlessly lingered at the edges of my mind, like a smoldering ember refusing to be extinguished.

Sophia's voice was smooth, measured, the kind of tone that carried authority without trying. I forced myself to focus on her words as the waiter took our orders. I settled on a light pasta dish and a sparkling water, while Sophia chose a seared salmon and a glass of sauvignon blanc. Her selections mirrored the impression she gave: refined, deliberate, and quietly commanding.

Once the waiter disappeared, Sophia leaned forward slightly, her dark eyes locking onto mine. "Ivy & Bloom has so much potential, Rosalie," she began, her hands lightly resting on the edge of the table. "It's already a gem, but with the right direction, it could be... luminous."

I tilted my head, intrigued despite the stubborn knot of

unease in my chest. "Luminous?" I repeated, the word feeling strange yet tantalizing.

Sophia's lips curved into a faint smile. "Yes. You've cultivated a space that resonates with people—elegance, charm, nostalgia. But it's more than just a floral shop, isn't it? It's an extension of you, your family, your history."

My stomach twisted at the mention of family, the image of my mother's photograph flashing in my mind. "It is," I said softly, gripping the edge of my napkin. "But it's also a business. One that's... evolving."

Sophia nodded, her expression empathetic but shrewd. "Evolving, yes. But evolution requires vision. And sometimes, an external perspective can shed light on opportunities that might not be obvious to those closest to the operation."

I wasn't sure if that was a dig at Lena's changes or simply a broader observation, but I let it slide. "What kind of opportunities are we talking about?"

Sophia's smile widened, a glint of satisfaction in her eyes as if she'd been waiting for me to ask. "Expanding your client base, for one. Ivy & Bloom has a distinct identity, but its reach is limited to those who happen upon it. Imagine leveraging your existing charm to attract high-end events, luxury brands, and even exclusive clientele who would value the craftsmanship your shop provides."

My pulse quickened slightly. High-end events? Luxury brands? It sounded ambitious, far beyond the intimate community connections Ivy & Bloom had built over the years. But was that a bad thing? I wasn't sure. And we had Julian's business now, he technically fit into that category...

"I've worked with businesses like yours before," Sophia continued, her tone gentle but persuasive. "Boutiques, florists, artisanal ventures. It's about amplifying what already makes you special. With the right marketing strategy, networking, and branding, Ivy & Bloom could be the name synonymous with exclusivity and sophistication."

I swallowed, trying to process the whirlwind of possibilities she was presenting. The idea of taking Ivy &

Bloom to those heights was thrilling, but it also felt overwhelming. The shop was my mother's legacy, a space built on love and memory. Could I really let it transform into something so... commercial?

"I don't know," I admitted, my voice quiet but steady. "It sounds incredible, but I don't want to lose what makes the shop unique. What makes it... home."

Sophia's gaze softened slightly, though her shrewdness never fully faded. "I understand," she said, her voice kind but firm. "And that's exactly why I want to help. My job isn't to strip away your identity—it's to elevate it. To ensure that the heart of Ivy & Bloom remains intact while expanding its reach to those who will truly appreciate it."

Her words settled over me like a warm yet heavy cloak. The idea of growth—of something new—was appealing, but it came with the weight of change. Change I wasn't sure I was ready for.

Sophia took a sip of her wine, letting the moment breathe before continuing. "Think about it, Rosalie. No pressure, no rush. I'm not offering a one-size-fits-all solution. What I'm offering is a partnership—one where we shape Ivy & Bloom's future together."

I nodded slowly, grateful for her patience but still unsure of how to respond. The waiter arrived with our meals, breaking the intensity of the moment. As the aroma of fresh herbs and delicate sauces filled the air, I forced myself to focus on the present—on the meal, on Sophia, on the opportunity she was laying before me.

Still, in the back of my mind, Cassian lingered like a shadow. What would he think of all this? Would he support me, or would he see it as another risk—another step into a world where vulnerability and ambition collided?

I twirled the edge of my fork through my pasta, gathering my thoughts before voicing my next question. Sophia had a way of presenting her ideas so seamlessly, yet they felt monumental to me. I couldn't shake the feeling that this was the start of something I might not fully control once it began.

"You mentioned branding and marketing," I said

carefully, looking up at her. "What exactly does that entail? Are we talking about changing the shop's look? Its logo?"

Sophia's smile was warm but purposeful. "Not necessarily a complete overhaul, unless you want one. What I envision is more of an enhancement. Ivy & Bloom has a timeless charm—that shouldn't be tampered with. But we could create elements that highlight its elegance: a signature scent, custom packaging, maybe even a seasonal line of limited-edition arrangements that appeal to high-profile clients."

I nodded slowly, trying to imagine the shop with her suggestions. It wasn't hard to see how they'd elevate the business. "And how would the events work?" I asked, pushing a rogue strand of hair behind my ear. "I mean, I've done weddings before, and a few exclusive events, but nothing on a... larger scale."

Sophia leaned forward slightly, her posture effortlessly commanding without being overbearing. "That's where my team comes in. We handle the logistics—the connections, the negotiations, the client relations. You focus on what you do best: creating beautiful, memorable arrangements. Of course, it would mean working closely with me on the design concepts for these events, but I think you'd find it fulfilling."

I considered her words, feeling a flicker of excitement despite my initial hesitation. The idea of focusing solely on the artistry without the stress of handling the business end was tempting. "Would you be willing to put something together? A proposal or maybe a few concepts to give me a clearer idea?"

Sophia's smile widened, satisfaction flickering in her dark eyes. "Absolutely. I'll draft an official proposal with a few design concepts and send it over within the week. You'll see—I think you'll love what we can create together."

I returned her smile, feeling a cautious sense of hope. "Thank you. I'd like that."

We finished our meals with lighter conversation, discussing trends in the industry and the types of clients Sophia had worked with. Despite my lingering reservations, I found myself drawn to her vision, her confidence, and the way she made everything seem possible.

As we left the restaurant, the cool afternoon air greeted us, flushing my cheeks as we stepped onto the bustling sidewalk. I reached into my purse to grab my phone when someone bumped into me, their shoulder colliding with mine. The force sent my bag tumbling to the ground, its contents spilling across the pavement.

"Oh!" I gasped, instinctively crouching to gather my things.

Sierra, who had been standing a few feet away, moved toward me with quick, purposeful strides. Her sharp blue eyes scanned the scene, her posture tense. "Miss Quinn, are you all right?" she asked, her voice firm but calm.

"I'm fine," I said quickly, waving her off before she could escalate the situation. "It was just an accident."

Sophia knelt beside me, her movements graceful as she picked up a stray lipstick and my phone. "Quite the entourage you've got there," she remarked, her tone light but inquisitive as she glanced toward Sierra.

I smiled faintly, tucking a stray strand of hair behind my ear as I grabbed my wallet and keys. "It's... a long story."

Sophia handed me the items she'd collected, her eyes lingering on Sierra for a moment before shifting back to me. "Well, I hope it's a story with a happy ending. Bodyguards usually suggest otherwise."

I let out a small laugh, though it lacked humor. "It's complicated; you have no idea."

Sophia studied me for a moment, her expression unreadable before she stood and dusted off her hands. "Complicated can be good—keeps life interesting."

I finished gathering my things and rose to my feet, slinging my bag back over my shoulder. "Let's go with that," I said lightly, though my mind was already elsewhere. Cassian's protectiveness, his insistence on keeping me safe—it all weighed heavier than I liked to admit.

Sierra lingered nearby, her sharp gaze still scanning the

crowd as we resumed walking. Sophia glanced back at her once, an amused smile playing at her lips, but thankfully, she didn't press further. For now, my focus was on the proposal and what it could mean for Ivy & Bloom—and on keeping the delicate balance of my life from tipping further into chaos.

The SUV door clicked shut behind me, and I exhaled, letting the relative quiet of the vehicle replace the bustle of the city streets. Sierra climbed into the front passenger seat while Marcus settled behind the wheel, his broad shoulders filling the space with an air of silent vigilance.

I set my bag down on the seat beside me, but something caught my eye. Something was off. A subtle prickle of unease crept along my spine, and I frowned as I reached for the strap to pull it closer. Opening the bag further, I immediately noticed an envelope nestled among my belongings. My heart skipped, the sight so out of place it stopped me cold.

I glanced toward the front of the vehicle. Sierra and Marcus were engaged in a low conversation about security protocols. Neither noticed as I slid the envelope free and held it in my lap.

The cream-colored paper was unmarked, no return address or indication of its origin. My fingers trembled slightly as I tore it open, curiosity battling the dread curling in my stomach. Inside was a folded sheet of paper and a photograph. The picture slipped from the envelope first, falling onto my lap. I caught a glimpse of it—a man seated at a café table, his face partially obscured by the brim of his hat. The name of the coffee shop was visible in the background, clear and deliberate.

What is this?

I set the photo aside, quickly unfolding the letter. The handwriting was precise, almost too perfect, as if someone had taken their time crafting each letter. My eyes skimmed the opening lines, and my breath caught.

You think you're safe with him, but you're not. The Reapers know who you are, Rosalie. They're watching. If you want to protect him, you need to find the connection between

Apex and Damon Cross.

My pulse pounded as I read further, but before I could make it halfway through, Marcus's sharp voice cut through the air. "Miss Quinn, what's that?"

I froze, the letter gripped tightly in my hand. "It's—" I started, but Marcus was already reaching over the console, his large hand outstretched.

"Hand it over," he said firmly, his expression unwavering.

Reluctantly, I passed him the letter, my heart racing as he scanned its contents. His eyes narrowed, his jaw tightening as he read. "Sierra," he said sharply, his voice low but commanding. He handed the letter over the seat to her.

Sierra's blue eyes flicked over the paper, her expression hardening with each line. "This needs to go to Mr. Moreau immediately," she said, her tone clipped. She pulled out her phone and began typing a message, her fingers moving quickly over the screen.

Neither of them noticed the photograph still resting in my lap. I glanced down at it, my hands brushing the glossy surface. The man in the photo was unfamiliar, but the coffee shop's name—Birch & Bean—was unmistakable. It was a cozy café near downtown, one I'd passed by a handful of times but never thought much about.

I slipped the photo into my pocket, my movements subtle and deliberate as Sierra and Marcus continued discussing the letter. Whatever this was, it felt personal in a way that went beyond Cassian's typical enemies. The unease I'd felt earlier deepened, knotting in my stomach.

"Miss Quinn," Marcus said, turning in his seat to face me. His dark eyes were serious, his tone leaving no room for debate. "We'll handle this. Mr. Moreau will be informed, and we'll ensure your safety."

I nodded, my throat tight with unspoken questions. The letter had rattled me, but the photograph—its quiet, chilling message—left me with a feeling I couldn't shake. Whoever had slipped it into my bag knew exactly what they were doing.

As the SUV pulled away from the curb, I pressed my hand against my pocket, my mind racing. Cassian would undoubtedly react with his usual blend of calculated fury and protectiveness, but this time, I wasn't sure if his world or mine was truly at the center of the threat.

CHAPTER SEVENTEEN

The mood in Cassian's office was taut, like a string pulled too tightly, vibrating with barely contained tension. I hesitated in the doorway, unsure whether to step into the whirlwind of activity or retreat unnoticed. Cassian was an island of calm amid the storm, seated behind his desk as Marcus delivered a low, urgent report. Sierra stood nearby, a picture of precision, her voice steady as she relayed instructions into her headset.

I clenched my fists, the envelope still in my hand. I'd come here for answers, but the scene in front of me gave rise to more questions. There were at least three other men I didn't recognize in the room, all dressed in the same sharp black suits Cassian's security team favored. They moved with purpose, exchanging clipped sentences that I couldn't make sense of.

This wasn't normal.

"Miss Quinn." Sierra's voice cut through my thoughts, sharp and professional. She stepped away from the monitors, her attention zeroing in on me like a laser. "You shouldn't be here."

I lifted the envelope. "We need to talk about this."

Sierra's gaze flicked to the envelope, her lips pressing into a thin line. "Mr. Moreau is already aware of the letter.

It's being handled."

"I don't care if it's being *handled*," I snapped, stepping further into the room. "I'm not just some bystander in all of this, Sierra. Someone put this in my bag, and I want to know who."

Before Sierra could respond, Cassian's voice rumbled from behind the desk, low and commanding. "Rosalie."

I turned to find him watching me, his gray eyes dark with an intensity that made my breath catch. His expression was unreadable, but there was no mistaking the tension in his posture or the steel in his gaze.

"This isn't the time," he said, his tone leaving dismissing me as quickly as I had arrived.

I lifted my chin, refusing to back down. "Then make time. This involves me, Cassian. You can't just keep me in the dark."

His jaw tightened, and he nodded to Marcus, who left the room without a word. The other men followed, leaving only Cassian, Sierra, and me in the suddenly too-quiet office. The air felt heavier, and I struggled to keep my composure under Cassian's piercing stare.

"Fine," he said finally, leaning back in his chair. "What do you want to know?"

I hesitated for a moment, glancing at Sierra. Her arms were crossed, her expression carefully neutral, but I could sense the undercurrent of disapproval. "The letter," I said, turning back to Cassian. "What does it mean? And why are there suddenly so many new people on your security team?"

Cassian's gaze flicked to Sierra, who gave a barely perceptible nod before speaking. "The letter is being analyzed for fingerprints and any other identifying markers. It's a threat, clearly, but it's also a distraction."

"A distraction?" I echoed, confusion tightening in my chest.

Sierra nodded. "It's meant to unsettle you, to make you question your safety. And while we're focusing on that, whoever sent it might be making moves elsewhere."

Cassian interjected, his voice calm but unyielding. "Which is why the team has been expanded. There's increased chatter about the Reapers moving into new territory. This isn't just about you, Rosalie. They want to see how I'll react."

I left Cassian's office without a word, the weight of the letter and everything it implied still pressing on my chest. Sierra had given me a sharp glance as I walked out, but I didn't stop, didn't explain. My feet carried me through the penthouse until I reached the solarium, a place that always felt a little softer, a little more detached from the chaos of Cassian's world.

The solarium was bathed in the soft glow of early evening, the greenery thriving under its windows of sunlight. I sank into one of the chairs, the plush cushion doing little to ease the tension in my shoulders. My phone was in my hand before I even realized it, my thumb hovering over my father's number.

It had been too long since I called him—longer still since I felt like I could talk to him without the weight of Cassian's world shadowing the conversation. But today, I needed the sound of his voice, the reminder of something untainted.

I hit the call button and brought the phone to my ear, listening to the ringing as my heart thudded in time.

"Rosalie?" My dad's voice was warm, the familiar timbre wrapping around me like a hug. "Hey, sweetheart. This is a surprise."

"Hi, Dad," I said, forcing a smile even though he couldn't see it. "I had some time and thought I'd check in."

"Well, I'm glad you did. How are you? How's the shop?"

I hesitated, the words catching in my throat. The shop. It felt like a lifetime ago that Ivy & Bloom had been my safe haven, my world. Now, it was something else entirely— something I wasn't sure I could claim as mine anymore. But I couldn't tell him that. Not without inviting questions I wasn't ready to answer.

"It's... good," I said finally. "A little busier than usual, but good."

"Busy's a good thing," he said, his tone light. "Keeps you out of trouble."

A laugh bubbled out of me before I could stop it, the irony

of his words hitting too close to home. If only he knew the kind of trouble I was neck-deep in. "Yeah, something like that."

There was a pause on his end, the kind of pause that meant he was thinking, weighing whether or not to push. "You sound different," he said finally, his voice quieter now. "Everything okay, Rosie?"

I swallowed hard, my grip tightening on the phone. "Of course," I said, too quickly. "Why wouldn't it be?"

"I don't know," he said, his tone careful. "You just... you sound like you've got a lot on your mind. Is it the shop? Something else?"

"No, it's not the shop," I said, exhaling slowly. "I guess I've just been busy. A lot going on, you know?"

"Mmm," he murmured, the skepticism in his voice clear. "You know you can tell me if something's wrong, right? Whatever it is."

I closed my eyes, the warmth of his concern washing over me. He didn't know—couldn't know—how much I wanted to tell him everything. But this wasn't his burden to bear. It was mine.

"I know," I said softly. "Thanks, Dad."

"Anytime," he said. "But remember, Rosie, you don't have to do everything alone. Whatever it is, I'm here."

My throat tightened, the words sticking like glue. I nodded, even though he couldn't see me, and forced another smile into my voice. "I'll remember."

We talked a little longer, the conversation shifting to safer topics—memories of Mom, updates on his projects, and his insistence that I come visit him soon. By the time we said goodbye, the ache in my chest had lessened, if only slightly.

I set my phone down on the small glass table in front of me, my gaze drifting to the greenery around me. The solarium was quiet, peaceful, but my thoughts were anything but. The picture in my purse, the letter, Cassian's growing tension—it all pressed against me, a reminder that the life I'd once known was slipping further and further out of reach.

And the worst part? I wasn't sure I wanted it back. Not entirely.

The solarium's calm had done little to soothe my restless mind. My father's voice, though comforting, lingered like a bittersweet echo. I leaned back in the chair, staring at the greenery around me, but my thoughts kept circling back to Cassian, his tightly controlled fury, and the weight of the letter Sierra had whisked away.

I couldn't sit still any longer. Pushing myself up, I started back toward Cassian's office. If he thought he could keep me in the dark, he was wrong. Whatever was happening, whatever had him so tightly wound, I deserved to know.

As I approached the office, the low murmur of voices carried down the hallway. I slowed my steps, my pulse quickening. The door was slightly ajar, just enough for the faint hum of conversation to slip through.

I paused just outside, my heart thudding in my chest as I caught fragments of their discussion.

"...Apex Logistics shipment," Marcus said, his tone clipped. "It's coming into the south docks tonight. Looks like it might be tied to Cross."

I froze, the name sending a chill down my spine. Damon Cross. Apex Logistics. The threads I'd uncovered in Cassian's files came rushing back, piecing together a picture I hadn't fully understood until now.

"We can't let it slip through," Marcus continued. "If what the intel suggests is true, it's a major play."

Cassian's voice followed, low and sharp, the kind of tone that brooked no argument. "We won't. Have the team ready to move by 2100. I want eyes on every angle—drones, scouts, everything. If Cross is using this shipment to funnel something for the Reapers, we're shutting it down."

There was a brief pause, then Sierra spoke up. "What about security? If the Reapers catch wind of this..."

"They won't," Cassian interrupted. "And if they do, they'll regret it. This ends tonight."

My breath caught, the weight of their words pressing down on me. They were planning an interception—a full-scale operation to stop whatever the Reapers were moving. And Cassian was going to lead it.

The thought made my stomach twist. I knew the risks he took, the danger that came with his world, but hearing it spelled out so plainly was different. It wasn't just a calculated move—it was a gamble. And the stakes were high.

I leaned closer, my hand resting lightly against the doorframe as I strained to hear more.

"We need to keep this quiet," Marcus said. "No leaks, no mistakes."

Cassian's voice was steel. "Agreed, keep the circle tight. I want the team briefed within the hour. Make sure everyone knows their role."

Footsteps sounded from inside, and I realized too late that the conversation was wrapping up. Panic shot through me as I straightened, stepping back from the door just as it swung open.

Marcus was the first to emerge, his sharp eyes locking onto mine immediately. His expression didn't betray anything, but the faint flicker of surprise in his gaze was enough to confirm he knew I'd overheard.

"Miss Quinn," he said, his tone neutral.

I forced a smile, trying to look as though I hadn't been eavesdropping. "Marcus."

Sierra followed, her sharp blue eyes narrowing slightly as she glanced between me and the door. "Is there something you need?" she asked, her voice cool but not unfriendly.

Before I could respond, Cassian appeared in the doorway. His gray eyes landed on me, their intensity pinning me in place. He didn't say anything at first, his gaze sweeping over me as though assessing the situation.

"Rosalie," he said finally, his voice calm but laced with an undercurrent of authority. "What are you doing here?"

I hesitated, my mind scrambling for an explanation that wouldn't betray how much I'd overheard. "I... wanted to talk to you," I said, meeting his gaze. "About earlier."

His eyes narrowed slightly, but he stepped aside,

gesturing for me to enter the office. "Come in."

As I crossed the threshold, I couldn't shake the feeling that I'd just walked into a storm I wasn't fully prepared for. Whatever was happening with the Reapers, with Damon Cross, and this shipment—it wasn't over. And I wasn't sure Cassian would ever let me be a part of it.

Cassian shut the office door behind me, the sound ominous in the otherwise quiet room. His presence loomed as he stepped toward the desk, his gray eyes scanning me with a sharpness that made my skin prickle.

"So," he said, leaning back against the desk and crossing his arms. "I thought we had this conversation already. What was so important that you needed to interrupt?"

I squared my shoulders, my heart racing but my resolve firm. "I overheard your plans about the shipment."

His expression didn't change, but a flicker of something—irritation, maybe—crossed his eyes. "You were eavesdropping?"

"I wasn't trying to," I said quickly. "But I heard enough to know you're planning to intercept something big. And I want to come with you."

Cassian's brow lifted, and for a moment, he just stared at me, as if waiting for me to realize how absurd my statement sounded. When I didn't falter, he pushed off the desk, his movements slow and deliberate as he approached.

"Absolutely not," he said, his voice cold and final. "You're staying here."

"No, I'm not." I stepped closer, refusing to back down. "You said yourself this could be a diversion. If the Reapers are planning something bigger, leaving me behind makes me a sitting duck."

Cassian's jaw tightened, his gaze darkening. "You'll have Sierra here. You'll be safe."

"Will I?" I countered, my voice rising slightly. "Because last time I was left alone, Victor shot me. Or have you forgotten?"

His expression turned stormy, the memory clearly striking a nerve. "That's exactly why you're not coming," he snapped. "You think I'm going to put you in the middle of this? Where you could get hurt—or worse?"

"I think I'm safer with you and your team than locked away in this penthouse," I shot back. "You can't control everything, Cassian. If the Reapers are as dangerous as you say, then nowhere is truly safe. At least if I'm with you, I'll have a chance."

His hands clenched at his sides, his control visibly slipping. "You have no idea what you're asking for, Rosalie."

"I'm not asking," I said, my tone firm. "I'm telling you. I'm coming. It's my choice, remember?"

For a long moment, the tension between us crackled like a live wire. His gray eyes bore into mine, unyielding and fierce, but I didn't waver. I couldn't. The thought of being left behind, vulnerable and alone, was worse than whatever danger I might face by his side.

Finally, he exhaled sharply, raking a hand through his hair. "I don't like it," he muttered, his voice low and frustrated.

I crossed my arms, waiting.

Cassian turned away, pacing to the window and staring out at the city for a moment. When he finally spoke, his tone was colder, more controlled. "Fine. You can come. But you're staying in the vehicle. No arguments, no exceptions."

Relief and a flicker of triumph surged through me, but I kept my expression neutral. "I'll stay in the vehicle," I agreed, knowing it was the only way he'd let me come.

Cassian turned back to me, his eyes narrowing as if to gauge whether I was truly being honest. "You're not to leave the vehicle, under any circumstance, Rosalie. Do you hear me? You don't leave the fucken car. Not for anything."

"I understand," I said, though I could feel his doubt lingering.

He sighed again, muttering something under his breath before stepping closer, his hand reaching out to cup my face. His thumb brushed over my cheek, the gesture surprisingly gentle despite the tension radiating from him.

"I swear, you're going to be the death of me," he murmured, his voice low but laced with something softer—

something that made my chest tighten.

I placed my hand over his, meeting his gaze. "Then don't leave me behind."

For a moment, we just stood there, the weight of unspoken fears and frustrations hanging between us. Finally, he stepped back, his expression hardening once more.

"Get ready," he said curtly. "We leave in an hour."

CHAPTER EIGHTEEN

The armored SUV hummed steadily beneath me, the low vibration doing little to soothe the restless energy coursing through my veins. Outside, the city blurred by, its neon lights and muted grays painting a canvas of chaos I barely noticed. I sat in the back seat, flanked by Sierra and Marcus, their silent presence a constant reminder that I wasn't supposed to be here.

Cassian was in the lead vehicle, his shadow long and ever-present, even when he wasn't physically near. I could feel him somehow, his protective energy wrapping around me like a shield—though at the moment, it felt more like a chain.

Sierra glanced at me from the corner of her sharp blue eyes, her movements economical as she checked the weapon holstered at her side. "You know the rules," she said, her tone clipped. "You stay in this vehicle, you heard Cassian's orders. This isn't the moment for you to be bold."

I crossed my arms and let out a huff, staring straight ahead. "I've heard the speech, Sierra."

"And you're going to hear it again," she shot back, her gaze darting between me and the surrounding streets. "This isn't a game, Rosalie. You step out of this SUV, and you could ruin everything."

Marcus, sitting on my other side, leaned forward slightly, his calm demeanor the polar opposite of Sierra's no-nonsense intensity. "She's right, you know," he said, his deep voice rumbling like distant thunder. "Cassian put us here to protect you. You have to let us do our job."

"I didn't ask to be protected," I muttered, gripping the edge of my seat. "I asked to be included."

"That's not how this works," Sierra said, her voice softening just enough to make the words sting. "And you know it."

The tension between us settled into a heavy silence, broken only by the occasional crackle of the radio as updates filtered through from the other vehicles in the convoy. I glanced out the window, the city giving way to industrial zones marked by sprawling warehouses and deserted streets. The glow of streetlights cast long shadows across the cracked asphalt, and an uneasy chill crept up my spine.

"What's the plan?" I asked, trying to mask the apprehension in my voice.

Marcus leaned back against the seat, his posture steady and unyielding, as if nothing could shake him. His calm presence was a stark contrast to the storm of thoughts raging in my head. "We're hitting the warehouse fast and clean," he began, his deep voice cutting through the tension in the SUV like a blade.

"Apex Logistics has been moving shipments through this facility for months," he continued, his gaze fixed ahead as the city began to give way to the desolate industrial outskirts. "We've pinpointed tonight's delivery as something significant—too significant to ignore. Cassian believes it could be a major piece of their operation. Potentially the missing piece to the puzzle."

I swallowed hard, the gravity of his words sinking in. "What exactly are you expecting to find?"

"Anything," Marcus said bluntly. "Drugs, weapons, people—it could be any of the above or all of them. Apex isn't sloppy. If they're moving something big, they'll have layers of security to protect it."

Sierra chimed in from the front seat, her sharp tone as precise as the weapon strapped to her hip. "That's why we're splitting into teams. One group secures the perimeter, cutting off any chance for reinforcements. The second team breaches the building, neutralizing threats and securing the shipment. Cassian's group will focus on extracting intel—documents, electronic devices, anything we can use to trace this back to Damon Cross."

"And me?" I asked, though I already knew the answer.

Marcus turned his head slightly, his calm gaze meeting mine. "You're staying here. Sierra and I will be with you the entire time. If anything happens, we'll get you out."

My hands tightened around the strap of my purse as frustration bubbled to the surface. "So I'm just supposed to sit here and do nothing?"

"Yes," Sierra said firmly, not even glancing back. "Because your presence outside this vehicle compromises the mission."

Her words stung, but I bit back a retort. Instead, I focused on Marcus, who leaned forward slightly, his voice softening but no less resolute. "I know this isn't easy but for every moment he is thinking of you, worrying about you, it's a split second his head isn't in the game. That when mistakes happen and we can't afford mistakes—not tonight."

I leaned back in my seat, exhaling sharply as I processed the weight of their plan. It was a military-level operation, precise and methodical, and I was an outsider—a civilian thrust into a world of calculated risks and dangerous stakes.

The radio crackled, and Cassian's voice came through, low and commanding. "Two minutes out. Final checks."

Sierra's hand moved to her earpiece, her attention shifting instantly to the mission. "Copy that. Perimeter teams are in position."

Marcus shifted, his broad shoulders blocking part of the window as the SUV slowed. "This will move fast," he said, glancing at me. "Stay alert. If anything happens, you follow our instructions without hesitation. Understood?"

"Understood," I murmured, though the uneasy knot in my stomach told me this was far from over.

The SUV came to a halt, the glow of streetlights casting long shadows across the cracked asphalt. In the distance, the warehouse loomed like a fortress, its silhouette dark and foreboding. The hum of activity outside was faint but unmistakable—this was Cassian's world, unfolding in real time.

I stayed silent, my pulse pounding in my ears as Marcus and Sierra exchanged a quick series of hand signals, their movements seamless and practiced. Whatever lay ahead, I wasn't sure I was ready for it—but there was no turning back now.

CHAPTER NINETEEN

CASSIAN

From our vantage point, the warehouse sprawled out like a fortress, its massive structure cast in a cold, industrial glow from the overhead floodlights. My men and I crouched low behind a line of rusting shipping containers, the sharp scent of oil and damp metal hanging in the air.

Through the binoculars, I could see them—guards patrolling the perimeter, their movements predictable but measured. They weren't amateurs, but they weren't exactly elite either. Cheap muscle, the kind Apex Logistics probably employed by the dozen. Their uniforms were dark, nondescript, and their weapons were slung casually across their shoulders. Too casual.

"They're overconfident," I muttered, lowering the binoculars and handing them to Dominic, who crouched beside me. His sharp eyes followed the path of the guards, his expression unreadable.

"Sloppy security for a shipment they're clearly trying to hide," Dominic replied, his voice low. "But there's enough of them to make this a problem if we don't move fast."

I nodded, my gaze shifting to the activity inside the warehouse. Crates were being loaded onto trucks with an efficiency that spoke of experience. Forklifts moved in and out like clockwork, the workers keeping their heads down and their movements quick.

"Any idea what's inside the crates?" I asked, my tone clipped.

Dominic adjusted the binoculars. "Not yet. No labels on the shipments. Could be weapons, could be contraband, could be something worse."

I clenched my jaw, the thought of "something worse" sending a sharp pulse of anger through me. The Reapers were bold, but this operation reeked of desperation—or ambition. Either way, it was dangerous.

My earpiece crackled to life, Sierra's calm voice cutting through the static. "Perimeter teams are in position. Ready on your signal."

I glanced at Dominic, who gave a curt nod, his hand resting on the stock of his rifle. The rest of the team waited behind us, their silhouettes blending into the shadows. My men weren't just muscle; they were precision tools, honed and ready to strike.

"Anything on the scanners?" I asked, my voice low but firm.

Dominic shook his head. "No unusual frequencies. If they're running comms, it's localized and rudimentary."

"Good," I said, my voice hardening. "We hit them fast and hard. Perimeter team cuts off their escape routes; breach team moves in to secure the building. Dominic, you and I focus on the shipment intel. Whatever they're moving, I want to know where it's going and who's paying for it."

I glanced over my shoulder at the rest of the crew, each of them waiting with a quiet tension. Their faces were shadowed, but their readiness was palpable.

"We've got maybe a ten-minute window before anyone notices we're here," I said, addressing them all. "No mistakes. No loose ends."

They nodded, their silence an agreement as solid as any spoken word. I pressed a hand to my earpiece. "Sierra, hold position until we breach. Marcus?"

"Still with the package," came Marcus's steady reply.

"All clear for now."

I exhaled sharply, the thought of Rosalie tugging at my focus. She was safe, for now. That was what mattered. But the memory of her defiance earlier in the evening lingered, a sharp edge that I couldn't quite dull.

"Eyes on the target," Dominic said, pulling me back to the moment. He handed me the binoculars, nodding toward the truck furthest from us. "That one's leaving first."

I raised the binoculars, focusing on the truck he'd indicated. A worker was sealing the back, his hands moving quickly as another man climbed into the driver's seat. My jaw tightened.

"Not if we have anything to say about it," I muttered.

I tapped my earpiece again. "Perimeter team, prepare to intercept. Breach team, move into position. On my signal, we go."

The air around us seemed to still, the hum of the distant forklifts and the occasional murmur of the guards the only sounds breaking the tension. My men moved into position with the practiced silence of predators closing in on their prey.

I took one last glance at the warehouse, at the guards who had no idea what was coming for them, and let the adrenaline sharpen my focus. This was my world, and tonight, the Reapers would learn that it didn't belong to them.

"On my count," I said, my voice calm but laced with steel. "Three. Two. One. Go."

The team moved like shadows, slipping through the gaps in the guards' perimeter with practiced precision. Every step was calculated, silent. My earpiece crackled as Sierra's voice confirmed, "All perimeter routes secure. No activity spotted on the south end."

Dominic gestured toward the warehouse's entrance, his hand signaling the next move. I nodded, my focus sharp as my eyes scanned the grounds. But as I shifted my gaze to the far side of the building, something stopped me cold.

An unmarked black van.

It was parked in the shadows, tucked between two

shipping containers on the northeast side. Its sleek, unassuming design might have escaped notice if I hadn't been searching for irregularities. The van's windows were heavily tinted, and there were no company logos—no identifiers at all.

"Dominic," I muttered, my voice low enough not to carry. "That van," my eyes fell on it again, drawing Dominic's gaze to it. "Has it been cleared?"

He followed my line of sight, his brow furrowing. "No. Not in the satellite images or the scout reports. Could be backup."

"Or something worse," I replied, the cold knot in my stomach tightening. The van felt wrong, like a splinter under the skin—an irritation that could fester into something deadly if ignored.

I pressed a hand to my earpiece, the cold plastic grounding me. "Sierra, eyes on the northeast corner. Black van parked near the containers. I want to know if it's active."

"Copy that," came Sierra's voice, calm and precise. "Deploying a drone now."

A soft hum broke the silence, barely audible against the faint rustle of the wind. One of Sierra's compact drones zipped out of her pack, a sleek, dark object that blended into the shadows. On my wrist monitor, the live feed flickered to life, displaying the van in sharp, stark detail.

The drone's camera zoomed in as it approached. The polished black exterior gleamed under the harsh glow of the floodlights, its reflective surface making it seem unnervingly blank. The van's windows were like mirrors, revealing nothing of what lay within. My breath slowed as I watched, every nerve on high alert.

"Thermal scan initiated," Sierra reported, her voice clipped but steady. "No immediate heat signatures inside the vehicle."

"Could be shielded," I muttered, half to myself.

The drone hovered closer, its tiny rotors barely whispering in the cool night air. On the screen, the camera shifted angles, capturing every inch of the van's exterior.

No decals, no license plate—nothing to identify who owned it or why it was there.

"Angle shift," Sierra said. The feed adjusted, zooming in on the van's undercarriage. "No tracking devices or explosive rigging detected."

I exhaled, but the knot in my stomach didn't loosen. "Keep scanning."

The camera panned to the back doors, and a faint glimmer caught my attention—tiny scratches near the lock, barely visible under the floodlights. My pulse quickened.

"Zoom in," I ordered, my voice sharp.

The image clarified, revealing what looked like marks from a hastily inserted tool. Someone had been here, tampering with the lock—but whether they'd been trying to get in or out, I couldn't tell.

"Sierra, you seeing this?" I asked.

"Affirmative," she replied.

"Possible decoy?" Dominic suggested, his voice low.

"Or bait," I said grimly, my chest tightening with unease. "Either way, it's deliberate."

Sierra's voice broke through again, tinged with tension. "Cassian, we've got movement—rear compartment doors just shifted. Looks like internal pressure adjustment."

My grip tightened on the monitor. A vehicle without occupants wouldn't adjust pressure like that—not without someone triggering it. My instincts screamed that this was wrong, that we were on the verge of uncovering something far worse than a simple shipment.

"Perimeter team," I snapped into the earpiece. "Hold position and monitor for any activity near the van. No one engages without my order."

Dominic's jaw tightened beside me. "What's the call?"

I glanced toward the warehouse, where the shipment was being loaded onto trucks, and back to the van. The two threats sat like twin wolves waiting to pounce, and I had no idea which one to face first.

"We stick to the plan," I said finally, though my gut churned. "We take the warehouse. But keep an eye on that van. If it moves, we hit it."

As Sierra's drone continued to hover, its camera unflinching, I couldn't shake the feeling that something was watching us in return—something patient, calculating, and far deadlier than I'd anticipated.

The moment I gave the signal, my team moved like clockwork.

"Go," I barked into the earpiece.

Dominic and the perimeter crew shifted forward, silent shadows against the dimly lit yard. The warehouse loomed ahead, its corrugated metal walls reflecting the sparse light from scattered floodlights. The air was thick with the smell of oil and damp concrete, mingling with the faint metallic tang of the harbor in the distance.

Sierra's voice crackled in my ear. "Drone confirms no new movement around the van. All quiet."

"For now," I muttered, my eyes flicking to the warehouse entrance. "Stay sharp."

The first team breached the outer fence, the faint snip of bolt cutters the only sound as they made an opening. Dominic was first through, crouched low as he scanned the area ahead. My eyes tracked the laser pointer from his rifle as it swept across the loading docks and the row of parked trucks. Nothing stirred.

"Clear," he whispered.

I signaled the second team forward, their footfalls muffled against the gravel as they moved toward the side entrance. The industrial-sized doors stood partially open, allowing a sliver of light to spill out. A pair of guards loitered nearby, their postures casual but their weapons slung in easy reach.

"Two guards, east side," Dominic reported.

"Take them," I said coldly.

Dominic raised his rifle, the faint click of his suppressed weapon breaking the silence. One guard dropped without a sound, his body crumpling to the ground. The second turned, his hand moving toward his radio, but a second shot took him down before he could react.

"Guards neutralized," Dominic confirmed.

I gestured for the team to push forward. The faint hum

of machinery buzzed from within the warehouse, accompanied by the occasional clang of metal against metal. My boots crunched softly on the gravel as I moved closer, my senses hyper-focused on every sound, every shift in the shadows.

The interior of the warehouse was a cavernous maze of towering metal shelves and stacked crates, their labels faded and illegible. Forklifts sat idle, their rusting frames glinting under the harsh fluorescent lights. Workers milled about near the loading docks, their movements brisk as they hauled large containers toward the waiting trucks.

"Count six workers near the docks," Sierra's voice came through. "Could be Reaper affiliates."

"They will be soon enough," I muttered.

The team split into two groups as planned. Dominic led one toward the offices on the mezzanine, where we suspected the shipment manifest would be kept. My group moved toward the loading area, hugging the shadows cast by the towering shelves.

The smell of diesel fuel and old wood hit me as I neared the docks. My team fanned out, weapons trained on the workers, who were too preoccupied to notice our approach.

"Hold," I said softly into the earpiece.

My gaze swept the scene, locking onto the shipping containers being loaded onto the trucks. Their serial numbers matched the ones flagged in the intel, confirming this was the shipment we'd been tracking. A flicker of satisfaction ran through me, but it was short-lived.

A voice barked an order in the distance, harsh and unfamiliar. My gut clenched. A man emerged from the shadows near the rear of the warehouse, flanked by two more armed guards. He was tall, broad-shouldered, and carried himself with the air of someone who knew exactly where the power lay—in his hands.

"Target identified," Dominic's voice came through. "That's Anton Ryker. Mid-level Reaper. Handles logistics."

I studied him for a moment, noting the confident swagger and the way his hand rested lightly on the grip of his pistol. He wasn't here by accident. This wasn't just a routine shipment.

"This changes nothing," I said into the earpiece. "Take the shipment and bring him in."

The team moved in unison, their weapons raised as they converged on the loading area.

"Down on the ground!" Dominic's voice rang out, sharp and commanding.

The workers froze, their wide eyes darting to the armed men surrounding them. One of them hesitated, his hand inching toward a crowbar, but a warning shot into the floor made him drop it with a clatter.

The guards with Anton reacted instantly, raising their weapons. I moved before they could fire, my own rifle kicking against my shoulder as I put one of them down. The second fired a wild shot that ricocheted off a metal crate before Dominic took him out with a clean headshot.

Anton raised his hands, his face carefully neutral as he sized us up. "You've made a mistake," he said, his voice calm but dripping with malice.

"No," I replied, stepping forward. "You have."

Before he could respond, the warehouse door on the far side slammed open. The sound echoed like a gunshot, and I turned to see figures pouring in—figures dressed in black, their faces obscured by masks. The Reapers weren't just shipping goods. They were staging an ambush.

It was a fucking ambush.

The first sign that something was wrong came as I barked another command into the earpiece. Silence.

"Sierra, status on the northwest—" I stopped, tapping the device against my ear. Nothing. The steady hum of comms chatter had gone dead. My stomach twisted.

"Marcus?" I tried again, my voice a growl of frustration. The silence was deafening. The realization hit hard—our comms were jammed.

"Damn it," I hissed, gesturing sharply to Dominic. "We're cut off. No tech. Old-school."

Dominic nodded, his jaw tight. "Understood."

The crackle of boots on concrete reached my ears as shadows moved in the distance. Whoever was jamming us wasn't just playing defense—they were moving in for the kill.

"Hold the line!" I bellowed to my men. The echo carried through the warehouse, bouncing off the steel beams and towering stacks of crates. This wasn't going to be clean. This was going to be brutal.

The first attacker emerged from the shadows, wielding a bat wrapped in barbed wire. I ducked the wild swing, slamming the butt of my rifle into his ribs. He stumbled, but another figure lunged at me from the side. I pivoted, drawing the knife from my boot and driving it into his shoulder. He dropped with a guttural scream, but there wasn't time to revel in the victory.

A deafening roar filled the air as one of the attackers fired a shotgun. The blast took out a row of crates, sending splinters flying like shrapnel. I dove behind a stack of pallets, my heart pounding. More and more I realized how wrong we'd been. We'd been baited right into the ambush.

Dominic was a blur of motion, disarming one of the attackers with a swift strike before delivering a crushing blow to his temple. "Cassian, we're boxed in!"

"No shit!" I yelled back, rising from cover to fire at the group advancing on us. Two went down, but more were coming.

The warehouse transformed into a battleground. The air was thick with the acrid smell of gunpowder and sweat. The sharp clang of metal on metal echoed as one of my men engaged in hand-to-hand combat, their blades flashing in the dim light. The Reapers weren't just here to defend their shipment—they were here to send a message.

A figure loomed out of the corner of my vision, swinging a lead pipe. I ducked, feeling the rush of air as it passed over my head. I countered with a swift uppercut, the impact sending him sprawling. Before I could recover, another grabbed me from behind, his arm locking around my neck.

I slammed my elbow into his ribs once, twice, until his grip loosened. With a snarl, I twisted free and drove him headfirst into the concrete floor. My breath came in short bursts, but the adrenaline kept me moving.

Across the room, Dominic was holding his own, using a broken crate lid as a makeshift shield against an attacker with a machete. He parried the blow and retaliated with a brutal punch that sent the man crashing into a pile of barrels.

"Cassian!" Dominic's voice cut through the chaos. "We've got movement near the van!"

I turned, my gaze snapping to the black van that had been parked at the edge of the loading dock. Its engine roared to life, and the back doors swung open. Two men jumped out, carrying what looked like a reinforced case.

"That's it," I muttered. My instincts screamed that whatever was in that case was the key to this entire operation.

"Cover me!" I shouted to Dominic as I bolted toward the van. The floor was a gauntlet of debris and bodies, but I didn't stop. Bullets zipped past me, one grazing my shoulder, but the pain barely registered.

The two men with the case saw me coming and turned to flee, but I was faster. I tackled the first one, the impact driving us both to the ground. The case skidded across the floor, coming to rest near a stack of crates.

The second man pulled a knife, lunging at me with a wild swing. I blocked with my forearm, the blade slicing through my sleeve but missing flesh. I countered with a headbutt, sending him reeling. Before he could recover, I delivered a sharp kick to his knee, and he collapsed with a howl.

Dominic reached my side, his rifle trained on the downed men. "We've got the case."

"Not yet." I grabbed it, my hands slick with sweat and blood. "We get out of here first."

But as I stood, a new wave of attackers poured in from the warehouse's far entrance, their sheer numbers overwhelming. We were outmanned and out of options.

"Fall back!" I barked, dragging the case toward the exit. Dominic covered me, his rifle spitting fire at the advancing Reapers. We retreated step by step, the weight of the case a reminder of what was at stake.

The battle wasn't over—not by a long shot—but for now, survival was the only priority.

CHAPTER TWENTY

ROSALIE

The sharp cracks of gunfire echoed faintly through the warehouse's thick walls, mingling with the flickering flashes of light that pierced the gloom. From my position in the SUV, I could feel the tension radiating off Sierra and Marcus like a storm about to break. They sat rigid in their seats, eyes scanning the dark expanse of the loading yard. The vehicle hummed quietly beneath us, ready to spring into action at a moment's notice.

My chest tightened with every second that passed. The longer the sounds of chaos stretched on, the harder it became to sit still. My hands twisted in my lap, knuckles white as I stared out the window, straining to make sense of the shapes moving in the distance.

"Is this normal?" I asked, my voice breaking the taut silence. My heart was racing, a relentless thrum in my ears. "The gunfire?"

Sierra's jaw tightened, avoiding answering me directly. "Stay calm. Cassian and his team know what they're doing."

Her words did little to ease my growing anxiety. Something felt wrong—off. The flashes of light weren't just sporadic bursts; they seemed concentrated, almost planned, like whoever was inside was fighting against more than they anticipated.

As I forced my gaze to the shadowed loading area, movement caught my eye. A vehicle emerged from the far side of the yard, its headlights cutting through the darkness like twin blades. My breath hitched as the unmistakable shape of a black van materialized, gliding toward us with ominous intent.

"Sierra," I whispered, my voice trembling. "There's another van."

Her head snapped in the direction I was pointing, her sharp blue eyes narrowing. Marcus leaned forward in his seat, his hand already moving toward the weapon holstered at his side. The tension in the SUV escalated to a fever pitch as Sierra grabbed her radio.

"Cassian, we've got a second black van incoming. East of the yard, heading toward our position." She waited for a response, but the radio remained silent. Her expression darkened as she tried again, her tone clipped. "Cassian, do you copy?"

Nothing.

"Comms are down," Marcus muttered, his voice a low rumble. "They must have jammed them."

Sierra cursed under her breath, her hand tightening around the radio. "Of course they have."

My pulse spiked as I watched the van inch closer, its dark windows gleaming under the faint light of the yard's overhead lamps. "What do we do?"

Sierra turned to Marcus, her gaze sharp. "We need to hold position. If they're coming for us, we can't lead them to Cassian's team. Rosalie stays inside no matter what."

Marcus nodded grimly, his large frame exuding calm authority. "Understood."

The van slowed, its movements deliberate, predatory. My heart was in my throat as I tried to make sense of its intentions. Was it scouting? A decoy? Or something worse? The weight of uncertainty pressed down on me, stealing my breath.

"I don't like this," Marcus muttered, his eyes never

leaving the approaching vehicle.

Sierra's grip on her weapon tightened. "Me neither."

The van came to a halt roughly fifty feet from us, idling ominously in the shadows. For a moment, everything was still, as though the world was holding its breath. Then the driver's side door opened, and a figure stepped out, shrouded in darkness.

"Stay low," Sierra commanded, her voice firm but calm. Her sharp gaze flicked to me. "Rosalie, don't move."

I obeyed, sliding down in my seat, my pulse hammering in my ears. The air in the SUV was suffocating, charged with unspoken fear and the tension of trained professionals preparing for the worst. Outside, the figure paused, their posture unnervingly casual as they surveyed the yard.

"Sierra—" I began, my voice barely a whisper, but she cut me off with a quick shake of her head. Her focus was razor-sharp, her finger resting lightly on the trigger of her weapon.

The figure retreated back into the van, and the vehicle's headlights flickered once, almost like a signal. My breath hitched as another set of lights appeared on the opposite end of the yard. A second vehicle.

"They're coordinating," Marcus muttered grimly. "This isn't random."

Sierra's voice dropped to a near growl. "It's a trap."

Panic clawed at my chest as I clutched at the edge of the seat. "Cassian's in there. We have to do something!"

Sierra's gaze flicked to me, her expression firm. "Our orders are to protect you. We can't risk drawing attention to this vehicle."

Her words were logical, even necessary, but they felt like a knife to my gut. Helplessness wrapped around me like a vice as I glanced back at the warehouse, the flashes of gunfire inside painting the dark windows with bursts of light. Cassian was in there, cut off, surrounded by danger—and now, so were we.

A third van tore into the lot with a deafening screech, its tires skidding across the gravel. The sound sent a jolt through my chest, and my breath caught as the vehicle came to a halt barely thirty feet from us. The doors burst open almost simultaneously, and several armed men spilled out, their movements precise and coordinated—practiced. My stomach plummeted.

"They're moving toward us!" I whispered urgently, my voice barely steady.

Sierra didn't hesitate. She yanked open her door and swung out, her weapon already in hand. "Marcus, suppressive fire. Keep them off the SUV!"

Marcus was already in motion, his massive frame shifting with experienced efficiency as he opened his door and crouched behind it for cover. "Stay down, Rosalie!" he barked, his deep voice cutting through the chaos.

Gunfire erupted, the sharp cracks of Sierra and Marcus's weapons echoing in the night. The SUV rocked slightly as bullets ricocheted off the armored exterior, sparks flying as the assailants returned fire. My heart pounded in my chest, a frantic rhythm that drowned out almost everything else.

I sank lower in my seat, clutching the edge of the seatbelt with trembling hands. The acrid smell of gunpowder filtered through the slightly cracked windows, mixing with the tension that thickened the air.

Sierra's voice cut through the cacophony. "Marcus, three on the left. I'll take the right!"

She popped up from behind the hood of the SUV, her movements swift and precise as she fired off several rounds. One of the men staggered back, his weapon clattering to the ground, but the others pressed forward, relentless. Marcus provided cover, his shots heavy and deliberate, forcing the attackers to scatter and take cover behind the third van.

I peeked over the edge of the seat, my pulse hammering as I caught a glimpse of the scene outside. The lot was chaos, flashes of muzzle fire lighting up the dark as Sierra and Marcus held their ground. The men from the van weren't just a threat—they were organized, their movements calculated as they tried to flank the SUV.

"They're moving around us!" Marcus called out, his voice

calm but edged with urgency. He ducked low, shifting his position to cover Sierra's blind spot. "Rosalie, stay down!"

I obeyed, curling into myself as the gunfire intensified. The sound was deafening, each shot reverberating through the SUV like a thunderclap. I squeezed my eyes shut, willing myself to stay calm, but the fear clawing at my chest was relentless.

Outside, Sierra moved like a force of nature, her golden hair gleaming under the floodlights as she fired with deadly precision. She crouched behind the front wheel, her voice steady as she relayed instructions to Marcus. "They're falling back on the left! Keep the pressure on!"

Marcus nodded, his movements fluid despite his massive frame. His weapon barked in rapid succession, forcing the assailants to retreat a few steps. "They're regrouping. Watch the right flank!"

Sierra didn't respond immediately. Instead, she rose slightly, her sharp blue eyes scanning the lot. "Marcus, something's not right. They're too disciplined for this to be random."

Her words sent a shiver down my spine. This wasn't just an ambush—it was a strategy, and I was beginning to realize it wasn't just about the warehouse.

"They're targeting us," Sierra growled, confirming my unspoken fear. She adjusted her grip on her weapon and fired again, her expression cold and unyielding. "They want her."

My stomach churned, the weight of her statement pressing down like a vice. This wasn't just about Cassian or the Reapers. I was part of this now, whether I wanted to be or not.

A sudden, deafening bang shattered the tension, and one of the assailants screamed, clutching his arm as he collapsed behind the van. Sierra didn't flinch, her focus razor-sharp as she pressed forward, her weapon spitting fire.

"Marcus, cover me!" she shouted, her voice cutting through the chaos like steel. She darted to the side, her movements swift and calculated as she repositioned herself for a better vantage point.

Marcus complied without hesitation, his powerful presence an unshakable anchor in the storm of chaos. His shots were precise, each one forcing the attackers to rethink their approach. "We need to end this fast. If Cassian's not out soon, we're pulling her out of here."

Sierra's jaw tightened, but she nodded, her resolve unwavering. "Agreed."

I watched them, my heart pounding as the realization settled over me: this wasn't just a fight for survival. This was war. And we were at its center.

I couldn't sit still anymore. My heart raced in my chest as the sound of gunfire rattled my nerves. I glanced out the window again, searching for some sign of relief or an end to the chaos. Instead, my gaze locked onto one of the attackers creeping along the far side of the lot, crouched low as he moved toward the SUV's blind spot.

He was close. Too close.

"Sierra!" I called out, my voice shaky but loud enough to pierce through the cacophony. She didn't turn, her focus fixed on the group pinned behind the van.

"Right behind you!" I shouted, my panic rising as I saw the glint of the man's weapon. Without thinking, I shoved the door open, my bare feet hitting the gravel as I stepped out.

"Rosalie, no!" Marcus's voice boomed, but I ignored it, adrenaline overtaking reason.

"Sierra! Behind you!" I screamed, pointing toward the advancing figure. My chest heaved with the weight of my fear as the man's attention snapped to me.

He swung his weapon up, the cold metal barrel pointed directly at me. My breath caught, every nerve in my body screaming at me to run, but my legs felt like they were made of lead.

Time seemed to slow.

Sierra twisted around, her sharp blue eyes locking onto the man in an instant. She didn't hesitate. Her weapon fired, the muzzle flash illuminating the night as the man staggered backward, a look of shock etched on his face before he crumpled to the ground.

The relief was short-lived. Sierra staggered, her hand flying to her thigh as blood seeped between her fingers. "Damn it!" she hissed, hobbling toward me with a limp. "Rosalie, get back in the car. Now."

Before I could respond, Marcus was there, his massive frame blocking my view of the chaos beyond. His hands gripped my shoulders firmly but not unkindly as he steered me back toward the SUV. "Inside. Don't argue."

I started to protest, but the look in his eyes—hardened, unyielding—silenced me. He opened the door and practically lifted me into the seat. "Stay down."

Sierra reached the vehicle a moment later, her face pale but her jaw set in determination. She climbed into the front passenger seat, wincing as she moved her injured leg. Blood streaked her pants, the dark stain growing as she adjusted her position.

"Drive!" she barked, her voice sharp despite the pain.

Marcus slammed the door shut, and the SUV roared to life. Gravel crunched under the tires as he reversed sharply, the vehicle jerking as he spun it around to head back toward the main road. My heart pounded as I glanced out the rear window, searching for any sign of Cassian.

"Wait!" I cried, panic surging through me. "What about Cassian? We can't leave him!"

"He can handle himself," Marcus said curtly, his hands steady on the wheel. His eyes flicked to the rearview mirror, scanning for any signs of pursuit. "Our priority is getting you out of here."

"But—"

"Rosalie," Sierra cut in, her voice strained but firm. "Cassian knows what he's doing. He gave us orders to protect you, and that's exactly what we're doing."

Tears stung my eyes as I clenched my fists, helplessness washing over me. The sound of gunfire faded into the distance as the SUV sped away, the night swallowing us whole. All I could do was sit there, my body trembling with adrenaline and fear, as the weight of everything crashed down around me.

CHAPTER TWENTY-ONE

The safe house was nothing like Cassian's penthouse. It was small and sterile, with bare walls and minimal furniture—functional, not luxurious. The faint hum of the overhead lights buzzed in the silence as I paced the narrow living room, my arms crossed tightly over my chest. Every nerve in my body felt frayed, tension coiling in my muscles as I replayed the chaos of the night in my mind.

In the adjoining room, Sierra sat on the edge of a worn leather couch, her leg stretched out as the doctor worked with grim precision. The sight of her bloodied pant leg and the bullet hole he was carefully tending to sent a fresh wave of nausea through me.

"Hold still," Dr. Ellison said, his tone calm but firm as he adjusted his tools. He was a composed man in his fifties, with steel-gray hair and steady hands, but there was a difference to him now—unlike our last encounter. Now, the bedside manner was gone, he was operating in an emotionless world of precision and professionalism. The sharp scent of antiseptic filled the air as he leaned over Sierra's leg.

Sierra barely flinched, her jaw clenched as she endured the procedure with a stoicism I couldn't fathom. The faint clinking of metal instruments made my skin crawl, and I turned away, trying to focus on anything else.

"She should have more pain medication," I muttered, breaking the oppressive silence.

Dr. Ellison didn't look up, his focus unwavering. "Pain slows the reaction time. She'll manage."

Sierra's sharp gaze flicked to me, her lips curving into a faint, almost teasing smirk. "I'll live, Quinn. This isn't my first rodeo."

Her casual tone did little to ease the knot in my chest. I stopped pacing and leaned against the wall, my fingers gripping the edge of a small side table. The sterile room felt stifling, like it was pressing down on me, but I couldn't sit still. Not after what had just happened.

I rubbed my temples, trying to will away the images burned into my mind—the gunfire, the men storming toward the SUV, the sound of Sierra's pained grunt as she was hit. And Cassian—God, Cassian. I'd left him there, in that chaos, without knowing if he was safe.

"This wasn't supposed to happen," I said under my breath, more to myself than anyone else.

Marcus, standing guard by the door, spoke up, his deep voice steady. "It's why we have contingencies. This safe house exists for situations like tonight."

I shot him a glare, but he didn't flinch. "This isn't normal," I snapped. "None of this is normal."

Marcus's calm brown eyes met mine, a faint flicker of understanding in his expression. "It's normal for us; you just never saw this other side of the world behind the counter of your floral shop."

The weight of his words settled over me like a heavy blanket, suffocating and unrelenting. I turned my gaze back to Sierra, who was biting down on a folded piece of cloth as Dr. Ellison worked the forceps deeper into her leg. Her fingers gripped the edge of the couch, white-knuckled, but she didn't make a sound.

I couldn't take it anymore. "Is it almost done?" I asked, my voice sharper than I intended.

Dr. Ellison glanced at me briefly, his expression impassive. "If you'd like to help, you're welcome to hold the light steady."

I stepped back, shaking my head. "I can't... I just can't."

Sierra let out a huff, pulling the cloth from her mouth. "Relax, Quinn. I've had worse. You should've seen what Cassian looked like after a knife fight a few years ago. Now *that* was messy."

Her attempt at levity fell flat, and I turned away, wrapping my arms around myself as I stared out the small, barred window. The night beyond was pitch black, offering no comfort, no reprieve.

Marcus came up from behind me, quickly drawing the curtain shut, a warning glance telling me to stay away from the windows.

I exhaled slowly, trying to ground myself, but the unease gnawed at me, relentless. Cassian had planned for this, yes, but that didn't make it any easier to accept. All I could do now was wait, hope, and pray that he would walk through that door unscathed.

Peering back at them, I watched as Dr. Ellison's hands moved mindlessly, his steady demeanor a stark contrast to the chaos earlier. Sierra had begun to slump down on the leather couch, her pale complexion already improving now that the bleeding had been controlled. The bullet had been removed, cleaned up with surgical efficiency, and a fresh IV dripped into her arm. The saline and transfused blood had given her a touch of color back, but she still winced faintly with each movement. She let out a weak laugh when I asked how she was holding up.

"Like I got shot," she said, her lips curving faintly. "But I'll live, I promise."

Dr. Ellison didn't even glance up from his work as he spoke. "You'll recover fully, but you need rest—and keep it elevated. That leg needs time to heal properly."

Sierra huffed. "Resting's not exactly part of the job, Doc."

Her humor did little to ease the tension clawing at me. I couldn't sit still; every fiber of my being was wound too tight. I paced the length of the small safe house, the floor creaking faintly underfoot. The sparsely furnished space felt more like a holding cell than a refuge. A basic kitchen, a worn couch, and a table littered with Dr. Ellison's medical tools—this wasn't where I wanted to be. It wasn't where I should be.

"How are we not hearing anything?" I asked, stopping mid-stride and turning toward Marcus, who was standing by the door like a statue. "Cassian should've checked in by now."

Marcus shifted slightly, his expression as unreadable as ever. "No word yet," he said evenly.

"No word yet?" My voice rose, edged with frustration and something sharper—fear. "What does that mean? How long are we supposed to sit here and wait?"

Marcus didn't answer right away, his gaze fixed on the door as if the answer to my question might burst through it. Sierra shifted on the couch, wincing slightly but saying nothing. The tension in the room felt suffocating, pressing down on me until I couldn't stand still.

I crossed my arms tightly over my chest. "How long are we staying here?" I demanded, my voice sharper now. "What's the plan?"

Marcus's jaw tightened, and he finally looked at me, his expression calm but unyielding. "As long as it takes to ensure your safety."

"That's not an answer," I snapped. "How long is that? Hours? Days? Weeks? You can't just expect me to sit here, doing nothing, while Cassian is—" My throat closed up, and I swallowed hard, unable to finish the sentence.

"He's fine," Marcus interrupted, his voice steady but with an edge of finality that told me not to push further. "There are protocols for moments like this. Cassian knows what he's doing, and will contact us when he's ready."

But there was something in his tone—something that didn't quite match his words. It wasn't outright fear, but it wasn't certainty either. It was calculated, measured, like he was shielding me from the truth. My stomach twisted painfully at the thought.

"Rosalie," Sierra said, her voice softer than I'd ever heard it. I turned to see her looking at me, her piercing blue eyes dull with fatigue but filled with an unexpected gentleness. "He'll come back. He always does."

I nodded, but the reassurance didn't touch the gnawing worry in my chest. My hands twisted together in my lap as I sank into the chair by the window, my legs shaky and weak beneath me. The silence in the room grew heavier with every second that passed.

I glanced at Marcus again, but he was resolute, his focus locked on the door. Sierra had closed her eyes, her head resting against the back of the couch as Dr. Ellison finished securing the IV. I wanted to believe them, to trust in Cassian's invincibility, but the knot in my chest tightened with every passing moment of silence.

The tense stillness of the room was shattered by the sound of heavy footsteps outside the front door. My heart jumped, a mix of relief and apprehension flooding through me in equal measure. Marcus straightened immediately, his hand going to his holster as he signaled Sierra with a sharp nod. She groaned quietly, pushing herself up despite the obvious pain in her leg, her gun already in hand.

The three of us froze as the doorknob turned. Sierra's breathing was shallow, her weapon trained unerringly on the entryway, while Marcus moved closer to block my view. My heart pounded in my chest, each beat echoing like a drum.

The door swung open, and Cassian stepped into the room, his imposing frame silhouetted against the dim light outside. His shirt was slightly torn, dirt smudging the fabric, and the faint sheen of sweat glistened on his brow. His gray eyes immediately locked onto mine.

Both Sierra and Marcus had their weapons drawn, their stances rigid and ready. "Stand down," Cassian commanded, his voice low and even, though the tension in it was unmistakable.

Marcus lowered his weapon first, stepping aside to allow Cassian to move further into the room. Sierra hesitated for a moment, her sharp gaze scanning him for any signs of threat, before reluctantly dropping her aim.

Cassian's gaze softened as he looked at me, the sharp edge in his eyes replaced by something raw and unguarded.

Relief washed over his features as he crossed the room in long strides, his steps sure and purposeful. Before I could say anything, his hands were on me, pulling me into his arms with an urgency that took my breath away.

"Cassian—" I barely managed his name before his lips found mine.

The kiss was deep and demanding, a clash of raw emotion and desperate need. His hands held me firmly, one at the small of my back, the other tangled in my hair. The world around us seemed to fade as he poured everything—relief, anger, fear—into that one searing kiss.

I melted into him, my fingers clutching his shoulders as if letting go would shatter the fragile moment. His presence, his touch, grounded me in a way nothing else could. All the fear and worry of the night seemed to dissolve under the intensity of his embrace.

When he finally pulled back, his forehead rested against mine, his breathing heavy. "You're safe," he murmured, his voice rough with emotion. "You're safe."

My chest tightened, the weight of the night's events catching up to me all at once. "You're the one who was out there," I whispered, my voice trembling. "I was so scared—"

"I'm here," he interrupted softly, his thumb brushing against my cheek as he cupped my face. "Nothing is going to happen to you. Not while I'm breathing."

Behind us, Sierra slumped back onto the couch, muttering something about Cassian's dramatics, while Marcus resumed his post by the door. But I didn't care about them or the safe house or anything else in that moment. All I cared about was Cassian, here, alive, and holding me like I was the only thing keeping him grounded too.

For the first time that night, I exhaled a breath I hadn't realized I'd been holding.

CHAPTER TWENTY-TWO

Cassian's hand was a steady, immovable weight on the small of my back as he guided me toward the waiting SUV. His grip wasn't harsh, but it left no room for rebellion. Sierra leaned heavily on Marcus as they helped her into the backseat, the tension between them palpable, and I suspected it was because she hated asking for help. The playful smirk on Marcus's face told me he was enjoying every second of their shared vulnerability.

"We're going straight to the penthouse," Cassian said, his voice low but clipped. The words weren't a suggestion—they were an order.

I opened my mouth to protest, to ask what he'd seen in the warehouse, why his jaw was clenched so tight and his gray eyes carried a storm of unspoken thoughts. But the look he shot me silenced any argument. His expression was resolute, brooking no defiance, and I swallowed my words.

The drive back to the city was stiflingly silent. The faint hum of the engine and Sierra's occasional sharp inhale were the only sounds. Cassian sat rigid beside me, his arm stretched protectively across the back of my seat, his knee just brushing mine as though ensuring he could reach me if anything else went wrong. Marcus drove with a sharp focus, his eyes darting to the rearview mirror at regular intervals.

When the elevator doors opened to the familiar, comforting warmth of the penthouse, Cassian ushered us inside with single-minded determination. Marcus and Sierra moved toward the sitting area, and I hesitated near the entrance, my gaze flicking between them and Cassian, who had already made his way to the bar.

Without a word, he poured four heavy glasses of whiskey, the amber liquid catching the light as it sloshed slightly against the crystal. He carried them to the sitting area, handing one to each of us. His hand lingered just a fraction of a second longer when he passed me mine, his gray eyes scanning my face as if assuring himself I was still whole.

"We'll talk after this," he said simply, taking a long, measured sip of his drink. His tone was flat, but the undercurrent of something deeper—anger, worry, maybe both—was unmistakable.

Sierra was the first to break the tense silence. She shifted on the couch, her injured leg stretched out awkwardly, the bloodied bandage visible beneath her ripped pants. She winced slightly as she adjusted, then raised her glass in a half-hearted toast. "To surviving the night."

The attempt at levity fell flat. Marcus's lips twitched, but his eyes stayed sharp and watchful as he drained his whiskey in one long gulp. Cassian didn't respond, his attention fixed on the liquid in his glass as though it held the answers to everything.

I took a tentative sip, the whiskey burning as it slid down my throat. My mind raced with questions, each one louder than the last, but I kept quiet, knowing Cassian's mood was volatile. His silence felt heavier than his words ever could.

Finally, I couldn't stand it anymore. "Cassian," I said softly, setting my glass on the table. "What happened out there?"

He looked up, his gaze sharp and guarded. For a moment, I thought he wouldn't answer, but then he leaned forward, his elbows resting on his knees as he rubbed a hand over his face. The movement was uncharacteristically weary, a crack in the armor he so carefully maintained.

"You want to know what happened?" he asked, his voice low, almost dangerous. "We walked into a trap."

Cassian's words hung in the air, heavy and suffocating. The crackling fire in the hearth seemed to grow louder as the silence stretched between us.

"A trap?" I asked, my voice trembling slightly despite my efforts to keep it steady.

Cassian's gray eyes locked onto mine, the intensity in them almost unbearable. He leaned back in his chair, the muscles in his jaw tightening as he clenched his fists on his thighs. "They were waiting for us," he said, his tone clipped, as if each word cost him. "The intel about the shipment—it was bait."

Marcus shifted uncomfortably in his seat, his fingers curling around his empty glass. Sierra's hand rested lightly on her bandaged leg, but her expression was unreadable, her lips pressed into a thin line.

"The Reapers knew we'd come for it," Cassian continued, his voice hard and cold. "The warehouse wasn't just a distribution hub; it was a staging ground. They had more men than we expected—heavily armed, positioned strategically. The moment we breached the perimeter, they moved in."

My stomach twisted as I imagined the chaos, the danger. I had seen the flashes of gunfire from the safety of the SUV, but hearing Cassian recount it was something else entirely. His words painted a grim picture, every detail like a stone sinking into my chest.

"They had a secondary force waiting outside," Marcus added, his deep voice quiet but steady. "That's what hit us near the SUV."

Cassian nodded, his expression darkening. "They split our team, forced us to engage on two fronts. It was calculated, brilliant even—no one expected a two-front battle..." He paused, his hands curling into tight fists. "...but we lost Dominic."

My breath caught, my heart lurching painfully at the name. Dominic. One of Cassian's most trusted men—the one with the easy smile and the quiet confidence. The one who had always seemed invincible, and invisible. I rarely ever saw or heard him, he preferred to operate in the shadows, and Cassian had always admired that.

Cassian's voice dropped lower, a dangerous edge creeping in. "Three others didn't make it either. They didn't stand a chance against the firepower the Reapers brought."

Sierra exhaled sharply, her face paling as she stared at the floor. "They were good men," she said quietly, her voice laced with a mix of sadness and anger. "And they died fighting."

Cassian's gaze flicked to her, and for a moment, the mask of control slipped, revealing the raw grief beneath. "They knew the risks," he said, his tone softer now but no less weighted. "But that doesn't make it easier."

A lump formed in my throat, and I swallowed hard, struggling to find the right words. "And the Reapers?" I asked, barely above a whisper.

Cassian's lips pressed into a thin line, his expression hardening again. "We took out far more of them than they did of us," he said, his voice like steel. "But it doesn't change the fact that they drew first blood. They wanted us to know they're not afraid to engage directly. That they're willing to lose men if it means sending a message."

"And what message is that?" I asked, my chest tightening with dread.

"That they're escalating," Cassian said grimly. "And they're not backing down."

The tension in the room was palpable, the weight of Cassian's words pressing down on all of us. Sierra stared at the fire, her fingers brushing absently over the edge of the bandage on her leg. Marcus leaned forward, his elbows resting on his knees as he studied Cassian with a mixture of concern and respect.

"And Dominic's family?" I asked hesitantly, my voice trembling as I thought of the loss they would be facing.

Cassian's expression softened, just for a moment.

"They'll be taken care of," he said firmly. "They always are."

I nodded, biting my lip to keep the tears at bay. The loss of life, the danger, the weight of it all—it was too much. But Cassian's unwavering resolve, his ability to shoulder it all, was both awe-inspiring and terrifying.

"Rosalie," Cassian said, drawing my gaze back to him. His eyes softened as he looked at me, the sharp edges of his anger and grief dulling slightly. "This is why I didn't want you involved. Why I didn't want you anywhere near this."

"I know," I said quietly, my voice cracking. "But I'm here now. And I'm not going anywhere."

For a moment, the room was silent except for the crackling fire. Then Cassian nodded, his lips pressing into a thin line as he raised his glass. "To the ones we lost," he said solemnly. "And to the ones still standing."

Marcus and Sierra echoed the toast, their voices low but resolute. I raised my glass as well, the weight of the moment settling deep into my chest. As I sipped the whiskey, the burn in my throat was nothing compared to the ache in my heart.

Cassian set his empty glass down with a deliberate motion, his fingers lingering on the rim for a moment as though collecting his thoughts. His gray eyes burned with intensity as he leaned forward, resting his forearms on his knees. The flickering firelight cast sharp shadows over his face, making him look even more resolute.

"We secured the warehouse," he began, his voice steady but laced with a grim edge. "It wasn't clean, and it wasn't easy, but we sent the Reapers running. Temporarily, at least."

Marcus gave a small nod, his expression approving.

Cassian continued, "Once we broke their formation, it was only a matter of time before they scattered." His gaze locked onto mine. "We had to think fast after the ambush. Their numbers were greater than we anticipated, and they had reinforcements waiting just outside the perimeter. If we'd stayed locked in a straight firefight, it could've ended a hell of a lot worse."

He exhaled sharply, rubbing a hand over his jaw before

leaning back. "Dominic and his team managed to secure a few drums of diesel stored near the loading dock. We used it to rig a controlled explosion, cut off the majority of their forces, and create enough chaos to drive the Reapers out."

I felt my breath hitch at the thought of the danger Cassian had faced, but he pressed on, his voice steady as a rock. "The explosion gave us the leverage we needed. Once their reinforcements were scattered, we pushed through and claimed the warehouse. And... they left behind intel we didn't expect."

The calmness in his tone was unsettling, a sharp contrast to the violent reality he was describing. My chest tightened, imagining the chaos and danger he had walked into. Cassian didn't look at me as he continued, his focus somewhere distant, as if replaying every step of the operation.

"The explosion gave us the leverage we needed," he said. "Once their reinforcements were scattered, we pushed through and claimed the warehouse."

I waited, sensing there was more. He hesitated for a fraction of a second, then leaned forward, bracing his elbows on his knees.

"And..." His voice dropped slightly, the weight of his next words hanging heavy in the air. "They left behind intel we didn't expect."

Marcus and Sierra both leaned forward, their attention laser-focused on Cassian. I held my breath, caught between dread and anticipation.

"What kind of intel?" Marcus asked, his voice steady but tinged with urgency.

Cassian's gray eyes met mine briefly, a flicker of something unreadable passing through them before he reached into his jacket pocket. He pulled out a small, bloodstained leather-bound notebook and placed it carefully on the coffee table between us.

"This," he said, his voice tight. "We pulled it off Anton Ryker."

The name sent a chill down my spine. I'd never heard it before and I never cared to again.

"Ryker was there?" Sierra's tone was sharp, her blue eyes narrowing as she glanced at the notebook.

Cassian nodded, his expression hardening. "He was leading the ambush. It cost us dearly to take him down, but we did."

Marcus reached for the notebook, flipping it open carefully. The pages were covered in cramped, precise handwriting, with numbers, names, and symbols that looked like shorthand for something far more sinister. His brows furrowed as he scanned the contents.

"What's in it?" I asked softly, unable to tear my eyes away from the bloodstained pages.

"Names," Cassian replied, his tone clipped. "Contacts. Shipping schedules. Locations. It's their bloody playbook, the damned fools. Every major player in the Reapers' operation is listed here, along with their roles and connections. Ties to logistical hubs. This notebook would cost a pretty penny on the black market, even the authorities would pay to get their hands on it."

"And this?" Marcus asked, pointing to a set of coordinates scribbled in the margins.

Cassian leaned forward, his expression grave. "That's Apex Delta. It's not just a logistics hub—it's their nerve center. If this notebook is accurate, it's where they're storing the bulk of their assets. Weapons, cash, drugs—it's all there. Apex Logistics is only the name of the organization, but Apex Alpha, Bravo, Charlie, and Delta are the hubs. The network is impressive, massive—far greater than anything I've ever seen. It would have taken years to build an empire like this…"

Sierra let out a low whistle, her injured leg shifting slightly as she adjusted on the couch. "That's the smoking gun."

"It's more than that," Cassian said, his voice hardening. "This ties them directly to Damon Cross. His name is all over these entries—payments, orders, supply chains. If we take out Apex Delta and expose Cross, we can gut the Reapers' operation from the inside out."

The room fell into a heavy silence as the weight of his

words settled. It wasn't just about taking out a warehouse or intercepting shipments anymore. This was a chance to dismantle the entire network, to cripple the Reapers in a way they couldn't recover from.

But it came at a cost.

"What else?" I asked, my voice barely above a whisper.

Cassian's gaze shifted to me, his expression unreadable. "We're not the only ones after this. The notebook makes it clear—they've got rival factions, people who won't hesitate to swoop in and take over the moment we leave an opening."

My stomach twisted at the implication. This wasn't just a fight against the Reapers; it was a battle on all sides.

"And Ryker?" I pressed, unable to stop myself. "What happened to him?"

Cassian's jaw tightened, his gray eyes darkening as he glanced to the blood on the notebook's cover. "He's where he deserves to be, rotting at the bottom of the river."

The room fell silent again, the weight of the night's events pressing down on all of us. I couldn't bring myself to look at the notebook anymore, the blood on its cover a stark reminder of the lives lost to bring it here.

"This changes everything," Marcus said finally, his voice low but resolute.

Cassian nodded, his gaze flicking to each of us in turn. "We hit Apex Delta next. And this time, we finish it."

CHAPTER TWENTY-THREE

The penthouse was cloaked in an almost unnatural stillness, the kind that only existed in the small hours before dawn. The soft buzz of the dishwasher in the kitchen and the distant whisper of the city below were the only sounds breaking the silence. The glow from the overhead lights illuminated the glassy surfaces of the living room, casting faint reflections that seemed to flicker with the movement of shadows.

Cassian's office was the only hub of activity, the door slightly ajar, allowing muted voices to filter into the otherwise quiet space. The low murmur of strategy and precision planning was accompanied by the occasional rustle of paper and the tap of a pen against the desk.

The rest of the penthouse had the air of a space waiting to exhale, a tension that settled into the corners and refused to dissipate. Sierra and Marcus stood near the windows, their postures relaxed but their eyes sharp, scanning the streets below as if danger might rise from the concrete itself.

I sat on one of the sleek leather chairs, my mind only half on the conversation. My fingers drummed against my thigh, restless. No matter how hard I tried to focus on the mission unfolding in front of me, my thoughts kept slipping back to the photo of the man at the coffee shop. His face, blurred at the edges from the grainy image, wouldn't leave my mind. Who was he? And why had he been important enough to slip into my bag during the chaos?

Cassian stood at the head of the table, his presence commanding as he spread out Ryker's notebook and a series of maps. His gray eyes scanned the group with that sharp, calculating edge that made it clear every detail had already been scrutinized in his mind. "We'll focus on this sector first," he said, pointing to an industrial zone on the map. "Apex Delta. It's a secondary hub—one Ryker confirmed in his notes. If they're moving anything significant, it'll funnel through there."

His words barely registered. My attention drifted to Sierra, who leaned against the far wall, her leg bandaged from the gunshot wound she'd suffered just hours ago. She looked pale, but her sharp gaze hadn't lost its edge. Marcus stood beside her, arms crossed and expression unreadable. Both of them had thrown themselves into this fight without hesitation, yet I couldn't help but wonder if any of us fully understood what we were up against.

"Rosalie?" Cassian's voice cut through my haze, snapping me back to the moment. His gaze pinned me, questioning but not unkind.

I straightened in my seat, masking the nerves swirling in my chest. "I'm listening."

He studied me for a beat longer, his expression unreadable, before turning back to the group. "Apex Delta isn't just a shipping hub; it's a stronghold. Ryker's notes indicated a highly secured facility. If we're going in, we need a well-defined plan, and then a backup for when shit hits the fan. We'll be trying to penetrate and impenetrable facility. It's a complex infiltration mission."

"Infiltration?" Sierra's voice was calm but pointed. "With all due respect, Cassian, what makes you think they won't see us coming?"

Cassian's lips twitched in what could've been a smile, though there was no humor in it. "They won't expect us to act this quickly. Ryker's death has them on edge, scrambling to cover their tracks. That gives us a window, but it's narrow."

I opened my mouth to argue, but the weight of his words—and the unspoken plea in his eyes—stopped me. This wasn't the time for rebellion. Not yet.

Marcus stepped forward, his deep voice grounding the tension in the room. "What's the objective once we're in?"

Cassian tapped the notebook, flipping to a series of cryptic symbols and annotations Ryker had scrawled in the margins. "There's a vault," he said. "Apex Delta uses it to store sensitive shipments before they're transported. If we can access it, we'll know exactly what the Reapers are moving—and where it's going."

The room fell into a heavy silence, each of us absorbing the enormity of the task ahead. My gaze drifted back to the notebook, the jagged handwriting sparking an unsettling curiosity. Cassian's confidence was palpable, but even he couldn't predict what we'd find behind those walls.

As the group dispersed to prepare, I lingered, my thoughts tugging me in two directions. The mission loomed large, but the mystery of the coffee shop photo refused to be silenced. I had a sinking feeling that the two were connected, though how, I couldn't yet say.

Cassian approached me, his steps quiet but purposeful. "You've been quiet," he said softly, his gray eyes searching mine.

"I'm just... thinking," I replied, avoiding his gaze.

He tilted his head, the corner of his mouth lifting in a faint, knowing smile. "Don't overthink it, Rosalie. Stay focused on what's in front of you."

His words were meant to reassure, but they only deepened my unease. Something about the photo felt like a loose thread in the fabric of everything we were fighting for. And if there was one thing I knew about threads, it was that they always led somewhere.

The tension of Cassian's words hung in the air as he turned and moved toward the planning table, his focus already shifting to the maps and intel spread before him. I watched him for a moment, his broad shoulders tense as he bent over the desk, issuing commands to Marcus and Sierra. He was calm, controlled, but there was an edge beneath his words—a sharpness that spoke of the stakes we faced.

I exhaled slowly and turned away, slipping out of the room while the others were distracted by the details of the operation. The sound of their voices faded as I moved down the hall, the click of my boots muted against the carpeted floor. The weight of the photograph in my purse felt heavier with each step.

By the time I reached the elevator, Marcus and Sierra had caught up to me, their presence a ever-present, looming shadow. I didn't bother explaining my destination. They wouldn't ask, not directly, but I knew the suspicion lingered in their sharp gazes.

The ride down was quiet, the hum of the elevator filling the space between us. When the doors slid open, I stepped out into the pre-dawn city, the chill of the air biting at my cheeks. The streets were still half-asleep, the occasional headlights cutting through the faint glow of streetlights. The coffee shop wasn't far, but it wasn't close either, and the route I took was deliberate.

"You're taking the scenic route," Marcus said, his voice a low rumble as he matched my pace.

"The air clears my head," I replied without looking at him.

Sierra didn't comment, but her sharp eyes swept the streets around us, ever-watchful. We walked in silence until the familiar sign of the coffee shop came into view, its flickering light casting a faint glow onto the sidewalk.

I pushed the door open, the chime overhead soft but distinct. The warmth of the shop enveloped me instantly, the scent of freshly brewed coffee and baked goods wrapping around me like a comfort I hadn't realized I needed. The barista glanced up briefly, offering a polite smile before returning to her work.

I scanned the room, my eyes moving from table to table, my pulse quickening. It was instinctual now, the need to compare each face to the one in the photograph. My gaze lingered on a man sitting by the window, his back to me. For a fleeting second, I thought it could be him, but as he turned slightly, my heart sank. It wasn't him. None of them were.

"What's the hold-up?" Sierra asked from her position near the door, her tone casual but her posture anything but.

"Nothing," I said quickly, stepping toward the counter. "Just deciding what to get."

The barista greeted me warmly, and I rattled off a list of orders for the group, my voice steady despite the slight tremor in my hands. As I waited for the drinks to be prepared, I glanced around the shop again, my stomach knotting with a mixture of disappointment and relief. The photograph remained a mystery, and for now, that was both a blessing and a curse.

When the order was ready, Marcus helped me carry the trays while Sierra held the door open, her sharp gaze sweeping the street before we stepped outside. The air was colder now, the sun still hiding beneath the horizon.

"You're awfully quiet," Sierra remarked as we walked back toward the penthouse.

"Just tired," I replied, keeping my voice light. "Long day ahead."

Neither of them pushed further, but I felt their suspicion like a weight on my shoulders. They weren't blind to my detour, even if they didn't say anything. As we approached the building, I glanced back at the coffee shop one last time, the flickering sign growing smaller with each step. The mystery of the photograph lingered in my mind, a shadow I couldn't shake.

By the time we reached the elevator, the trays of coffee and pastries felt heavier than they should have, but I forced a smile as we stepped inside. The hum of the elevator filled the silence, but my thoughts were anything but quiet. The photograph had to mean something—it was a thread leading somewhere. And sooner or later, I was going to find out where.

Back at the penthouse, the atmosphere was a swirl of activity. Cassian's sharp commands and the constant bustle of his team's chatter echoed through the halls. Maps were spread across the dining table, documents pinned to walls, and screens flickered with security footage and data analysis. Everyone was focused, their energy feeding into the tension that seemed to pulse through the very air.

I set the trays of coffee and pastries on the kitchen counter, silently grateful to step out of the chaos for a moment. My body still buzzed with lingering unease from the coffee shop trip, but I pushed it aside, knowing now wasn't the time to dwell on it. Marcus and Sierra disappeared into the fray, their roles demanding their immediate attention, while I leaned against the counter, taking in the scene around me.

Cassian was at the center of it all, of course, his presence commanding even when he wasn't speaking. He stood by the dining table, a tablet in hand, his gray eyes scanning the data with a precision that made it clear he missed nothing. His shirt sleeves were rolled up, revealing the strength in his forearms as he gestured to one of his lieutenants.

I wanted to approach him, to tell him about the strange weight of the photograph in my purse, but the words felt lodged in my throat. Instead, I stayed where I was, watching him work. He hadn't glanced my way since I'd come back, his focus entirely consumed by whatever intel they were dissecting.

The buzz of the intercom interrupted the moment, cutting through the noise like a sharp blade. One of the security guards answered it, and a brief exchange followed before he approached Cassian.

"Delivery for you, sir," the guard said, holding out a small envelope, its edges embossed with gold filigree.

Cassian waved a hand dismissively, his attention fixed on the screen in front of him. "Give it to Rosalie."

I blinked, surprised, but I stepped forward and took the envelope from the guard. The material was heavy, the kind of stationery that reeked of expensive perfume and elegance. My fingers traced the gilded edges as I flipped it over, breaking the elegant wax seal with a touch of hesitation.

Inside was an invitation, the calligraphy bold and regal:

You are cordially invited to the
New Dawn Foundation Charity Masquerade Gala
Hosted by Julian Lancaster
Date: Saturday
Time: 8:00 PM
Location: Disclosed the evening of the event
Dress Code: Formal Attire & Mask Required

At first glance, it seemed like any other high-society event. But then my gaze dropped to the names at the bottom, and my breath hitched.

Addressed to: Mr. Cassian Moreau & Miss Rosalie Quinn

My name wasn't just tacked on as an afterthought—it was deliberate, equal. A clear acknowledgment of my association not just with Cassian but with his world. The underworld. The kind of distinction that couldn't be ignored, especially considering who Julian Lancaster was.

The weight of it settled over me, a mixture of dread and something I couldn't quite name. It wasn't just an invitation to a gala; it was an invitation into their circle, their rules, their expectations. And there was no escaping what that meant.

Cassian's voice broke through my thoughts, low and commanding as always. "What is it?"

I looked up to find his gray eyes fixed on me, his attention finally pulled from his work. Holding up the invitation, I crossed the room and handed it to him. His expression darkened as he read it, his jaw tightening ever so slightly.

"It's addressed to both of us," I said softly, though the words felt heavy in my mouth.

Cassian folded the invitation slowly, his gaze unreadable as he set it on the table. "Julian's games," he murmured, almost to himself. Then his eyes locked onto mine, sharp and unrelenting. "We'll go, despite everything else right now."

It wasn't a question, and I didn't argue. Because as much as I wanted to resist, I knew there was no point. This was the world I'd stepped into, and there was no turning back now.

CHAPTER TWENTY-FOUR

The shop smelled of eucalyptus and lilies, the sharp yet soothing scent mingling with the earthy aroma of freshly cut stems. Sunlight streamed through the large front windows, glinting off the vases and jars that lined the shelves. The faint sounds of activity outside filtered through the glass, a stark contrast to the quiet, almost meditative atmosphere inside Ivy & Bloom.

I wiped my hands on my apron, stepping back to examine the arrangement I'd just finished. Vibrant tulips, soft pink ranunculus, and cascading ivy spiraled together in a glass vase, a splash of spring come to life. It was beautiful, but I didn't feel it. The act of creating— something that used to center me—was now just another way to keep my mind occupied.

Behind me, Sierra leaned casually against the counter, her sharp gaze flicking between the door and the street outside. Marcus sat at one of the small café tables near the front window, pretending to read a newspaper but clearly scanning the surroundings like a hawk. Neither of them said anything, though I could feel their judgment weighing heavy on the air.

"Don't start," I muttered, turning to grab another bundle of greenery from the workstation.

"Who's starting?" Sierra asked innocently, though the corner of her mouth twitched. "I didn't say a word."

I shot her a look. "You don't have to."

"You know he's going to lose it, right?" she said, tilting her head toward the window. "When he finds out you're here."

"Cassian doesn't get to dictate my entire life," I snapped, a little sharper than I intended, my unresolved frustrations making their way to the surface. "This is my shop. My responsibility. I can't just sit around doing nothing."

"You're not doing nothing," Marcus interjected, his deep voice calm but firm. "You had an entire work station set up exclusively for you at the penthouse. You're choosing to be here rather than in the safety of the penthouse."

I clenched my teeth, my hands tightening around the bundle of greenery. "You enjoy siding with him, don't you." I huffed, "Ivy & Bloom is my family's legacy, but I don't expect you to understand. Nonetheless, I won't let it fall apart because he's wants to keep me locked up."

Marcus folded the newspaper neatly, setting it on the table. "As long as you recognize that, I won't stop you."

I turned away from them, focusing on the delicate task of trimming the stems. The rhythmic snip of the shears was a small comfort, a grounding force in the middle of the storm my life had become.

Not settled with the conversation, I turned back around. "If the Reapers are going to come for me, they'll find me whether I'm here or locked away in his penthouse," I said quietly. "At least here, I'm doing something that matters."

The rhythmic snip of the shears filled the silence that followed, but the weight of Marcus's calm gaze lingered in the back of my mind. I knew he didn't approve, but he wouldn't challenge me outright. Not when I'd made my stance so clear. Still, his presence was a constant reminder of the invisible leash Cassian had placed on me, one I was determined to gnaw through.

Across the shop, Lena hovered near the cash register, flipping through the ledger with a meticulousness that seemed unnecessary. Her lips pressed into a thin line when

I glanced her way, her body angled as if shielding the contents from view.

"I can finish out the month's accounting if you'd like," I offered casually, hoping to bridge the growing distance I felt between us.

She looked up sharply, her eyes narrowing slightly before her expression smoothed over. "That's alright. I've got it covered."

The response was clipped, her tone guarded. I didn't push the issue, though unease prickled at the back of my mind. Lena had always been diligent, but this level of secrecy felt... off. Making a mental note to revisit the ledger later, I turned my attention back to the bouquet in front of me, forcing myself to focus on the vibrant spray of roses and tulips.

The day wore on, customers coming and going in a steady rhythm. The shop emptied as evening approached, and eventually, even Marcus and Sierra gave up their silent watchfulness and stationed themselves outside. It was a small victory, but one I savored.

By the time Lena packed up for the night, the shop was bathed in the warm, golden glow of the overhead lights. She lingered by the door, her hand on the lock as she hesitated. "You sure you don't want me to stay?"

I waved her off, forcing a smile. "I'm fine. Just a few more arrangements to finish before tomorrow."

She nodded, her movements stiff as she locked up and slipped into the night.. The moment the door clicked shut, the shop felt emptier, quieter. I slipped my headphones in, letting the pulsing bass of my playlist drown out the silence as I worked through the leftover stems and greenery.

Sierra and Marcus had opted for the warmth of the vehicle parked on the curb, and I didn't mind, the place was secured already

Time slipped away as I lost myself in the repetitive motions of cutting, arranging, and binding. The music thudded in my ears, a comfort against the growing unease that always seemed to creep in when I was alone.

I didn't hear the front door open, the subtle creak of the

hinges muffled by the pounding beat. It wasn't until a shadow fell across the counter that I looked up—and screamed, nearly dropping the shears in my hand.

Cassian stood there, his tall frame silhouetted by the dim light spilling in from the street outside. His expression was carved from stone, his gray eyes piercing as they bore into mine.

"Enjoying your rebellion?" he asked, his voice low and laced with a dangerous calm.

I yanked the headphones out, my heart hammering in my chest. "Jesus, Cassian! You scared the hell out of me."

He didn't move, his gaze flicking to the shears in my hand before settling back on my face. "You've got a habit of ignoring my orders."

I straightened, bracing myself for the storm I knew was coming. "Sometime I like to think that the Reapers are allergic to roses, or peonies—that usually helps." When my playful jab fell short, I added, "I'm not about to let a little danger uproot everything my family built. And I'm not a soldier—I don't follow your orders."

Cassian's lips twitched, the barest hint of a smirk breaking through his stony expression. "Not a soldier, huh? Because you're certainly on a battlefield."

I sighed, setting the shears down on the counter with deliberate care. "The only battlefield here is between me and this shipment of cherry blossoms. And frankly, I'm winning."

He stepped closer, the low thud of his shoes against the hardwood floor reverberating through the quiet shop. The tension in the air shifted as his gaze swept over the arrangements I'd been working on, lingering on the delicate blooms before returning to me.

"This place," he said, his voice softer now, "it's a part of you. I see that. But if the Reapers catch even a whisper that you're here alone—"

"I'm not alone," I interrupted, gesturing toward the street where Marcus and Sierra were undoubtedly keeping watch. "And I'm not reckless. I know what's at stake, Cassian. But you can't ask me to abandon the one piece of normalcy I have left."

His jaw tightened, the conflict in his gray eyes unmistakable. "Normalcy doesn't matter if you're not alive to enjoy it."

"Neither does hiding," I countered, my voice steady but firm. "I need this, Cassian. You might not understand it, but I do."

For a moment, he didn't reply, his expression unreadable as he studied me. The shop was silent except for the faint rustle of leaves as a draft moved through the room. Finally, he exhaled, running a hand through his hair in frustration.

"You're so goddamn stubborn, you know that?" he said, a hint of exasperation coloring his tone.

I allowed myself a small smile. "So I've been told."

Cassian shook his head, but there was no mistaking the flicker of amusement in his eyes. "Fine. If this is where you insist on being, I'll make it work. But," he added, stepping even closer, "there will be rules."

I raised an eyebrow, crossing my arms. "Rules?"

"Non-negotiable ones," he said, his tone brooking no argument. "Marcus and Sierra stay glued to you at all times. You don't close up alone. And if anything, anything feels off, you leave immediately."

I considered him for a moment, the intensity of his gaze making it clear there was no room for debate. "Deal," I said finally.

Cassian leaned in, his voice dropping to a low murmur. "You think the Reapers are allergic to roses, huh?"

The warmth of his breath brushed against my ear, and I couldn't suppress the slight shiver it sent down my spine. "I like to think they'd rather avoid the thorns," I said, trying to keep my voice steady.

He straightened, a smirk tugging at the corner of his mouth. "You keep surprising me, Rosalie."

"And you keep underestimating me," I shot back.

Cassian gave a short laugh, shaking his head as he turned to survey the shop and its new changes. "Try not to give me a reason to regret this, but let me ask you this," he paused, his eyes finding mine once more. "What if I wasn't me, Rosalie? What if I'd been someone with less... agreeable intentions who?"

I rolled my eyes, setting down the bouquet I'd been arranging. "The doors were locked, Marcus and Sierra were just outside, and I had my shears." I held them up like a trophy. "What more could I possibly need?"

"Your head on a swivel, for one," he replied, leaning casually across the counter. His gray eyes sparkled with amusement, but there was something deeper beneath his playful tone—a note of protectiveness that made my stomach twist. "And maybe a little less faith in the locked doors."

"I'm not completely helpless, you know," I retorted, placing my hands on my hips. "Besides, you're here now, so I think I'm covered."

His smirk grew as his gaze flicked to the shears still within my reach. With a quick motion, he reached out, his hand brushing mine as he gently plucked them away. "Covered? Sure," he said, holding up the shears and twirling them lazily between his fingers. "But maybe let's keep the sharp objects out of this, hmm?"

"Hey!" I protested, making a grab for them, but he was faster, holding them just out of my reach.

He leaned closer across the table, his voice dropping to a soft murmur that sent a shiver down my spine. "Tisk, tisk. You're adorable."

"I prefer 'resourceful,'" I countered, though my breath hitched as his eyes locked onto mine. The space between us felt suddenly charged, the banter melting into something heavier, weightier. His smirk softened into something more genuine, his thumb brushing over the handle of the shears before he set them down out of reach.

"There," he said, his tone still teasing but with a gentleness that disarmed me completely. "Now you can focus on what you're supposed to be doing instead of pretending to be some floral ninja."

I opened my mouth to argue but stopped myself. He was still leaning close, his proximity sending my heart into overdrive.

"My sweet little petal, what will I ever do with you?" he muttered instead, his gaze lingered, with a hot fever—a look I was all too familiar with.

It was the look he gave me when he was about to unravel ever sin, every desire, every lustful thought I ever had...

CHAPTER TWENTY-FIVE

Cassian leaned against the counter across from me, his jacket discarded and his sleeves rolled up to his elbows. His watch glinted under the dim light, the leather band taut against his strong wrist. He was watching me, his gaze steady and deliberate, but I didn't dare look up. I knew that look—it was one part amusement and two parts predatory.

"Rosalie," he said, his voice low, pulling my name out like a slow drawl.

"Mm-hmm?" I responded, not sparing him a glance as I adjusted the placement of a daisy.

"Put the flowers down."

"I'm almost done," I replied absently, already reaching for the sprigs of lavender waiting to be arranged.

Cassian's footsteps were soft but deliberate as he crossed the shop floor. I barely registered him behind me until his hands moved to my waist, his fingers deftly untying the knot of my apron. He slipped it off me and tossed it carelessly onto the nearest table.

"Hey!" I turned, half-laughing, half-indignant. "I need that."

"No, you don't." His gray eyes locked onto mine, darkened with mischief. "You've done enough for tonight."

"Cassian, there's so much still to—"

His finger pressed to my lips, silencing me instantly. The simple gesture was commanding, but the softness in his touch stole the heat from my protests.

"Shh," he murmured, his tone low and velvety. "No lists. No excuses. You're mine tonight, Rosalie."

Before I could protest—or agree—his mouth claimed mine in a kiss that erased any argument I might have had. His lips were firm, insistent, and my breath hitched as his hands slid to my hips, pulling me against him. The edge of the table pressed into the small of my back, anchoring me as the kiss deepened.

His fingers brushed the folds of my skirt aside, the movement slow and deliberate as though daring me to stop him. He broke the kiss just long enough to lean down, his lips grazing my ear as he whispered, "You work too hard, little petal. Let me help take the edge off."

A shiver raced down my spine at his words, his breath warm against my skin. My hands found their way to his shoulders, gripping him for balance as his lips trailed down my neck, leaving a path of heat in their wake.

"I can't—" I started, my voice barely a whisper.

"You can," he interrupted, his voice rough but tender. His hands gripped my thighs, lifting me effortlessly onto the edge of the counter. "And you will."

He stepped closer, his body pressed against mine as his lips returned to mine with a renewed intensity. Whatever reservations I'd had melted away under his touch, leaving nothing but the pulse of desire coursing through me.

All thoughts of unfinished work and long to-do lists vanished, replaced by the singular focus of him—Cassian, relentless and consuming, pulling me into his desire-filled moment with every touch.

"Cassian," I gasped as his lips moved to my neck, nipping and sucking at the sensitive skin. "The windows—someone might see."

He chuckled against my throat, the vibration sending shivers down my spine. "Let them look," he murmured, his voice husky with desire. "I want the whole world to know you're mine."

His fingers deftly unbuttoned my blouse, pushing it off my shoulders. The cool air of the shop raised goosebumps on my skin, quickly chased away by the heat of Cassian's touch. He cupped my breasts through the thin lace of my bra, his thumbs brushing over my hardened nipples.

I arched into his touch, a soft moan escaping my lips. My hands fumbled with the buttons of his shirt, desperate to feel his skin against mine. Cassian helped me, shrugging out of the garment and tossing it aside.

His sculpted chest pressed against me as he claimed my lips once more, his kiss fierce and possessive. I wrapped my legs around his waist, pulling him closer, feeling the hard length of him through his trousers.

"Mmm, it's hungry" I whispered, my hips rocking against him instinctively.

Cassian's eyes, dark with lust, met mine. "Tell me what you want, little petal," he growled, his fingers teasing along the hem of my skirt.

"You," I breathed. "I want you. Now."

A wicked grin spread across his face. "Your wish is my command."

With a swift motion, Cassian hiked up my skirt, bunching it around my waist. His fingers hooked into the waistband of my panties, sliding them down my legs with agonizing slowness. I shivered as the cool air hit my exposed skin, but it was nothing compared to the heat of Cassian's gaze as he drank in the sight of me.

"I've wanted to take you on this counter since the first day I saw you," he murmured, his hands caressing my thighs. "And now, you're mine."

I reached for him, fumbling with his belt buckle. Cassian chuckled, gently batting my hands away. "Allow me, little petal."

He made quick work of his trousers, pushing them down along with his briefs. My breath caught in my throat at the sight of him, hard and ready. Cassian stepped between my legs, positioning himself at my sex.

With a groan, he thrust forward, filling me completely. I gasped at the sensation, my palms gripping the counter firmly, holding me in place. Cassian stilled for a moment, allowing me to adjust to his size, but the moment was brief.

"God, Rosalie," he breathed, his forehead resting against mine. "You feel incredible."

He began to move, slowly at first, then building to a steady rhythm. The counter creaked beneath us, petals from nearby arrangements fluttering to the floor with each thrust. I clung to him, lost in the sensation of our bodies moving together.

Cassian's lips found mine once more, swallowing my moans as he picked up the pace. One of his hands snaked between us, his thumb finding my sensitive bundle of nerves. I broke the kiss with a gasp, throwing my head back in pleasure.

"That's it, little petal," Cassian growled, his voice rough with desire. "But don't you dare come—not yet."

His words sent a thrill through me, heightening my arousal even as I struggled to obey. Cassian's thrusts grew more forceful, each one driving me closer to the edge. I clung to him desperately, my fingertips curling around his hair, as I fought against the building pressure.

"I can't hold it back much longer, please," I whimpered, my body trembling with the effort of suppressing the orgasm that threatened to break through the surface of my desire-ridden body.

He chuckled darkly, his breath hot against my ear. "Not yet, little petal. I'm not done with you."

Suddenly, he pulled out, leaving me feeling achingly empty. Before I could protest, he spun me around, bending me over the counter. The cool surface pressed against my flushed skin as Cassian's hand tangled in my hair, pulling my head back gently.

"Is this what you want?" he murmured, his lips brushing the nape of my neck.

"Yes," I gasped, pushing back against him. "Please, Cassian."

With a growl, he thrust into me once more, setting a punishing pace. The new angle sent shockwaves of pleasure through my body, and I bit my lip to stifle my cries.

Cassian's free hand snaked around to my front, his fingers finding my clit and circling it mercilessly.

"Come for me, Rosalie," he commanded, his voice rough with desire. "Now."

His words were all it took to send me over the edge. I came with a cry, my body clenching around him as waves of pleasure washed over me. Cassian followed soon after, his hips stuttering against mine as he found his release.

We stayed like that for a moment, both of us panting and trembling with the aftershocks. Slowly, Cassian released his grip on my hair, his hand moving to stroke my back soothingly. He placed a gentle kiss on my shoulder before pulling out, helping me stand on shaky legs.

As I turned to face him, a small smile played on his lips. "I think," he said, tucking a stray strand of hair behind my ear, "that we've found a much better use for this counter than arranging flowers."

I couldn't help but laugh, leaning into his touch. "I suppose you're right," I admitted. "Though I'm not sure how I'll ever get any work done now."

Cassian's eyes sparkled with mischief. "Who says we're done, little petal? The night is still young, and I have plans for every surface in this shop."

I laughed softly, still catching my breath, and playfully swatted at his chest. "Your sex drive is insatiable."

Cassian's smirk deepened, his hands steadying me as I wobbled slightly. "And you wouldn't have it any other way."

My heart was still racing, but reality started to seep back in, chasing away the haze of desire. I glanced around the shop, the smell of flowers mingling with something far more intimate. A blush crept up my neck.

"We have to go," I said, my voice firm despite the lingering tremor. "Lena's going to open the shop in the morning, and the last thing she needs is to walk into—"

Cassian raised an eyebrow, amused. "The smell of us?"

I huffed, swatting at him again. "Exactly. You might not care about things like that, but I do. Ivy & Bloom is still a place of business, you know."

Cassian chuckled, reaching for my coat. With a

surprising amount of tenderness, he wrapped it around my shoulders, his hands lingering just a moment too long on my arms. "As you wish, but I quite enjoyed staking my claim. First the shop, and now you..." he said smoothly, though the glint in his eye promised this conversation wasn't over.

Before I could protest further, he swept me up into his arms like I weighed nothing. "Cassian!" I squealed, clutching at his shoulders.

He grinned, clearly enjoying my reaction. "What? You said we have to go."

I rolled my eyes but didn't fight him, secretly relishing the strength of his arms around me. He carried me to the door, pausing so I could lock it behind us. I fumbled with the keys for a moment, my mind still half-lost in the whirlwind of him, before finally securing the lock.

"All set," I murmured, breathless.

Cassian didn't respond, instead carrying me to the waiting SUV. Marcus was already at the wheel, his expression carefully neutral as he opened the door for us. Sierra sat in the front seat, glancing back with an arched eyebrow but wisely staying silent.

Cassian settled into the back seat with me still in his arms, placing me on his lap. "Lie down," he instructed, his voice low but warm.

I hesitated for only a moment before shifting, stretching out across the seat with my head resting on his lap. His hand immediately found its way to my hair, his fingers threading through the strands in a soothing rhythm.

The motion, combined with the hum of the car and the lingering exhaustion from the night, lulled me into a hazy calm. My mind drifted, and despite myself, I found myself thinking about the night's events—about Cassian, about us, and about the sharp edges and undeniable pull of what we were becoming.

Thorns and desire.

The words wove through my thoughts like a whispered mantra, pulling me deeper into the quiet complexity of what Cassian and I had become. Thorns, sharp and unyielding, the parts of him that kept the world at bay—his guarded heart, his razor-edged control, the dangerous undercurrents of his life. And then there was desire, raw and undeniable, the pull that ignited between us like a match struck in the dark.

Thorns kept us distant, but desire brought us together.

Cassian was a paradox—powerful and unrelenting, yet capable of moments so tender they left me breathless. I thought of the way his hands moved tonight, first demanding and consuming, then soft and reverent, as though I were something precious. How he could shift from teasing dominance to genuine care in a heartbeat, making me feel both overwhelmed and cherished.

But the thorns were always there. Lurking beneath his surface, hidden in the shadows of his world—the danger he wore like armor and the secrets he held close. They pricked at me, a constant reminder that his life was not meant for someone like me. Yet I couldn't stop reaching for him, even as the thorns threatened to cut me.

Desire was the salve, the counterpoint to the jagged edges. It was what pulled me closer when I should've stayed away, what made me want to uncover every hidden part of him, no matter the risk. Desire made me reckless, but it also made me brave.

I shifted slightly in the back seat, my head nestled against Cassian's lap. His fingers continued their soothing rhythm through my hair, his touch grounding me even as my thoughts unraveled. I glanced up, catching the faint outline of his profile in the dim light of the passing streetlamps.

He was staring out the window, his expression unreadable, but his hand in my hair never stopped moving. That was the thing about Cassian—he was always two people at once. The man who kept the world at a distance and the man who pulled me close. The protector and the predator. The thorns and the desire.

And me? I wasn't sure which part of him I was falling for, or if it was both.

The SUV hit a small bump, jostling me just enough to

bring me back to the moment. I closed my eyes, letting the gentle hum of the car and the steady motion of his hand lull me into a calm I hadn't felt in days.

Thorns and desire. The thought lingered, sharp and soft all at once, until sleep finally claimed me.

CHAPTER TWENTY-SIX

The sun had barely risen when I stepped into the crisp morning air, clutching my coat tighter against the lingering chill. For the past week, I'd followed the same ritual: leave the penthouse under Marcus and Sierra's watchful eyes, stop by the coffee shop, and spend a few minutes scanning the faces of the patrons before heading to Ivy & Bloom. It had become a quiet obsession, searching for the man in the photograph.

I couldn't explain why I felt so drawn to it—why the grainy image of a stranger sitting at a coffee shop refused to leave my mind. Maybe it was the mystery, the unspoken connection to everything unraveling around me. Or maybe it was just a distraction from the slow, creeping realization that my life wasn't my own anymore.

As I stepped into the coffee shop, the familiar scent of freshly ground beans and warm pastries greeted me. It was comforting, in a way, like a piece of normalcy in a world that had become anything but. Marcus held the door open, his broad frame blocking the entrance as he scanned the room with the same quiet vigilance he carried everywhere.

"Clear," he muttered, stepping in behind me.

I ignored the curious looks from a couple of early risers as I made my way to the counter. Sierra took up her usual post near the door, her sharp blue eyes tracking every movement in the room.

The barista greeted me with a smile, already reaching for a cup. "Morning, Rosalie. The usual?"

"Yes, thank you," I replied, my eyes sweeping over the room. The small tables were mostly occupied—students with laptops, professionals scrolling through their phones, a couple huddled over a shared pastry. But none of them matched the man from the photograph.

I lingered at the counter, pretending to check my phone as I watched the door. My heart gave a faint, irrational flutter every time someone new walked in, but it always sank just as quickly. Whoever he was, he hadn't shown up.

"If I didn't know better, you look like you're expecting someone" Marcus said quietly, his voice low enough that only I could hear.

I shook my head, tucking my phone back into my bag as the barista slid my coffee across the counter. "Just trying to be more vigilant," I said, more to myself than to him. "Let's go."

By the time we reached Ivy & Bloom, the shop was already buzzing with activity. Lena's car was parked out front, and through the window, I could see a couple of her new hires arranging displays.

The sight made something twist in my chest. Lately, it felt like the shop was slipping away from me, piece by piece. Inside, Lena was directing one of the delivery drivers, a clipboard in hand. She looked up as I walked in, her expression bright but professional. "Morning, Rosalie," she said, her tone brisk. "We're making good progress on the arrangements for Julian's charity event. I've got the new team handling the prep work, so you don't need to worry about that."

"Great," I said, forcing a smile as I set my bag down behind the counter. "Anything else that needs my attention?"

Lena hesitated, glancing at the clipboard. "Actually, I've already taken care of most of the paperwork for this week. And I finalized the standing orders with our suppliers yesterday."

"Oh," I said, the smile slipping slightly. "Well... good."

I wandered over to one of the workstations, running my fingers over the petals of a bouquet someone had left half-finished. The colors were beautiful—soft pastels perfect for spring—but it felt like someone else's work, not mine.

The truth was, Ivy & Bloom didn't feel like mine anymore. Lena was efficient, capable, and had taken over so many of the tasks that used to define my days. And while I appreciated her help, it left me feeling untethered, like I was just a guest in the place that had once been my home.

I spent the rest of the morning arranging a few custom orders, trying to lose myself in the familiar motions. But even as I worked, I couldn't shake the nagging sense that I was becoming obsolete—both here and in my own life.

When the shop finally emptied out for the afternoon, I found myself standing at the counter, staring at the ledger Lena had left open. She'd done a flawless job of balancing the books, as usual, but something about the precise, impersonal numbers made my chest ache.

Taking control into my own hands, I reached for my phone and called Sophia to inquire if the proposal was ready. To my surprise, it was—so we agreed to talk it through over dinner.

The evening sky stretched like a deep indigo blanket as I stepped out of Ivy & Bloom, the cool air brushing against my skin. I adjusted my coat, tucking my scarf closer around my neck as Cassian's sleek black SUV idled at the curb. Marcus opened the door for me without a word, his usual stoic expression unchanging, but I could feel his eyes sweeping the street for any signs of trouble.

Cassian was already inside, the glow from his phone screen casting faint shadows across his face. His expression was sharp, his brow furrowed in concentration as he scrolled through what looked like a detailed report. The sight of him so engrossed made my stomach twist, the weight of his world creeping into mine once again.

I slipped into the seat beside him, smoothing my skirt as the cold from outside still clung to my skin. "What are you reading?" I asked softly, my curiosity outweighing my hesitation.

He glanced up, and for a moment, the tension in his features melted. His gray eyes softened as they met mine, and a faint, genuine smile tugged at the corner of his lips. "Just the follow-up on Apex Delta," he replied, locking his phone and slipping it into his jacket pocket. "It's a win in some ways, but we've got new fires to put out."

I tilted my head, studying him. "Overwhelmingly good or bad?"

His hand reached for mine, his touch grounding as he intertwined our fingers. "The hit on Apex Delta was successful. We managed to push the Reapers back and secure valuable intel on what they're transporting," he said, his tone steady. "But retaliation came fast. Two of my properties were hit overnight—likely as payback."

I frowned, the weight of his words sinking in. "Are they okay? Your people?"

"Everyone's accounted for," he reassured me, his thumb brushing lightly against the back of my hand. "The damage is just... expensive. And messy. It's their way of reminding me they won't go down quietly."

I let out a slow breath, the reality of his world once again pressing into mine. "I'm sorry," I murmured, my free hand resting on his arm.

His lips quirked into a faint smile, his gaze lingering on me for a moment longer than necessary. "Don't be," he said softly. "Seeing you has already made the day better."

I felt warmth rise in my cheeks, his words disarming me in a way I wasn't prepared for. "I—"

The driver started the engine, the hum of the car filling the space as we pulled away from the curb. Cassian leaned back in his seat, his fingers still laced with mine. "I'm surprised you invited me, are you sure you want me to join you and Sophia for dinner?" he asked, his voice lighter now.

The drive to the restaurant was smooth, the city lights casting fleeting reflections across the sleek interior of the SUV. Cassian's fingers remained intertwined with mine, a steady, source of warmth that I didn't know I needed until it was there. His earlier words echoed in my mind, softening some of the tension I hadn't realized I'd been carrying.

"I'm not sure 'invited' is the right word," I replied with a wry smile. "You're not exactly easy to say no to."

His lips quirked, the faintest hint of amusement playing on his face. "Good. I'd hate to think I was losing my edge."

I rolled my eyes but couldn't help the small laugh that escaped me. His ability to make me feel at ease, even amidst the chaos surrounding us, was one of the many things about him that unnerved me—and that I found impossible to resist.

When we arrived at the restaurant, Sophia was already waiting at a table tucked into a quiet corner. She rose as we approached, her polished demeanor never faltering as she offered a professional smile. As Cassian approached, she took him in, but what was that... a flash of recognition? She recovered quickly, shaking Cassian's hand, clearly respecting the authority he demanded.

Cassian and I slid into the seats across from her, and after a brief exchange of pleasantries, the server arrived to take our orders.

Sophia wasted no time diving into the proposal, sliding a thick folder across the table toward me. "This outlines the initial concepts for Ivy & Bloom's rebranding and growth strategy," she said, her voice as smooth and practiced as ever. "It's ambitious, but I believe it's a realistic vision of where the shop can go."

I opened the folder, flipping through the meticulously detailed pages. The words and charts seemed to blur together, their meaning just out of reach as I struggled to focus. Bold ideas jumped out—expanding the shop's online presence, introducing upscale floral subscriptions, partnering with luxury brands. All exciting, all innovative... all unfamiliar.

I wasn't reading about Ivy & Bloom. I was reading about someone else's shop—someone else's vision. My stomach twisted, and my hands stilled on the pages.

Cassian, who had been quietly watching me, picked up

on the change almost immediately. His fingers brushed against mine under the table, the gentle contact pulling me from my spiraling thoughts.

"What do you think?" he asked softly, his tone free of judgment but heavy with understanding.

I hesitated, my voice catching as I forced a smile. "It's... impressive," I managed, my throat tightening around the words. "Sophia, you've clearly put a lot of thought into this."

Sophia beamed, mistaking my hesitation for approval. "I believe Ivy & Bloom has untapped potential. With these strategies, we can position it as a premier name in the industry."

I nodded, though my grip on the folder tightened. "It's just a lot to take in," I admitted, my voice quieter now.

Sophia didn't seem to notice, diving into an explanation of the projected growth numbers, the partnerships she envisioned, and the market opportunities she wanted to pursue. Her enthusiasm was genuine, her expertise undeniable, but every word felt like it was driving a wedge further between me and the shop my mother had built.

Cassian's hand tightened briefly on mine beneath the table, anchoring me. When I glanced at him, his gray eyes met mine, steady and calm. He didn't say anything, but the silent reassurance in his gaze was enough to help me keep my composure.

As Sophia continued, I found myself retreating into my thoughts. This wasn't just about the shop. It was about losing pieces of myself—pieces of my family—to a world that was increasingly beyond my control. The realization hit me with a sharp pang of grief that I wasn't prepared for.

Finally, Sophia paused, looking between Cassian and me expectantly. "So, what do you think? Are we ready to move forward?"

I forced a smile, nodding once. "I think it's a strong direction, but I need some time to mull this over before giving you a final answer."

Sophia seemed satisfied with that, her smile brightening. "Of course. Take all the time you need."

The server returned with our meals, breaking the

tension as plates were placed in front of us. The conversation shifted to lighter topics as we ate, though I could feel Cassian's gaze on me, assessing, waiting. He didn't press, didn't push, but his presence was a constant reminder that I wasn't as alone in this as I felt.

By the time dinner ended, I was emotionally drained. As we rose to leave, Sophia gave me a quick hug, promising to send over a few more details for review. Cassian stayed close, his hand resting lightly on the small of my back as we exited the restaurant.

As we slid into the SUV, the weight of the evening pressed heavier against my chest. The city lights streamed by in fleeting blurs, their brilliance doing little to illuminate the uncertainty I felt. I sat quietly, the smooth hum of the vehicle soothing but not enough to distract from the knot in my stomach.

Cassian, seated beside me, was silent too, his attention shifting between his phone and the passing skyline. His gray eyes occasionally flicked my way, but he didn't say anything. I appreciated in this moment that he didn't pry or ask for an explanation. I'm sure he could see the conflict in my eyes, see the distress I had with Sophia's grand plan, but it was exactly that—a plan. I didn't have to go through with it.

I took a breath and leaned forward, catching Marcus's eye in the rearview mirror. "Marcus, could you drop me off at my apartment tonight?"

The tension in the car shifted immediately. Cassian's gaze snapped to me, his phone forgotten as he straightened slightly. "Your apartment?" he repeated, his voice calm but laced with a sharp undertone.

I nodded, trying to keep my voice steady. "Yes. I need to be in my own space for a little while."

Cassian's jaw tightened, his expression unreadable as he leaned back against the seat. Marcus glanced between us in the mirror but didn't say anything, waiting for Cassian's response. The silence stretched, heavy and charged.

Finally, Cassian exhaled, his gaze softening as it settled

on me. "If that's what you need," he said slowly, his voice quieter now, "but I'm coming with you."

It wasn't a question, and I wasn't surprised. I met his eyes, searching for a hint of compromise, but found only resolve. There was no point in arguing. Part of me was relieved, though I wasn't ready to admit it.

"Fine," I said softly, my shoulders relaxing just slightly. "But I want to sleep in my own bed tonight. No guards. No plans. Just... quiet."

Cassian's lips twitched into the faintest of smiles, though it didn't quite reach his eyes. "Quiet sounds good," he murmured, his hand reaching for mine. He laced our fingers together, his grip firm but reassuring.

Marcus turned onto the familiar street leading to my building, the SUV slowing as we approached. I hadn't been here in what felt like weeks, and seeing it again was both comforting and bittersweet. The building stood tall and unassuming, its simple facade a stark contrast to the gilded world I'd been living in with Cassian.

The SUV came to a stop, and Marcus stepped out to open my door. Cassian was already moving, his hand still wrapped around mine as he helped me out of the vehicle. He didn't let go as we walked toward the entrance, his presence steady and protective even in the relative quiet of the neighborhood.

Inside, the familiar scent of my apartment greeted me, a mixture of lavender and something faintly floral. I let out a soft sigh, the weight in my chest easing slightly as I stepped into the space. Cassian followed close behind, his gaze sweeping over the room like he was cataloging every detail, every possible threat.

I set my purse on the counter and turned to him, my hands fidgeting slightly. "Thank you," I said quietly. "For understanding."

He shrugged out of his coat, draping it over the back of a chair. "I'm not sure I do," he admitted, his tone light but his eyes serious. "But I'll try."

Something about his honesty made me smile, a small, genuine curve of my lips. "That's all I can ask for."

Cassian closed the distance between us in a few easy steps, his hands settling on my hips as he leaned down to press a soft kiss to my forehead. "Get comfortable," he said, his voice low. "I'll get us something to drink."

I nodded, retreating to the bedroom to change into something more relaxed. As I slipped into a soft sweater and leggings, I couldn't help but feel the tension in my chest loosening, just a little. For tonight, at least, I wanted to forget all about grandiose signs, country-wide expansions, and absurd marketing strategies.

CHAPTER TWENTY-SEVEN

The busy Tuesday morning chatter of the coffee shop consumed me, a constant rhythm of business conversation, clinking cups, and the hiss of the espresso machine. It had become an oddly comforting routine over the past week—my small rebellion against the carefully controlled chaos of my life. Marcus and Sierra were stationed in their usual places: Marcus by the door, scanning the room with his usual stoic intensity, and Sierra near the counter, pretending to scroll through her phone while her sharp blue eyes missed nothing.

They hadn't been thrilled about my insistence on coming here every morning. Marcus had muttered something about patterns being dangerous, and Sierra had sighed dramatically, reminding me that predictability was a liability. But I needed this, a sliver of normalcy amidst the storm.

The coffee shop's warmth wrapped around me as I sipped my drink, my gaze idly drifting to the window. And then I saw him.

My breath caught in my throat.

The man from the photograph.

He was seated near the back, a newspaper spread out before him. He looked ordinary—dark hair combed neatly, glasses perched on his nose, his posture relaxed. But my heart raced, the image of the photograph flashing in my mind like a warning light. It was him. It had to be.

I glanced toward Marcus, who was now watching me intently. He must have noticed the shift in my demeanor. I forced a calm breath, setting my cup down before rising to my feet.

"Rosalie," Sierra's voice cut through the noise as she took a step toward me. "What are you doing?"

I ignored her, my focus locked on the man as he folded his newspaper and stood. He slipped a satchel over his shoulder and began making his way to the door. My legs moved before I could think, and I followed him out onto the busy street, the cool morning air biting at my cheeks.

"Rosalie!" Marcus's voice called behind me, firm and sharp, but I didn't stop. I couldn't.

The man walked with purpose, his long strides brisk and determined. I stayed several paces behind, weaving through the crowd as he made his way down the sidewalk. My heart hammered in my chest, the adrenaline coursing through me drowning out the city's noise.

He turned a corner, and I quickened my pace to keep up, careful not to get too close. My mind raced, questions colliding in a whirlwind of confusion. Who was he? What connection did he have to the Reapers? And why was he in the photograph at all?

The man stopped abruptly, and I ducked into the doorway of a small boutique, pretending to examine the display. He glanced over his shoulder briefly before continuing on, heading toward a nondescript brick building. My stomach knotted as I watched him walk up to an unmarked door, his hand reaching into his pocket to pull out a keycard.

I froze as I read the small sign above the door: EMPLOYEES ONLY – DEPARTMENT OF MOTOR VEHICLES.

The *DMV*?

My confusion deepened as I watched him swipe his card and step inside, the door clicking shut behind him. I stayed rooted to the spot for a moment, my mind struggling to connect the dots. The DMV? That didn't make any sense.

A hand on my arm startled me, and I turned to see Marcus, his expression dark with barely contained frustration. Sierra stood a few steps behind him, her jaw tight as she scanned the area.

"Miss Quinn," Marcus said, his voice low and clipped. "What are you doing?"

I opened my mouth to answer, but the words didn't come. What was I doing? What did I even hope to find?

"I…" My voice trailed off as I glanced back at the door, now closed and unremarkable, as if nothing unusual had happened. "I thought I saw something."

"Something, or someone?" Sierra asked, her tone laced with exasperation.

I hesitated, my gaze flicking back to the door. "It doesn't matter. I was wrong," I confessed, "Let's just get to the shop. There is still a lot to be done today."

Without waiting for their response, I turned and started walking back toward the floral shop, my mind spinning with the strange, inexplicable puzzle I'd just stumbled into. The man from the photograph worked at the DMV? Why? And what did it mean?

I didn't have answers, only a growing sense of unease that settled deep in my chest. Whatever this was, it wasn't simple—and it wasn't over.

Sierra muttered under her breath, her pace slower than usual as she limped slightly behind me. "This much walking isn't exactly what the doctor ordered, Rosalie. In case you've forgotten, I've got a bullet wound that says I'm supposed to be resting."

I slowed down just enough to glance over my shoulder, guilt threading through my frustration. "Which is why you should be on convalescent leave. You're *supposed* to be resting, Sierra, not babysitting me."

Her glare was sharp enough to pierce through steel. "And leave you to get yourself into more trouble? Not a chance."

Marcus, ever the silent sentinel, walked a step ahead of

us, his posture as unyielding as always. But even he gave a slight side-eye toward Sierra, clearly gauging her limits. The tension between the three of us was thick, and I desperately needed to steer the conversation away from my impulsive chase and Sierra's injury.

Spotting a quaint little trinket shop tucked between a café and a bookstore, I made a split-second decision. "Come on, I've always wanted to check this place out" I said, changing direction abruptly and stepping through the shop's door. A bell overhead jingled, announcing our arrival.

Sierra groaned audibly as she followed. "You're lucky I like cute shops. This better be worth it."

The interior was charming, lined with shelves displaying handmade goods, from candles to miniature sculptures. The faint scent of lavender hung in the air, mingling with the soft hum of instrumental music playing in the background. The shopkeeper, an elderly woman with kind eyes, offered a warm smile from behind the counter but didn't press us as we wandered.

My eyes caught on a small glass case filled with intricately carved chess pieces, each one unique. Something about the set drew me in—the craftsmanship, the detail, the quiet power of the pieces themselves. Among them, two stood out: a King, strong and regal, its lines sharp and purposeful; and a Queen, elegant but fierce, her crown adorned with the finest touches of artistry.

"I'll take these two," I said, pointing to the King and Queen. The shopkeeper nodded, her smile deepening as she unlocked the case and retrieved them with careful hands.

Marcus watched me with a raised brow. "You play chess?"

"No," I admitted, holding the pieces in my palm and studying their detail. "But I like what they represent."

"Power?" Sierra guessed, leaning heavily against a display shelf, her irritation momentarily dulled by curiosity.

"Balance," I said softly, turning the Queen over in my hand. "Two halves of a whole. They work best when they're together."

The shopkeeper wrapped the pieces in tissue paper, placing them gently into a small velvet pouch. I thanked her and slipped the pouch into my coat pocket, already imagining the look on Cassian's face when I gave them to him. A small token, but one that felt significant. He was my King, and I wanted to remind him that I could be his Queen.

As we stepped back outside, Sierra's limp was more pronounced, and Marcus's gaze lingered on her for a moment before falling on me. "Satisfied?"

"For now," I said, offering him a faint smile.

They didn't press me further about the coffee shop, and I was grateful. The oddity of the encounter still nagged at me, but for now, I needed to focus on getting the arrangement for Julian's event completed. Cassian would want to know where I'd been, and I wasn't ready to explain everything—at least not until I figured out what it meant.

Sliding my hand into my pocket, I ran my thumb over the smooth edge of the chess pieces. Whatever was coming, I would face it with him, side by side.

CHAPTER TWENTY-EIGHT

The stillness of the cool midnight air felt heavier than usual. Shadows clung to the walls of Cassian's penthouse like quiet sentinels, the soft drumbeat of the city below, even at this hour was unmistakable. Despite the late hour, my eyes snapped open, my chest tightening with an unshakable unease. Something was wrong—or maybe not wrong, exactly, but *missing*. The feeling clung to me like a phantom, refusing to let go.

I glanced at the digital clock glowing faintly on the nightstand. 3:17 a.m. Cassian's breathing was even beside me, his strong arm draped protectively over my waist. Normally, the warmth of him would lull me back to sleep, but tonight, the restless gnawing in my chest refused to relent.

Carefully, I slipped out from under his arm, pulling on the silk robe draped over the foot of the bed. My bare feet moved silently across the cool floor, the faint sound of my heartbeat filling my ears. The penthouse was steeped in darkness, save for the soft glow of the city skyline filtering through the curtains.

The office door creaked slightly as I pushed it open, the sound unnaturally loud in the stillness. Cassian's office had always felt like a sacred space—a room where decisions were made, lives altered, and secrets locked away. The weight of his world was tangible here, in the dark wood of the desk, the sleek monitors that hummed softly even when idle, and the stacks of papers meticulously organized yet bursting with tension.

My gaze swept the room before landing on the notebook sitting neatly on the desk. It was the same one Cassian had recovered from Ryker, its edges worn from handling. Something about it had gnawed at me ever since he'd first mentioned the intel they recovered.

I hesitated, my fingers hovering over the leather cover. Would he be angry if he caught me reading it? Probably. But the unease twisting inside me left no room for hesitation.

Flipping it open, I scanned the pages quickly, careful not to disturb the meticulous placement of notes. Handwritten lines of Cassian's sharp, deliberate script filled each page— names, locations, fragmented details of an operation I didn't fully understand. My heart pounded as I turned page after page, searching for... I didn't even know what.

Until I landed on it.

A page filled with license plate numbers and VINs, their significance circled in a distinct penmanship. My brow furrowed as I traced the numbers with my finger, the lines connecting them to dates and seemingly unrelated notes. There was something here, something that tugged at the edges of my mind like a whisper I couldn't quite hear.

I grabbed my phone from my robe pocket and took a quick picture of the page. The light from the screen cast eerie shadows over the notebook, and for a moment, I felt a pang of guilt. Cassian had been trying to protect me and more since that day; protect me from the darkness that consumed him daily. But how could I stand by, knowing I might be able to help?

The notebook closed with a soft *thud,* and I stood there for a moment, the weight of my discovery pressing against me. Whatever these numbers represented, they weren't random. And they might just be the thread that unraveled the entire operation.

I froze as the low, familiar sound of Cassian's footsteps echoed softly in the hallway, drawing closer with each step. My heart leapt into my throat as his tall frame filled the doorway, his gray eyes sharp despite the late hour. He was dressed in nothing but dark pajama bottoms, the expanse of his chest catching the faint glow of the city lights outside. His expression was unreadable, but his silence said everything.

"Cassian," I began, my voice soft, almost apologetic. I couldn't think of a single explanation that wouldn't make this worse.

Without saying a word, he crossed the room, his hand extending toward the notebook. Reluctantly, I relinquished it, the leather cool and weighty as it left my fingers. Cassian's jaw was set, his movements deliberate as he turned away, heading toward the large portrait on the far wall. It was an oil painting—classic and imposing—a piece I'd always thought was purely decorative.

He pressed a concealed button on the edge of the frame, and the portrait slid aside with a quiet mechanical vibration, revealing a built-in safe embedded into the wall. The keypad lit up as he entered a code, his shoulders tense with an energy I couldn't quite place. The safe door swung open, and he placed the notebook inside with a finality that made my stomach twist.

With the same deliberate motions, he shut the safe and pressed the button again, the portrait sliding back into place as though nothing had happened.

When he turned back to me, his expression was softer, but no less determined. "You don't need to concern yourself with this anymore, Rosalie," he said, his voice low and firm. "It's not your burden to carry."

"Not my burden?" I repeated, incredulous. "Cassian, you can be so hot and cold sometimes. I want to help, I want to figure out what is going on and to be done with this nightmare as quickly as possible."

His lips pressed into a thin line, and he exhaled sharply, crossing the room to stand in front of me. "It's not a fight you're equipped for," he said, his tone tinged with both frustration and something gentler—something that sounded a lot like fear. "I've spent my entire life navigating this world, protecting myself and the people I care about.

I met his gaze, my frustration bubbling to the surface. "You don't get to decide what I can or can't handle, Cassian. This affects me just as much as it affects you. I have a right to know."

His hand came up, brushing a strand of hair from my face, the motion as tender as his words were sharp. "What you have is a right to live. To breathe without this weighing you down. I won't let you drown in this, Rosalie. Not when I'm the one pulling you under."

The rawness in his voice stole the air from my lungs, but it wasn't enough to quell the fire in my chest. "And what if I don't want to be left out of it? What if I want to stand by you, not behind you?"

Cassian's jaw tightened, his gaze holding mine with an intensity that made my pulse quicken. He didn't answer immediately, the silence between us stretching taut. Finally, he exhaled, his hand falling to his side. "You deserve better than this world," he said quietly, almost to himself. "Better than me."

I reached for his hand, holding it tightly between both of mine. "Then it's a good thing I have better taste than you, Cassian. I'll choose who I want to be with."

For a moment, he didn't move, his gray eyes searching mine as though looking for something he couldn't name. Then, with a sigh that sounded like defeat, he pulled me into his arms, his embrace firm and protective.

"I'll protect you, Rosalie," he murmured against my hair, his voice a quiet promise. "Even from yourself."

I didn't respond, the weight of his words settling heavily in my chest. As much as I wanted to fight him, to argue my place in this mess, I couldn't ignore the fear I saw in his eyes—the fear of losing me.

And for now, that fear was enough to silence my protests.

Cassian's hand slipped into mine, his grip firm but warm as he tugged me gently toward the hallway. "Come now," he said softly, his voice losing some of its earlier edge. "Back to bed."

I let him guide me, the weight of his earlier words still pressing against my chest. The safe was locked, the notebook out of my reach, but my thoughts wouldn't relent. They circled back to the scraps of information I'd glimpsed—the numbers, the names, the fragments that refused to fall into place. A sense of urgency throbbed in the back of my mind, as if the answers were just out of reach, waiting for me to connect them.

When we reached the bedroom, Cassian pulled me close, his arms wrapping around me as he eased us onto the bed. The scent of cedar and spice surrounded me, his presence grounding yet not enough to quiet the storm in my head. I rested my head against his chest, feeling the steady rise and fall of his breath. His fingers brushed through my hair, a soothing rhythm that lulled my body but left my thoughts untamed.

"Cassian," I murmured after a long silence, the words barely audible against the darkness. "What if... what if there's something we've missed? What if there's a way I could help?"

He sighed, his lips brushing against the top of my head. "You're helping by staying out of the way, Rosalie. That's all I need from you."

I wanted to argue, to tell him that wasn't enough—not for me. But his grip tightened slightly, as if he could feel the battle waging inside me.

"Sleep," he murmured, his voice low and commanding but laced with a softness that broke something in me. "Please."

I closed my eyes, not because I was ready to surrender, but because I knew he needed this moment of peace as much as I did. His heartbeat echoed in my ear, steady and strong, but even as my body relaxed into his, my mind stayed sharp.

The numbers, the names, the fragments—they were all there, waiting. And I wouldn't stop until I figured out how they fit together.

CHAPTER TWENTY-NINE

The sun filtered through the delicate curtains of Cassian's penthouse, casting golden light across the polished floors. Despite the warmth of the morning, an unease clung to me like a second skin. Only a few hours had passed since I'd stared at those vehicle VINs in the journal, and the puzzle pieces still refused to fit together. The frustration had become a low annoyance in the back of my mind, constant and gnawing.

I tossed aside the blanket tangled around my legs and padded barefoot to the kitchen. Cassian had already left, no doubt pulled into whatever silent war he was waging. The penthouse felt cavernous without him, the muted distant commotion of the city below doing little to fill the void. A half-drunk cup of coffee sat abandoned on the counter, his ritual as predictable as the tension that always followed.

As I poured myself a fresh cup, the idea struck. I was done sitting on the sidelines, spinning my wheels without traction. Cassian might have locked his secrets away, but he couldn't keep me from digging elsewhere.

When I arrived at Ivy & Bloom an hour later, the shop was bustling with activity. Lena barely glanced up from her clipboard as I walked in, her sharp voice rattling off instructions to a delivery driver. "Morning," I said, more out of habit than enthusiasm.

Lena nodded absently. "Morning. I've got the books to balance, and the event orders to finalize, and last night's deposit to take to the bank."

"Why don't I take care of that for you," I offered, "It's a warmer morning and I could use a good walk to clear my head."

"That would be great!" She beamed from behind a several boxes of imported flowers.

"No problem," I replied smoothly, though my mind was already far from Ivy & Bloom. I scooped up the deposit bag and slipped it into my tote, keeping my movements casual. "Anything else?"

"Nope, that should do it."

Marcus and Sierra hovered near the door, their presence a constant reminder of Cassian's overprotectiveness. I met their watchful gazes with a practiced smile. "Let's make this quick," I said, heading for the door.

The streets bustled with morning energy, a mix of coffee-seekers and commuters moving in hurried streams. The deposit bag felt heavier than it should in my tote, its weight an anchor to the lie I was about to tell. My steps were measured, casual, as though the bank were my intended destination. Marcus and Sierra flanked me, their silent vigilance a constant anchor at my sides.

When we approached the corner where I should have turned toward the bank, I veered left instead, heading straight for the DMV. Sierra's sharp gaze didn't miss a thing.

"You missed the turn," she said, her voice neutral but questioning.

"I know," I replied smoothly, my tone light. "I need to pay for my father's vehicle registration. It's expired and the DMV always has a longer line than the bank tellers."

"That's not what we're here for," Marcus said, his voice low and firm. His steps slowed slightly as though he was debating pulling me back.

"It'll only take a minute," I assured them, keeping my pace brisk. "It's overdue, and I might as well take care of it while I'm out."

Sierra gave Marcus a glance, her expression unreadable, but neither of them argued further. They followed as I stepped into the DMV, the sharp, sterile smell of the building washing over me. The fluorescent lights buzzed faintly above, casting a washed-out glow over the dull gray walls and rows of plastic chairs.

The DMV was a stark contrast to the elegance of Cassian's world, but it had a peculiar kind of energy—chaotic and mundane. I scanned the room quickly, my heart pounding as my gaze darted from one face to the next. There he was, the man from the photograph, seated behind a counter marked *Registration Services*.

I approached the line for his station, my palms growing damp despite the chill of the building. Marcus and Sierra stayed close, their eyes scanning the room as though expecting trouble to leap from behind the laminated posters and stacks of forms.

When it was my turn, I stepped up to the counter, clutching the deposit bag tightly in one hand and a thin file folder in the other. The man looked up, his expression bored as he said, "How can I help you?"

I slid the folder across the counter, keeping my movements calm and deliberate. "I need to pay for a vehicle registration renewal," I said, my voice steady.

He opened the folder, glancing briefly at the outdated papers inside. "This vehicle hasn't been active for over a year," he noted, raising an eyebrow.

"I'm getting it ready again," I replied smoothly. "Figured I'd start with the basics."

His eyes flicked to mine, and for a moment, something unreadable passed between us. He didn't seem startled or suspicious—if anything, he seemed vaguely amused. But he processed the paperwork without further comment, his fingers moving efficiently over the keyboard.

He typed away, the clacking of keys punctuating the sterile quiet of the DMV. I watched him carefully, noting the precision in his movements. This was someone who was used to working under pressure, someone who could manage more than mundane registration renewals.

As he processed my father's paperwork, I leaned forward slightly, lowering my voice. "I need something else."

He didn't stop typing, but his brow furrowed slightly. "This is the wrong counter for 'something else,'" he replied dryly.

I reached into my tote, pulling out the deposit bag and placing it discreetly on the counter. His fingers hesitated on the keyboard, his eyes flicking to the bag and then back to me.

"I need information," I said, sliding a folded piece of paper across the counter. "On these VINs."

The man glanced at the paper, his jaw tightening ever so slightly. He didn't pick it up but studied it for a beat too long before meeting my eyes. "That's not the kind of thing we handle here."

"It is," I countered softly. "And you can handle it—for the right price."

I nudged the bag forward slightly, the unspoken offer hanging heavily in the air. His gaze darted around the room, but no one was paying us any attention. Marcus and Sierra hovered near the door, their presence a quiet but constant reminder that I wasn't alone.

He sighed, closing the folder on my father's registration. "Wait here."

Without another word, he stood and disappeared into the back room, the paper with the VINs tucked under his arm. My heart hammered against my ribs as the seconds stretched into minutes. Marcus and Sierra shifted uncomfortably by the entrance, their sharp eyes scanning the room.

"What's taking so long?" Sierra muttered under her breath.

"Paperwork," I said, forcing a calm tone. "These things always take longer than they should."

Sierra raised an eyebrow but didn't inquire further, though her posture remained taut with suspicion.

Finally, the man reappeared, a printout in his hand and the paper with the VINs folded neatly beneath it. He set the registration and receipt on the counter first, then handed me the folded sheet.

"That's everything," he said, his tone clipped. "I'd suggest you keep this to yourself."

I nodded, slipping the documents into my tote and sliding the deposit bag toward him. He hesitated for half a second before taking it, his expression carefully neutral.

"Pleasure doing business," I said quietly, turning on my heel and heading for the exit. Marcus and Sierra fell into step behind me, their watchful gazes burning into my back as we left the DMV.

The walk to the bank was uneventful, save for the simmering tension I could feel emanating from Sierra. Her sharp blue eyes tracked every movement, her injured leg slowing her pace slightly but not enough to dull her vigilance. Marcus walked beside her, his calm demeanor a counterweight to her restlessness.

When we reached the bank, the air inside was cool and inviting, minus the faint scent of disinfectant lingering in the air. I approached the counter with measured steps, my bag clutched in one hand and my debit card in the other.

When the teller turns her attention toward me, I quickly ask to make a withdrawal of a hundred bucks—I needed an excuse to be at the counter with Marcus and Sierra watching so closely.

She handed over the receipt, and I tucked it into my tote, keeping my expression neutral as I turned away from the counter. Sierra and Marcus were waiting near the entrance, their gazes flicking over the other patrons before settling on me.

"All set?" Marcus asked, his tone casual but his eyes sharp.

"Good to go," I replied, walking past them toward the exit. My heart raced slightly, but my steps were steady, confident.

We stepped back onto the sidewalk, the late morning sun casting long shadows across the pavement. Sierra adjusted her jacket, her eyes scanning the street with practiced precision. "Where to now?" she asked, her tone clipped.

"Back to Ivy & Bloom," I said, slipping my sunglasses on to hide the unease simmering in my eyes. "Maybe all this walking will make you reconsider that convalescent leave you've been avoiding."

Sierra gave a slight glare, and we fell into step, heading back toward the shop. The streets bustled with the usual midweek activity—businesspeople hurrying to meetings, couples strolling hand in hand, and street vendors calling out to passersby. But the world felt quieter, more insulated, as I turned the events of the morning over in my mind.

The list of VINs and corresponding details burned in my tote, its weight heavier than it should have been. The hundred-dollar bill in my purse felt like a small rebellion, a sliver of autonomy in a world where every move felt scrutinized. I kept my face neutral, my steps purposeful, as Marcus and Sierra flanked me, none the wiser to the small secrets I carried.

As we approached Ivy & Bloom, the familiar scent of primroses and fresh cherry blossoms drifted through the open door. I paused for a moment on the sidewalk, the weight of the morning settling in my chest. Something about the shop's warm glow felt like a stark contrast to the shadows I was now chasing. And as much as I wanted to push it all aside, I knew I was already too deep.

CHAPTER THIRTY

The next evening, the penthouse seemed to hold its breath, anticipation seeping into every corner like a tangible thing. Shadows danced on the walls, cast by the flickering glow of chandeliers, and the faint hum of the city below felt distant, muted by the weight of what the night promised. Cassian had disappeared into his study hours ago, his focus sharp and unwavering, leaving me to the capable—and relentless—hands of a stylist team determined to sculpt me into their vision of perfection.

Brushstrokes of makeup swept across my skin, each touch delicate but deliberate. Hairpins clicked into place with a precision that felt surgical, and the silken whisper of fabric being adjusted around my body was the only sound besides the soft murmurs of the team. When they finally stepped back, their work complete, I was left staring at a reflection that felt like a stranger.

The woman in the mirror was regal, untouchable. Her gown clung to her like a secret, deep crimson silk that shimmered with every subtle shift. Black lace crept up her bodice like ivy, delicate and dangerous, before tapering off to bare her shoulders.

The pièce de résistance, however, was the necklace. Cassian had it commissioned specifically for tonight.

Jewels sparkled at her throat, woven into a necklace that could have been stolen from a queen's vault—or a weapon's collection. The rubies glinted like droplets of blood among blackened thorns, bold and unapologetic. The thorns, sharp and menacing, pressed lightly against my skin—not enough to hurt, but enough to remind me of their presence. It was a symbol, I realized, of him. Beauty wrapped in danger. Desire cloaked in restraint.

She was stunning.

She was lethal.

She was me.

I reached out, my fingertips grazing the mirror as if I needed proof that the woman staring back wasn't some phantom conjured for the evening. "Is this what it feels like?" I murmured under my breath. "To make every man fall at my feet?"

No one answered, but I wasn't speaking to them anyway. I wasn't even sure if I wanted the answer.

Cassian appeared in the doorway, dressed in a sharp black tuxedo with a crisp white shirt and a black bow tie. His presence filled the room, his gray eyes scanning me with an intensity that left me breathless.

"I would bow at your feet." He whispered, as the rest of the stylist team made themselves sparse. "You'll make it impossible for anyone to focus on the charity tonight," he said, his voice a low, velvety murmur as he approached. His gaze lingered on the necklace before meeting mine. "It suits you."

"It's beautiful," I whispered, unable to hide the awe in my voice. "You had this made?"

"For you," he replied simply, his fingers brushing a strand of hair away from my face. "To remind everyone exactly who you belong to."

I ran my fingers across the beautiful necklace, and realized now was as good as any time. I went to the chair where my jacket was draped over the edge, and fished out the King chess piece from my pocket, holding onto it tightly. When I turned around, his eyes were following me curiously. I moved in front of him, holding out my hands, revealing the tiny trinket.

"It isn't much," I confessed, "and no where nearly as expensive, but when I saw this, I thought of you."

He picked up the piece, a genuine smile forming at the corner of his lips.

"I have one too, I said—the Queen. So you know exactly who you belong to."

Cassian laughed, pleased to hear his words thrown back at him.

"My sweet petal, thank you. I'll carry this with me forever."

Heat rose to my cheeks, but I didn't look away. Instead, I stepped closer, letting the fabric of my gown sway around me like a living thing. "And what happens if the Queen steal the spotlight from you tonight?"

His lips quirked into a smirk, his hand coming to rest on my hip. "I'm counting on it, but just for tonight—otherwise, I might have to remind them."

The sound of Marcus clearing his throat from the doorway interrupted the charged moment. "The car is ready, sir."

Cassian's hand lingered for a moment longer before he stepped back, his expression softening as he extended his arm. "Shall we?"

We made our way down to the waiting SUV. The cool evening air greeted us as Cassian held the door open for me. I gathered the heavy fabric of my gown, the silk whispering against my skin, and stepped out with his assistance. His hand was warm and steady, a grounding force in the whirlwind of everything tonight represented.

As I straightened, the lights of the event venue sparkled ahead of us. Cassian's grip tightened slightly as he leaned in, his lips brushing against my ear. "Remember, there are still threats out there, and no matter what happens, you're the queen of this game."

With those words, he led me forward, the weight of the gown and the thorns at my neck a reminder of the power we were stepping into together.

As the SUV spurred to life, Cassian reached into the

center console and retrieved two masks. He handed mine over with a quiet smile—a delicate creation of black lace that mirrored the intricate designs adorning my dress. The lace was elaborate, web-like, and threaded with tiny glimmers of silver, subtle enough to catch the light without overpowering.

His mask, by contrast, was simple and commanding—a stark black with sharp edges that emphasized the strong lines of his jaw and the intensity of his gaze. There was no ornamentation, no softness. It was pure dominance, a reflection of the man who wore it.

I ran my fingers over the lace of my mask, letting its texture ground me as he adjusted his own. The silence between us felt charged, but not uncomfortable. Cassian's presence filled the space effortlessly, his confidence a steady pulse that I could feel without needing to look at him.

When the vehicle pulled up to the venue, Cassian stepped out first. The flash of cameras and the murmurs of the crowd outside barely fazed him as he turned and extended a hand to me. "Take your time," he murmured, his tone low, inviting, and brimming with something unspoken.

I accepted his hand, the warmth of his touch steadying me as I stepped out of the SUV. The hem of my gown brushed against the pavement as I stood, the chill of the evening air brushing against my bare shoulders. The glow of the building ahead spilled out onto the street, casting long shadows and painting everything in gold and silver.

Cassian slid his hand to the small of my back as we walked, his fingers resting lightly but with purpose. The clamor of the crowd faded into a background hum as we ascended the steps side by side, his presence shielding me from the world as much as it showcased me to it.

"What have you been up to lately, little petal?" he asked, his voice casual, almost lazy, but the sharp undertone wasn't lost on me.

I glanced up at him, the edge of my mask framing my face in shadows. "Why do you ask?" I countered, keeping my tone light, playful, though I could feel my pulse quicken.

Cassian's lips curved into a faint smile, one that didn't quite reach his eyes. "No reason. Just curious if you've been keeping yourself out of trouble—or finding new ways to dive headfirst into it."

I felt his words slide under my skin, calculated and intentional, designed to keep me guessing, to remind me that nothing escaped his notice. "I've been busy," I said smoothly, the practiced ease in my voice disguising the flicker of unease that his question ignited. "You know, arranging flowers, taking care of the shop—normal things."

"Normal," he echoed, as though testing the word, tasting its simplicity. His smile deepened, though it carried an edge of mischief that sent a shiver down my spine. "How refreshingly mundane."

I shot him a sidelong glance, a faint smirk tugging at my lips. "Not everyone thrives on chaos, Cassian."

His chuckle was low, vibrating through the space between us. "Don't mistake this for chaos, Rosalie. It's order—just on a scale most people can't comprehend."

The doors to the venue loomed ahead, two grand arches framed in cascading roses and flickering candlelight. As the attendant stepped forward to admit us, Cassian's hand pressed gently against my back, guiding me inside. His lips brushed close to my ear, his voice a soft murmur meant only for me.

"Let's hope tonight doesn't test just how well you comprehend it."

Cassian's hand tightened slightly against the small of my back as we navigated the grand staircase. The soft murmur of the crowd below faded with each step, replaced by the echo of our footsteps on polished marble. The opulence of the venue enveloped us, but I couldn't ignore the weight of Cassian's words—or the subtle tension laced beneath them.

"You've been awfully quiet tonight," he said, his voice smooth but edged with something sharper.

"I'm enjoying the atmosphere," I replied lightly, keeping my tone neutral. "It's beautiful here."

Cassian's lips curved into a small smile, though his eyes betrayed none of the warmth his expression suggested. "Beautiful, yes. But not as beautiful as the truth."

I faltered slightly, the heat of his gaze brushing over me like a tangible force. "I don't know what you mean."

He stopped at the landing, turning to face me fully. The low light caught the sharp planes of his face, the mask framing his gray eyes in shadow. "Don't you?" His words were a quiet challenge, spoken so softly they almost didn't reach me.

I met his gaze, holding firm despite the unease twisting in my stomach. "Of course, I do. I told you—I've been busy with the shop."

The smile on his lips deepened, a predatory curve that sent a ripple of something between fear and anticipation through me. "You've gotten better at lying, I'll give you that. But do you remember what I said would happen if you ever lied to me, Rosalie?"

My pulse stuttered as he reached into his pocket, retrieving a small key. Without breaking eye contact, he stepped toward the door at the top of the stairs, unlocking it with unrelenting determination.

I hesitated as he pushed the door open, revealing a lavishly decorated private room. The space was intimate, draped in dark fabrics and soft lighting. A table set with crystal glasses and an unopened bottle of champagne waited in the center, but my focus remained fixed on Cassian.

"Why are we here?" I asked, my voice quiet as I followed him inside.

Cassian closed the door behind us, the soft click of the lock sending a jolt of awareness down my spine. He leaned casually against the doorframe, his posture deceptively relaxed as his eyes fixed on mine. "To give you one more chance."

"Chance for what?"

"To tell me the truth," he said simply, his voice as calm as if he were discussing the weather. But his gaze, piercing and unyielding, left no room for misinterpretation.

I swallowed hard, the weight of his presence pressing down on me. "I've told you everything," I said, forcing my voice to remain steady. "There's nothing else to say."

Cassian stepped closer, each movement deliberate and controlled. He stopped mere inches from me, his head tilting slightly as he studied my face. "One more chance, Rosalie," he murmured, his voice dropping to a low whisper. "Think carefully."

Cassian's hand slipped into the pocket of his suit jacket, his movements deliberate as he retrieved something folded and small. My breath hitched as he held it up between two fingers—a photograph. *The* photograph.

"Recognize this?" he asked, his tone calm, almost casual. But his eyes, dark and penetrating behind the mask, betrayed his displeasure.

I froze, the blood draining from my face. "Where did you get that?"

"From you." He unfolded the photograph, holding it up so the light caught the image. "You've been carrying this around. And that's not all I know." His voice dropped, sharp with authority. "The money you took from the deposit bag— was that for your little investigation?"

"It's my money," I said quickly, trying to match his calm.

Cassian's expression didn't shift, but the weight of his gaze bore down on me like a crushing force. "It's *my* money," he corrected, his voice icy yet still controlled. "Every dollar in that shop is mine, Rosalie. Just like every move you make should be within the bounds I've set for your safety. But instead, you've been making trips to coffee shops and DMV counters, lying to my face. And this?" He held up the photograph again. "This was your endgame?"

I shook my head, taking a step back, but Cassian's hand shot out, gripping my wrist firmly but not painfully. "No, I wasn't—"

"Enough," he cut me off, pulling me closer. "You've had your chances to tell me the truth, little petal."

My stomach twisted at the nickname, the way it dripped with both affection and reprimand. Before I could protest, he pulled me forward and guided me over his knee, his grip strong but careful. "Cassian—"

"Quiet," he said simply, his voice calm but resolute. "You've been pushing boundaries, Rosalie, and it's time you remembered where they are."

I barely had time to process his words as he hiked up the folds of my dress; his palm landed against me, the sharp sting surprising and hot. I gasped, my heart pounding as he delivered a second, then a third. The strikes weren't hard, but they were firm enough to send a clear message.

"Care to jog your memory now?" he asked, his voice low and smooth. His hand rested on the small of my back, grounding and commanding all at once.

"I—I found it in the letter," I stammered, the heat rising to my cheeks and radiating through my body. "It was slipped into my purse after the meeting with Sophia."

Cassian paused, his grip steady. "Go on."

"I don't know who sent it," I admitted, my voice trembling. "It wasn't signed. And I didn't know who the man in the photo was when I received it. I swear."

He hummed, the sound vibrating deep in his chest. "So, you decided to play detective with stolen money, risking not just your safety but mine. You've learned nothing from the trouble you've already stirred up."

"I was trying to help," I said, my voice cracking.

"Help?" Cassian's fingers skimmed the curve of my hip as he straightened me up, his palm lingering on my flushed skin before guiding me back to stand in front of him. "You've done the opposite of help, petal."

I tried to meet his gaze, but the intensity in his eyes made me look away. "You don't trust me."

"You've made that difficult," he said bluntly. Then, leaning forward, he grabbed my chin, tilting my face up to meet his. "You don't get to play coy with me, Rosalie. Not after this."

My lips parted, but no words came out. Cassian smirked faintly, the edge of his earlier anger softening into something more dangerous—controlled desire. His thumb brushed over my lower lip as his voice dropped to a low murmur. "You're mine to protect. Mine to guide. And when you get yourself in trouble, mine to punish. Understand?"

The knot in my chest tightened, the heat of his words sending a flush through me. I nodded slowly, my breath hitching as his hand slipped to the back of my neck, pulling me closer until his lips grazed my ear.

"Good," he whispered, his voice dark with promise. "Now, let's see if you can behave, or if you're just as willful as the petals of those roses you seem to love—soft and pliant on the outside but with thorns that can't help but draw blood."

My pulse quickened at the nickname, and despite my unease, I couldn't help but lean into him. Cassian's grip on my neck tightened slightly, a subtle reminder of his control, before he brushed his lips over mine in a kiss that left me breathless and craving more.

CHAPTER THIRTY-ONE

The grand ballroom shimmered, a perfect blend of opulence and spring's delicate beauty. Every detail reflected the careful attention I had poured into the floral arrangements, yet I couldn't shake the unease bubbling beneath my pride.

Towering centerpieces commanded attention, their gilded stands wrapped in trailing vines of clematis and adorned with soft pink peonies and golden ranunculus. Lily of the valley peeked shyly from beneath clusters of astilbe, their sweet fragrance mingling with the heady aroma of garden roses. Blue delphinium added a surprising pop of color, grounding the ethereal displays with a touch of boldness.

On the banquet tables, the arrangements felt intimate, drawing the eye with hellebores and anemones nestled in beds of moss. Jewel-toned petals seemed to glimmer like treasures under the soft glow of the chandeliers, while thistles—my personal addition—hinted at the strength that often lay behind beauty. Even the bar bore my touch, delicate sprigs of freesia and lisianthus framing the polished menus like a whisper of spring.

I sipped my champagne, my fingers idly tracing the stem of the glass as I surveyed the room. Guests swirled around me, their laughter and the soft strains of a string quartet blending into the background. It was breathtaking, yet I felt like an outsider watching it all unfold.

"This is your handiwork, isn't it?" Cassian's voice pulled me from my thoughts, his presence grounding me immediately.

I turned, finding him holding two glasses of whiskey. His gray eyes were sharp but warm as he handed me one.

"It is," I admitted, heat creeping into my cheeks at the rare softness in his expression.

"You've outdone yourself," he said simply, his tone carrying weight that went beyond the words.

"Thank you," I murmured, the compliment settling in my chest like a soft glow.

We moved through the crowd together, exchanging pleasantries with Cassian's associates and their spouses. The interactions felt easier with him beside me, his steady presence anchoring me in the sea of silk and tuxedos.

But, as always, duty called. A man approached Cassian, his manner sharp and businesslike, leaning in to murmur something urgent. Cassian's expression darkened briefly before he turned to me.

"Stay here, please" he said, his voice firm but gentle. "I won't be long."

I nodded, forcing a smile. He gave me one last glance before disappearing into the crowd, leaving me standing at the edge of the room with my champagne and the swirl of my thoughts.

I barely had time to settle my nerves before someone else approached—a man whose presence carried the same commanding weight as Cassian's, though his charm felt smoother, more calculated.

"Rosalie," Cassian's once-presumed-dead-father greeted, his voice deep and resonant, with a faint hint of amusement that put me on edge.

"Mr. Moreau," I replied politely, straightening as he stopped in front of me.

"Damien," he corrected smoothly, a faint smile playing on his lips. "No need to make me sound older than I feel."

Damien Moreau exuded a quiet menace, the kind that made a room still without so much as a word. His features, sharp and uncompromising, seemed molded by a lifetime of hard decisions. High cheekbones and a pale complexion gave him an almost spectral quality, while the deep lines around his eyes and mouth hinted at battles fought in shadows. His eyes, dark and unyielding, had the unsettling ability to dismantle a person with a single glance, peeling back layers of pretense to expose what lay beneath. There was no warmth in his gaze, only the cold calculation of a man who had seen too much and trusted too little.

A faint scar bisected his right eyebrow, disappearing into iron-gray hair combed back with the kind of meticulous discipline that spoke not of vanity, but of control. His neatly trimmed beard framed a strong jawline, flecked with silver strands that glimmered like frost in the low light. Everything about him—his tailored midnight-blue three-piece suit, the crimson silk tie that offered a striking contrast, and the heavy gold signet ring on his left hand—radiated an aura of power that went beyond wealth. This was a man who carried legacy like a weapon, wielding it with quiet authority.

His mask, a work of dark, burnished metal, was sleek and angular, its edges etched with delicate patterns that caught the room's golden light. It obscured the upper half of his face, leaving his mouth visible—a faint, knowing smirk playing at his lips. The mask's weight matched the somber depth of his gaze, as if it was not meant to disguise, but to amplify his presence. He wore it like a second skin, effortlessly merging its sharp elegance with his own quiet intensity.

His hands, clasped loosely in front of him, provided a stark contrast to his refined attire. The knuckles bore faint scars, the skin roughened by a history of hard work and violence—a reminder that he hadn't always walked among the elite. They were the hands of a man who had clawed his way to power and carried the lessons of that climb in every movement.

As he approached, a faint, woodsy cologne lingered in

the air—earthy and grounding, as though he brought a piece of the wild with him into the sophistication of the room. His sharp eyes swept the room, lingering for a moment on one of the towering centerpieces. "You've done a remarkable job tonight. These arrangements—they're exquisite. A reflection of their creator, no doubt."

"Thank you," I said, the compliment feeling oddly weighted.

His gaze shifted back to me, his smile deepening. "Dance with me."

I hesitated, my hand tightening slightly around the stem of my glass. My eyes flicked toward the edge of the room where Cassian had disappeared. Surely, he wouldn't approve of this.

But Damien's hand extended toward me, his invitation more of a command than a request. "Come now, Rosalie If I didn't know better I'd say you're scared of me." He chuckled, "Doll, it's a party, not a shakedown. Surely Cassian wouldn't begrudge his father one dance."

I swallowed hard, glancing around for a familiar face. None were nearby, and Damien's sharp gaze was unrelenting. My options were limited, and refusing him felt like a risk I wasn't ready to take.

Taking a steadying breath, I placed my hand in his, forcing a smile. "One dance," I said softly.

Damien's smile widened, though it didn't quite reach his eyes. "Of course."

As he led me toward the dance floor, a chill ran down my spine, though I couldn't quite place why.

Damien's hand was firm, his grip guiding but not rough as he led me to the center of the dance floor. The room felt bigger suddenly, as though everyone had taken a step back, leaving only the two of us under the soft glow of the chandeliers. The music shifted to something slower, more deliberate, and I was keenly aware of every pair of eyes that might be watching.

He placed one hand at my waist, the other holding mine with an almost paternal care that belied the razor's edge in his demeanor. His smile was polite, almost charming, but his eyes were calculating, dissecting me with every step.

"You've surprised me," Damien began smoothly as we started to move. His voice was calm, almost conversational, yet the undertone carried a weight that made it impossible to relax. "I admit, I didn't think you'd last this long."

I blinked, keeping my face neutral. "I didn't realize I was something to endure."

He chuckled low in his throat, the sound like a predator toying with its prey. "Not in the way you think. But I've seen women come and go in Cassian's life—none of them could handle what it truly means to stand beside him. Yet here you are."

"I'm not most women," I said evenly, though my heart raced. I wasn't sure whether it was from the tension of his words or the weight of his scrutiny.

"No, you're not," he agreed, his tone thoughtful. "Which is why I'm curious, Rosalie. What is it that drives you? What keeps you anchored to my son and his...profession, despite its... challenges?"

I hesitated, my mind racing for a diplomatic response. "I care about Cassian, can't it be as simple as that?" I said finally, meeting his gaze head-on. "And I believe in him."

His lips twitched into a faint smile, though his eyes remained cold. "A noble answer. But caring for Cassian, believing in him—those are not easy tasks. Especially now, with the Reapers circling like vultures."

I didn't respond immediately, letting the sway of the dance ground me. Finally, I said, "Cassian is capable, and isn't going to be intimidated or backed into a corner. He'll figure a way out, and when he does... they'll never see it coming." I faintly smiled, remembering our first encounter and how it had blindsided me then.

"Capable, yes," Damien said, his grip tightening slightly at my waist. "But even the strongest need allies. Family. Guidance."

His words hung between us, a subtle challenge wrapped in fatherly concern. My chest tightened as I realized where this conversation was headed.

"You want me to convince him to work with you," I said

quietly, cutting through the niceties.

Damien's smile widened, but it didn't soften. "I want what's best for the Moreau name. For our legacy. Cassian's pride is admirable, but it's also dangerous. He thinks he can fight this war alone, and it's only a matter of time before that arrogance costs him everything."

"And you think you're the solution," I replied, my voice steady despite the knot forming in my stomach.

"I think," he said, his voice dropping to a near-whisper, "that you're in a unique position to help him see reason. You care about him, don't you?"

"Of course I do," I said, my jaw tightening.

"Then prove it," Damien said, his eyes narrowing slightly. "Before the Reapers take everything he's built—including you."

The weight of his words hung heavy in the air, but Damien wasn't finished. His voice lowered further, a shadow of menace beneath his calm tone. "The best way to win a war is not to fight fair—it's to strike where your enemy least expects."

I frowned, something about the remark unsettling me, though I couldn't put my finger on why. "Cassian isn't trying to play dirty. He's just trying to protect what's his."

"And that's precisely why he'll fail," Damien replied smoothly. "Blood ties mean nothing without loyalty—remember that, Rosalie. You might think he's untouchable, but the Reapers don't just aim for the head. They dismantle from within, piece by piece. And by the time the damage is done, even the strongest legacy can crumble."

My chest tightened at his ominous words, and I hesitated, trying to decipher the layers behind them.

Cassian's voice cut through the tension like a blade, sharp and commanding. "Father."

Damien's grip on my waist eased, his hand falling away as he turned to face Cassian with a practiced smile. "Ah, Cassian. Perfect timing. I was just about to let your lovely Rosalie return to you."

The tension in Cassian's jaw was unmistakable, though his expression remained controlled. "How generous of you," he said, his tone clipped.

Damien inclined his head slightly, his polished demeanor unshaken. "I never cared much for charity events anyway," he remarked, stepping back with the smooth confidence of someone who always left on their own terms. "They're all corrupt, masking greed with good intentions."

"I never trust a man's buried six feet down, unless I've done it myself—and yet, here you are. Stay the fuck away from her—I thought I made myself clear the last time."

"Then I suggest you don't leave her side," he quipped, glancing at both of us a second too long. "Good night, Rosalie. I enjoyed the conversation."

Cassian's sharp gray eyes followed his father's retreat, a muscle ticking in his jaw. He didn't say anything until Damien had disappeared into the crowd, his commanding presence dissolving like smoke in the chaos of the gala.

I exhaled slowly, the weight of the encounter settling in my chest. My hands trembled slightly at my sides, and Cassian's gaze snapped to me, his expression softening instantly. Without a word, he placed a warm hand at the small of my back, guiding me away from the dance floor and toward the bar.

He signaled the bartender, ordering a glass of champagne before sliding it into my hand. "Drink," he instructed gently, his fingers lingering over mine for a moment.

I took a sip, the bubbles sharp on my tongue, but it did little to settle the nerves Damien had unraveled.

Cassian leaned against the bar, his attention entirely on me. "What did he say to you?"

I shook my head, unsure how to explain the strange dance of threats and persuasion woven into Damien's words. "He just... he wanted me to help convince you to work with him. He said you couldn't fight this alone."

Cassian's eyes darkened, his lips pressing into a thin line. "And did he happen to mention why he's suddenly so interested in my business?"

I hesitated, the echoes of Damien's ominous remarks

lingering in my mind. "He said the Reapers struck three more of his businesses tonight. That they're closing in on you, on everything."

Cassian exhaled sharply, his gaze flicking away for a brief moment before locking back onto mine. "My father always has an angle," he said finally, his voice low. "Don't let his concern fool you. He's as much a threat as anyone else."

I studied him, the weight of his words settling over me like a shroud. "Do you think he's lying about the Reapers?"

"No," Cassian admitted, his fingers brushing against my arm in a fleeting touch meant to ground me. "But his solution to the problem is where the real danger lies."

I nodded slowly, taking another sip of champagne as Cassian's hand slid from my arm to rest possessively at my waist. The protective gesture should have calmed me, but the undercurrent of tension in his touch only heightened the unease curling in my stomach.

"Whatever he said," Cassian continued, his voice soft but firm, "don't let him get into your head, Rosalie. My father doesn't play fair, and he doesn't take prisoners."

His words were a warning, but also a reassurance. I wasn't alone in this—not with Cassian by my side.

"Let's get through this night," he said, his tone shifting slightly as he placed a kiss on my temple. "And then we'll deal with whatever comes next."

I nodded, leaning into him as the chaos of the gala continued to swirl around us, but the chill left behind by Damien's words refused to fade.

CHAPTER THIRTY-TWO

The solarium was quiet, save for the soft rustling of papers as I flipped through the proposal again. The sunlight filtered through the glass ceiling, casting dappled patterns across the room, but even the warm glow couldn't soften the knot of frustration tightening in my chest.

I sipped my coffee, the bitter taste sparking something within me as I stared down at the glossy renderings spread across the table. The future Sophia had envisioned for Ivy & Bloom looked nothing like the shop I'd grown up in.

The first image was a sleek, modern storefront—polished glass windows framed by matte black trim, the name *Ivy & Bloom* in minimalist gold lettering. It was undeniably beautiful, the kind of design that would draw the eye of the elite clients Sophia worked with, but it felt... classic. Cold.

I flipped to the next rendering. The interior was spacious, with towering shelving units and strategically placed floral displays under dramatic lighting. The rustic charm of the original shop was gone, replaced by something curated and commercialized. It wasn't bad. In fact, it was the kind of shop that could win awards, the kind that could turn Ivy & Bloom into a destination rather than a neighborhood staple.

But as I studied the polished marble countertops and the perfectly arranged rows of flowers in color-coded perfection, I couldn't shake the feeling that it wasn't mine.

I sighed, setting my coffee mug down as I shuffled the papers into a neat stack. The more I looked at these proposals, the harder it became to picture the soul of the shop in these pristine renderings.

The shop as it stood now wasn't perfect—far from it. The wooden floorboards creaked in spots, and the faint scent of soil and eucalyptus always lingered in the air no matter how often we cleaned. But it felt *real*. The mismatched pots and vases, the small bursts of color from flowers that weren't in any arrangement but simply there because they made us happy—that was what made Ivy & Bloom special.

I leaned back in my chair, rubbing my temples. Sophia's vision was everything the shop *should* be if I wanted it to succeed in this new world—Cassian's world. But it was also everything it *shouldn't* be if I wanted it to remain the heart of the neighborhood.

Reaching for my coffee, I took another sip, the heat seeping through the ceramic warming my fingers. My gaze flicked back to the renderings, and I found myself staring at a particular photo. It was of a section designed to mimic a library, with flowers arranged in tall vases alongside bookshelves. Aesthetically, it was stunning, but it lacked the charm of the actual reading nook we'd set up with a threadbare loveseat and a coffee table filled with magazines from the early 2000s.

I smiled faintly, the memory of a customer dozing off there after browsing the hydrangeas tugging at the edges of my frustration. *That's what Ivy & Bloom is,* I thought. A place where people lingered, not because they had to, but because they wanted to.

The smile faded as I picked up another image, this one showing a sleek, corporate-inspired workspace in the back for consultations. It was worlds away from the cozy, often chaotic space where Lena and I worked side by side, sometimes with a cat from the alley sprawled out on the counter.

As much as I respected Sophia's expertise, I couldn't shake the feeling that her Ivy & Bloom would lose the essence of what made the shop *home.*

I sighed again, setting the papers down and staring at the sunlight streaming through the glass. Maybe I was holding on too tightly to the past. Maybe this new version was what Ivy & Bloom needed to survive.

I stacked the renderings neatly and tucked them back into the folder, my frustration simmering under the surface. This wasn't a decision I could make sitting in the solarium, staring at pictures that felt more like someone else's dream than mine.

Grabbing my coat and bag, I decided to go straight to the source. Sophia needed to hear this from me directly, and I needed answers—real answers, not glossy proposals.

The brisk air outside cooled the tension in my chest as I slipped into the waiting SUV. Sierra glanced at me from the passenger seat, her eyebrow arched in curiosity. "Where to?"

"Sophia's office," I replied, pulling the folder closer to my chest.

Marcus glanced at me in the rearview mirror but said nothing, starting the engine. The drive to Sophia's office was mercifully short, though I used every second of it to rehearse what I wanted to say. I needed to be firm but respectful, to make it clear that while I appreciated her work, this wasn't what I envisioned for Ivy & Bloom.

Sophia's office was just as elegant as she was—sleek, modern, and polished to perfection. Her assistant ushered me into her glass-walled office, where Sophia was seated behind a pristine desk, her laptop open and a cappuccino steaming beside it.

"Rosalie!" She looked up, her expression brightening. "This is a surprise. What can I do for you?"

I set the folder on her desk, offering a small smile. "I wanted to talk about the proposal. It's beautifully done, really. But... it's not what I'm looking for."

Sophia's smile faltered slightly, though she recovered quickly, leaning back in her chair. "Not what you're looking for?" she repeated, her tone careful.

I nodded, flipping open the folder to the first rendering. "This is stunning, but it doesn't feel like Ivy & Bloom. The shop has always been a little messy, a little personal, and this—" I gestured to the image of the modern storefront "—isn't that. It's corporate, sleek, and while I understand the appeal, it doesn't feel *right*."

Sophia studied me for a moment, her fingers steepled beneath her chin. "I see," she said slowly. "But Rosalie, these changes aren't just about aesthetics. They're about growth—about taking Ivy & Bloom to the next level."

I hesitated, wondering how to phrase what I wanted to say without sounding dismissive. "I'm not sure I want Ivy & Bloom to become something it's not just for the sake of growth. It's always been a part of the community, not just another high-end shop. I'm worried this expansion will strip away everything that makes it special."

Sophia's lips pressed into a thin line, and for the first time, I saw a flicker of frustration in her usually composed demeanor. "Rosalie," she said carefully, "I understand your concerns, but these changes weren't entirely my idea."

I frowned. "What do you mean?"

She hesitated, glancing down at the folder before meeting my gaze. "Cassian was the one who insisted on the expansion. He was very specific about which cities the new locations should target—New York, Los Angeles, Miami, London. He wanted Ivy & Bloom to become an international brand."

The words hit me like a cold wave. I stared at her, trying to process what she was saying. "Cassian insisted?" He had never once mentioned his involvement in this. Not once.

Sophia nodded, her expression softening slightly. "He didn't want to overwhelm you with the details, but he made it clear that this was the direction he wanted to take. He believes in Ivy & Bloom's potential, Rosalie. He sees what it can become."

My mind raced, a storm of emotions churning in my chest. Cassian had made this decision—this monumental decision—without consulting me. And while his intentions might have been good, it felt like yet another reminder that the shop was slipping further and further out of my control.

I forced a tight smile, nodding slightly. "I appreciate the insight, Sophia. Thank you."

She smiled, though it didn't quite reach her eyes. "Of course. If you'd like, we can revisit the designs and find a way to blend the old with the new. But trust me, Rosalie, this expansion could be the best thing to ever happen to Ivy & Bloom."

I stood, gathering the folder and forcing my voice to remain steady. "We may have to disagree on that one." I said, grabbing my bag and walked out. My thoughts were a tangled mess. Cassian believed in the shop's potential—but at what cost? And why hadn't he trusted me enough to discuss it with me first? The questions lingered, heavy and unanswered, as I climbed back into the SUV.

"Ivy & Bloom," I instructed, my impatience at an all time-high.

The air inside Ivy & Bloom was thick with the scent of fresh lilies and freesia, a comforting reminder of the shop's roots amidst the chaos of everything else in my life; they did little to comfort me in that moment with a dreadful gut feeling creeping up. The soft bell over the door chimed as I entered, and Lena glanced up from where she was rearranging a bouquet at the counter.

"Hey, Rosalie," she said brightly, though there was a slight edge to her tone, as if she were trying to keep something in check. "Perfect timing. Can you give me a hand? I want to move some of the display stands into the back storage space to free up some room for the new inventory."

"Of course," I replied, shrugging off my coat and draping it over a chair. "Marcus, can you help with the heavier stands?"

Marcus, leaning against the doorframe with his arms crossed, raised an eyebrow but nodded, pushing off the wall. "Sure."

As the two of them headed toward the displays, I waited a beat, listening for the sound of movement in the back. The moment I was sure they were occupied, I slipped behind the counter and into the office.

The familiar space greeted me with a sense of both nostalgia and unease. It was the same office where my father used to keep his neatly stacked invoices and scribbled notes on customer requests. Now, it felt foreign—too orderly, too impersonal. Lena's touch was evident in the way everything was labeled and color-coded.

I stepped up to the desk, my heart thudding as I pulled open the top drawer. Inside was the ledger Lena had been using, its pages meticulously filled out in her careful handwriting. I flipped through it quickly, scanning for any inconsistencies, but everything seemed in perfect order. Every expense, every transaction, every deposit—it all balanced seamlessly. Even the ten thousand and some change that I'd diverted for my own purposes.

Frustration prickled at the edges of my mind. Something felt off, and yet this ledger didn't reveal anything. I closed it and glanced around the room, my gaze landing on Lena's bag sitting on the chair in the corner.

Breaking girl-code was the last thing I wanted to do, but the nagging suspicion in my gut wouldn't be silenced. Swallowing my guilt, I stepped toward the bag, glancing over my shoulder to ensure I was still alone.

I unzipped it carefully, my hands trembling slightly. Inside was a cluttered mix of personal items—lipstick, a wallet, a small notebook. And then I saw it: another ledger. This one was smaller, its black cover unmarked and inconspicuous.

My breath hitched as I pulled it out and flipped it open. Unlike the official ledger, this one wasn't neat or precise. The handwriting was rushed, almost frantic in places, and the numbers scrawled across the pages told a completely different story. Transactions that didn't match the ones in the official ledger. Expenses that shouldn't exist. And deposits that were suspiciously large.

A chill ran down my spine as I realized what I was holding. This was the real ledger—the one Lena didn't want anyone to see.

The realization hit me like a freight train, cold and unforgiving. My fingers tightened around the edges of the small ledger as the implications of what I was reading sank in. The discrepancies, the hidden transactions, the unexplained deposits—it all pointed to one thing.

Cassian.

My knees felt weak, and I lowered myself into the chair behind the desk, the creak of the wood barely registering in my ears. Page after page detailed sums of money funneled through Ivy & Bloom, cloaked in layers of fake transactions that would look innocent enough to the untrained eye. But I knew better. This wasn't a true representation of the shop's profits.

He was using my shop to launder his dirty money.

My throat tightened as I stared at the incriminating numbers, my mind racing to piece together what this meant. He'd never said anything, never hinted that the shop was anything more than a business he was protecting for me. But now, it was clear. This wasn't just my father's legacy anymore—it was a tool. A cog in the complex, dangerous machine Cassian controlled.

A bitter laugh escaped my lips, though it sounded more like a strangled gasp. Of course. Of course, Cassian would do this without telling me. It was just like him to keep me in the dark, to decide what I needed to know and what I didn't, all under the guise of protecting me. My hands trembled as I flipped through the ledger, each entry feeling like another betrayal.

How long had this been going on? Since before the shop became his? Or was it only after? The questions clawed at my mind, each one more painful than the last. And Lena— did she know? Was she complicit in all of this, or was she just another pawn in Cassian's game?

The sound of footsteps from the storage room jolted me out of my thoughts. I slammed the ledger shut, stuffing it back into Lena's bag with shaking hands. My heart pounded as I zipped the bag closed and straightened, trying to mask the storm raging inside me.

A moment later, the office door opened, and Lena poked

her head in. "Everything okay in here?" she asked, her tone light but her eyes sharp.

"Yeah," I managed, forcing a tight smile. "Just... organizing a few things."

Her gaze lingered on me for a moment longer before she nodded. "Good. I was just about to grab some inventory sheets. Marcus and I finished moving the stands."

"Great," I said, my voice too high, too forced. "I'll be out in a minute."

She left without another word, and I exhaled shakily, my mind racing. I couldn't confront Lena—not yet. Not without more answers. And Cassian... I wasn't sure I was ready to face him, either. Not until I figured out how to navigate the truth without losing everything in the process.

For now, I would keep this to myself. But the seed of doubt had been planted, and there was no turning back.

CHAPTER THIRTY-THREE

"Do you trust me, Rosalie?"

Cassian's voice cut through the hum of the SUV as we sped toward the Marquess. I turned to look at him, his gray eyes locked on mine, piercing as ever. The question lingered between us, heavy and loaded, as if he already knew the answer but wanted to hear me say it.

I hesitated, my hands tightening in my lap. "Should I?" He'd given me plenty of reasons to trust him, and then... others that threw all of that away.

His lips curved into a faint, unreadable smile. "You should."

I looked out the window, watching the city lights blur into streaks of gold and silver against the darkness. The tension in the car was palpable, though neither Marcus nor Sierra spoke a word. They were both focused, their postures rigid as they scanned the road ahead.

"You still haven't told me why we're doing this," I said quietly, breaking the silence. "Why the sudden change of heart? A truce isn't exactly your style."

Cassian leaned back, his expression darkening. "Because even a leader knows when to pause a war to rebuild his resources; at this rate, the Reapers plan to bleed us dry and we can't continue to striking them at this rate."

The tension inside the car pressed down on me, the weight of unspoken truths and lingering doubts making it hard to breathe. Outside, patrons lined up under the iconic polished brass plaque bore its name—*The Marquess*—etched in elegant, understated script.

"You still haven't told me why this truce matters now," I said, keeping my voice even. "What's changed?"

Cassian leaned back, his fingers drumming lightly against his knee. "The Reapers are pushing harder than we anticipated. The last strike cost us more than I'm willing to admit. Sometimes, you have to step back and realign the board."

"A strategic pause," I said, turning to face him fully. "Will they agree to a temporary peace?"

"I don't know, but I'm covering all of my bases. If they want their empire to remain intact, they'll listen, but if not, there are other means at work," he paused, shaking his head, "I just don't want to get to that point."

His words were calculated, deliberate. But there was something beneath them—something darker. I didn't press further, though my chest tightened with the weight of everything he wasn't saying.

As the SUV rolled to a stop, Cassian turned to me, his expression softening ever so slightly. "You've been distant," he said, his gray eyes searching mine. "What's on your mind?"

I opened my mouth, then closed it, the words tangling in my throat. "Nothing," I said finally. "Just ready for this to be over."

Cassian's gaze lingered for a beat too long, his jaw tightening before he nodded. Without another word, he stepped out of the car, extending a hand to me as the valet opened my door.

The low thrum of the club's music vibrated through the soles of my shoes as I stepped onto the sidewalk. Cassian's hand was warm, steady as he led me toward the entrance, but his grip tightened ever so slightly.

"Whatever it is you're keeping from me," he murmured as we approached the double doors, "just remember—I always find out." It was a low threat, but his words didn't scare me. If anything, I wanted to laugh, but I was damned sure he already knew about the money laundering. I wanted to laugh because I'd been such a fool, this entire time, but the moment this was all over, the moment I didn't have a threat against my life looming overhead...

I shook the thought free of my mind, focusing on the present.

The familiar wave of tension greeted us as we stepped into the club's polished interior. The Marquess, with its muted lighting and understated luxury, buzzed with the kind of energy only power could command. Cassian's hand remained firmly on my back as he guided me through the dimly lit corridors, past velvet-draped alcoves where secrets were whispered and deals brokered.

The same meeting room awaited us, its heavy oak doors already ajar. Inside, the space was exactly as I remembered—dim, deliberately imposing, with a long table flanked by leather chairs. The air carried a faint scent of expensive cigars and aged whiskey, a subtle reminder of the men who ruled here.

Cassian led me to our seats, pulling out my chair with grace of a gentleman that bordered on mechanical. His movements were careful, deliberate, as if each step were part of a larger game, always being watched, analyzed, scrutinized. The players were already in place, their expressions a mix of curiosity and wariness as they watched us enter.

Several of them stared at me, suddenly dismissing their gaze to fall on Cassian—the one with the true power.

At the head of the table sat a man who looked more like the enforcer of a gang than the leader of an empire. His arms, corded with muscle, were bare beneath the rolled-up sleeves of a faded plaid shirt, revealing a tapestry of ink that stretched from his knuckles to the curve of his neck. The tattoos were a chaotic mix—tribal patterns, skulls, barbed wire, and symbols that seemed to hold meaning only to him, creating a mosaic of intimidation. A black snake coiled around his left forearm, its head poised just above his wrist like it was ready to strike.

His jeans, worn and frayed at the edges, were a stark contrast to the meticulously polished boots he wore, scuffed only at the toes, as though they'd seen their share of confrontation. His fingers, adorned with heavy rings, tapped against the scarred wood of the table in a rhythm that betrayed his impatience. The knuckles on his right hand were red and slightly swollen, hinting at a recent fight or punishment dealt.

His face, angular and weathered, bore the marks of a life lived hard—a faint scar bisected his right eyebrow, and another cut across his chin. His dark hair was cropped short, but not carefully maintained, and stubble shadowed his jawline, giving him a perpetually rough look. His eyes, dark and narrow, flicked around the room, sharp and searching, but lacking the weight of true command.

He slouched slightly in his chair, exuding a kind of lazy confidence, but there was something performative about it—like a man playing a role he wasn't entirely suited for. His movements were calculated, his posture relaxed but deliberate, as if he were trying to mask unease with bravado. Yet it was the way he glanced—quick, almost nervous—to the man seated at his right that gave him away. Despite the ink, the swagger, and the scarred hands, it was clear he was a figurehead, a puppet whose strings were being pulled from the shadows.

My heart quickened as the realization settled. This was deliberate—an illusion crafted to keep outsiders guessing. And for a brief moment, I wondered if Cassian already knew or if this was something I'd have to decide how to handle.

I glanced at him out of the corner of my eye. Cassian was composed, his gray eyes cold as steel, his body relaxed but ready. He didn't let a single flicker of doubt cross his features, though I could feel the weight of his determined strategy pressing down on the room.

Cassian sat down beside me, his every move deliberate, exuding authority without needing to utter a word. His calm exterior was a sharp contrast to the tension crackling in the air. I glanced at him briefly, his jaw set, his gaze piercing as he surveyed the table. This wasn't a negotiation—it was a battlefield disguised in civility, and everyone here knew it.

The tattooed man at the head of the table leaned forward, his fingers still tapping against the table in an uneven rhythm. The metallic clink of his rings against the wood punctuated his words as he spoke.

"Seven million," he said, his voice gravelly but steady. "Untraceable. Gold, gemstones, diamonds—you know the drill. And a cut of your operations in the north sector. Say... a thirty percent stake."

My eyes went wide at the mention of so much cash. I shook my head, having realized more than ever that I didn't truly know the man I sat next to.

Cassian's gray eyes narrowed slightly, the subtle shift in his expression enough to silence the low murmurs from the men seated around the table. He let the demand hang in the air for a moment before leaning back in his chair, his arms resting casually on the armrests. It was a deliberate move—one that would cripple Cassian and his operations for years to come—or so I suspected.

"That wasn't the deal," Cassian said, his tone even, but edged with authority. "The agreement was a ceasefire in exchange for operational access—not permanent ownership."

The tattooed man's fingers stilled, his eyes narrowing as he leaned back in his chair. His façade of confidence cracked slightly, but he quickly masked it with a crooked grin.

"You've got to understand," he said, his voice laced with faux amiability, "the streets don't care about your pride." His voice dropped to a dangerous level, "You want to keep what's yours? Then pay for the privilege, or we'll carve it out of your territory."

Cassian's lips pressed into a thin line. His eyes flicked briefly to the man seated at the tattooed man's right—a wiry figure with glasses and teardrop tattoos trickling down his face.

"I can get you the stones," Cassian said, his voice cutting through the room like a blade. "But thirty percent of the north sector? That's off the table."

The tattooed man's grin faltered, and his gaze shifted to his companions for just a fraction of a second before he caught himself. He leaned forward, folding his arms on the table. "Then we've got a problem, Moreau. My people are done playing your games. You want peace? Show us you're serious."

Cassian didn't flinch. "You'll have your assurance in the form of seven million in untraceable assets. And you'll have it within hours. That's the deal. Take it or leave it."

The room fell silent, the weight of Cassian's words settling heavily on everyone present. The tattooed man hesitated, his eyes darting toward the men who flanked his sides. I followed his gaze, catching the faintest of nods from several of them.

A collective decision, or was there something more?

"Fine," the tattooed man said finally, dragging the word out like it pained him to say it. His fingers curled into a fist on the table, the inked snake on his forearm coiling as his muscles tensed. "But you'd better deliver fast. We're not in the habit of waiting, and patience ain't exactly our strong suit."

His tone carried more than just a threat—it was a challenge, daring Cassian to falter. Around the room, a few of the other men shifted in their seats, their wary glances speaking volumes about the volatile air.

Cassian inclined his head slightly, his composure unshaken. It was a gesture of agreement, but not submission. His voice was low, measured. "You'll have what you need. We'll reconvene here in two hours."

The tattooed man smirked, leaning back in his chair as if to mask his irritation. "Two hours," he repeated, tapping a heavy ring against his glass. "Clock's ticking, Moreau. Don't make me regret this truce."

Cassian's gaze flicked briefly to the man's hand before returning to meet his eyes, unflinching. "You'll get your package," he said, the weight of his words pressing into the room like a storm cloud.

Without waiting for a reply, Cassian pushed back his chair and stood, his movements eager to be free of the Reaper's presence. I followed suit, struggling to keep my pulse steady as the eyes of the room burned into our backs. The tension hung heavy, thick as smoke, as we stepped into the hallway and left the negotiation chamber behind.

The moment the doors shut, the silence between us crackled with unspoken words. Cassian walked a step ahead of me, his shoulders set, his stride purposeful. His outward calm didn't fool me—I'd spent enough time with him to notice the small signs of stress: the way his hand flexed at his side, the slight clench of his jaw.

I matched his pace, my heels clicking softly against the polished floor. "Are you alright?" I asked quietly, glancing up at him.

Cassian's jaw tightened, his gaze locked straight ahead. "No," he said after a beat, his voice clipped. "But I will be."

I pressed further, unable to shake the unease that had settled in my chest. "What do they really want?"

He exhaled sharply, his hand brushing over the back of his neck before falling to his side again. "Control. Territory. Leverage. Same as always." His tone was neutral, but I caught the edge of frustration simmering beneath it.

The weight of his words settled heavily on my shoulders, and I looked away, my mind racing. "Do you think they'll honor the truce if you meet their demands?"

Cassian's lips twitched, though it wasn't quite a smile. "Honor's not exactly their currency," he said dryly. "They'll take what they can get until they think they've got the upper hand. Then they'll come back for more."

I swallowed hard, the reality of his world pressing in on me once again. "Then why agree at all?"

He stopped abruptly, turning to face me. The intensity in his gaze was startling, and I had to fight the urge to take a step back. "Because sometimes, Rosalie, you have to give a little to win a lot. I'm simply buying time until the next move. This won't be the last battle, not in a long shot."

That's what worried me—this world he lived in, the

constant danger, ever-present threats, gun fights and robberies—they never seemed to end.

His words were cold, calculated, and I realized then that this wasn't just strategy—it was survival. Cassian wasn't playing for peace; he was playing to outlast them.

I nodded, though the knot in my stomach tightened. "Two hours," I murmured, echoing the tattooed man's words.

Cassian's expression softened slightly, his hand brushing against mine in a fleeting gesture of reassurance. "That's all I need," he said, his voice quieter now but no less determined. "Come on. Let's get what we need."

As we walked on, the tension between us eased, but it didn't disappear entirely. Cassian's world was one of shifting alliances and dangerous gambles, and I couldn't shake the feeling that we were standing on the edge of something far more precarious than I could yet see.

The jewelry store was a paradox of faded grandeur and dubious dealings, its polished counters and velvet-lined cases clashing with the faint scent of cigarette smoke that clung to the air. Glass displays sparkled under harsh fluorescent lights, their brilliance almost too forced, as if to compensate for the threadbare carpet beneath and the peeling gold leaf on the edges of the shelves. The unmistakable sound of voices lacked the refinement one might expect, punctuated instead by muttered negotiations and the occasional glance over a shoulder. A faint edge of tension underpinned the atmosphere, the kind that hinted this wasn't just a place for legitimate business—but one where fortunes were both made and laundered.

The moment we stepped inside, the sharp scent of metal and polish greeted me, mingling with the faint musk of too many bodies in too small a space. Cassian moved with purpose, his gray eyes sweeping the room, assessing every angle, every potential threat, while Marcus and two others flanked him like a silent phalanx.

The owner, a pudgy man with a nervous smile and a gold chain as large for his thick neck, greeted Cassian with a deference that bordered on fear. "Mr. Moreau, always a pleasure," he said, wringing his hands as he gestured toward a back room. "Right this way."

The room was cramped but secure, its walls lined with locked cases and the constant buzz of a security system thrumming through the air. A large metal table dominated the center, and on it lay several gleaming velvet trays, each laden with an assortment of gemstones—rubies, emeralds, sapphires, and diamonds that caught the harsh overhead light like captive stars.

Cassian didn't speak, simply gestured to Marcus, who set the first briefcase on the table with a solid *thunk*. The wiry man's eyes widened as he opened it, revealing neatly stacked bundles of cash. His trembling fingers traced one of the bundles reverently before he nodded and began assembling the gems into a waiting case.

I stayed close to Cassian, my heart thudding in my chest as I watched the transaction unfold. The gemstones were weighed, inspected under magnifying glasses, and carefully loaded into a black case lined with padded compartments. It was meticulous, almost hypnotic, and I could feel the tension in the room shift—business was business, but everyone knew what this exchange represented.

Cassian's phone buzzed, breaking the silence. He frowned, pulling it from his pocket, his focus momentarily diverted as he scanned the screen. Marcus leaned in, murmuring something low and urgent, and Cassian stepped away slightly, his attention split between the call and his lieutenant's report.

It was the distraction I hadn't dared to hope for.

My hands trembled as I reached for the black case, the weight of it heavier than I expected as I cradled it against my chest. My breath hitched, and I forced myself to move, my heels clicking against the tile floor as I made my way toward the door.

There was no going back now, not after this, and I knew in some ways, I was sealing my fate, and maybe even ending my life—but I trusted my instincts far more than anyone else in the moment.

Alarmingly, no one stopped me.

Not Marcus, whose sharp eyes were fixed on Cassian, and not the wiry man, who was too busy counting the second briefcase of cash. My pulse roared in my ears as I slipped out of the back room, through the showroom, and into the cool night air.

The city was alive around me—bright lights, distant laughter, the hum of engines. My eyes darted frantically, searching for escape, and then I saw it—a yellow cab idling at the curb.

Without a second thought, I yanked open the door and slid inside, the case pressed tightly to my chest. "Drive," I said, my voice sharp, urgent.

The driver turned, his expression confused. "Where to?"

"Just go," I snapped, not daring to look back.

As the cab pulled into traffic, the adrenaline began to crash over me. My hands were clammy, my heart racing. I didn't know what I was doing, only that I had to do *something*—for myself, for Ivy & Bloom, for all the pieces of my life that had been swallowed by Cassian's world.

CHAPTER THIRTY-FOUR

The scent hit me first—a heady mix of charred oak barrels, yeast, and the faintest whiff of caramelized sugar that clung to the air like a ghost of stories past. The dim, amber lighting cast long shadows across the cavernous whiskey distillery, its industrial beauty both intimidating and alluring. Rows of gleaming copper stills towered like sentinels, their curved bodies reflecting the faint glow of exposed Edison bulbs strung across the ceiling. The rhythmic hum of machinery pulsed faintly in the background, blending with the occasional creak of timber from the stacked barrels lining the far walls.

I stepped inside, the echo of my heels swallowed by the sheer vastness of the space. The briefcase hung heavy in my hand, its significance outweighing its physical mass. My heart pounded with each step, the gravity of what I'd done settling deeper into my chest. The air was thick with history, as though the walls themselves bore witness to the clandestine deals and whispered betrayals that had unfolded here.

Cassian's name flashed across my phone for the fifth time in as many minutes. My fingers hovered over the screen, but I didn't answer. I couldn't. Not yet.

The screen dimmed before lighting up again, the

persistent vibration gnawing at my nerves.

Cassian: Answer the phone.
Cassian: Rosalie, where the hell are you?
Cassian: *Do not make me come looking for you.*

My grip tightened on the briefcase handle as the weight of his words hit. The tone, even through text, carried the promise of retribution—not just anger but something deeper, more desperate.

The phone buzzed again, the screen illuminating his name like a beacon I wasn't ready to face.

Cassian: *You have no idea what you've done. So help me.*

My heart raced, his words digging under my skin.

Sliding the phone back into my pocket, I ignored the next vibration, the noise fading into the background of the distillery's sounds. Whatever fury or frustration Cassian had for me could wait. There were things I needed to figure out—truths I couldn't uncover while trapped under his thumb.

The distillery was colder than I remembered, or maybe it was just me. My pulse roared in my ears, a steady drumbeat of apprehension as I approached the tall, massive doors near the back of the room. Pushing them open to reveal the familiar conference room where this all began, I realized the irony was not lost on me.

A man stood there, his back to me, inspecting the contents of a decanter held up to the light. He turned at the sound of my approach, his face shadowed but familiar.

Damien's expression shifted subtly as I approached, the faint smirk playing on his lips deepening into something sharper, more sinister. He stepped away from the long wooden table, his broad frame moving with deliberate ease, like a predator circling prey that had just stumbled into its den.

"Well," he said, his voice smooth and dripping with condescension, "look at you. Clever little Rosalie, walking straight into the lion's den." His dark eyes flicked to the briefcase in my hand before meeting mine again. "And alone, no less. I must admit, you've surprised me."

I tightened my grip on the handle, forcing my voice to

remain steady. "I wasn't sure at first. It didn't all add up—Cassian, the Reapers, the attacks. But then I dug deeper, connected the dots, and it started to make sense."

"Did it now?" he asked, the faintest trace of amusement in his tone. He crossed his arms, the movement casual yet defensive—as if he needed protection against me.

"It started with the license plates," I said, my voice stronger now. "The vehicles—they were sold under aliases, but they all came from the same dealership. On paper, it looked clean. But when I checked the business registry..." I paused, my chest tightening. "I'll be honest, I expected to come across the name Damon Cross or one of this known associates, but imagine my surprise when that wasn't the name I saw... Was it?"

Damien laughed, full bellied and rich, pure amusement rolling off his shoulder.

"It was you." I said, my voice louder, braver. "Damon Cross isn't just some rival, is he? He is a person you invented to operate in the shadows, under the guise of your enemies."

The room felt like it froze, the weight of my words hanging heavily in the stale air. Damien's smirk widened, a slow, deliberate movement that sent a chill down my spine.

"Well done," he said softly, his tone equal parts admiration and mockery. "You're sharper than I gave you credit for. I knew I had underestimated you, Rosalie, but bravo—you've truly outdone yourself." He took a step closer, his presence foreboding. "But tell me, what exactly do you plan to do with that knowledge?"

I swallowed hard, my fingers flexing against the leather of the briefcase. "That depends. Are you going to deny it?"

"Deny it?" He laughed, the sound low and dark, echoing off the walls of the distillery. "Why would I deny it? Yes, I'm Damon Cross. And yes, everyone was so foolish to see what they wanted to see—including my son—that by the time the Reapers and Cassian's men realize it, there won't be much left of them at all."

"The Reapers? They're useful, but only just. Puppets,

really—unsuspecting soldiers in a war they don't even realize they're fighting. I gave them a target, fed their ego, and pointed them at Cassian's facilities like a loaded gun." He paused, his voice dropping to a razor's edge. "It's not about them, Rosalie. It's never been about them."

I felt my stomach churn as his words sank in. "You manipulated them," I said, my voice quieter but no less accusatory. "You turned them into pawns to wear Cassian down."

Damien's lips curved into a slow, deliberate smile. "Manipulated? Perhaps. I prefer to think of it as setting the stage. The Reapers thought they were in control, that they were pushing Cassian to the brink. But in reality, they've been doing my work for me, eroding his empire piece by piece, while I remained comfortably in the shadows."

"And Cassian?" I demanded, anger rising to the surface. "What about him? Is he just another pawn to you?"

Damien's smirk faded, replaced by something colder, sharper. "Cassian left me to die—my own son," he said, his voice cutting through the air like a blade. "He's too proud, too stubborn to see the bigger picture. He's fighting battles he doesn't understand, bleeding resources for the sake of a war he's already losing."

Damien leaned back against the table's edge, his posture casual, but the glint in his eyes was anything but. He studied me for a moment, as though gauging how much to reveal. Then, with the air of a man savoring a final move in a long game, he began.

"Everything I've done up to this point was just setting the board," he said, his voice carrying an eerie calm. "Manipulating the Reapers, dismantling Cassian's empire piece by piece, bleeding his resources dry—it was necessary groundwork. But now, we're entering the final stage."

My breath hitched. There was something chilling in his tone, in the ease with which he spoke about such destruction. "What do you mean, final stage?" I asked, my voice steadier than I felt.

Damien's lips curved into a cruel smile. "The cargo, Rosalie. The shipments Cassian's been so desperate to intercept. The ones even the Reapers didn't fully know what they were transporting. They weren't rifles, or drugs. Weapons, sure—at least not in the traditional sense."

He leaned forward, his voice dropping to a conspiratorial whisper. "They're explosives. Untraceable, undetectable, and more advanced than anything the world has seen. A marvel of science and destruction. One device is enough to take down a building without leaving a shred of evidence. Entire empires could fall, and no one would even know who to blame."

A cold chill ran down my spine. "That's what this has all been about?" I said, my voice rising despite myself. "Smuggling explosives? Using Cassian's operations to move them without him even knowing?"

Damien's laugh was low, dark, and devoid of humor. "Cassian made it far too easy. His pride blinded him, made him predictable. He saw the Reapers as a threat and focused all his energy on them, never thinking to look at the shadow puppeteer pulling their strings. Meanwhile, I used his own facilities to store and transport the devices, and the Reapers for protection."

I stared at him, the weight of his confession settling like a stone in my chest. "Why are you telling me this?" I asked, though the answer was already forming in my mind.

Damien's expression hardened, his gaze cutting into me. "Because you're not leaving here alive, Rosalie. You've become a complication I can't afford. You're clever—cleverer than I gave you credit for—but that only makes you dangerous. And I can't risk you running back to Cassian with this. Surely, you understand that, don't you?"

As if Damien had sent a silent command, the doors behind me sealed shut, the metal clank of a lock secured in place from the outside. I pounded on the door, pushing and pulling with all my might but it didn't give.

I forced myself to stop and turn to face him. The flames in the fireplace's hearth flickered a sinister glow across the room, the heat become a smidge too stifling with the doors sealed now. Everything seemed to close in around me, the dim light casting ominous shadows over Damien's face.

My heart thundered in my chest, but I forced myself to stay calm, to think. "You don't have to do this," I said, grasping for any leverage I could find. "If you're as untouchable as you think, what's the harm in letting me go?"

When he didn't answer me, I brought the brief case to the surface of the table, opened it, and turned it toward him so he could see its contents clearly. "Then I'll buy my freedom."

He shook his head, tisking under his breath. "I'm sorry love, but your life is worthless to me. I could just kill you here and now, and consider those gemstones a bonus well deserved."

"Please, just let me go," I pleaded again.

Damien's smile was cold, merciless. "No," he paused, letting his gaze fall on mine. "You've already seen too much. And I don't take chances, Miss Quinn. Ever."

The sound of muffled voices outside the door sent my heart racing. Damien's attention snapped to it, his brows knitting in confusion as the door's lock clicked open.

It swung inward, revealing Cassian standing there, his silhouette framed by the harsh light spilling in from the hallway. His gray eyes were sharper than steel, his expression cold and unreadable, but the rigid line of his jaw and the pistol in his hand made it clear—he was out for blood. Behind him loomed Marcus, Sierra, and a few others, their shadows casting ominous figures on the walls.

"Well, isn't this a touching reunion?" Damien drawled, though the faint crack in his voice betrayed him.

Cassian stepped into the room, his movements deliberate and controlled. The tension in the air was suffocating, each step he took magnifying the lethal calm that radiated off him. "I figured you'd try to pull something like this, Father," Cassian said, his voice low, measured, and laced with venom. "The moment you crawled out of whatever grave you were supposed to be in, I knew you were up to something. Always playing a fucking game."

Damien chuckled, though it lacked its earlier bravado. "Chess, is it? You think you've got me in checkmate?"

Cassian's gaze didn't waver. "You were never ahead. Every move you made was predictable—feeding the Reapers, using them as pawns, leveraging my assets to cover your tracks. It was all so... sloppy. I let you play, let you think you were winning, because I wanted to see where it led. And here we are."

Damien's lips curled into a sneer, though there was a flicker of unease in his eyes. "Maybe so, but you never figured out the most important part..."

Cassian raised an eyebrow, his grip tightening on the pistol. "Haven't I?"

Before Damien could respond, he reached into his jacket, pulling out a small black detonator. My blood ran cold as I realized what it was, the faint gleam of the button like a death sentence.

"Don't!" I screamed, turning to face Cassian, "he's planted bombs all over the city, he intends to set them off, to cripple you. Cassian, you need to warn your people!"

He laughed a wicked, evil sound from the pit of his belly. "It's a bit too late for warnings," Damien hissed, his voice dripping with malice. "Those shipments—or rather explosives—you've been chasing—they're already in place. Strategically positioned across the city, ready to bring it all crashing down. You want to know what a real empire looks like, then watch yours fall."

"No!" I cried out, stepping forward instinctively, but Cassian's arm shot out, holding me back.

"Don't," Cassian said sharply, his eyes never leaving Damien. "My empire won't fall today; this isn't over."

"Oh, but it is," Damien said, his thumb hovering over the button. "And there's nothing you can do to stop it."

The soft click of the detonator echoed in the room like a death knell. The ground beneath us trembled violently, a deep, guttural rumble that felt as though it were tearing through the bones of the earth itself. Dust cascaded from the ceiling in fine, choking streams, and the iron beams of the distillery groaned ominously, protesting the force of the tremor.

I staggered, clutching the nearest table for support, my

heart hammering in my chest. The vibrations rattled through the metal tanks, causing their contents to slosh and echo in the cavernous space. Bottles fell from shelves, shattering in explosive bursts of glass that mirrored the chaos erupting in my mind.

Damien, however, wasn't triumphant. His smirk faded into a deep, furrowed scowl. His finger jabbed the button again, then again, his movements becoming increasingly erratic.

"What... what's happening?" he hissed, his voice laced with confusion and mounting panic. His dark eyes darted to the walls, to the vibrating machinery, then back to Cassian, who stood eerily still in the middle of the chaos.

The corners of Cassian's lips curled into a slow, deliberate smile, a look so lethal it sent a shiver down my spine. "Something wrong, Damien?" he asked, his tone mockingly calm, though his gray eyes gleamed with unrestrained fury.

Damien's jaw tightened, the detonator shaking in his grip. "This... this isn't right. The bombs aren't close enough to cause this. They couldn't..."

"Couldn't shake this place to its core?" Cassian supplied, his voice cutting through the cacophony like a blade. "No, they couldn't. Not the way you planned." He stepped forward, his pistol hanging loosely at his side, his presence dominating the space despite the chaos around him. "But I made a few adjustments."

Damien's eyes widened as realization began to dawn, his face paling beneath the flickering industrial lights. "What did you do?" he demanded, his voice cracking with desperation.

Cassian tilted his head, his expression almost pitying. "What I always do—clean up your mess. You see, Father, I intercepted the plans for your little explosives. It wasn't hard. You've always been predictable, relying on arrogance to carry you through." He gestured toward the trembling walls, his voice dropping into a deadly whisper. "Every bomb you set up, every strategic position you thought would cripple me... I relocated them."

Damien's lips parted in disbelief, his composure unraveling with every word Cassian spoke. "You're lying," he spat, though the tremor in his voice betrayed him.

"Am I?" Cassian countered, his smile turning sharp and dangerous. "Right now, those bombs are doing exactly what they were designed to do—eliminate threats. Except the threats they're targeting aren't mine." He stepped closer, his gaze boring into Damien. "Apex Logistics. The Reapers' central compound. And every other little illegitimate business you've been building behind my back."

The color drained from Damien's face. "You wouldn't..."

"I would," Cassian cut in coldly. "And I did. You've underestimated me for the last time, old man."

The room trembled again, the vibrations growing stronger, more pronounced. The lights flickered, casting shadows that danced wildly across the walls. Damien's composure shattered completely, his breathing ragged as he staggered backward, clutching the useless detonator like a lifeline.

"You bastard," he hissed, his voice a broken growl. "You've destroyed everything."

"No," Cassian replied, his tone as sharp and unyielding as steel. "I've restored what was always rightfully mine. You've been playing a game you never had the pieces to win. Checkmate."

The distillery fell into a tense silence as the tremors began to subside, leaving only the heavy breathing of those in the room and the faint creak of the settling building. Damien looked at Cassian, then at me, his face a mask of fury and defeat. For the first time, he looked truly powerless—a man who had gambled everything and lost.

Cassian's movements were unnaturally calm, yet every inch of him radiating unrelenting fury as he raised his gun. The click of the hammer pulling back was deafening in the stunned silence of the distillery. Damien froze, his eyes wide, his lips parting to form words that never came.

"Cassian," I whispered, my voice trembling as I stepped forward, instinctively reaching for him. But his steely gaze didn't waver, fixed solely on his father.

"I warned you," Cassian said, his tone devoid of emotion, hollow in its finality. "You've betrayed me for the last time."

Damien's mouth twisted, caught between a sneer and a plea, but Cassian didn't give him the chance to speak. The gunshot rang out, splitting the air with a thunderous crack.

For a moment, everything seemed to slow. Damien's head snapped back, the force of the bullet driving him into the wall behind him. Blood sprayed in a gruesome arc, a hot, metallic mist that splattered across my face and coat. I stood frozen, my breath catching in my throat as my mind struggled to process the sheer brutality of what had just happened.

Damien's body crumpled to the floor, lifeless, his fingers slack around the detonator. The dull thud of his collapse reverberated through the room, followed by an eerie silence.

Cassian lowered his arm slowly, his gun still clenched in his hand. His breathing was steady, almost unnervingly so, as if the act had cost him nothing.

"Cassian," I managed, my voice shaking as I wiped at the blood on my cheek with a trembling hand. The coppery scent was overwhelming, clinging to my skin and dress, turning my stomach.

He turned to me then, his eyes softening ever so slightly as they met mine. "Are you hurt?" he asked, his voice low and calm, as if the chaos and violence hadn't just erupted around us.

I shook my head, unable to form coherent words. My heart pounded in my chest, every nerve in my body screaming at the shock of what I'd just witnessed.

Cassian stepped closer, his presence commanding even in the aftermath of violence. His hand found mine, steadying the tremble that had overtaken my fingers, but I stepped back, out of his reach. Shaking my head, I brought my eyes up to his, saw the storm calming behind his deadly gaze. My breath froze, trapped in lungs that refused to expand.

He stepped forward, and again I stepped back, "Don't," I said, "just don't."

CHAPTER THIRTY-FIVE

The metallic scent of blood saturated the air, thick and cloying, wrapping around me like a noose. Damien's body lay crumpled at my feet, his lifeless eyes staring up at the ceiling. A dark pool of crimson spread outward, reaching the edges of the conference room like an accusation.

I couldn't look away. My chest heaved, each breath a struggle as I tried to reconcile what had just happened. Cassian stood a few feet away, his pistol still in hand, though lowered now, his posture unnervingly calm.

"Rosalie, are you alright?" He asked again, but the words seemed so distant.

I shook my head, but my knees threatened to give out beneath me. The world tilted dangerously, and I stumbled back a step, my heel catching the edge of the bloodstain. I barely suppressed a sob as the slick sensation clung to my skin.

"You're shaking." Cassian's voice was closer now, the sound of his shoes against the floor a harsh reminder that he was moving toward me.

"Don't," I managed, holding up a hand to stop him. My eyes met his, and the ice in them sent a chill down my spine. "Stay back."

His steps faltered, and for the briefest moment,

something that looked like pain flickered across his face. "Rosalie," he said quietly, his voice threading with something almost like pleading, "I had to do this."

"But did you?" I shot back, my voice rising despite the tremor in it. "Everything you do, every choice you make— it all comes back to you. And now... now there's blood pooled at my feet because of you. Another man murdered in front of me."

His jaw tightened, the softening in his expression replaced by something harder. "He was going to kill you if I hadn't stepped in," he said, his words cutting through the tension like a blade. "My father was a threat—the worst kind, Rosalie. Not just to me, but to everything we've built."

I laughed bitterly, the sound hollow and broken. "Built? What have we built, Cassian? Lies? Manipulation? Bloodshed?" My voice cracked as I gestured to the corpse between us. "This—this isn't building anything. It's destroying everything."

Cassian's lips pressed into a thin line, his shoulders squaring as he stepped closer despite my protests. "I did what had to be done," he said, his voice low and unrelenting. "You might not understand it now, but I protected you. I've always protected you."

"By turning me into a pawn?" I snapped, my hands shaking as I clenched them into fists. "You use people, Cassian. You used me, you used them—" I gestured vaguely toward the door, where Marcus and Sierra waited outside, "—and you used him."

Cassian's eyes darkened, the calm mask slipping just enough to reveal the storm beneath. "Damien was no pawn," he said coldly. "He was once a king in his own right, but he was just a man trying to claw his way to the top. He would have gutted us all if I'd given him the chance."

"Maybe," I admitted, my voice quieter now, "but you didn't just stop him, Cassian. You *became* him."

The words hung between us, heavy and damning. For the first time, Cassian didn't have a quick response, his silence louder than anything he could have said.

I wrapped my arms around myself, the weight of

everything—of Damien's death, of Cassian's choices, of my own complicity—threatening to crush me. "I can't do this," I whispered, tears streaming down my face as I took another step back.

Cassian's eyes softened, and he reached for me, his hand hesitant. "Rosalie—"

"No," I said, cutting him off. "You scare me, Cassian. What you've done, what you're capable of—it terrifies me."

His hand dropped to his side, his expression unreadable. "I never wanted to scare you," he said quietly, his voice laced with something dangerously close to vulnerability.

"But you do," I replied, my voice barely audible. "And I don't think I can be the person you need me to be."

Cassian's gaze locked onto mine, and for the first time, I saw the faintest crack in his armor. But it was too late. The blood on the floor, the weight of his choices—it was all too much.

I turned away, my legs unsteady as I headed for the door. "I need to get out of here," I said, more to myself than to him, but at I stood in the doorway, I stopped, feeling the weight of the familiar piece in my pocket. I pulled it out, examining the delicate features in the glow of the fireplace, before I turned and set the Queen chess piece on the table beside him.

I wasn't his Queen anymore than I was a pawn; I realized that now.

"Rosalie," he called after me, his voice sharp but tinged with desperation.

I didn't look back.

Enjoy a sneak peek at Book Three of Ivy & Bloom!

BLOSSOMS OF LUST

BY LINDSEY FINCH

CHAPTER ONE

The gunshot rang out, sharp and unforgiving, and I watched the body fall again. The sound reverberated through the crumbled distillery, a cruel echo that refused to fade. Blood sprayed across the cold concrete floor, stark and vivid against the shadows. My chest heaved, but my legs refused to move, frozen in place as if bound by invisible chains.

Damien's lifeless eyes locked onto mine, unblinking and accusing. The betrayal in their empty depths seared into me, branding itself behind my eyelids. The coppery scent of blood filled the air, thick and suffocating, mingling with the acrid tang of gunpowder. My stomach twisted as the crimson pool beneath him spread like ink, its dark tendrils creeping outward, unstoppable.

I wanted to scream, to run, to do *something*. But I couldn't. My body was rooted in place, heavy with the weight of fear and disbelief. My pulse thundered in my ears, drowning out everything except the sharp clip of Cassian's footsteps as he approached, unbothered by his actions, or the murder of his father.

His voice, low and calm, cut through the haze, a blade slicing cleanly through my spiraling thoughts. "This is what loyalty costs," he murmured, his words laced with

265

finality, each syllable a nail driven into the coffin of my trust.

I turned to look at him—no, *forced* myself to look at him—but the face I knew was gone. His expression was impassive, his steel-gray eyes colder than I had ever seen them, devoid of the tenderness I had once foolishly believed was real. There was no remorse, no hesitation, just the unyielding presence of a man who had calculated every step, every consequence.

A sob clawed its way up my throat, but it refused to escape. My chest ached, the pressure unbearable, like I was suffocating under the weight of my own helplessness. "Why?" I wanted to ask, but the word never left my lips.

Damien's hand twitched, a final, involuntary spasm, before falling still. The sight broke something in me, a sharp crack that reverberated through my entire being. The bloodied walls of the conference room seemed to close in, the air thick and suffocating, trapping me in this waking nightmare.

And then Cassian's gaze turned to me.

"You knew this was coming," he said, his tone as smooth as velvet, yet devoid of any comfort. He stepped closer, the soles of his polished shoes clicking against the floor with a rhythm that matched the frantic pounding of my heart.

"I didn't..." I tried to speak, but the words felt heavy and broken, caught in the tangle of emotions choking me.

"You didn't *want* to see it," he corrected, tilting his head slightly, as though examining a curious artifact. "That's the difference."

His shadow stretched long over the bloodied floor, over Damien's lifeless form, over me. I couldn't breathe. The room darkened, the flames in the fireplace suddenly snuffed out, the edges of my vision closing in until all that remained was the crimson pool and Cassian's unyielding presence.

The blood crept closer, inching toward my feet, and I stumbled back, finally able to move. But no matter how far I retreated, it followed, relentless and unyielding.

I tried to close my eyes, to block out the scene, but the

darkness behind my eyelids held no solace. The sound of the gunshot echoed again, louder this time, splitting the silence apart.

I woke up gasping, my heart clawing its way out of my chest.

The sound of my ragged breaths filled the room, and for a moment, I wasn't sure if I was awake or still trapped in that nightmare. My fingers dug into the bedsheets, the smooth fabric bunched tightly in my fists as though I could anchor myself to reality.

But the weight of Damien's gaze lingered, and Cassian's words were etched into my mind, haunting me even in the light of dawn.

The clock on the nightstand glared at me with its relentless red numbers: 5:13 a.m. It had been three weeks since I'd walked away from everything—Cassian, Ivy & Bloom, and the wreckage of who I thought I was. And yet, every night, the dreams brought me back to that warehouse.

I swung my legs over the side of the bed and sat there, my hands gripping the edge of the mattress. The cold floor against my bare feet was a small mercy, grounding me in the present. My chest felt heavy, like the weight of everything I'd been avoiding was pressing down harder with each breath.

The curtains were drawn, but I didn't need to look outside to know they were there—Marcus and Sierra, the ever-watchful bodyguards Cassian had stationed near my building. I'd changed the locks on my apartment again after the last time he let himself in. I wouldn't let him corner me, not here. Not anymore.

My phone buzzed on the nightstand, the screen lighting up with his name. I didn't need to check the message. It was the same as always—short, commanding, dripping with that quiet dominance he wielded so effortlessly.

"We need to talk."

I stared at the phone, the ache in my chest flaring. The urge to respond was there, sharp and undeniable, but I pushed it down. Ghosting him was the only thing I could control anymore.

Shoving the phone aside, I forced myself to stand. My reflection in the mirror across the room caught my eye, and I almost didn't recognize the woman staring back. Hollow eyes, dark circles, and tangled hair that hadn't seen a brush in days. My favorite old robe hung off my frame, the faded floral print a painful reminder of a time when my life felt simpler.

I wrapped the robe tighter around me and shuffled to the kitchen. The morning routine of the city outside was muted through the windows, and for a moment, I let the mundane ritual of brewing coffee distract me. The aroma filled the small space, comforting in its familiarity, but even that couldn't chase away the gnawing emptiness.

I hadn't set foot in Ivy & Bloom since the day I walked away from Cassian, convinced that seeing the shop would mean seeing him. It was easier to stay away, to bury myself in this half-life where the only company I had was my own guilt and the memories I couldn't escape.

The coffee maker sputtered, pulling me from my thoughts. I poured a mug, the warmth seeping into my hands as I held it close. But before I could take a sip, my phone buzzed again.

I stared at it from across the room, the glow of the screen taunting me. Another message. Another thread tying me to him. My chest tightened, and without thinking, I crossed the room and grabbed the phone.

The message was simple: *"You can't avoid me forever, Rosalie."*

A bitter laugh escaped me as I set the phone back down with a sharp click. He was wrong. Avoiding him was the only thing keeping me from completely falling apart.

Moving back to the kitchen, I leaned against the counter, the mug still warm in my hands, and stared out the window at the city waking up. Somewhere out there, Cassian Moreau was waiting. Watching. And I hated that some part of me wanted to let him in.

But I couldn't. Not after what I'd seen. Not after what he'd done.

I took a shaky breath and whispered to no one, "You can't fix this, Cassian."

The words felt hollow, but I repeated them anyway, hoping that if I said them enough, I might start to believe them.

The silence in the apartment wrapped around me like a suffocating blanket, broken only by the annoying putter of the refrigerator and the occasional creak of the floorboards beneath my feet. I stayed rooted by the counter, clutching the coffee mug as if the warmth might seep deeper into my chilled bones. But it wouldn't.

It never did.

My gaze drifted back to the vase of flowers on the table, their brittle stems leaning precariously, petals curled inward as if retreating from the world. They mirrored how I felt—worn, lifeless, and incapable of holding any beauty that had once existed.

The vase hadn't moved since I'd brought it home, an afterthought from the shop when I thought I'd be back in a few days. Couldn't face the memories. Couldn't face him.

I set the mug down with a soft clink and ran a hand through my hair, wincing as my fingers caught on the tangles. My body felt heavy, leaden with exhaustion that no amount of sleep—or avoidance—seemed to ease. Even now, standing here, I wanted nothing more than to crawl back into bed, pull the covers over my head, and pretend the world outside didn't exist.

But the world did exist. And so did Cassian.

The phone buzzed again. He was persistent, unrelenting.

I didn't move this time, letting it vibrate against the nightstand until the sound faded into silence. The message wasn't going anywhere. Neither was he.

With a sigh, I grabbed the mug again and shuffled into the living room, the cluttered space feeling smaller with every passing day. I sank onto the couch, careful to avoid the stack of unopened mail teetering on the cushion beside me. My legs curled beneath me as I cradled my coffee, my eyes drifting to the window again.

What would it feel like to walk into Ivy & Bloom, to see the flowers, the customers, the shop that had been my life for so long? The thought twisted something deep inside me. Ivy & Bloom had been in my family for as long as I could remember—until Cassian had tainted it, turned it into something I couldn't recognize.

I pressed the mug to my lips, letting the warmth burn my mouth, a small, grounding pain that distracted me for half a second. That's all it ever was now: distractions. Small, fleeting moments to keep me from drowning in the bigger picture.

I should clean. I should eat something. I should open one of those letters or call someone who might remind me what it felt like to live instead of just exist.

Instead, I sat there, the coffee growing cold in my hands, staring out the window and wondering how long I could keep avoiding everything before it finally caught up with me.

The truth was, it already had.

CHAPTER TWO

The shower was meant to wake me up, to shock my senses and force me into some semblance of normalcy. I stood under the spray, the hot water pounding against my shoulders as if it could wash away the layers of exhaustion clinging to me like a second skin. But the effort felt hollow. The water cascaded over me, down my back, pooling at my feet as I stared blankly at the tile, unmoving.

At some point, I turned off the shower and sank into the tub, letting it fill around me. The steam fogged the mirror and blurred the sharp edges of the bathroom, cocooning me in a hazy silence. I rested my head against the cool porcelain and closed my eyes, the water lapping softly against my skin.

It wasn't until the chill began to seep into my bones that I realized the water had turned cold. My fingers were pruned, and the goosebumps on my arms made me shiver as I finally forced myself to move. The sluggish pull of my body felt like wading through molasses, but I grabbed the detangling brush from the edge of the tub and began pulling it through my wet hair.

Each stroke of the brush tugged at the knots, and I winced at the sharp pricks of pain as it caught on tangles. The mirror, once fogged, cleared just enough to reflect the woman staring back at me.

Gaunt. Hollow. A shadow of who I'd been.

My cheekbones, always subtly pronounced, now jutted out sharply, the skin beneath them pale and stretched thin. My lips were dry and cracked, their natural blush faded into a muted pink that barely stood out against my sallow complexion. My eyes were the worst of it—dark, heavy shadows painted the skin beneath them, the kind that no amount of concealer could mask. They were glassy, distant, like they didn't belong to me anymore.

I leaned closer to the mirror, my damp hair falling forward to frame my face. My fingers brushed against my cheeks, tracing the hollows where fullness had once been. Even my collarbones seemed more pronounced, the ridges stark against the delicate curve of my neck.

The woman staring back wasn't someone I recognized.

I swallowed hard, forcing the lump in my throat down as I ran the brush through the last section of my hair, detangling it into submission. The process was automatic, mechanical—another distraction to fill the minutes of my day.

The urge to crawl back into bed whispered in the back of my mind, but something deeper stirred—a small flicker of rebellion against the monotony that had consumed me for weeks. My reflection stared at me, her eyes bleak but resolute, and for the first time in days, I listened to her.

I was going to leave this apartment.

I pulled on the first clothes I could find—a pair of faded jeans that hung looser on my hips than they used to, and a soft, oversized sweater that smelled faintly of lavender fabric softener. It was enough.

The air outside was damp and cool, the kind that hinted at the lingering grip of spring's early days. A light drizzle fell, the rain soft and gentle, soaking into the cracked pavement and darkening the edges of my jeans as I walked. The sweater I'd grabbed hung loose on my frame, but it was warm enough to keep the chill from sinking too deep into my skin. At the last moment, I'd grabbed a thin knee-length coat which had lost its form fitting appeal as well.

I didn't bother with an umbrella. The rain felt more cleansing than oppressive, the tiny droplets cool against my face as I tucked my hands into my pockets and kept moving.

The corner coffee shop came into view, its familiar awning sagging slightly under the weight of rainwater. The soft glow of its interior lights spilled out onto the sidewalk, a warm invitation that drew me closer. I pushed the door open, the harsh chime of the doorbell blending with the low rumblings of chatter and the hiss of the espresso machine.

I'd spent a fair portion of my time surviving off of takeout and coffee—lots and lots of coffee.

My shoes squeaked slightly against the tile floor as I approached the counter, scanning the menu even though I already knew what I wanted.

"One medium black coffee and... a blueberry muffin," I said, my voice soft but steady as I handed over a crumpled bill.

The barista nodded, her polite smile not quite reaching her eyes, and I stepped aside to wait. My fingers traced the edge of my sweater sleeve as I stood there, feeling the damp fabric cling to my skin.

Out of the corner of my eye, I spotted them.

Marcus and Sierra.

They were seated at a small table near the back, their heads tilted slightly as if they were in conversation, but I knew better. Their presence was too deliberate, too coincidental. Even at this distance, I could feel their watchful gazes following my every move.

I turned back to the counter as the barista called my name, grabbing the coffee and the small paper bag containing the muffin. The warmth of the cup seeped into my hands once more.

Sliding into a booth by the window, I set the coffee and muffin on the table in front of me. The rain outside had picked up, streaking the glass and blurring the view of the street beyond. It gave the world a soft, dreamlike quality, as if everything outside this little coffee shop existed just out of reach.

I peeled the wrapper off the muffin slowly, my

movements absent-minded as my thoughts were elsewhere—they always were these days. The smell of blueberries and sugar wafted up, sweet and nostalgic. I broke off a piece and brought it to my lips, letting the flavor linger on my tongue before setting the muffin back down.

One bite. That was all I could manage.

The coffee was easier. I cradled the cup in both hands, taking small sips, letting the warmth spread through me. It didn't fill the hollowness, but it dulled the edges, made it a little easier to sit still.

I could feel Marcus and Sierra even without looking. Their presence was like a weight pressing against my back, their eyes ensuring I wasn't truly alone. Cassian's shadows, always there, always watching. I wondered if he had sent them to protect me—or to make sure I hadn't run to the cops.

Although I had considered it, the thought hadn't resurfaced again. A nod to my corrupted moral compass.

Turning my gaze to the window, I let my mind wander, following the trails of raindrops as they slid down the glass. The streets outside were quiet, the occasional car passing by, its tires hissing against the wet pavement. A woman hurried by with a bright yellow umbrella, her laughter audible even through the rain.

For a moment, I envied her.

The corner coffee shop was my first step outside in weeks, my first attempt to feel human again. But even here, in this small bubble of warmth and normalcy, the weight of everything I'd left behind loomed large.

I gripped the coffee tighter and whispered to myself, "One step at a time." Having sat there for nearly an hour, I contemplated every possible excuse to prevent me from going there, but none of them seems worthy enough.

When the rain lightened up, I pushed open the coffee shop door, the bell giving a cheerful chime that didn't match the knot twisting in my stomach. The rain had softened to a mist, fine droplets clinging to my hair and coat as I stepped onto the sidewalk.

The muffin, still mostly whole, felt like a lead weight in

my hand. With a sigh, I dropped it into the nearest trash can, its paper bag crumpling softly against the metal bin. The taste of blueberries lingered faintly on my tongue, bittersweet and hollow, much like everything else lately.

The coffee stayed in my grip, its warmth a small comfort as I walked aimlessly, letting the drizzle blur the edges of the city around me. I didn't need to look over my shoulder to know Marcus and Sierra were nearby, trailing me at a distance that wasn't far enough to forget but just far enough to pretend.

I wasn't sure if I could do this until I saw it: *Ivy & Bloom*.

The sight of the shop was a jolt to my system, like stepping into a puddle and realizing too late that the water was ice cold. The windows were just as I remembered, filled with carefully arranged blooms in every color. Roses, daisies, tulips—they looked vibrant, alive, and utterly out of place against the grayness of the day.

The coffee in my hand suddenly felt too hot, burning against my palm as I stood frozen on the sidewalk. My chest tightened, the ache sharp and familiar, as my gaze traced the curves of the painted sign above the door.

For a fleeting moment, I imagined pushing the door open, hearing the soft chime of the bell and breathing in the heady scent of flowers and earth. I could almost feel the smooth counters beneath my fingertips, hear the murmur of customers, and see the faint smile my mother always wore when she worked.

But the image shattered, replaced by the memory of Cassian standing in the center of the shop, his voice low and commanding as he unraveled the truth. My sanctuary, my mother's legacy, had been nothing more than a front for his schemes.

I took a step back, the motion instinctive, like touching a flame and realizing too late how much it burns. My heart was pounding, and the warmth from the coffee wasn't enough to steady my trembling hands.

I couldn't go in. Not yet.

With a sharp inhale, I turned on my heel and walked away, my footsteps quick and uneven against the wet pavement.

The walk back to my apartment felt heavier than it should have, the rain soaking into my coat and sweater and chilling me to the bone. By the time I reached my building, my fingers were stiff, and the coffee cup was cold and forgotten in my hand.

But it wasn't the rain or the chill that stopped me in my tracks. It was the single rose waiting for me, perched neatly in the center of my door.

The bloom was soft and delicate, its creamy white petals almost glowing against the dark wood. A black ribbon was tied in a neat bow around the stem, its stark contrast making the gesture feel more ominous than romantic.

I didn't need to touch it to know who had left it.

Cassian.

My pulse quickened, the sharp thrum of my heart pounding in my ears as I stared at the rose. It was elegant and deliberate, like that side of him that I fell in love with. White roses meant forgiveness—I knew that much. But this wasn't just about forgiveness. It was a message, one as clear as if he'd carved it into the door himself.

I reached for it hesitantly, my fingers brushing the ribbon. The softness of the petals under my touch felt wrong, too perfect for something that carried the weight of so many unspoken words.

A part of me wanted to throw it down, to toss it into the dumpster and let the rain wash it away. But I couldn't. Instead, I pulled it free, the stem cold and damp in my hand as I unlocked the door with trembling fingers.

The apartment was just as I'd left it—silent, stale, and suffocating. I placed the rose on the kitchen counter, the black bow unraveling slightly as it rested against the chipped surface.

I stood there for a long time, staring at it, the warmth of forgiveness and the chill of manipulation coiled tightly around its delicate petals.

Cassian always had a way of making his presence known, even when he wasn't there. And no matter how far I ran, he always seemed to find me.

CHAPTER THREE

I stared at my phone, Abram's name glowing on the screen, his call pulling me from the haze that had settled over me in the last few days. For a moment, I debated letting it ring, but guilt gnawed at me until I reluctantly answered.

"Dad," I said, my voice flat as I sank into the couch, tucking my legs beneath me.

"Rosalie," Abram said, his voice carrying a familiar warmth beneath its gruff exterior, the way it always did when he was trying not to worry too much. "I was starting to think I'd have to come knock on your door myself. You know, just to make sure you're still alive."

His attempt at lightness was painfully transparent, a thin veil over the concern I could hear plain as day.

I sighed, pressing a hand to my forehead. "I've been... busy."

"Busy doing what? Sitting in that apartment? I stopped by the shop the other day, they said you haven't been there in weeks." His voice carried a sharpness that I hadn't missed. "This isn't you, Rosalie. You used to be full of joy... and—" His words fell short, but anything else would have been the truth. "Now, look at you. You're just—"

"Don't." My voice cracked, and I cleared my throat,

277

forcing the lump back down. "Please, don't do this right now."

Abram paused, the silence between us stretching long enough that I almost thought he'd hung up.

"You know," he said finally, softer this time, "you were happier when you were with him."

The words hit me like a punch to the gut, stealing the air from my lungs. I squeezed my eyes shut, the image of Cassian's face flashing in my mind—his intense gaze, the way he used to look at me like I was the only thing that mattered in the world.

"You didn't even like him," I shot back, my voice rising slightly.

"No," Abram admitted, "I didn't. And I still don't. But at least you weren't like this—hiding, sulking, wasting away."

I clenched my jaw, anger and hurt bubbling to the surface. "You don't get to say that to me. Not after everything."

Another pause. When Abram spoke again, his voice was softer, almost hesitant. "I'm worried about you, Rosalie. That's all. I just want my daughter back."

"I have to go," I said abruptly, standing and pacing the small space of my living room. "I'll call you later."

"Rosalie—"

I ended the call before he could say anything else, dropping the phone onto the couch and pressing the heels of my hands against my eyes. His words echoed in my head, louder than I wanted them to be.

You were happier when you were with him.

I took a deep breath, letting it out slowly as I lowered my hands. Abram was wrong. He had to be.

But as the quiet of the apartment settled over me again, I realized I couldn't sit here anymore. The suffocating weight of my own thoughts was too much.

I rifled through my closet, pulling out a black leather jacket and a pair of dark jeans. The sweater and jeans I'd been wearing for days felt like they were holding me back, a reminder of the inertia I'd been drowning in. I didn't want to feel it anymore.

Once dressed, I stood in front of the mirror and pulled my hair into a loose French braid, smoothing the strands with trembling fingers. My reflection looked sharper now, more purposeful, even if the hollowness in my eyes remained.

Grabbing a small bag and slinging it over my shoulder, I turned off the lights and moved toward the window in my bedroom. The fire escape outside was barely used, the metal grates slick with rain from earlier in the evening. I opened the window carefully, the cool night air rushing in as I stepped out onto the fire escape.

I glanced down at the alley below, my heart thudding as I climbed down the steps. The thought of Marcus or Sierra catching me made my stomach twist, but I didn't hear the low hum of their SUV or see the flash of their silhouettes.

Once I reached the alley, I slipped into the shadows, the sounds of the city buzzing intoxicatingly around me. The air was cool and damp, the streets alive with the rhythm of traffic and the chatter of people moving from one place to another. I kept my head down, blending into the blur of the night.

The lights and sounds of downtown Chicago pulsed around me, the energy both overwhelming and grounding. For the first time in weeks, I felt something other than the weight of my own thoughts. The chaos of the city enveloped me, numbing the ache in my chest, even if just for a moment.

The rain fell softly at first, barely noticeable as it mingled with the mist rising from the pavement. I turned down one street, then another, following the shifting glow of neon signs and the faint strains of music escaping from bars and restaurants. My steps felt aimless, each one carrying me further from my apartment and the suffocating stillness I'd left behind.

By the time I glanced up again, the rain had turned heavier, soaking through my jacket as I walked, the drizzle from earlier now a steady patter against the pavement. My hair stuck to my neck, and my jeans clung uncomfortably to my legs. I didn't have a destination in mind, just the need to keep moving.

The streets shifted as I ventured further from my usual haunts, the familiar glow of coffee shops and corner stores replaced by dim alleyways and tightly packed buildings with facades that blurred in the rain. Neon lights reflected off the wet ground, their soft hum and electric colors cutting through the haze.

That's when I saw it.

A single, unassuming door tucked into the side of a building, its glossy black paint glinting under a narrow beam of light. Above it, the word *Nocturne* was etched in sleek silver letters, illuminated just enough to catch the eye. The name hummed with intrigue, and the faint sound of music—low, rhythmic, and intoxicating—seeped through the cracks.

I hesitated on the sidewalk, my breath fogging in the cool air. People moved in and out of the door with careless ease, their movements fluid, their expressions calm but guarded. The allure of the place tugged at me. I told myself it was curiosity, nothing more. But deep down, I knew it was the need to escape—if only for a little while—that pushed me forward.

The bouncer at the door gave me a quick once-over, his brow arching slightly. I straightened my back, forcing myself to meet his gaze, even as I felt out of place in my rain-dampened jacket and scuffed boots. He didn't say a word, just stepped aside and pushed the door open.

Warmth spilled out as I stepped inside, the low thrum of bass-heavy music pulsing through the air. The amber glow of pendant lights cast soft, flattering beauty over the space, illuminating deep forest-green booths and polished black tables scattered haphazardly to encourage conversation—or something more intimate.

The crowd was a mix that immediately put me on edge. Some were dressed to impress, their sharp suits and elegant dresses exuding effortless confidence, while others leaned casual but stylish, in fitted jeans, designer jackets, or crisp button-downs with the sleeves rolled up. A few groups clustered around the bar, their voices raised in laughter, while others lounged in booths, their movements languid and deliberate, as though they had all the time in the world.

The scent of expensive perfume mingled with the tang of spilled liquor and something musky I couldn't quite place. It wasn't unpleasant, but it added to the charged atmosphere that filled the room.

On one side of the club, a narrow stage was set up with low lighting, a DJ perched behind an impressive setup of turntables and equipment. The music was loud but not overwhelming, its rhythm thrumming through the floor and into my chest. It was upbeat, a mix of electronic and hip-hop, with the kind of energy that invited people to dance—or to disappear into a corner with someone under the pretense of conversation.

A group near the dance floor caught my eye—two women in glittering dresses laughing loudly, their drinks sloshing as they moved to the music, while a man in a tight v-neck and black blazer leaned close, his words lost in the noise. A few feet away, a couple stood pressed against a wall, their faces close, oblivious to everything around them.

The bar, however, was the center of it all. It stretched along the far wall, its glossy black surface catching the golden light from above. Bartenders moved in the controlled chaos with ease, shaking cocktails and sliding drinks across to waiting hands.

I hesitated near the entrance, feeling out of place in my damp jacket and jeans. My hair still clung to my neck from the rain, and I had none of the polished, put-together confidence the people here seemed to wear so easily.

But if I didn't adjust quickly, I'd stick out more than I already did.

Straightening my shoulders, I let my eyes drift over the room, feigning a casual disinterest while I took everything in. My fingers brushed my jacket's zipper as if debating whether to remove it, but I left it on for now—armor against the unfamiliar.

I headed toward the bar, keeping my pace steady and my expression neutral, as though I belonged here as much as anyone else. Around me, the conversations and laughter rose and fell, a symphony of energy and intent, but I couldn't shake the feeling of being watched.

I made my way to the bar, weaving through the crowd with measured steps. The energy in the room was infectious, and I could feel it creeping under my skin despite myself. Conversations hummed around me, snippets of laughter and raised voices blending into the rhythmic thrum of the music.

When I reached the bar, I leaned lightly against the sleek black surface, scanning the shelves of bottles glowing softly under the golden light. A bartender caught my eye and approached with an infectious smile.

"What can I get you?" he asked, his voice smooth, nearly drowned out by the noise.

"Whiskey sour," I said, louder than I intended, my voice cutting through the low hum around us. A smile slowly crept up as I realized that I had deliberately avoided anything with whisky until Cassian introduced me to it. His vice slowly became my own...

He nodded and turned to mix the drink. I glanced over my shoulder, letting my eyes roam the room. Groups gathered and scattered like shifting constellations, conversations flickering between laughter and low, urgent murmurs. The air was thick with the heady mix of expensive perfumes and sharp alcohol, undercut by the faint, unexpected sweetness of floral arrangements tucked into the darker corners. Their blooms were striking—nothing but black flowers, glossy and dramatic under the dim amber light. The combination was intoxicating, almost overwhelming, but strangely comforting in its indulgence. For once, the chaos around me felt easier to breathe in than the silence I'd left behind.

The bartender slid the drink toward me, the condensation already gathering on the outside of the glass. I handed him a bill, not bothering with change, and took a sip. The tart sweetness of lemon and the warmth of whiskey flooded my senses, igniting a fire in me as I turned from the bar and searched for a quieter spot.

I found it in a booth tucked into the farthest corner of the room, partially obscured by shadows. Sliding into the seat, I positioned myself so I could see the crowd without being too conspicuous. The velvet fabric beneath me was cool and smooth, and the table had the faintest stickiness that came from countless spilled drinks, but I wasn't too bothered by it.

For a moment, I just watched.

The crowd moved like a living thing, shifting and undulating as people came together and broke apart. At one table, two men leaned close, their conversation intense and hurried. A few feet away, a woman in a red dress threw her head back in laughter, her companion leaning closer, clearly captivated. On the dance floor, the glittering dresses and sharp lines of jackets blurred into a kaleidoscope of movement under the shifting lights.

I took another sip of my drink, the warmth spreading through me as I leaned back against the booth. For the first time in weeks, the weight in my chest felt lighter, pushed aside by the buzz of the room and the whiskey loosening its hold.

A group near my booth caught my attention—a woman with a sleek ponytail and sharp cheekbones who radiated confidence, her laughter infectious as she leaned into the man beside her. They noticed me watching, and she offered a faint, knowing smile.

"You look like you've got a story," she said, her voice cutting through the music as she shifted slightly to face me.

I blinked, caught off guard. "I think everyone here does," I replied, my tone wry, the drink in my hand giving me a touch of boldness I wouldn't have found otherwise.

Her smile widened, and she raised her glass toward me. "Fair enough. I'm Lydia."

"Rosalie," I said, tipping my glass in return.

For the next few minutes—or maybe longer; time was slippery in this place—I found myself talking to Lydia and her companions. Their conversation was easy, light, filled with anecdotes and teasing jabs at one another. None of it felt pointed or prying, just the kind of banter that came from people who knew how to enjoy the night.

I let myself laugh, the sound unfamiliar in my throat but not unwelcome. The whiskey dulled the sharp edges of my thoughts, and for a little while, I forgot about Cassian, about the shop, about everything waiting for me outside of these walls.

The music changed, the beat slower and heavier, and Lydia turned back to her group, leaving me with a warm smile and a casual, "Come find us if you want more company."

The booth felt more comfortable now, or maybe it was just the whiskey. I wasn't sure how many I'd had—three or four? Maybe five? The glass in my hand was lighter than I remembered, the amber liquid inside dwindling faster with each sip. My stomach churned faintly, reminding me that I hadn't eaten dinner, but I ignored it. For the first time in weeks, I felt alive, like my body wasn't weighed down by the ache I'd been carrying.

The music had shifted again, slower now, with a pulsing rhythm that seemed to match the faint buzz in my veins. The dim amber light of the room blurred at the edges, softening the hard lines of the tables and the shadowy figures moving past. I leaned back in the booth, a faint, lazy smile tugging at my lips as I watched the people on the dance floor sway to the tantalizing music.

A man approached my booth, his confident stride cutting through the haze of the room. He was tall, with a cocky smile and sharp features that might have been charming if my head wasn't swimming. His dark shirt was unbuttoned at the collar, and he carried himself with the kind of casual arrogance that seemed to thrive in a place like this.

"Mind if I join you?" he asked, his voice smooth as he gestured to the empty seat across from me.

I shrugged, too relaxed—or maybe too tipsy—to argue. "Sure, but I'm not much for good company. I have a habit of attracting the wrong kind."

He slid into the booth, setting his drink on the table. "Or maybe the wrong kind are attracted to you, sweet, innocent enough, gorgeous ," he said, his tone light, his eyes scanning my face.

"I'm the magnet then, huh?" I replied, raising my glass with a wry smile. "Here's to attraction—the magnetic kind."

For a while, the conversation was pleasant enough. He asked where I was from, what brought me here, and I gave him vague answers, the kind that didn't invite too much prying. He laughed at my sarcasm, leaning in closer with each passing minute, the space between us shrinking.

The alcohol made it easier to talk, easier to smile, easier to forget the sinking feeling that always lingered at the edge of my thoughts. I felt a flicker of something I hadn't felt in a long time—lightness, freedom.

But then his hand brushed against mine, lingering for just a moment too long.

I tensed, the haze in my head clearing slightly as he leaned closer, his voice dropping into something softer, more intimate.

"You really are gorgeous, you know that, right?" he murmured, his breath warm against my cheek.

I shifted back instinctively, the smile slipping from my face. "Thanks," I said, my tone flat now, the warning clear in my voice.

He didn't seem to notice—or care. Before I could react, he leaned in, his lips aiming for mine.

I turned my head just in time, his kiss landing awkwardly near my temple. "Hey," I said sharply, my voice louder than I intended.

"Come on," he said, his hand moving to rest on my arm. "I thought we were having a good time."

Before I could respond, another voice cut through the air, low and commanding.

"She said no."

The man froze, his hand still on my arm as someone grabbed his wrist. The grip wasn't violent, but it was firm—unyielding.

I looked up, my heart skipping as my gaze locked onto Cassian.

He stood there, his sharp gray eyes a strange concoction

of disarmingly cold and furious flames, a flicker of something dangerous dancing behind them. His fingers tightened just enough to make the man wince, forcing him to stand.

"Let go," the man hissed, his confidence crumbling under Cassian's steady gaze.

Cassian leaned in, his voice calm but laced with a quiet fury that sent a shiver down my spine. "You don't want to make me repeat myself. Fuck off."

The man hesitated, glancing between Cassian and me, before yanking his wrist free and stumbling away, muttering curses under his breath.

The booth felt impossibly small as Cassian turned to me, his presence filling the space. My chest tightened as his eyes met mine, the storm in his gaze softening slightly.

"Rosalie," he said, his voice lower now, but no less intense.

The sound of my name on his lips sent a rush of heat through me, cutting through the alcohol in my system like a blade. For a moment, I couldn't speak, couldn't move.

I would never forget the way he looked at me in that moment—like I was something fragile and precious, something he'd break the world to protect.

The chaos of the room faded, the music and voices becoming distant, drowned out by the weight of his gaze.

I swallowed hard, my voice barely above a whisper. "What are you doing here?"

Cassian didn't answer immediately. Instead, he slid into the booth across from me, his expression unreadable as he rested his forearms on the table, leaning closer.

"I should be asking you the same thing," he said finally, his tone soft but edged with something I couldn't quite place.

And just like that, the fragile peace I'd found tonight shattered, leaving me alone with the one person I'd been running from—and the emotions I could no longer ignore.

ABOUT THE AUTHOR
LINDSEY FINCH

Lindsey Finch is a devoted mother, loving wife, and self-proclaimed hopeless romantic who has been crafting heart-pounding love stories for over a decade. Her passion for storytelling began with a simple idea: love, no matter how dark or twisted, has the power to transform and heal. This belief shines through in every one of her novels, where strong heroines meet brooding, complex heroes, and happily-ever-afters are anything but conventional.

A ten-year veteran of the romance genre, Lindsey has penned multiple bestselling series, including *The White Lotus* and *The Citadel*, captivating readers with her signature blend of emotional intensity, steamy chemistry, and richly imagined worlds. Her stories often explore the fine line between love and danger, drawing readers into tales of power, betrayal, and unrelenting desire.

When she's not writing, Lindsey enjoys spending time with her husband and children, sipping wine over a cozy dinner, or getting lost in her ever-growing library of romance novels. Whether she's dreaming up her next dark and twisty romance or indulging in a guilty pleasure binge-watch, Lindsey's heart always gravitates toward love stories that push boundaries and defy expectations.

Stay connected with Lindsey Finch for updates on upcoming releases, sneak peeks, and exclusive content:

Author Page: **www.amazon.com/author/lindseyfinch**
Instagram: **@AviaryPublications**
Goodreads: **Lindsey Finch**

With each book, Lindsey invites readers into a world where passion cuts deep, love is worth the risk, and even the darkest hearts can be redeemed.